KU-402-578

‖‖‖‖‖‖‖‖‖‖‖‖‖‖‖‖‖‖‖‖‖‖‖‖‖‖

Terence Strong was brought up in south London, after the Second World War. He has worked in advertising, journalism, publishing and many other professions. His bestselling novels (which have sold more than one million copies in the UK alone) include *President Down*, *The Tick Tock Man*, *Wheels of Fire*, *Cold Monday* and *White Viper*. He lives in the south-west of England.

WITHDRAWN FROM
NEWCASTLE LIBRARIES

Visit www.twbooks.co.uk/authors/tstrong.html

Acclaim for Terence Strong

'Belongs to the action-man school of writing, backed up by hands-on research' *The Times*

'Tension ratchets up wickedly – a strong sense of reality is reinforced with powerful emotion and gritty characters' *Daily Telegraph*

'An edge-of-the-chair thriller with the chilling grip of authenticity' *Independent on Sunday*

'Well plotted and genuinely exciting' *Sunday Telegraph*

'An extremely good topical thriller' Jack Higgins

'Breathless entertainment' *Guardian*

Also by Terence Strong

President Down
That Last Mountain
Whisper Who Dares
The Fifth Hostage
Conflict of Lions
Sons of Heaven
This Angry Land
Stalking Horse
The Tick Tock Man
White Viper
Deadwater Deep
Cold Monday
Wheels of Fire
Rogue Element

Dragonplague

Terence Strong

POCKET
BOOKS

LONDON • SYDNEY • NEW YORK • TORONTO

First published in Great Britain by Hodder and Stoughton Ltd, 1987
This edition published by Pocket Books UK, 2010
An imprint of Simon & Schuster UK Ltd
A CBS Company

Copyright © Terence Strong, 1986

This book is copyright under the Berne Convention.
No reproduction without permission.
® and © 1997 Simon & Schuster Inc. All rights reserved.
Pocket Books & Design is a registered trademark
of Simon & Schuster, Inc.

The right of Terence Strong to be identified as author of this
work has been asserted in accordance with sections 77 and
78 of the Copyright, Designs and Patents Act, 1988.

1 3 5 7 9 10 8 6 4 2

Simon & Schuster UK Ltd
1st Floor
222 Gray's Inn Road
London WC1X 8HB

www.simonandschuster.co.uk

Simon & Schuster Australia
Sydney

A CIP catalogue record for this book is available from the British Library

ISBN 978-1-84739-258-9

This book is a work of fiction. Names, characters, places and
incidents are either a product of the author's imagination
or are used fictitiously. Any resemblance to actual people,
living or dead, events or locales, is entirely coincidental.

Typeset by Hewer Text UK Ltd, Edinburgh
Printed and bound in Great Britain by Cox & Wyman

For Princess
with love

Author's Note

'*The most serious peacetime threat to our national well-being.*'

That is how a Commons all-party Home Affairs Committee described the menace of drug-addiction today.

One MP, on returning from a research visit to the United States, commented: 'We have seen the future – and it is frightening.'

An officer of the Home Office Drugs Branch said chillingly: 'It's everywhere. Drug abuse used to be confined to certain parts of major conurbations – but now it's all over the place, from Southport to stockbroker-belt Surrey.'

The plague of the 'dragon' is with us.

And this story is part of it.

It is based on a factual drug-trafficking organisation operated by the IRA in collusion with Colonel Gadaffi's Libya. Its tentacles spread from the Middle East, through Europe, to Dublin – then back into Britain.

Other supplies may be forwarded to the east coast of the United States and Canada.

Many of the characters in this book are the fictitious counterparts of those involved in the *actual* 'ring': 'Frankie Lewis', 'Bernadette', 'The Mulqueen Brothers', 'Maltese Max', and 'The Man' – who in reality remains a shadowy and mysterious figure.

As is the way in the most secret world of narcotics, the full facts will probably never be known. Much has to be 'informed' speculation. One such speculation is the drift of the IRA into international crime, filling the vacuum left by a Mafia retreating under relentless pressure from police in America and Italy.

Theories of global conspiracy are not new, and should be treated with caution.

Certainly there are hundreds of drugs barons throughout the world, operating to satisfy their own personal greed. It would be of little concern to them if their efforts were being knowingly orchestrated by others.

But who would benefit from such an international conspiracy aimed at the social fabric of 'decadent' Western democracies?

Suffice to say that the Bulgarian KGB's involvement in drugs-trafficking and co-operation with international terrorist groupings is well-documented. And Soviet KGB officers are known to be extremely active at remote source villages in the 'Golden Crescent'.

But how will the plague be stopped? Historically, whenever there is a demand, there will always be a supply.

Eventually it can only be stopped on the streets, and particularly by young people who have the courage to say one simple, single word.

'NO.'

TERENCE STRONG,
LONDON, 1986

Acknowledgments

I have an exceptional number of individuals and organisations to thank for their help in my investigations – starting with 'Georgina', who uncovered it.

Members of the Metropolitan Police, Customs & Excise, the Probation Service, the Society of Civil and Public Servants, the Royal Marines, and 'The Christian Science Monitor', have all played their part, as well as Carol for her on-going supply of information.

In Britain: Sam; Roger Lewis and Richard Lock for their history lesson; the Institute for the Study of Drug Dependence; Margaret; writers Tony Shippam and Andrew Tyler; Steve, Em and Jo. And, as always, Paulie and Colin.

In Malta: Amy; Mary-Jane; Giovanni; Helena and Archie; Charles; Peter, and Bill.

In Paxos: Terry.

In Eire: Matthew; Sean; Padraig, and Tom.

In Boston: Dick.

Prologue

The solitary camel picked its way down the stony slope; it seemed to know exactly where it was going.

It looked no different from any other camel, its coat mangy and matted with dried mud. The only unusual thing about it was that it carried a pannier load strapped across its back, and yet was unescorted.

Only its agitated manner and the glazed expression in its eyes gave clues to the fact that it was addicted to opium.

At the bottom the animal stopped and stiffened. The big imperious nose lifted nervously and the nostrils flared, detecting the scent of humans on the hot, dry wind.

Across the valley Ahmed Rahmani, a captain in the Iranian gendarmerie, lowered his binoculars.

He was responsible for this remote mountainous section that bordered with Afghanistan. He knew about the camel 'couriers' that had regularly been fed opium gum and conditioned to follow a special secret route in the knowledge that they'd get more at the journey's end.

Captain Rahmani also knew that on one of those craggy heights to the east a group of heavily-armed bandits was watching the camel's progress. They were dangerous men. Normally the gendarmerie would only give chase in armoured vehicles. And nowadays, since the war with Iraq, those were in very short supply.

'Well, is there any sign of it?' demanded a high-pitched voice in Farsi behind him.

The policeman turned to face the squat, bearded mullah. 'It is coming, *agha*.' He hid his irritation at the cleric's impatience. The man didn't like hanging about getting his nice brown robe and turban clogged with dust. Still it didn't do to upset the religious men of Allah nowadays.

Captain Rahmani beckoned to the two armed policemen who stood beside the dilapidated truck talking to the civilian driver. They came at once and, following his curt instruction, started down the hillside to meet the camel as it came into view around an outcrop.

It gathered speed. The smell of humans meant another tit-bit of opium gum.

Ten minutes later the packages taken from the panniers had been thoroughly examined. Satisfied, the religious man extracted a wad of money from the leather pouch around his waist. He handed it to the policeman who peeled off a few notes for his two officers. They seemed well-pleased; these were hard times in Iran.

They all climbed aboard the truck which began its long journey away from the wild mountains and their hidden dangers. Without any instruction the camel turned and started back the way it had come, as though by remote control.

At a local village Captain Rahmani and his two officers climbed down and watched the truck disappear from view towards the barren waste of desert that stretched before it.

Idly he wondered how the mullah had ever got to know the bandits. Perhaps he had a relative or a contact amongst the clerics in Afghanistan on the other side of the mountains. But it didn't really matter. The important thing was that they should not be found out. Officially the Ayatollah Khomeini's regime frowned on the growing or smuggling of opium, but Captain Rahmani knew that there were plenty of others like the impatient mullah with the squeaky voice.

What he did not know – and little really cared – was that the truck would continue on to the desert city of Yazd.

Before it reached the vaulted, flag-stoned streets of the centre it turned into a dusty estate of modern prefabricated factory units. It drove into the lofty loading bay of one of them and parked beside a refrigerated container trailer.

When the bay doors were closed, the air was rich with the smell of recently defrosted meat from the butchery department.

But that was no concern of the mullah. He took his precious packages to the European who waited beside his trailer. After thoroughly checking the dozens of small polythene packets contained in the larger packages, the man clambered into the back of his empty container trailer.

Two workmen stood inside. They had already removed one of the aluminium panels and extracted the thick slab of solidified insulation foam behind it.

They watched with bored disinterest as the European lifted off the top half of the four-inch thick slab to reveal a series of neatly-cut pockets. Each recess was shallow, otherwise giveaway patches of frost might form on the outside of the trailer later. So it took the man half-an-hour to carefully fit the dozens of tiny packets into the recesses.

Satisfied, he nodded to the workmen. With practised skill they refitted the two halves of the foam slab together and inserted it back into the trailer wall.

A new aluminium panel, which had already been left to oxidise in the factory cold-store, was put into position and pop-riveted. To have re-used the old panel would almost certainly have left tell-tale signs of tampering. The rivet-heads themselves would soon discolour.

And then no one would ever find the illicit cargo. Not unless his was unlucky enough to be the one in 200 rigs to be checked by British Customs. And not unless they were prepared to risk contaminating his cargo. And not unless they were rash enough to rip the container apart.

A million to one chance. The consignment was already as good as delivered.

He stood back momentarily to examine the handiwork then strolled back down to the tailgate. To the mullah's irritation he laconically sat down and lit a cigarette.

'Right. They can load up the fruit now and I'll be on my way.' The Irish accent murdered the pidgin Farsi it attempted.

But the mullah had got the message. And he had already received the money.

The driver ambled back to his cab and threw the refrigeration switch. Inside the trailer the unit began to thrum as the space was filled with a blast of cold air.

He stubbed out his half-finished cigarette and stretched. He had a long, long drive in front of him.

One

The door crashed shut behind him.

He was out.

Billy Robson didn't believe it. He hadn't allowed himself to believe it, even when the bolt on the cell door had been rattled at six-thirty that morning. He'd been awake most of the night, snatching just the odd few moments of fitful sleep, waiting for the dawn. Waiting but still not believing.

After five years' anticipation of one moment, it was difficult to believe when it eventually came.

He had been the last one to leave; the last one to bow his head and step through the door in the front gate of Wormwood Scrubs. Now he stood, clutching the small holdall, and watched. The rest of the released parolees sorted their friends and relatives from the small knot of people waiting at the end of the short, snow-covered drive.

Greetings were muted, abruptly curtailed by the cons who were anxious to be away from the grim Victorian walls.

Only one of them remembered him. 'See ya around, Billy-boy. Be lucky.'

Robson inclined his head and watched impassively as the door of the man's taxi slammed. After five years it was like stepping out of a dark cinema into bright daylight. Everything was too vivid and too loud, all bustle and movement. Too much to take in at once.

The remaining people on the corner began drifting towards a waiting Cortina mini-cab.

There was no sign of Sandy. Perhaps she'd missed the bus, or couldn't get a taxi.

Exhaust from the Cortina belched into the sharp cold air, drifting across his line of vision in a billowing cloud. Slowly it eddied away.

There was no one left.

He was aware of the cold of the snow starting to seep up through the thin leather soles of his shoes. His nose had started to run, dampening the black hairs of the moustache he had kept since his days in the Royal Marines.

In fact, coming out today reminded him of the day, six years earlier, when he'd stepped outside Bickleigh Barracks in Plymouth as a civilian. At twenty-seven he had been free again after nine years' service to the Crown.

The memory flooded back. He had a small fist of apprehension in his gut then. A well-founded apprehension as it turned out. Within twelve months he was doing another sentence, much less pleasant. Five years for driving a bank-robbery getaway car.

Never again.

Robson began to walk. A slow smile crossed his face. He could keep on walking now. Not just a hundred yards to the prison's perimeter wall. But a thousand yards. Miles. As far as he wanted.

In a way, he was pleased that Sandy was late. He knew which way his wife would come, so it wouldn't hurt to indulge himself in the unfamiliar sights and smell around him.

Just the air. Crisp and clean. Not like the cloying fug of stale sweat, cigarette smoke and urine buckets you got with three men sharing a thirteen-by-seven cell each night. Even the air in the yard smelled nothing like the sweet free air on the other side of the wall.

Idly he watched as an electric milk-float rattled to a halt and the milkman carried four pints over to a shop doorway, whistling as he went.

Robson's heart soared. What a sight for sore eyes. He grinned stupidly to himself. He was, after all, beginning – just beginning – to believe it.

BLEEP! BLEEP! ... Hitler has only got one ...!

The loud sing-song blast on the musical horn made him jump. He turned to see the custom-painted E-type swerve past the milk-float. It slipped neatly across the road, through the oncoming traffic, and jerked to a halt beside him.

Angry hooters united in protest. Andy Sutcliff's head grinned up from the open window and his hand came out to cheerfully V-sign the aggrieved motorists.

'Well, if Billy-boy isn't on the run again. You didn't hang about, did you?'

Robson grinned down at the unruly mop of fair hair. 'With jokes like that, Andy, you and I *could* just fall out!'

'And ruin our long-running relationship? Schoolboy chums, and Best Man and all that crap ...'

'Piss off.'

Aren't you going to get in ... ?'

Robson leaned on the purple roof. 'I'm expecting Sandy.'

'I know you are, Billy-boy, but you'll have to make do with me. Sand was a bit poorly this morning. She asked me if I'd do the honour of picking up our fallen idol.'

'Is she ill?'

Sutcliff shook his head. 'No, nothing serious. Just sick. Probably woman's troubles. Or maybe it was the few jars we had last night to celebrate you comin' out.'

Robson laughed. 'You could have waited until I was there.'

He had scarcely opened the door and settled into the mauve fleece-covered passenger seat when Sutcliff had released the clutch with a vengeance. The exhausts rumbled with menace as the garish E-type leapt forward, prising its way through a gap in the oncoming stream of traffic and back to the left-hand lane. A second cacophony of hooters protested as the drivers were forced to brake.

'You haven't changed,' Robson observed with a grin. It was good to be with his old friend again. No one else's company was ever quite as enjoyable. Even if it was embarrassing on occasions. 'You never mentioned your new motor.'

Sutcliff chuckled as he jumped the traffic-lights. 'Didn't want to make you jealous. Like it?'

'Truthfully?'

'Course.'

'It's bloody awful. Who in God's name chose the colours?'

'Some pop star whose roadie absconded with all the assets – except this car. It was a finance company reclaim, so I got it cheap.'

'I can see why.'

Sutcliff scratched at the thick scrub of fair curls at his chin. 'It pulls the birds, no trouble. You can see the footprints on the roof.'

'Time you settled down, Andy, and found yourself a wife.'

'In time, Billy, in time. I can't afford to run an E-type and a wife.'

'How's the motor trade, then?' Robson plucked at the sleeve of his friend's suede jacket. 'That must have cost a bob or two.'

The E-type swerved to overtake a dawdling car on the inside. 'Well, I'm scratching a living, Billy-boy, you know how it is. Shifting the odd motor off the forecourt, and doin' a bit of duckin' and diving on the side. To keep the old head above water. But what with the tax man and the VAT inspector, it ain't easy.'

Robson smiled to himself. Some things never changed. But he hadn't been really listening. His mind had moved on to the prospect of being reunited with Sandy. For a moment he allowed himself to imagine the creamy complexion that made her look younger than her twenty-nine years. Those stunning grey eyes that were so often clouded with some obscure minor worry, but could be bright and laughing at the slightest provocation. And that hair. That's what made everyone fall in love with Sandy. Her hair. Soft, light, red-blonde waves with a natural hint of ginger.

In his mind's eye, his gaze travelled down her pale, slender body. Suddenly the smell of her hair seemed to fill the car . . .

The effect of it shook Robson for a moment. For two years now he hadn't allowed himself to think of her in that way. Not since that Christmas after her visit, which had left him feeling desperately aroused. They all knew the gentle tell-tale tremor of the bunk-beds. His cell mates had said nothing. Just exchanged knowing smirks and continued the game of Hangman that they played obsessively.

'You listening, Billy?'

Robson realised they were nearly at the Mile End Road. 'Sorry, Andy. Miles away.'

'Dirty sod.' Sutcliff grinned.

'How'd you guess?'

'I'd be the same. It's got to be either Sandy, or young Dan.'

The words pulled Robson up short. He realised that he had hardly thought about his son since he'd walked through the gates of the Scrubs. He also knew why.

Dan had been only four when he'd gone inside. Scarcely more than a toddler. Now he was nine. Almost an adult. Soon it would be school studies and girls. Hopefully in that order.

Sandy had wanted to bring him in for the occasional visit, but Robson had steadfastly refused. He wasn't sure of his reasons. Shame or pride. Guilt? A bit of both. Like erotic thoughts of his wife, he'd not allowed his son to enter his conscious mind. Now he felt distinctly nervous.

'Andy, stop at the corner, will you. I want to get some snouts.'

'Thought you'd given it up.'

Robson suddenly saw the funny side of it. Afraid of meeting his own son. 'I've just started again.'

He'd smoked two in the short time before the monolith of Newey House could be seen above the East End rooftops, like a finger poking a rude gesture at the sky. It had been one of the first tower blocks built in the early 1960s. An architect's vision of the better world to come – a vision that, no doubt, he made sure he didn't have to live anywhere near.

Andy Sutcliff parked the car in a side street where a group of schoolchildren were playing football. After warning them of the dire consequences of even looking at its gleaming paintwork too hard, he walked with Robson through the maze of council houses and maisonettes to the entrance of Newey House.

Already the window in the newly-installed security door had been smashed. Anyone could reach in and open it without punching in the code number. Aerosol graffiti was the only decoration on the rough slab walls of the lobby which had the souless smell of accumulated dirt and damp concrete.

A tall West Indian in a bright bomber-jacket was waiting

impatiently by the lifts with a roll of carpet. Beside him stood an elderly woman loaded down with a tartan bag.

The West Indian grinned at Robson. 'Hope you're feelin' fit, man. Looks like they're both outa order again. Mashed.'

Sutcliff rolled his eyes in despair. 'Not again? They break down every time I bloody come here. Got it in for me, they have.'

'It's them Chinese on the top floor,' the old woman muttered accusingly. 'They jam matchsticks in the buttons.' She didn't elaborate as to why they should want to commit such a sabotage.

Robson said: 'If someone's holding it, I'll send it down. What floor you live on, love?'

She told him it was the twelfth.

He picked up her bag. 'I'll drop it outside your door for you on our way up.'

The wizened face peered up at him from under the floral nylon headscarf. 'You're Billy Robson, aren't ya?' She didn't wait for confirmation. 'I 'eard you was out.'

Robson smiled gently. 'I didn't go inside for nicking old ladies' shopping, love.'

She cackled with mirth. 'Na, course you didn't, dear. You're a good 'un. Everyone round 'ere knows that.' She waved a warning finger at him. 'Just you stay outa trouble, Billy-boy, and look after your wife an' son proper. She's a lovely girl, that 'un. You make sure you deserve 'er.'

'Shall do, Gran,' Robson assured her.

The West Indian then insisted on shaking his hand. 'Name's Spiro,' he introduced. 'I've heard about you. If there's anything I can do, man, just knock me up. On the floor below.'

Robson was beginning to feel like the neighbourhood's prodigal son as they began the climb.

'Twenty-four floors,' Andy Sutcliff complained, 'That's forty-eight soddin' flights. Like climbing bloody Everest. Why'd you have to pick the top floor?'

'I didn't choose it, Andy. When we lost the house we had to take what the council offered. It was all they had.'

By the time they reached the eleventh, Robson's unused leg muscles were screaming for rest.

The two friends faced each other, breathing heavily and laughing at the stupidity of their shared agony.

Suddenly Robson sniffed the air. 'What's that smell?' He moved towards the landing door.

Quickly Sutcliff placed a restraining hand on his friend's shoulder. 'Careful, Billy. Someone's using smack. Heroin.' For a moment Robson held his friend's gaze, then turned and gently eased open the door.

There were three of them. Two youths sat on the concrete floor beside the lifts, one with his legs oustretched, his head lolling. The second was crouched over with knees drawn up to his chest, supporting a sheet of aluminium foil in his hands. A third was standing, slightly bent as he played a cigarette lighter beneath the foil for his friend to sniff up the fumes.

Robson went to say something, but Sutcliff silenced him. 'C'mon, Billy. You've got a home to go to, remember?'

Quietly, he let the swing door close. Somehow the scene had really sickened him. They were not much older than his own son. An evil tableau of hunched dwarfs, so feverishly intent on their deeds that they hadn't even noticed him.

'They call it chasin' the dragon,' Sutcliff said as they started to climb the stairs again. 'All the kids are doin' it now. It's nothing to them. They're even pushin' it outside the schools. Call it "Happy Powder". Give it free until the kids get hooked.'

'What's been happening to the world while I've been inside?'

Sutcliff gave a brittle laugh. 'It's a meaner place, Billy, that's all. And the kids see smack as a way out. Accordin' to the papers, it's a bleedin' epidemic, especially in the big towns. You know, teenagers out of work, no future and all that.'

They dropped off the old woman's shopping outside her door on the twelfth, and continued on up.

As they neared the top floor, Robson forgot about the incident with the young junkies. Instead he was aware that his elation at being free again was tempered by wondering how he'd be able to cope again with normality. The trivia of life suddenly seemed momentously important. Helping in the home, going shopping with Sandy, assisting his son with sums he couldn't fathom himself, lying in on a Sunday morning . . .

Abruptly they were there. Through the swing-door and onto the landing. The same graffiti-smeared walls, the same odour of soiled concrete and faint tang of someone cooking cabbage.

But this floor was different. This was home. He'd heard about them so often that even the pile of black polythene bags that emanated from the flat opposite seemed familiar. No one knew what the Chinese family did, but the speculation was that they were running some kind of "sweat shop". One of the lifts, at least, he noted, was working now.

The cheerful ding-dong doorbell chimed behind his front door. He heard a muffled voice somewhere inside. A sudden scuffling movement as something was hastily tidied away. A cushion being plumped.

The distant blurred form on the other side of the frosted glass grew in size, outlined against a shaft of wintry sunlight.

Through the pane he could almost distinguish his wife's familiar features. Pale fleshy blobs through the patterns. His heart pounded. He heard her hand on the Yale lock. The click and faint creak of hinges that needed oil.

'Hello, Sand.' He was aware that his grin was stupidly huge.

She seemed smaller than the last time he had seen her. More slender, and more vulnerable. She looked tired, too, her skin paler than he remembered. But it did nothing to detract from the dancing light of pleasure in her grey eyes.

'Billy . . .'

For a second they just stood and looked at each other. Neither quite believed it. Andy Sutcliff shifted his feet.

'Oh, God, Billy . . .'

She threw herself at him, her arms tight around his neck. It seemed like an age that they clung together. Not speaking, just drawing strength from each other, feeling the ebb and flow of unspoken emotion.

Andy Sutcliff cleared his throat. 'Er, well, you two, I'll – er – leave you to it. I guess you've a lot to talk about. I'll see you around.'

Robson gently eased back from his wife, his eyes not leaving her face. 'Sure, Andy, and thanks for all you've done, mate. I'm grateful, really.'

Sandy peered over her husband's shoulders and roughly wiped the tears from her eyes. 'Yes, thanks, Andy, for picking Billy up. I don't know what I'd have done without you.'

Sutcliff dismissed it with a wave. 'Worth it, just to see the smile on your face, love.' He hesitated by the lift. 'Oh, by the way, Billy, I saw Rich Abbott yesterday evening. He asked if you could drop round the club tonight for a drink. Celebrate, for old times' sake.'

Robson's back stiffened. Without turning around he said: 'There's no old times *to* celebrate, Andy. I've spent the last five years trying to forget Rich Abbott. Tell him thanks but no thanks.'

Sutcliff scratched at his beard. 'He might not like that.'

'I don't give a toss what he likes.'

Robson's friend went to say something, then thought better of it, as Sandy led her husband inside.

The door closed, and for the first time Robson noticed young Dan. His son was standing uncertainly by the living-room door, his skinny four-foot-six frame dressed in jeans and a faded Royal Marines T-shirt that was several sizes too big for him. He had his father's straight black hair, but cut in a fringe; the same blue eyes. The freckles and the mouth, now set in a sullen pout, belonged to Sandy.

'Hey, aren't you going to come and say hallo to your Dad?' his mother asked.

Dan's eyes flickered, unsure.

Robson dropped to one knee. He could hardly believe that this was the same wild and hairbrained four-year-old he'd last seen. 'Hallo, son. It's good to see you again.'

Dan made no attempt to move. His eyes dipped to study his tatty trainers with profound interest.

Robson and Sandy exchanged glances. 'Come on,' she repeated. 'Come and say hallo to your Dad.'

Grudgingly Dan advanced across the threadbare carpet, still diverting his eyes from Robson's. His father reached out slowly to take hold of the boy's shoulders, and draw him close, hugging him tightly to his chest.

Dan still said nothing. It was then that Robson felt the charged emotion well up inside him, tearing aside the barriers of protection he had built up so carefully over the years. He could do nothing to stop the tremors and the thin trickle of tears that ran onto his son's hair.

When the door of Dan's bedroom closed for the last time at eight o'clock that night, Robson had to admit to a sense of relief.

It had been a long day and it hadn't been easy. Only slowly, very slowly, had Dan begun to accept him. For the most part he answered in monosyllables; rarely did the boy allow his eyes to meet those of his father.

Robson sat down on the sofa and stretched out his legs. Home sweet home, perhaps, but it was hard work.

The room was more sparsely furnished than he remembered. Just a well-worn sideboard and coffee table, and the tatty three-piece suite. Different from the ones they'd had before he went inside.

Sandy came in with a tray of coffee. It looked as though the day had taken its toll on her, too. Her eyes were dark-rimmed, her straggly hair in need of a shampoo.

'You look all in, Sand.'

She smiled wanly. 'It must be all the excitement. Not every day you get your old man back after five years. And Danny didn't make things easier. You'd think he'd be pleased to see his Dad.'

Robson stirred his coffee. 'He just needs time to adjust. We all do. By the way, I haven't asked you what happened this morning? Why you sent Andy?'

She shrugged and settled down on the floor by his feet. 'I felt a bit sick. Shivery, you know. Must be one of those flu bugs floating about. Danny's always picking up something from school and passing it on. I seem to get everything that's going since that glandular fever last year. It's a devil to shake off. Doc reckons it can recur on and off for months, years even. Leaves you feeling so bloody lethargic and run-down.'

'Have you been sleeping okay?'

Absently she scratched at her arm. 'It's all right if I use Valium or Mogadon, but then I can't get it together the next day.'

He reached down and held her wrist. She was trembling. 'You'll sleep all right now, Sand. You won't need your pills. You've got me.'

Her laughter was brittle as she drew her hand away. 'You reckon that now you're back, God's in His heaven and all's right with the world?'

Robson grinned. 'Well, for us.'

Suddenly she looked angry. 'I can't just switch on and off like that. Have you any bloody idea what I've been through during the past five years?'

'Of course.' Consoling.

Her eyes bore into his, the pupils small and hard. 'I don't think you have, Billy. I don't think you've a bloody clue. It was bad enough those nine years when you were playing soldiers in the Marines. But at least we had a home of our own at the end of it. A little terraced house. Furniture that wasn't on HP.'

Her words cut like a razor. 'Christ, Sand, I know what I've done. I've paid, though. Paid for five years.'

She climbed unsteadily to her feet. 'Paid, Billy? You haven't even started. It's me who's done the paying. ME!

I've had my house repossessed and I've had to sell off our furniture to meet the bills.'

Robson blinked. Glancing around the room he realised just how much had gone. Not only the furniture, but paintings and ornaments. Earlier he'd noticed how bare the kitchen was. The food-mixer, the fridge, the washing machine. Even their best canteen of cutlery that had been a wedding present from her mother.

'Why didn't you tell me just how bad things were, Sand?'

The anger burned in her eyes. 'And what the hell could you have done about it?' She turned abruptly, clutching her arms about her, squeezing at her sleeves in an effort to suppress her rage.

Quietly Robson climbed to his feet and stepped behind her. He slid his arms around her waist and pressed his face against her hair.

'We've got to start again, Sand,' he murmured. 'I'll make it up to you and Danny, honest I will.' He let his eyes wander around the bare painted walls. 'I'm staying out. An honest job. Like I always intended when I left the Corps. I won't get side-tracked or tempted. I promise you that.'

Slowly she swivelled around in his embrace. Her eyes were moist. 'You poor, poor darling. You don't see it, do you?'

'What?'

She shook her head in slow exasperation. 'You thought it would be easy when you left the Marines. But you weren't qualified *then*. Now we've got three million on the dole and you've got a record.'

'I'll do it.' Determined.

Idly she twisted at the hairs at the top of his open shirt. 'We'll need help from our friends, Billy. I can't continue bringing up Danny in this slum. Too ashamed to bring his mates back. We've got to have money.'

'We've got each other now.'

After a pause she said softly. '*I* need money, Billy. A woman needs a decent home. That means if you want to keep me, you'll have to get a good job.' She hesitated. 'And I don't know if you *can*.'

Suddenly Robson thought he knew what she was driving at. 'Is this anything to do with Rich Abbott?'

'I think you ought to see him.'

'Has he been around here?'

She shook her head. 'Not like that, Billy. In fact he's made sure no one bothers me. Even that randy milkman was told not to get any ideas if he didn't want his legs broken. Rich is very sweet. He cares about us. And about Danny. More than once, when I couldn't cope with the bills, he's dropped me a few hundred . . .'

'Jesus!' Robson pulled away abruptly.

Rich Abbott cares. So Rich Abbott bloody well might. As far as Robson was concerned, he was the reason he'd spent the last half decade of his life rotting at Her Majesty's pleasure.

Rich Abbott and his cream Roller. Rich Abbott with his fat roll of banknotes and his dollybirds. Rich Abbott who had it all worked out. No risks. Just a little driving. Fast driving with no questions asked.

Even now he could recall that fateful talk in the pub six years ago as though it was yesterday.

Rich Abbott had cared then. Worried that his old school chum couldn't get a decent job and needed the name of a good moneylender so he could pay off his mortgage instalments. Concerned that an ex-Royal Marine couldn't get it together in Civvy Street.

He'd offered the job and in a moment of desperation Robson had been tempted. He was being invited back to the community in which he'd grown up before he'd joined the Marines. Amongst friends. One of the lads again, trusted. Even the prospect of some real excitement appealed. But mostly it was the chance to square things with Sandy. To give themselves and their son a chance. Even if it did mean compromising his ideals – just once.

Just a morning's work. That's what Rich Abbott had said. A morning's work and fifteen grand in cash for his troubles.

But it hadn't worked out like that, had it? It ended up as five years' work and bugger all to show for it.

'It wasn't Rich's fault it went wrong.' Sandy's voice cut through his thoughts.

Robson turned. 'Told you all about it, has he?'

His wife realised she was out of order. She lowered her eyes. 'No, of course not. Just that it was bad luck.'

He stared at the ceiling in desperation, trying to prevent the scene that had haunted him for so long from re-forming in his mind.

Sitting there in the souped-up Jaguar, drumming on the steering wheel with his fingers, palms moist with sweat. Watching ahead. Watching the rear-view mirror. Glancing at the open door of the bank. Heart thumping, trying to burst out of his chest.

Wondering just how long it had been since he'd heard the crack of the shotgun. Shock tactics. Both barrels into the ceiling. Stun everyone into instant obedience as the plaster showered down on them. Their cartridges had only been loaded with rice grain, but no one realised. The bank clerks and customers didn't know Rich Abbott had insisted that no "civilians" got hurt.

How many minutes had it been? It was the longest wait of his life. The street seemed packed with traffic. Every car in London was on this stretch of road. Every pedestrian walking the pavement by his car. And each one of them, it seemed to Robson, peering in at him as they walked past.

He could have sworn he could hear his wristwatch ticking, so aware was he of each long second.

Then they were out. Three men in boiler-suits and grotesque stocking masks. Out into the bright sunlight, exposed to the world.

Robson revved the engine. The doors flew open and the car rocked as the gang leapt in. Hard on the gas, up with the clutch. A roar of exhaust and the screech of dry rubber on tarmac. The rear door swung wildly as he drove straight out into the path of a double-decker bus.

More squeals of brakes and the great red monster slewed across the road and nosed violently into the back of a baker's delivery van. Loaves of Mother's Pride scattered all over the pavement.

It had been a nightmare drive. It had gone wrong from the very start. A sudden fault in the carburettor, and a police car where it shouldn't have been, saw to that. The white Rover had been sitting on their tail right from the start. They didn't have a chance.

Rich Abbott's carefully laid getaway route had to be abandoned. Instead, Robson had to go through the back-doubles, accelerating hard down car-lined residential streets. Making turn after turn to allow each gang member to leap out as he slowed, and to run for safety before the pursuing Rover came round the last corner, the siren screaming in his ears.

He was the only one left when his luck ran out and he rammed the second police car sent to head him off.

At the station, he learned they'd caught the man with the money. Arnie. Neither he nor Robson ever said who else had been with them.

That silence had ensured him an eight-year sentence.

Sandy said: 'It was your decision, Billy. You didn't have to do it. No one forced you. You can't blame Rich. He made nothing out of it, you know that. The police got the money back. But he's looked after us. He didn't have to . . .'

'I know, I know.' Robson gazed out of the window. A glittering panoramic view of East London by night; the one compensation Newey House had to offer.

'There's still time,' Sandy spoke hesitatingly, 'if you want to meet Rich tonight, like Andy said.'

He breathed in deeply and shut his eyes. 'No, Sandy, forget it. I've finished with Rich Abbott. And all his cronies.'

Sandy shrugged. 'Rich says villains always look after their own . . .'

He didn't reply. He didn't trust himself. Slowly he walked to the sideboard and took out a bottle of Tesco's own Scotch. His hands were trembling as he poured the generous measures into a couple of tumblers.

Sandy watched cautiously as he held out a glass to her.

'Thanks,' she whispered.

'Sand, let's go to bed. I've waited five years for this. Five years and one day. And I think that last day was the worst.'

She sipped at her drink, seemingly distracted. 'I'm afraid I'm not feeling very sexy, Billy. Tired. Perhaps we'd do better to wait.'

Robson ran his hand through her hair and planted a kiss gently on her forehead. It said it all. She knew he ached for her.

'All right, Billy.'

*　　　*　　　*

But it wasn't.

It had been a disaster. Robson had sensed Sandy's lack of enthusiasm and his own body had failed to respond. Perhaps it had been the prolonged period of abstinence. He'd heard that long terms in jail could end with impotence or sterility. Or both. It was common prison folklore.

He had slept fitfully until seven. A luxurious extra half-hour over the Scrubs regime. No doubt it would be some time before his inbuilt body-clock would allow him to take full advantage of the extra hours.

He climbed out of the double bed and wrapped a blue terry towelling dressing gown around his naked body, before reaching for the cigarette pack. Only two left.

He grimaced as he lit one of them and stared out at the expanse of grey London sky. It was full of the threat of more sleet.

Out there, somewhere, he told himself, his future lay waiting. All he had to do was find it.

The front door slammed suddenly, jolting him. Danny?

Quickly, he made his way through to his son's bedroom where 'Duran Duran' posters vied for prominence with portraits of West Ham football players.

On the blanket he found the hastily scrawled note: *Sorry, Mum, forgot to tell you I've got to be at school early today. Dan.*

Robson rubbed his eyes and shuffled to the kitchen. As he put the kettle on the stove, he couldn't help wondering what on earth his son had to do at school at seven in the morning?

But as he made the tea, he was sure he knew the answer. His son just hadn't wanted to run the risk of having to talk to his father again before he left.

He put it from his mind and took the tray through to the bedroom. He wasn't sorry to have some more time alone with Sandy.

He had difficulty in rousing her, and when he did she was shivering.

'You got that flu back?' he asked.

She held the cup in both hands and sipped at it. 'Seems like it.' He remembered how edgy she'd seemed sometimes on her visits to the prison. Not herself.

'You ought to see the doctor again. Even I can see you're run-down.'

The suggestion appeared to irritate her. 'I'll be all right: I've got tablets. For Christ's sake, don't fuss me!'

He raised his hands in mock surrender. 'Okay, okay! Sorry I spoke!'

She smiled thinly. 'I didn't mean that. Just don't get at me, eh? I'm not used to it. I sort myself out nowadays.'

'Sure.'

Ding-dong, ding-dong. The door chimes echoed throught the flat.

Robson frowned. 'Who the hell can that be?' He glanced at his watch. 'It's only eight.'

'Perhaps it's Andy.' In a sudden scurry of activity, she threw her legs out from under the bedclothes onto the floor and stood up. The flash of her slim naked body and pert breasts whipped at his senses. She grabbed her dressing-gown from the end of the bed and gathered it around her shoulders. 'Let me get to the loo before you answer. I don't want people to see me in this state.'

Robson laughed. He'd lost his own sense of privacy during his years in the Scrubs. 'It's probably only Andy You said so yourself.'

She grabbed her sponge bag from beneath the bed and moved towards the door. 'No need to make a thing of it,' she said irritably. 'I just don't want to be seen looking like some slag.'

He followed her through to the hall, waited until she had disappeared into the bathroom, then opened the front door.

' 'Allo, Billy-boy. How are you then?'

Rich Abbott hadn't changed. He looked to be in his mid-thirties, but then he always had. The swarthy, square-chinned face with its blunt features had a sort of inbuilt maturity. Robson guessed he would never look much older. The tan helped, of course, even if it wasn't natural. It certainly set off the thick waves of black hair.

'Sorry to call so early, Billy-boy.' He indicated the open-necked tuxedo and black dinner suit beneath the dark overcoat. 'But I was on me way back from a poker game up West. Thought I might miss you if I left it. 'Ope I didn't disturb nothin'.' One of his icy blue eyes winked knowingly.

Robson felt the hairs on the back of his neck bristle. 'We've nothing to say to each other, Rich. I asked Andy to tell you.'

Rich Abbott's smile was disarming: perfect white teeth glistened through his morning shadow. 'Yes, Billy, I got the message. I was upset, but I understand. You missed a good party.' He peered into the hall. 'May I come in? Just a couple of mo's to say thanks to an old school chum . . .'

With a flourish, he produced the magnum of champagne he'd been concealing beneath his overcoat. 'If you've a drop of orange juice, we could have a champagne-breakfast. I 'ad a lucky night.' The bright white smile persisted.

Robson's shoulders relaxed. Some things never changed, not around here. 'Five minutes then.'

The older man stepped smartly in, walking through to the living-room without further invitation, in a search for glasses.

Robson tapped on the bathroom door. 'It's Rich. Brought a champagne-breakfast, if you're interested.'

He heard a mumbled curse. 'Oh, shit! . . .' Then loudly: 'Okay, Billy, I'll be out.'

He went through to find Rich Abbott holding out a glass of sparkling orange liquid. 'Helped meself from the sideboard, Billy-boy. Hope that's in order?'

Robson took the glass.

'To freedom. Cheers!' Abbott downed it in three successive gulps.

It wasn't his style, but Robson took a sip. 'What is it, Rich? It won't do me any good with the fuzz if you're seen coming here.'

The man raised a disparaging eyebrow. 'Another reason for the early call, Billy-boy. But if the mountain won't go to Mohammed . . .' He topped up his glass. 'I just wanted to thank you, Billy, personal like. For not grassing. If I'd gone inside again, they'd have thrown away the key. I'm honestly grateful for that.' He sounded as though he meant it.

'What are you doing now?' Rich Abbott didn't miss the implication.

The smile dazzled again. 'I've gone legit, Billy. Well, you know, within reason. That business with you really turned me up. I thought, Rich, I thought, your luck is running out. So I organised a couple of jobs from a distance. Quiet stuff. A nice line in 'jars' – you know, replica jewellery – and some quiet 'tweedles'. Switched jewellery in some real posh houses up in Mayfair. Each job well clued-up first. Even today, some old dowagers don't know they're wearin' zircons round their necks instead of gems.'

He took another swig of the Buck's Fizz. 'That's the way of the future now, Billy. Sophistication. No more going into jugs like we did, or jumpin' up lorries. The Bill's all

computerised now. Even cheque books and cards are gettin'
impossible. Holograms an' all. You've got to specialise.'

'I thought you'd gone legit?'

Rich Abbott tapped the side of his nose. 'So I have, Billy-
boy, so I have. I've invested in a couple of clubs, and I'm
doing a little research into the computer business. Hi-tech.'

Robson shook his head in slow disbelief. 'Times *have*
changed.'

'Villainy's changing, Billy.' Abbot spoke almost with regret
in his voice as he perched himself on the arm of the sofa.
'Since the Battle of the OK Corral in Glasgow, I suppose.
The Brothers Grimm and the Richardsons – shit, there was
respect in them days, Billy. You could trust people. There was
a pecking order and mutual trust. Now it's all cowboys and
wogs.' Suddenly, he straightened his back. 'Thank God, I'm
young enough to move with the times. Adapt. You know,
Billy, I did a three- and a five-year stretch, when I was in me
twenties – while you was tear-arsin' around the world in the
Marines shootin' people. Next time I went in it would have
been for a ten. I couldn't face that. Coming out, I'd 'ave been
pushin' fifty. So I've adapted.'

The door opened and Sandy came in. She had made a
half-hearted attempt to comb her hair but had forgotten
to remove the smudged mascara from the night before.
Nevertheless, her complexion had lost its waxy pallor, and
she looked better.

As she took the glass from Rich Abbott, her husband
noticed that the fever seemed to have passed.

'You're lookin' as lovely as ever, Sand,' Abbott said, but he
didn't sound very convincing.

She smiled. 'I've got some bug, but I'm feeling better
now.'

Abbott nodded as though she had confirmed something he was thinking. 'It's like I was saying, Billy, crime don't pay nowadays. An' it's not just us. Like your good lady here. Pretty though she is, you can tell she's been through a rough patch. Run-down . . .'

Robson felt his anger rising. But Rich Abbott saw it coming, and raised a hand in protest. 'Sorry, Billy, but it's got to be said. We look after our own here, don't forget that. I know you did your bit in the Forces, but you're *still* one of us.' He glanced at Sandy who had seated herself on an armchair allowing an expanse of shapely thigh to show below her care- lessly arranged dressing-gown. 'For Christ's sake, you, me and Andy were all at school together. In the same gang. Playing 'Knock-down-Ginger' and runnin' around the old bomb-sites when we should've been in class. And I can remember Sand down the road at the secondary-modern. We were all trying to get down her knickers behind the bicycle-sheds.'

'Rich!' Sandy protested half-heartedly.

Abbott roared. 'No offence, love. None of us succeeded, till lover-boy here came and swept you off your feet.' His laughter subsided. 'What I'm getting at, Billy, is that you've got *mates*. They may be villains, but you've known most since you was a nipper. And since you went in the frame for that bank job, you've earned their *respect*.'

'I'm flattered,' Robson muttered sarcastically.

Rich Abbott climbed to his feet and came to stand with his face only a few inches from Robson's. 'You should be, Billy-boy. And there are several faces in my spieler who owe you as a result of keeping stüm. They'd be happy to show their appreciation.'

Robson shook his head in disbelief. 'If you mean a whip- round, Rich, forget it. I don't need it.'

'Listen to 'im, Billy, for Christsakes,' Sandy pleaded. 'And get off that high-horse of yours before you fall off . . .'

Rich Abbott placed his empty glass on the sideboard and moved towards the door. 'Well, remember what I said, Billy. You're always welcome down the spieler, and a lot of you ol' mates will be there tonight. So, if you've a mind, come an' have a few jars on me. Right?' He raised his hand. 'Be lucky.'

The front door closed a few seconds later, and Robson paced thoughtfully back into the room.

Sandy looked up at him. 'Well?'

'Well what?'

'Are you going?'

He glanced around for his cigarettes. 'What do you think?'

'I think you're a bloody fool, Billy Robson.'

Angrily, he snatched the pack from the coffee table. It was empty.

Two

Detective Chief Superintendent Ray Pilger felt lousy.

As the dark blue Ambassador 1.7L squealed around another corner, he felt distinctly bilious. The driver was new and Pilger didn't care for his rally-cross style.

The car began a series of intermittent hard accelerations and jolting stops as they negotiated around Westminister. It almost made him wish he hadn't gone on the town last night. Almost, but not quite. It wasn't often that the Central Drug Squad of the Metropolitan Police had something to celebrate these days. They'd scored a lot of hits all right, more and more frequently. But in recent years the more narcotics they took out of circulation, the greater was the volume they missed.

He pressed his cheek against the window. Like taking away a teaspoonful from a mountain of sugar.

Outside the Houses of Parliament flashed by behind a curtain of grey sleet. Now at last, they'd had a big one – Mustaq Malik – known by the glamorous name of 'The Black Prince'.

He'd been caught thousands of miles away from London near his palatial mansion in Karachi. At last the Pakistani authorities had had their hand forced by outside pressures to make the arrest. And with it, the single biggest and most influential heroin supplier in that source country had been snuffed out.

It was a gratifying result to the eighteen-month-long 'Operation Fisherman', during which over £2 million worth of heroin had been seized as it was ingeniously smuggled into Heathrow. Of course, it was mostly a Customs and Excise victory. But Pilger was pleased that his Squad had played an important role in the vast international co-operation, and the trap that actually brought Mustaq Malik to book. It was so rare to ever get the men who mattered.

Yes, Pilger decided, it had been worth the night on the town. Without doubt.

But he also had little doubt that the billionaire Malik wouldn't stay in custody for long. That was the most insidious thing about drugs. The profits were so huge that anyone could be bought. Anyone. It was proven history. It was bad enough in Western democracies, but in a place like Pakistan where bribery was endemic . . .

Pilger sighed as the Ambassador turned into Broadway. Even if Malik was sentenced, how long before another mastermind stepped in to take his place? On the streets of London, he had no doubt that the fall of 'The Black Prince' would cause no more than a brief hiccup in the continuing supply.

With a quick flick of the wheel, the driver turned the car into the New Scotland Yard sliproad and pulled to an extravagant halt outside the glass doors. His passenger was thankful to get out into the sharp February air, and then into the comfortable warmth of the white and grey marble foyer where the 'eternal flame' flickered in its glass case. In memory of those Metropolitan Police members who had died during two World Wars.

The check on his warrant card by the uniformed police officers on guard was perfunctory. The short, neat ginger hair and ruddy complexion of the stern, clean-shaven face was well known to the duty staff. As familiar, in fact, as the man's inevitably impeccable turnout. Today it was an immaculately pressed lightweight suit, expertly cut about a slim muscular frame that carried its forty-odd years well.

Detective Chief Superintendent Ray Pilger's appearance and open manner spoke volumes. It was a statement of incorruptibility – a rare quality amongst the narcotics police of the world. Even one of his predecessors had fallen from grace – not to mention lesser officers in the Drug Squad who'd become enmeshed in the spider's web of bribery and double-dealing that the trade created.

On taking the appointment, he had decided that his approach had to be different from his contemporaries' in other branches of the force. He knew no villain, fellow policeman or informer would ever fully trust him. He knew that the slightest slip-up would be the end of his career. And sometimes, even now, that hurt.

'Squeaky clean,' he had confided to a friend once. 'That's how I've got to be and to be seen to be. Squeaky clean.' It was an underworld expression that said it all. And he liked it.

He had vowed that, except for reasons of security with cases in hand, he would be totally frank with the press. Keep an open door, with no questions hedged and no unpleasant truths withheld. And likewise he would run the Squad with a rod of iron.

Strict discipline and everything by the book. No deals or horse-trading that was a necessary way of life with the rest of the Met.

'A politician, not a policeman' was the unkind verdict of some old-timers in the Force. But they were only half-right. A politician he might be, but Pilger had a private, almost evangelical mission to purge society of its most evil cancer.

It was a mission, he knew, that would never be achieved.

He passed through one of the stainless steel blast-doors and around to the lifts. On the sixteenth floor he turned right, away from his office, and past the large Squad Room to one of the 'secure' conference rooms.

Today was going to be different, of that he was sure. Something was in the wind, although he didn't know what. He had only had the call from the Commissioner about the 'special briefing' the evening before. All very mysterious. And too late to cancel the night's celebrations.

He just hoped WPC Gifford would move her pretty little backside and keep the coffee flowing as instructed. It wasn't unknown for admiring officers to distract her.

Outside the teak door he paused, flipped the sign to CONFERENCE IN PROGRESS, took a deep breath, and entered.

Pilger instantly recognised two of the three men seated at the large table in the bare and featureless conference room.

Opposite sat Fred Roxan, the dour Customs drugs investigation chief with the florid, heavily jowled face, and a body to match. The thick thighs beneath the crumpled suit fitted tightly between the arms of the tubular steel chair.

As usual the grey eyes were totally deadpan when he spoke. 'Given you up for lost, Ray. Good party last night, was it?'

Pilger replied with a tight half-smile. Roxan always had a Customs man's dyspeptic sense of humour.

'Worth celebrating so I hear,' Derek Dillinger came in quickly to diffuse the antagonism before it had a chance to become established. The softly spoken, dark-haired detective inspector from the Anti-Terrorist Squad had only met Pilger previously on the squash court. In their few encounters, the older man had thrashed him soundly, but he had liked him neverthless. Which was more than he could say about this first encounter with Fred Roxan.

'Absolutely right, D. D.,' Pilger confirmed. 'All work and no play, as they say . . .'

Roxan grunted. 'I suppose it was the snow and traffic this morning.' Once he got hold of a bone, the Customs chief wasn't renowned for letting go.

'I trust, gentlemen, we can start. Even if it isn't *quite* yet nine.'

It was the stranger who spoke. The sing-song accent was immediately identifiable as Welsh.

Roxan's eyes hardened and he wrinkled his bulbous nose with suppressed irritation as he cast his gaze disparagingly at the short, stocky figure at the head of the table.

'Major Harper's the name. Bill or "Boyo" Harper. Take your pick.' The smile on the rotund, balding head was quite disarming. 'The coffee smells good. Shall I be Mum?'

He didn't wait for a reply but began to fill the cups on the tray deftly. As he did so he continued cheerfully: 'I don't know how much you've all been told. If our usual British bureaucracies are running true to form, precious little I expect. ''Fact is, I'm here as a representative of the "TIGER" Committee. That's short for Terrorist Intelligence Gathering Evaluation Review. I'm sure you're all aware that it was set up in response to the British bombing last year when the Provisional IRA nearly succeeded in taking out the entire British cabinet.' He looked up and smiled. 'Who's for milk and sugar?'

Major Harper swiftly serviced the orders and slid the cups across the polished surface of the table. 'The role of TIGER

– as Derek Dillinger will know – is to channel and co-ordinate information from Special Branch, the Anti-Terrorist Squad, the Secret Intelligence Service, MI5 and other agencies, at home and abroad. In short, it's so that our left hand knows what the right is doing. And to see that vital information gets properly circulated and not left sitting at the bottom of someone's in-tray. We've got access to the country's best computer facilities to ensure that all aspects of each intelligence input are fully cross-referenced and indexed . . .'

He paused to ensure he had carried his audience with him. He had. 'It's early days, but things look promising. Nevertheless, it's one hell of a task. It's not just the Provos we have to worry about nowadays, but a whole gamut of international terrorist organisations. From the Red Army Faction – or Baader Meinhof – and France's Action Directe, etcetera, etcetera, to the Libyans and the PLO. They're all communicating, doing each other favours, and exchanging information. So you can see what we're up against.'

After a couple of hard gulps of black unsweetened coffee, Ray Pilger was feeling distinctly revived. 'So where does my Squad fit in to all this, Bill? If I can call you Bill?'

Harper nodded. 'Course you can. I prefer informality. In my experience, respect has to be earned. Titles are worth nothing unless we all respect each others' judgement. And that's why we're here today, because it is your judgement I'm interested in.

'Until recently, I was serving with the Army based at Hereford in a special intelligence unit. Now I'm back at Whitehall seconded to TIGER as a liaison officer. I've been given the specific task of reporting on terrorist funding. Everything from armed robbery and extortion to kidnap ransoms – and drug-peddling.'

'Ah,' Pilger said. 'I see.'

Major Harper smiled and settled back in his chair. 'And what do you see, Ray? I'm interested to hear.'

The detective extracted a new pack of small cigars from his waistcoat pocket and began to unwrap the cellophane. 'Well, Bill, for a start we don't really see any terrorist connections. Not in our business here in the UK. Internationally, of course, it's a different story. It's well-documented that the PLO used to finance itself with cannabis grown in the Bekaa Valley in Lebanon, which is why the place was defended so vigorously against the Israelis when they invaded. And the Turks are heavily into heroin grown in their part of the world. That's used to finance the right-wing Grey Wolves who've got such a hold over there. But most of that stuff finds its way into Germany and mainland Europe, rather than here.' He paused. 'Mind you, Turkish dealers in North London have been coming on a bit heavy in the last year.'

'And it's heroin that's the biggest problem in the UK currently?' Harper prompted.

Pilger smiled gently. 'You've been reading your newspapers, I see. Yes, you could say that. Cocaine is the other problem and we're expecting trouble. But that comes from South America – it's largely protected by the Latin governments – and, until recently, distributed mostly by the Mafia in the States. It's generally fed into the UK via Spain. National family connections. That's an expensive route for an expensive product. A small select market. It also helps us that the Mafia have never really got a foothold in the UK But that's history'

He lit his cigar and exhaled a thick plume of blue smoke before continuing: 'Heroin on the other hand, that's coming in at such a rate that I sometimes feel like that Dutch dyke boy with his finger in the hole. It's a flood. An epidemic.' He was vaguely aware of Fred Roxan shifting uncomfortably in his seat opposite. 'Officially, we in the police estimate there are actually some fifty thousand addicts in the country, bearing in mind that only a maximum of one in five addicts are ever registered. And that usually only happens when they're arrested by us or turn up in hospital. But personally . . .' He hesitated.

Fred Roxan glowered across the table. Whatever Ray Pilger said wasn't going to reflect well on the Customs and Excise.

'And personally . . . ?' Major Harper urged.

'Personally, I'd say we're in for one hell of a shock. In fact the union which represents the Customs and Excise has put forward the possibility of 140,000 addicts. The problem is that "snorting" or sniffing has become fashionable. The thought of a needle turns off most people. But after a period of "snorting" regularly, it's just not enough. The transition to the needle is virtually inevitable. It just takes some longer than others.'

'Jesus,' breathed Derek Dillinger. 'That is a terrifying statistic.'

Pilger's hard brown eyes darted in the Anti-Terrorist Squad man's direction. 'What's really frightening, D. D., is that those people are usually finished, wasted. Once you're hooked, it's almost impossible to get off it. The long-term success rate at clinics is little more than thirteen in every hundred.'

For a second there was total silence in the room; the clink of china as Major Harper replaced his cup on its saucer was uncannily loud. 'I'd never heard that before, Ray.'

'The authorities keep it quiet,' Pilger said. 'It won't stop people from starting, but it can deter addicts from at least *trying* to get treatment.'

Harper nodded slowly and he shifted his gaze to some point beyond the partitioned wall. His eyes had lost their humour. 'Where in God's name did it all start? It seems to have hit this nation like a sledgehammer.'

'Do you want a brief history lesson?' Pilger offered.

The major smiled sadly. 'If it'll help my understanding. Yes, of course.'

Pilger stubbed out his cigar. 'Until the late 70s, we had no great problem. Mostly it was doctors over-prescribing, sometimes from good but ill-informed motives. Then we had some trouble with the Chinese communities smoking the stuff, but we put pressure on the Triads over here and it fizzled out. It was always containable.

'The trouble really started when the Shah fell in Iran back in '78 and '79.' He glanced around the table. 'It's an ill-wind. Well, middle-class Iranians fled for their lives to the West, bringing out their money in the form of heroin. Drugs are the easiest way to carry wealth in your hand luggage. And it's international currency. In fact, flights to Heathrow from Teheran were referred to by Fred's people as "The Heroin Express".

'The stuff hit London in a big way. And simultaneously, Los Angeles from the same source. But the Ayatollah came to power and the trade dried up virtually overnight. But it had given a lot of poor sods the taste. And a few villains, ideas.

'It was about then that the Russians invaded Afghanistan – another major production area for the opium poppy. If you recall, there was no money made available from the US Congress to aid the Afghan resistance movement. Well – and you, Major, would know this better than I – it's ten-to-one that the CIA encouraged the hill tribes bordering

Afghanistan and Pakistan to build up their existing opium trade to finance their resistance.'

If Pilger was hoping for a hint of acknowledgement from Harper, he was disappointed. Yet somehow the poker-faced mask told him he was probably right. 'Anyway, it's strange that at about that time heroin started moving out of the region in a big way. Also a lot of Pathan heroin chemists left Iran to set up shop there.

'Soon the stuff started hitting the UK. It was brought in by Pakistanis from the Midlands. But they couldn't then find a market for it up there, so they came down to London. It was pathetic, really. They were just wandering around trying to sell it openly on the streets. We picked them up by the score . . .'

Roxan interrupted. 'That's one thing about drugs. You can't just set up shop. You've got to go through an established infrastructure. That helps to pinpoint movement of the stuff between countries. And also the traffickers' need to trust the people they deal with implicitly.'

'Like the Mafia?' Derek Dillinger suggested.

Roxan nodded. 'Exactly. Italian communities deal with each other in Italy and Sicily itself, the US, Australia. Same with the Pakis and the Turks. It's both the advantage of their system and the weakest point. Once we know the source at least we know where to start looking.'

Major Harper understood exactly what the Customs chief was saying. He had found that it applied equally to other areas. Like international finance. And terrorism. 'So what happened to these Pakistanis, Ray?'

'Finally, some of them made contact with London villains. Some East End outfits who knew the amphetamine market, and Irish gangs who were active in cannabis. Since that link-up it's gone from strength to strength. In Pakistan, they queue up to be couriers. If they get away with it, the profits are so high, you see. Quite amazing, really.'

Harper nodded slowly and looked towards Fred Roxan. 'Is this where Customs and Excise reckon that most of our heroin is coming from?'

'Yes,' Roxan confirmed. 'It's what's termed the "Golden Crescent". That's Iran, Afghanistan and Pakistan. Stuff grown in Mexico and the other main area – the "Golden Triangle" of Burma, Thailand and Laos – finds its way to the States. A lot of that also goes to Australia.'

Major Harper jotted on his notepad. 'I understand you've got an intelligence presence in Pakistan, Fred?'

'Yep. That's right. And it's been an effective operation. Nearly everything we pick up comes from that source.'

Harper raised his eyebrows. 'And yet you're only picking up ten to fifteen per cent of everything that's smuggled in. Right?'

Fred Roxan pulled a handkerchief from his top pocket and blew into it. 'If we're lucky. But you're talking ball-park figures. If we think it's ten to fifteen per cent, it might as well be five to ten per cent.' He dabbed carefully at his nose. 'Trouble is there're so many at it. They come in by air or sea, sometimes overland. Nothing centrally organised. Sometimes via central Europe or even Africa. Government cutbacks haven't helped in Customs staffing levels, either. There are "Mr Bigs", of course. Like Mustaq Malik. A lot of them.'

'Rather knocks the terrorist theory on the head,' Derek Dillinger observed.

'Mmm,' Harper grunted thoughtfully. 'Maybe. But not necessarily. You see, if I am to understand you correctly, there are many international villains working in the heroin business. Asians and Europeans, including the Italian Mafia. Yet, despite an apparently effective intelligence operation in the main source country, we're only stopping a small percentage of the stuff from getting in . . .'

'That's hardly a bloody fair interpretation,' Roxan grunted.

Major Harper waved aside the protest. 'No criticism intended, Fred. Far from it. All I'm saying is that amidst this eighty-five to ninety percent of heroin that *does* get past your chaps, there could be a major operation of which you know nothing. Maybe trading ten per cent, say, with total impunity?'

Roxan had his handkerchief out again, and his glare told Ray Pilger that his cigar was responsible. The Customs man snuffled into the material, then said: 'For all we know, there could be several major outlets of which we know nothing, each shifting five or ten per cent of the total. 'S not impossible. Or even one outfit shifting half of the lot.' He gave the major a hard stare. 'If you *want* to speculate. Or fantasise.' The hostility was unmistakable. Who does this upstart Army wallah, who knows bugger-all about it, think he is?

Ray Pilger found it hard to suppress a smile at Roxan's irritation. 'I think Fred's saying we can speculate all we like, but it doesn't get us nearer to discovering who or what these organisations might be . . .'

'Fred will say what Fred thinks,' Roxan snarled, '*thank you, Mr Pilger.*'

The Drug Squad chief ignored the rebuke. 'You've obviously been doing a spot of speculating on the TIGER Committee, Bill. But, presumably, there's a reason for it?'

Before replying, Major Harper consulted his notebook on the table, then extracted a pair of gold-rimmed halfmoon spectacles. Carefully he hooked them over his ears. 'Do you recall, gentlemen, the interception of the *Marita Ann* last year?'

Derek Dillinger nodded; this was more his territory. 'The IRA gun-running trawler that was intercepted by the Irish Navy? Sure. We received information from the CIA that a Boston boat, the *Valhalla*, was carrying arms across the Atlantic. They tracked it by satellite when it transferred its cargo at sea to the *Marita Ann*. We used Nimrod aircraft in surveillance until the Irish Navy caught them red-handed.'

'That's it,' Major Harper acknowledged. 'The biggest IRA arms haul ever recovered. Some 200 guns and weapons of every description. At a cost of some £1½ million.'

Pilger frowned. 'I still don't see . . .'

Major Harper held his gaze. 'We understand the money paid was profits from drug-dealing.'

The remaining three men around the table exchanged glances in silence, absorbing the relevance of the Army major's revelation. The hum of the air-conditioning seemed to grow in volume.

Fred Roxan leaned forward with his elbows on the table and an inscrutable Customs officer expression on his florid face. 'You said £1½ million for some 200 weapons . . . Maybe my arithmetic is at fault, Major, but on that basis, your intelligence is bullshit. Not even the Irish pay £7,500 for a gun.'

Light twinkled mischievously in Harper's eyes behind the half-moon spectacles. 'Your arithmetic is not at fault, Fred. Neither is our intelligence, believe me.'

Derek Dillinger said: 'On the assumption that you can get an automatic weapon on the legit market for – what? – £250 to £400. Say, double it, or even treble it on the black market . . . Fred's definitely right. Either a lot of money was paid by the Provos for something else, or the Irish navy missed other shipments off-loaded from the *Valhalla*. Maybe the *Marita Ann* wasn't the only trawler.'

Major Harper nodded. 'That's what concerns us. Intelligence reports from Dublin suggest that the *Marita Ann* may have been deliberately given to us. Along with some Provos that the IRA Army Council wanted to get rid of. It also suggests, as you've just indicated, that other loads went ashore from *Valhalla*. In Republic circles some rumours talk about arms. Others, cocaine.'

Pilger let out a long slow whistle. 'That's an odd one. Cocaine. From the States?'

Pointedly Harper said: 'I understand that Eire has a major heroin problem, Ray?'

It took a second for the Drug Squad chief to muster his concentration. 'Sorry, Bill. Yes, it has. In fact, per head of population, it's probably the worst in Europe. That's the trouble with Ireland – as I'm sure you know – it's very much the back door into the UK and we've no jurisdiction there. Shannon Airport takes direct flights from all over. And we know heroin does reach us from across the Irish Sea. But how much and how it comes in we've no idea.'

'Or who's behind it?' Harper prompted.

Fred Roxan fiddled thoughtfully with his handkerchief as he spoke. 'If you mean the IRA, I doubt it. In certain areas where there's been a public outcry over heroin addiction, I gather Sinn Fein has organised vigilante groups in Dublin. You know, to sort out the dealers. Successfully, I believe.'

It was Dillinger's turn. 'Come on, Fred. Think it through. There's a lot of mileage in covertly introducing a public evil, then publicly doing something about it. In fact, I gather one of the worst-hit areas was in the Minister of Health's own constituency. A real vote-winner for the opposition. After all, vigilantes can only pick up dealers at street-level. That would be several removed down the pyramid from the importers. No one could ever prove the connection. One thing is certain, like in Ulster, no major crime or racket happens in Eire without the IRA's say-so. That's fact.'

Fred Roxan took refuge in his handkerchief. 'There *could* be something in what you say, Major,' he conceded. 'The London Irish have been moving cannabis for years. Since the 70s, in fact, as Ray mentioned earlier. Mostly South London Irish outfits from Peckham and Balham. They bought it from the PLO in Lebanon. So there *could* be an IRA involvement.'

Ray Pilger raised his hand. 'Hang on a minute, Fred. There could be another connection here.' He turned to Harper. 'Well-placed members of the Syrian ruling clique are known to run heroin labs in Damascus and route the stuff either direct out of Syria or through Lebanon. So the contacts would be there.'

At that moment a knock came on the door. Pilger opened it to find WPC Gifford with a fresh tray of coffee.

She grinned widely. 'I expect you could do with this, sir.'

'Never a truer word.' He raised an eyebrow. 'Obviously none of your boyfriends are in today?'

'Sir?'

He laughed at her puzzled expression and took the tray as the policewoman closed the door.

'I think a coffee-break is most welcome,' Major Harper said. 'I feel we've made a great deal of progress already. Which is just as well.'

Pilger placed the tray on the table. 'Why's that, Bill?' he asked absently.

Harper blinked. 'Because the PM has got her teeth into this one, gentlemen. She wants the drugs traffic smashed. Especially the heroin trade. It was bad enough before she learned about the IRA's involvement. But now she's fighting mad.'

Ray Pilger stared across at the quiet Welshman. Just what on earth was his game? Was he holding something back? He'd been a detective long enough to sense when he wasn't being told the entire truth. 'Forgive me, Major, but apart from your intelligence reports, any connections between the IRA and heroin in the UK are tenuous, to say the least. We've just explained that.'

Major Harper pursed his lips thoughtfully, then slowly removed his half-moon spectacles. 'Gentlemen, I want you to think again. After this meeting, I want you to go away and review everything from a new angle. The Irish angle. The poppy and the shamrock, if you like. *Assume* that is the case and just see how much fits into place.'

Pilger could resist it no longer. 'You're holding back on something,' he challenged. 'What is it?'

After a thoughtful pause, Harper lowered his voice to a whisper. 'Just before Christmas, we received an intelligence report from Dublin. We in TIGER believe it to be one hundred per cent reliable. At present, there is a thousand kilos of the finest heroin poised to be distributed in Britain. That is a *fact*.'

Momentarily, Detective Chief Superintendent Pilger closed his eyes. A thousand kilos. Nearly two-and-a-half thousand pounds weight.

With a street value of £25 million in Britain. In the United States it would fetch £100 million.

He suddenly felt sick.

'Yes, dear? Can I help?' The woman with the purple rinse and ornate, plastic-framed spectacles peered through the glass partition into the spartan waiting room.

'Billy Robson for Mr Heathers.'

She smiled the standard 'feel-at-ease-I-understand' smile she used for all the wayward visitors who trampled into the Probation Office. She consulted the appointment book on her desk.

'It won't be Mr Heathers, dear. He's moved to Richmond. Now, let me see . . .'

'I only saw him last Thursday,' Robson said, feeling a pang of regret. He'd got on well with old Heathers. There had been a soft heart beneath the tough no-nonsense hide. He was from the old school and had once been an officer in the Army. No doubt that had helped. After all their meetings, he'd miss the worn tweed jacket and that infernal pipe which left a trail of tobacco wherever Heathers went.

'Yes, dear, it was a bit sudden. A vacancy he wanted suddenly came up. Oh, yes, you've been given Mr Vance.' Reassurance beamed at him again. 'A younger man. More your age, I should think, Mr Robson.' He wasn't sure that it sounded like a recommendation.

And when they came face-to-face, after Robson had waited for twenty minutes, he was quickly sure that it hadn't been.

Without apology for the delay, Vance motioned him to a hard plastic chair facing the desk. Heathers' old leather one, with the stuffing squeezing out of the seams, had gone.

Robson sat silently whilst his new probation officer flicked over his file. The man was a million miles apart from his predecessor: new generation, a slim athletic build from regular jogging, and dressed in a Reading University T-shirt, jeans and trainers. The ginger hair was close-cropped and his eyelashes were so pale that it gave the impression that he didn't have any.

Robson rummaged idly in his pocket and drew out his cigarettes. He guessed Mr Vance was a do-gooding type with degrees in modern psychology and sociology under his belt; that could be painful.

'I'd rather you didn't.'

Robson looked up. Very pale blue eyes that belonged to a much older man held his gaze. The ashtray was conspicuous by its absence. Robson replaced the cigarette in the pack.

To his increasing irritation, Mr Vance returned to the file for a further few minutes before finally closing it.

'So, Robson, I see you came out yesterday.' His voice was crisp and matter-of-fact. 'Did you know it's customary to report on your first day?'

Robson shrugged. 'Mr Heathers was understanding. We got on well. He believed it would be better for me to spend the day at home with my wife and kid. Rather than bother coming here.'

A smile flickered on Vance's thin mouth. 'Bother? It's not a question of bothering, Robson. You're out on licence, remember that. And that licence is subject to certain conditions. I have to approve your proposed "Release Plan" and carefully consider your "Home Circumstances Report". You, Robson, have to allow home visits at any time.'

Robson felt the hairs start to crawl at the back of his neck. He hadn't been prepared for the new man's attitude. Curtly, he said: 'Mr Heathers explained all that.'

'And did he tell you that if you so much as put one big toe out of line, we can have you back inside? You'll have no recourse to the courts. It's down to *me*, got it?'

Robson's eyes narrowed. 'I get the message.'

The thin smile on Vance's face spread a little wider and he relaxed back in his chair. He had made his point. Established who was boss.

'You'll find me different from Heathers,' he said, somewhat unnecessarily. 'He had a bit of a reputation for being a soft touch. I understand he was transferred to Richmond because it's less demanding. Less strain. Fewer old lags to deal with, to con him with their yarns.' His blue eyes hardened. 'I can deal with that, Robson, because I come from these parts. I know the people around here. *I* know the people *you* know. There'll be no wool pulled over my eyes. Understand?'

Robson sat motionless, a waxwork.

Vance leaned forward. 'I see the Parole Board turned down your first review. D'you know why?'

It was true. All sentences are automatically reduced by a third on the condition of good behaviour. But the EDR, or Earliest Date of Release, may be at any time after the first third has been served – subject to a review by the Parole Board and continuing probation until the conviction is served. For some reason, the Board had seen fit to turn down Robson's review after thirty-two months. That had been over two years ago.

'Prisoners aren't told,' Robson reminded him icily.

'Want to guess?' Vance warmed to his subject. 'Gauging from your report, I'd put it down to two factors. You were involved in a very serious crime, using firearms. That means you could still be a risk to the community . . .'

'I didn't use a gun,' Robson replied. 'The others did, but just for shock-effect. They were loaded with rice, not pellets. Besides, it was nothing to do with me.'

Vance continued as though he hadn't heard. 'And the other likely reason is your remorse – or lack of it. That didn't sound very remorseful. Nor the fact that you have continued to refuse to cooperate with the police regarding the other men on the raid who escaped. That didn't sound very remorseful either.

'In fact, I'm surprised the Board have seen fit to change their mind, to be perfectly honest, Robson. And I'm going to make sure they haven't made a mistake by keeping you on a very short lead.' He tapped the file with a well-manicured forefinger. 'I see Mr Heathers described you as "quiet, independent and determined". Typical ex-Forces, he said. Those same qualities *could* be interpreted as resentment and dumb insolence.'

Robson said very slowly: 'Mr Heathers and I built up a mutual trust and respect over a long period.'

Vance sniffed heavily. 'Yes, well, we'll have to start all over again, won't we? And see if we can do the same.'

He reached forward and retrieved the file again, flicking it open. 'You had agreed for Mr Heathers to visit your home. I took the opportunity on Saturday . . .'

Robson opened his mouth to protest, but decided against it. The thought of this antagonistic bastard snooping around his home raised his bile. Sandy hadn't mentioned it, but perhaps that was hardly surprising.

'I wasn't impressed, Robson. It's my assessment that your wife's not well. The place was untidy, to put it mildly. She's obviously under a strain, finding it hard to cope. And I was disturbed to find you hadn't allowed your son to visit . . .'

Robson was on his feet like a released spring. 'It's *none* of your *bloody* business . . . !'

The probation officer looked up at him without expression and crooked one eyebrow. 'Sit down, Robson. And no more outbursts like that. From now on *everything's* my business. Family life can affect your ability to stay on the right side of the law. Remember that. As can work opportunities . . .'

Reluctantly, Robson sat down again.

'I gather you had lorry driving in mind,' Vance continued. 'You hold an HGV licence from your time in the Marines.'

Robson nodded. 'Mr Heathers agreed that was the best prospect.'

Vance's smile melted away. 'As I've told you, I don't necessarily share my predecessor's opinions. I also said I come from these parts. I know the man convicted with you – the man known as Arnie. He's out shortly and he has a record for lorry hi-jacking. Another associate of yours, Abbott – Rich Abbott – is well-known as a "fence". He's lived around this neighbourhood for years.' The blue eyes blinked in mock apology. 'So, you see, in the interests of the community, I can hardly allow you to go driving consignments of cigarettes and spirits around the country.'

'I wasn't thinking of working for Securicor!' Robson snarled.

'What about building work?'

'I'm not skilled.'

'Labouring then.'

Robson saw his whole future disintegrating before his eyes. 'In case you hadn't heard, the construction industry's at rock-bottom. There're more labourers on the dole than anyone else. I may have been inside, but even I know that.' Desperately, he looked into Vance's eyes, trying to see what was going on in the mind behind them. 'Why the hell have you got it in for me?'

Vance climbed from his chair and leaned forward with his fists on the desk. 'I don't have it *in* for *any* of my clients, Robson. I'm just doing my job, and the first requisite of that is to serve the interests of the community. And *I* have to be convinced that *your* freedom is in those interests.

'But I'll tell you one thing. Every day I get kids in from around here who've never stood a chance. Black kids, Jewish kids, and white kids. Kids from broken homes and a social system that's spat them out. Driven to petty crime out of boredom and frustration and lack of understanding. Parents and teachers who don't care. Employers who don't want them. Kids who've got nothing, never have had and never will have.'

The blue eyes remained hard and deadpan. 'But you . . . you, Robson, had it all. Nine years in the Royal Marines. Sergeant, wasn't it? Mister Tough-Guy. Hard bastard, tough. Sod you, jack, I'm all right. Spoon-fed by the system. Then you come into Civvy Street and don't want to take what the rest of us have to put with all our lives.'

Robson began to understand; perhaps his original estimate of his new probation officer hadn't been that wrong after all.

'You think you can continue your military bully-boy tactics and intimidation on the public. Armed hold-ups, getaways.' Vance straightened up. 'Did you know that the manager of the bank you held up died of a heart attack three months later? Well, I did and everyone knew why. And the police-car you rammed? The driver had to retire from the force three years later because of recurring back trouble . . . And you calmly say it was nothing to do with you.' Vance stabbed a finger at Robson. 'The money spent on people like you in the Army and in jail, could be spent on those kids I was telling you about. The kids who've *really* got *nothing!*'

Robson said quietly: 'That was quite a speech, Vance. You deserve a Nobel Prize.'

'*Mister* Vance, Robson.'

Robson stood up. 'Then you can do me the same courtesy.'

'Don't push your luck. Just remember what I've said. It's your job to convince me I'm wrong about you. Now go down to the Social and sign on. Then go on to the Job Centre.'

Robson smiled, but his eyes were like flint. 'Apart from driving, my only other qualification in the Marines was killing people.'

'Was that supposed to be a joke? Or a threat?'

'It was a joke – if you've got a sense of humour, Mr Vance.'

'Same time next Tuesday.' He watched as his client moved towards the door. 'Mr Robson.'

Three

Sandy Robson had made her decision only seconds after husband had shut the front door.

Without bothering to wash properly, she just rinsed her face and tried repairing the previous night's make-up. After a half-hearted attempt she gave up. She felt slightly dizzy and the gentle curve of her mouth seemed to elude the tip of her lipstick.

Hurriedly, she returned to the bedroom and opened her wardrobe. God, it was a mess, she thought, as she flicked through the half-dozen hangers. Once she'd had quite a selection to choose from, cheap but smart. Now it was down to the best the Oxfam shop could offer. And half of those were in need of needle-and-thread, or blood-stained.

She pulled out a pretty red dress. Pretty, but years out-of-date. And definitely summerweight material.

Sod it. It would have to do.

Stripping naked, she rummaged in the linen basket for yesterday's bra and pants. In a minute she was dressed. After running a comb through her hair, she pulled on her overcoat and grimaced. The dress hung beneath the hem by three inches.

Then, stuffing her spongebag into the pocket of her coat, she moved into the hall towards the front door.

She paused with her hand on the lock.

Danny's fire? Why not? The flat was warm enough. Besides, spring wasn't far away.

Opening his bedroom door, she entered and picked up the two-bar electric fire and dumped it into a Tesco plastic bag.

It took her ten minutes to reach the ground floor. The sky was low and threatening, and there was an icy edge to the north-easterly wind that cut straight through her coat and the thin stuff of her summer dress. It reminded her that her circulation wasn't getting any better.

A short walk brought her to the narrow-fronted show-room of used cars. It was filled to brimming with resistible models. Most had rust patches and milometers which read Andy Sutcliff's standard 30,000 miles. His secretary Sue told her that he'd phoned in sick. He wouldn't be in for the rest of the day.

A fifteen-minute bus ride took her to the Victorian terraced street lined with cars.

She stopped outside No. 36. A low wall topped by a low hedge guarded the bay window. There was no gate, just six feet of chequered tiling leading to the front door with its stained glass window, fashioned after a galleon.

The purple E-type was still parked outside. She hesitated.

No, she told herself, she knew her decision was right. If she tried to fool herself, it would just blow everything. She'd waited five years for Billy; it would be stupid to foul up after going through all that.

The noise from the black lion's head knocker reverber-ated down the empty street. Nothing. She tried again and waited. Nothing.

Becoming agitated, she tried once more. Christ, he *had* to be in!

Then she heard the distant cough behind the door and the pad of footfalls in the hall.

After a rattling of bolts, Andy Sutcliff's head peered round the door. His hair was in the same dishevelled state as his beard.

He blinked into the daylight. 'Sorry I was so long, Sand. Didn't know it was you. Had to check from the upstairs window.'

He opened the door wider, sufficient for her to notice his bare hairy legs beneath the tartan dressing-gown.

She smiled. 'Why, who are you expecting? The taxman?'

He half-heartedly returned her smile. 'Closer than you think. Anyway, what do you want?'

Sutcliff seemed different, she thought. 'Aren't you going to invite me in?'

He looked uneasy. 'Is that a good idea? Er, I mean Billy's back.'

Sandy's patience was wearing thin. 'Don't be bloody silly, Andy. He's gone down the Probation Office then over to the Job Centre. You know what they're like. He'll be out all day.'

Sutcliff made no attempt to move. 'Still, it don't seem right.'

'Please, Andy, don't keep me standing here. I feel like a bloody encyclopaedia salesman. It'll only take a minute.'

Reluctantly, he stepped aside to let her in to the long dingy hall with its dado of brown anaglypta. By contrast, the rear living-room was smartly furnished with a deep-piled cream carpet and bright red Habitat furniture.

Immediately she noticed the two half-finished glasses of wine on the table and the overflowing ashtray.

'You're not ill, then?' she challenged. 'Sue said you were off sick.'

He smiled thinly. 'Heavy night. Celebrating Billy coming out. You know.'

Sandy's eyes hardened. 'Who've you got upstairs?'

For a moment he was undecided whether to lie. 'It's no one you know.' Then he added defensively: 'I've got my own life to lead.'

She shrugged and tried to appear indifferent. 'Sure, Andy. Of course you have.'

He relaxed now that there wasn't going to be a scene. 'So what do you want?'

Sandy's smile was as sweet as she could muster. 'I wondered if you could lend me a few quid, Andy. Just until Friday when I get my Child Benefit Giro.'

'Oh, Sand, come on . . .'

She shook her head vigorously. 'No, it's not what you think. I promise. It's just that I had extra expense with Billy coming back. Extra food and some booze. A new dress. You know, I sort of bust the budget.' Her eyes pleaded. 'I'm not very good with money, Andy. You know that.'

His expression softened. 'How much?'

She shrugged again and glanced casually around the room. 'Oh – I don't know – just to tide me over. Say – what? – a hundred quid . . . ?'

'You lying BITCH!' His words exploded in the confines of the small house. 'CHRIST! I don't believe it! After all those bloody promises! You're bloody well back on it again.'

She'd jumped back, startled by the ferocity of his outburst. Now she stood her ground, her lips contorting into a snarl of self-defence. 'No, I'm not, Andy. I've got it under control. Really I have. It's just that this last week there's been a lot of strain waiting for Billy.'

Sutcliff's eyes blazed. 'Well, he's back now, so end of strain, right?' She didn't answer, just bit her lower lip. '*Right?*' he repeated.

She looked up defiantly. 'And how's it going to look if I'm doing cold turkey on his first week home? Billy's not stupid, Andy. He'll know.'

'You should have thought about that before.' He turned abruptly away and glared out through the patio doors to the long narrow garden.

'I *did*, Andy. I told you.'

'You said you were *off*,' he retorted. 'That clinic cost me a packet. And now, you silly cunt, you're back on. God give me strength . . . !'

She stepped round to face him again. 'I told you, Andy, I've got it under control. Just the odd shoot-up. Maybe once a fortnight. I'm weaning off. Then it'll be a three-week gap. Then a month. That's what the clinic said.'

'Balls!' He refused to look at her. 'The clinic said no such thing and you know it.'

She began to feel desperate. '*Please*, Andy. Just a hundred miserable quid. It's not much. Just enough to get me over this first couple of weeks with Billy. To give us both a chance.'

Sutcliff spun round on her. '*Just* a hundred quid, Sand! For God's sake, I'm up to my neck in debt. And that's largely down to you and your fucking habit. You've bled me dry.' He paused, trying to see into her eyes. Somehow he couldn't get any reaction from the pinpoint pupils. 'Billy's back now. You're *his* problem. You can only do so much for your best mate.'

'Does that include screwing his wife?' Sarcastic.

He blanched. 'That's unfair, Sand. And it's over. We agreed.'

'Then one last fifty quid. For old times' sake?'

Sutcliff sighed and dropped down onto the cream leatherette settee. 'Look, Sand, I'm at my wits' end. You joked about the taxman. Well, the truth is it's the VAT. They've been chasing me for weeks and finally pinned me down to a meeting today.'

She sat by his side and reached for his hands as he wrung them in despair. 'So that's why you've decided to go sick?'

'It's the only way I could put them off.'

'I am sorry.' She leaned forward and kissed him on the cheek. 'Really I am.'

He looked sideways at her, hardly trusting himself. 'You're a soppy tart, Sand. You know that?'

She smiled and nodded. 'We make quite a pair.'

For a second he held her gaze, then abruptly stood up. He crossed to the mantelpiece and extracted some notes from an envelope.

'Fifty quid,' he said. 'It was for the showroom rent. It's all I've got. You'd better take it before I change my mind.'

Gleefully, she sprang to her feet and threw her arms around him, kissing him full on the mouth.

He eased her away and she pouted disappointment as she stepped back, the five notes in her hand.

'Thanks, Andy, really. Thanks.' She picked up her Tesco bag as she moved towards the passage.

'And, Sand?'

'Yes?'

'Don't come back. Not ever again.'

'How much?'

Sandy Robson waited anxiously on Bella's reply. Bella was a cow. All the fixers in the area knew it; she was always a last resort.

That was unfair, of course. She'd known Bella on the estate for the past four years. A tall, thin girl in her mid-twenties, her face was emaciated and white, which made her big dark eyes look large and innocent, like a child's. She'd been devastatingly beautiful once, but now her high aristocratic cheekbones just served to emphasise her skeletal appearance.

She was sweet and considerate, too. Often willing to talk for hours, to listen and to give soft words of comfort and understanding over the endless black coffee on which she survived.

Until it came to business. And then Bella was a cow.

'Seventy quid.'

Sandy was horror-struck. 'I've only got fifty.'

'Sorry, love. You've got a problem.' Bella was adamant.

In despair, Sandy looked around the ground-floor flatlet for some inspiration for a persuasive argument.

But there was no inspiration. The place was a pig-sty and it stank. A sweet, musty smell wafted from the carpet where Bella habitually emptied out her syringe with its residue of blood from her arm. In the kitchenette, the sink and drainer were overflowing with leftover Chinese take-aways and the remains of half-eaten Kentucky Fried Chicken. Nothing had been touched for days. Even the living-room was littered with dirty ashtrays, scraps of tinfoil, and empty vinegar and lime bottles.

It was the home of a fixer who was beyond redemption. And it was a scene that frequently haunted Sandy's dreams and woke her up in a cold sweat.

She said: 'My regular dealers only charge forty quid. And for quite good stuff.'

'Then go to them.' Cold.

'I can't, not now. They're only around at night.'

'So?'

'For God's sake, Bella, you know why! Billy's back home. I'm trying to get things together. I can't go out trying to score. You're my friend, you know that.'

'Fine, Sand.' Bella lit a cigarette with thin hands. Her finger-nails were painted black and chipped. 'Then just pay the seventy quid.'

Cow! Bloody cow!

Sandy held out the Tesco bag. 'There's an electric fire. You'll get twenty quid for that, no problem.'

The other woman ignored her and folded her arms. 'Sand, you know my rules. Strictly cash. Otherwise I'd have this place full of garbage.'

Sandy bit her tongue.

Bella blew out a long stream of smoke into the centre of the room and thought for a moment. She turned to face the older woman, who seemed so much younger and more innocent than herself. 'Look, Sand, for once I'll make an exception. This flat's been soddin' cold the last few days. I could use a fire. But *never* again. Right?'

Relief swept over Sandy. 'Oh, God, Bella, thanks. I can't tell you.'

Bella reached out and took Sandy's wrist. 'Listen, love, you're goin' to have to sort things out.'

'What d'you mean?'

Bella smiled. The business done, she was again the dear, sweet friend and confidante. 'When did you last shoot-up?'

Sandy hesitated. 'This morning. Why?'

'And you're ready for another one now.'

'No, I'm not.'

Bella's laugh was harsh. 'Who do you think you're foolin', love? Look at your hands. They're trembling.'

Involuntarily, Sandy withdrew her hands and shoved them deep into her coat pockets. 'I've kicked it, Bella, you know that. I just want some in case things get heavy with Billy.'

'Have it your own way, love.' Bella stubbed out her cigarette and moved towards a corner cupboard. Her long body, sheathed in a tight black dress, had the fluent movement of a cat. 'But I bet you also fixed yesterday morning. And if that's the case, this score won't last you more than a couple of days . . .'

'That's my problem.'

Bella returned with a small foil packet from the cupboard. 'But I am your friend, Sand. You're going to need bread.' She laughed. 'And I'm not sure how many electric fires you've got left.'

Sandy snatched the packet more eagerly than she had intended. 'Billy will soon get a job.'

'Sure, love. And he'll be able to afford – what did you say? – forty quid a day for your habit, no problem.' She reached out and held her friend's wrist again. 'Listen, love, get wise. Either tell the old man and get to a clinic again and kick it proper.' She hesitated. 'Or get a well-paid job yourself.'

Sandy shifted warily. 'I lost the part-time one at the baker's.'

'Christ!' Bella raised her eyes to the ceiling. 'Not that sort of job. That wouldn't pay for a pack of Valium. Besides, we all know why you lost it.'

'What sort of job then?' Sandy asked cautiously, although she expected she knew the answer.

'I could get you one at my club . . .'

'No!'

Bella didn't appear offended; she calmly lit another cigarette. 'You could tell your old man you were a bar-girl or waitress.'

62 *Terence Strong*

'I couldn't strip. Not that way. Not – not – like . . . ?' She fumbled for the word.

'Like *me*?' Bella's eyes were hard. 'Well at least you've got a decent pair of tits and an arse that's worth lookin' at. A lot of fixers ain't that lucky.'

'No. No, Bella, I couldn't.'

'Well, if you don't, love, you're goin' to have to go on the game, or resort to crime. Or dealin' yourself . . .'

'Never!'

Bella shrugged. 'Okay, Sand, just don't leave it too late. My offer stands. I don't want you gettin' hurt.' She smiled. 'Good luck with lover-boy tonight.'

Sandy hesitated by the door. 'Bella?'

'Yep.'

'Can I use your loo?'

Bella smiled slowly and knowingly. 'No need to ask, love.'

Once behind the closed door, Sandy quickly opened the foil packet. Sod! It was the usual crap that Bella mixed to sell. Badly cut stuff that could be dangerous to use, but gave a tremendous flash.

Hastily she pulled the small plaster that hid the open sore of pinpricks on her arm and went for a vein. Immediately she drew blood.

'Oh shit!' The needle point had clogged. She cursed again. If the blood in the syringe clotted she'd have to throw the lot away.

She couldn't pull it out. Instead she pushed as hard as she could to force the fine grit through the needle. She was in luck. It gave, and the load shot in. Quickly she drew back the plunger to squirt in the last remnants into her vein.

Christ! It happened again. Would you bloody believe it! She was mad with anger. There were only seconds before the flash hit. Using every ounce of strength she forced the syringe as hard as she could.

The plunger snapped and blood exploded all over the basin. Then the flash came.

It hit her head like a brick just a split second before the cramp caught in her heart. It was like someone twisting a knife in there. Her scalp crawled with a million electric sparks as she collapsed backwards onto the lavatory seat.

For an age she sprawled, dazed, against the low cistern, her paralysed left arm hanging limply at her side.

Sandy Robson felt curiously detached as she watched the bright crimson splashes on the white china basin as they dripped onto her outstretched legs.

The exhaust of the E-type snarled angrily as Andy Sutcliff accelerated away from Newey House. He was unperturbed by the slippery feel of the tyres on the polished ice of the road.

'Sorry I was late, Andy. Sand got in late and wasn't too well.'

'Yeah.' Sutcliff was more concerned with seeing through the smear of slush that the wipers were fighting to clear.

Robson lit a cigarette. 'She reckons it's another bout of that glandular fever. Or some bug Danny picked up at school. Her mate Bella from across the way brought her back. She'd passed out over coffee apparently. Anyway, we got her to bed and she went out like a light. I had to get Danny's tea. Didn't go down too well. I've forgotten how to fry a bloody egg while I've been inside.'

Andy's beard parted in a grin. 'Dan's a good kid. He talks a lot about you. You know, what the two of you would do when you were out.'

'You wouldn't think so.'

They took the next corner in a spectacular four-wheel drift. To Sutcliff it was nothing. 'He'll need time to adjust. Lots of villains – sorry – cons have family problems when they first get out. Is he all right by himself tonight?'

Robson laughed. 'I got the old dear we met yesterday to babysit – Gran'ma Jacobs. Cost me a half-bottle of gin, mind. Still, I expect she loves the idea of a nose around. Sand'll kill me when she hears about it.'

Sutcliff shot a set of red lights without a moment's hesitation. 'And how was the Job Centre? Got you lined up as a chauffeur to Princess Di, have they?'

'Bad joke that, Andy,' Robson replied tersely. 'Bunch of wankers. Them and the Probation Office. Jesus! That's why I decided to go tonight, after all.'

'Rich Abbott will be pleased.'

'I'm not worried about him, Andy. I just thought it would give me the chance to put a few feelers out. Old friends. I mean they know a lot of legit people too. There might be a job going somewhere.' He peered through the worsening sleet. 'I don't think I know this place we're going to. What's it called – the Sloane Sporting Society? Sounds a bit posh.'

'It's Ronco's old spieler. You'd have known it as the Field Sports and Shooting Club.'

Robson pulled a face. 'That dump.'

Andy Sutcliff said: 'Rich Abbott bought it a couple of years ago. You wouldn't recognise it now.'

Billy Robson didn't

The Sloane Sporting Society had changed beyond belief. Its entrance was still the same faded unmarked door between two antique shops in Pimlico Road. The tatty wall-papered stairway, too, was the same. But beyond the top floor door, with its discreet brass plaque, a whole new world existed. A gilt-and-red flocked lobby, where a pretty hat-check girl looked after the rows of Crombie, Burberry and Borg overcoats, led to the main lounge bar. Despite the low lights and overdone Victorian brass, the place bustled to the movement of the sharply-dressed patrons and the crackle of their equally sharp conversation.

Robson felt mildly uncomfortable as he followed Sutcliff through the crush to the long, well-stocked bar. It was a long time since he'd been in one of these underworld haunts. It was a private sanctum providing total refuge from the outside world. It had its own culture, rules and customs, which set it apart from the law-abiding normality beyond its heavy door.

One or two faces he recognised; others just looked vaguely familiar. Many more were new to him. Younger, harder faces. The new generation of up-and-coming villains perhaps. There were no women in the place.

They found spare stools at the bar and Sutcliff waved a tenner at the barman.

Robson smiled to himself as he remembered that small denominations of currency were taboo. Usually no one traded in anything less than twenties, which were invariably drawn from a fat roll kept in the back pocket.

'Put that away, my son.'

Rich Abbott's white dinner jacket and black bow tie stated that he was the proud owner of the joint. 'There's a coupla ice-buckets of Moët on the bar for you two. Compliments of the 'ouse. Be my guests. And a slate' – he lowered his voice as he beckoned the barman to do the honours – 'provided you don't take liberties.'

Instinctively, Robson felt incensed by Abbott's flamboyant offer. But he bit his tongue and merely nodded his appreciation. He didn't like champagne, any more than he cared for the flash spirits that were the fashion in the underworld. He'd have settled for a lager any day.

The corks popped loudly and attracted attention from the patrons, some of whom gathered around to congratulate Robson on his release and – more by implication – his silence when inside.

'So what do you think of it?' Rich Abbott enthused as the well-wishers returned to their own conversations. 'Bit different, eh?'

It certainly was, Robson had to admit. Even if the changes were only skin-deep. Instead of one ancient set, there were now two blank, slimline televisions in the far corner, surrounded by plush armchairs. In the afternoons, they would be occupied by villains gambling heavily with their ill-gotten gains. All their bets were handled by a 'tame' bookmaker who deducted only three per cent instead of the ten paid by the public. That three per cent found its way back to Rich Abbott as commission for business. And as for tax – that didn't even enter into the equation.

'There's a coupla gaming-rooms out the back,' Abbott added with a wink. 'If you fancy a stake. Blackjack at the moment.'

The chance would be a fine thing, Robson thought bitterly. 'I'll have to give it a miss, Rich. Not exactly flush at the moment. And Andy here's on the run from the VAT-man.'

'Oh dear, stupid of me!' Abbott said suddenly. And Robson sensed that the man had only been awaiting his cue. 'Just a small welcome-home gift from some of the lads . . .'

The crisp white envelope came out of the dinner jacket pocket with a flourish. It waved enticingly before him.

'Go on, Billy,' Andy urged. 'Take it.'

Abbott grinned widely as it dropped into Robson's palm. 'Two grand there, Billy-boy. Just to let you know you've still got friends.'

Despite the spieler-owner's obvious self-satisfaction, Robson couldn't help feeling emotion at the generosity. After all, Rich Abbott had gained nothing from the attempted robbery five years earlier – except his continued freedom.

Society had already wreaked its vengeance on Robson and, after his interviews that afternoon, it was obvious that it still wanted more blood.

Yet here he was, among unscrupulous villains who were supposed to have no honour . . .

'I'll never be able to pay this back . . .' he began.

Rich Abbott laughed loudly. 'No need, Billy. I said it's a *gift*. If you was a regular here – if you get my meaning? – I'd offer an interest-free loan facility. A few more grand with no collateral. But since you reckon on treading the straight and narrow . . .' He placed his arm around Robson's shoulder in a fatherly fashion. 'If you take my advice you'll get yourself some wheels. And not off that crooked mate of yours.' He winked at Sutcliff to show it was meant in good fun. 'Drivin's what you're good at. Besides, wheels give you a bit of freedom to move around. Find work.'

Robson swallowed the last of his champagne along with his pride; he pocketed the envelope. 'That's what I need, Rich. Desperately. A job. Anything legal, even if it means no questions asked. If you hear of anything . . .'

'That's what I like to hear. An *honest* man! A rare breed.' The voice came from behind him.

He turned to see a slightly built man in his mid-thirties with neatly cropped fair hair. But the thing that really first registered was the ready smile and deep blue eyes which had a mischievous good-humoured glint to them.

'Sorry about that!' The newcomer laughed. 'Bad habit of mine, listening to other people's chatter. As my old mum used to say, never come in half-way through a conversation. Can prove embarrassing.'

'That's never worried you yet!' Rich Abbott boomed and greeted the man with a vigorous two-handed shake. 'How are you, Frankie? Nice to see you.' He stepped back to introduce Robson and Sutcliff. 'Don't think you know these friends of mine. We go back a long way. Andy . . . Frank Lewis . . .'

'How'do?' Lewis' eyes gave a quick flicker of shrewd appraisal.

'And Billy,' Abbott said. 'Billy Robson. Who only came out from doing a five yesterday.'

The grip on Robson's right hand was firm and he felt the pressure of the heavy gold signet ring. 'So obviously *you're* the man looking for a job, eh?'

'Trying,' Robson replied, taking an instant but grudging liking to Lewis. He always envied those with the knack of putting others at their ease – even if it was all a bit smooth. 'I reckon it's going to be an uphill struggle. Went to the Job Centre earlier today. Zilch.'

Frank Lewis looked genuinely concerned. 'Nothing doing?'

Robson laughed bitterly. 'Not putting too fine a point on it, they reckoned my only qualifications were driving geta-way cars and killing people.'

'Good God!' Lewis stepped back in mock horror. 'What you get your five for? Manslaughter?'

Abbott passed over Lewis' Bacardi which the barman had
prepared at a signal from his boss. 'On me, Frankie. No –
Billy used to be in the Royal Marines before his little run-in
with the Law. First offence.'

'Ah!' Lewis replied. 'See, I was right. Never come in
half-way through a conversation. I thought you'd knocked
off your old granny for a minute.' He sipped on his Bacardi
for a moment. 'So how long did you do in the Marines
then?'

'Nine years.'

Lewis let out a low whistle. 'That's great, Billy. That's
something I always wanted to do. The Forces. Paras, or
Marines, or somesuch.' He laughed as he flexed the muscle
in his left arm: an arm in the very expensive grey silk jacket
of an immaculately-cut suit. 'But I don't reckon I had the
physique for it.'

'Brawn isn't everything,' Robson replied. He was well-
used to this mild form of hero-worship from the past, and
it always made him feel a little awkward. 'Staying power
and brains is what counts.'

'Yes, I can see that. Maybe I should've had a shot, then.
National Service was finished by the time I was eighteen.
Besides, I was heavily into birds and making a quick buck.'

'Still are from what I heard,' Abbott guffawed.

Frank Lewis nudged the club-owner in the ribs. 'Don't
you let her Ladyship hear you say that. So, Billy, you left the
birds and making a million in favour of cavortin' round
the world, I suppose?'

Robson nodded. 'Something like that.' He was always
reticent to offer too much; there was nothing worse than
worldy-wise bores.

'Lucky sod,' Lewis encouraged. 'Where'd you serve?'

'Oh, all the usual. Hong Kong, Cyprus, Norway, Belize, Ulster, Malta—'

'Malta?'

'Yes, spent quite some time there.'

Lewis clinked the ice in his glass thoughtfully. 'Know it well do you?'

Robson laughed. 'Too well. I've still got a few contacts there. Mind you, times have changed.'

Suddenly Frank Lewis' manner became more serious. 'Mind if I ask a personal question?'

'Try me.'

The blue eyes fixed Robson's attention. 'How do you handle yourself? You know – trouble-wise.'

It was Andy Sutcliff's turn to laugh; perhaps it was the drink on an empty stomach.

Lewis was mildly irritated. 'What's so funny?'

Sutcliff caught his breath. 'Didn't mean to be rude. It's just if you know Billy ... He used to instruct on unarmed combat. We got in this scrap once when he was on leave. Three muggers jumped us down the tube. I was useless – pole-axed. But Billy-boy here dealt with 'em like they was three toddlers. Ah, well, not exactly. One fractured jaw and the other with his ribs stove in. I think the third run off.'

Rich Abbott grinned. 'That's our Billy. Real hero type. Quiet and unassuming until you get a bit of action. Good lad.'

'High praise indeed.' Lewis seemed to come to a decision. 'Listen, Billy, I've got a little business to attend to in Malta soon. That's why I was interested. I don't know the place. Why don't you come with me? You can show me the ropes and get a tan at the same time. Call it a holiday. I'll cover your ex's, and pay you a consideration. You married?'

Robson found himself drawing back. 'Yes.'

Lewis slapped his forearm reassuringly. 'Well, then, bring Mrs Robson as well. She'll be company for Her Ladyship. I expect you could both do with a spot of sun and sand and the other, after doing a stretch? What d'you say?'

Robson was dubious. 'Look, Mr Lewis, that's very kind, but I'm – I'm not looking for any trouble. I can't get *involved* in anything.'

Rich Abbott intervened. 'Billy-boy, Frankie Lewis is probably the only legit operator in the club tonight. He's only welcome here because I've known him from way back. An East Ender like ourselves. Runs a big building firm, and – what is it? – catering . . . ?'

'Catering and contract cleaning,' Lewis added with more than a hint of pride. 'Little empire-builder, that's me. In fact, my lads did the renovation to this club for Rich.'

'And it's *all* legit,' Rich Abbott confirmed.

Robson could hardly believe his luck.

'So?' Frank Lewis' smile was contagious. 'What do you say?'

'How can I refuse?'

'Jammy sod,' Andy Sutcliff muttered.

Four

Dee's palms were sweating.

Of the three men behind the dark-tinted windows in the rear compartment of the Rolls Royce, Dee should have been the least nervous.

He had, after all, personally killed or mutilated ten British soldiers and seven Ulster Protestants. Some in the cross-hairs of a sniper rifle, the remainder blown to bits by high explosives. But that had been a long time ago. Since then he had directed and organised countless more 'executions' from a distance.

Yes, he told himself, he should have the least to fear from the godfathers of the Provisional IRA. So, if his palms were sweating, the Almighty only knew what his two companions were feeling as the Rolls swished through the still Eire countryside.

Beside him sat Eamon Molloy. A big ugly man with fleshy jug ears and a wet lower lip that protruded belligerently. His heavy body, wrapped in an astrakhan coat, filled most of the back seat, but as usual, he was oblivious to the discomfort he caused others around him. Years ago, he had inherited vast farmlands and stud farms in County Cork and Tipperary. Since that time his empire had expanded with the speed and ruthlessness of a Wild West cattle baron. Now business interests also stretched into shipping, construction and horse-racing. Eamon Molloy had friends in very high places, right across the political and religious divides.

Despite his vast wealth and seemingly limitless influence, he was still the most miserable man Dee had ever known. Tonight, in the dim light cast from the dashboard, Eamon Molloy looked more disgruntled than ever.

The third passenger did not complain about Molloy's thick thighs that crushed him against the side of the car every time the chauffeur took a left-hand bend. That was not Tom Rabbit's style. Typically, he said nothing as he peered out at the tree-lined road with the dark gypsy eyes he had inherited from his father's tinker family. Those eyes were his most striking feature. Deep and unfathomable, able to dance with wicked humour or switch, without warning, to burning malevolence.

Those eyes sat well in the swarthy face below the sleek black hair that his Sicilian mother had contributed. Tom Rabbit's quicksilver temper was another gift from her, along with an understated vanity. That manifested itself in his dress – he was given to dark and expensive mohair suits – his shoulder-length hair and sideburns that cut like scimitars across his cheeks. And the single gold ring in his left ear.

It was just possible, Dee thought, that Tom Rabbit could have something to fear. He was not a born-and-bred Republican with grandparents who had ever rejoiced at the Easter Rebellion. He was tinker-stock. A 'knacker'. Unpredictable and unreliable. It would not have surprised Dee to learn that his ancestors had sold information to the Black and Tans.

No, Rabbit came from a line of rogues; he even boasted his family name came from its traditional way of earning a living in ancient times, by poaching. To Dee, that was as likely an explanation as it was colourful.

Today, Rabbit's daily deeds were less romantic. He was a ruthless villain who knew his way around the Dublin underworld. Extortion, protection, armed robbery, and abduction were his stock-in-trade. He had no interest in politics or historical injustice.

He had never volunteered to join the Provisional IRA; he had been ordered to. No major criminal activity had been tolerated in Eire since the early 1970s without the Provo godfathers' permission. And that was only permitted in return for a percentage. There could be no other grouping, criminal or political, allowed to grow to any size. Any gang with too much power, wealth or underworld influence was seen as a possible threat.

So, one day, Tom Rabbit was told that he had new business partners. The Provos would provide the back-up, additional intelligence, guns, protective influence in the police and judiciary, and front-money in return for a fifty-per cent share of the cake. A cake that they promised would get bigger by the year.

The alternative, as it was put to him gently, was to have all the small bones in his hands and feet crushed to pulp with a builders' sledgehammer.

Rabbit took the soft option. And Dee was certain he had never forgiven the godfathers for it.

Several other gang leaders had been similarly persuaded where their true interests lay. But Tom Rabbit was more important than them.

Much more. His Sicilian mother had introduced him to the Palermo families at the centre of the worldwide Mafia brotherhood, which stretched from America to Australia.

Whilst those blood-ties doubled his value to the Provo godfathers, it also meant that he could just be a man with divided loyalties.

And that alone could mean that Tom Rabbit had every reason to worry.

As Dee allowed himself a small private smirk at the thought, the Rolls Royce glided through the tall gates between the pillars and into the drive. Even as he glanced back through the rear window, he saw the security guards were already locking the gates again. One of them restrained a slavering pit-bull fighting dog as it growled after the vehicle. The creature was totally untrainable, except to do the one thing that came naturally to it. To kill.

'The Man' liked his privacy.

Ten minutes later, The Man himself entered the darkened drawing-room to meet his three guests. His arrival completed the Special Finance Committee of the Provisional IRA.

Dee watched warily from the deep leather chair as The Man passed through a puddle of light on the Persian carpet, cast by the silk-shaded standard lamp.

It was the only illumination in the large room, and the vast area of shadow had the effect of shrinking it down to almost claustrophobic proportions. That, and the all-pervading scent of beeswax polish from the oak-panelled walls made Dee feel surrounded, trapped.

Yet the figure that passed the standard lamp was scarcely threatening. It was that of a slightly-built man in his late sixties or early seventies. Only the stoop to the shoulders, and the hint of a flagging belly beneath the thin primrose sweater, suggested it was not the physique of a much younger man.

The Man liked to keep to the shadows. He rarely ventured beyond the highly-guarded confines of his mansion. Even at meetings like this, he had a knack of selecting a darkened corner in which to sit. Momentarily, the light reflected on the silver hair, then, as he turned, Dee caught sight of the small, thin-lipped mouth with tiny, even white teeth. Then the face melted back into shadow.

From previous meetings, Dee recalled the well-scrubbed texture of The Man's skin, and the small colourless mole on one cheek. But most of all, he remembered those striking cornflower eyes.

Now seated opposite his three guests, their chairman appeared to be ready. On the low antique table between them, a bottle of Irish whiskey stood with some cut-glass tumblers in open invitation.

The soft, gravelly Irish brogue confirmed it. 'Pour yourselves drinks, me lads.' It was scarcely higher than a whisper. 'And we'll get started.'

Tom Rabbit leaned forward and slopped a large measure into one of the tumblers. He offered no one else a drink, and no one else spoke. Deep in the heart of the mansion, a clock chimed.

'Well?' The Man's voice was as soft as always but the faint rasp from his throat suggested he was growing impatient. 'You called for this extraordinary meeting, Bunny, so I suggest that you start.'

Rabbit sat on the edge of his seat, his forearms resting on his knees whilst he nervously toyed with the tumbler between his fingers. His dark eyes glared. They all knew he hated the name Bunny. It had been used by their chairman in a deliberately provocative way.

'I am not happy,' Rabbit stated at last, suddenly deciding to get the matter off his chest. His accent was thick and would have been almost incomprehensible to an Englishman.

'Are you not?' The sarcasm in The Man's tone was light and playful.

'No, sir, I'm not.' Rabbit glanced at his companions for their reactions. Eamon Molloy just lay back in his chair, fingers clasped across his gross belly, and studied the ceiling as though the conversation was nothing to do with him. As usual, his lower lip jutted obstinately. Dee just looked, watchful and alert, as always.

Rabbit bought himself thinking time by lighting a cigarette. This was going to be difficult. 'I am not happy about the seizure. Not at all. Somethin' is goin' on that I don' know about and don' understand. Yet no one else seems concerned. I find tha' a mite puzzlin'.'

'There's nothing for you to understand.' They strained to catch The Man's words. 'You have no doubt read about it in the newspapers. The Dublin government seized one of our covert accounts containing over one million pounds sterling. End of story.'

'They were tipped off!' Rabbit snarled.

'It was sacrificed.' Quietly.

Rabbit's face contorted like a grotesque carnival mask. '*Sacrificed?* Sacrificed! For what?'

'The Cause.'

He shook his head in disbelief. 'Without funds there *is* no bloody cause. You talk about it being sacrificed as though 'twas some sort of *honour*. You can't make a martyr out o' a bloody bank account, y'know.'

For a moment no sound came from the shadows. Dee at first thought that The Man was angry, but then he sensed the mocking, silent smile. It somehow filled Dee with admiration, and not for the first time. 'There are other accounts, Bunny. Larger, much larger, than the one we have traded.'

The dark eyebrows frowned demonically. '*Traded?* What is this, some kind o' sick joke? I've spent three years accumulatin' those funds. At great risk. And now y' calmly say 'twas *traded*! Traded for *what*, in the name o' the Holy Mother?'

'For peace and quiet. So that we will be left alone.'

A passionate light gleamed in Rabbit's gypsy eyes, but momentarily he was speechless.

Dee, on the other hand, remained totally without expression. However his head was reeling with the implications of The Man's statement. Dee knew for a fact that the 'knacker' was assuming that the answers he got were soft rhetoric to hide the importance of the Dublin government's recent seizure of vast terrorist funds. But Dee knew The Man better. He was not given to rhetoric. He was a realist and a pragmatist. He moulded events. Events did not mould him.

Enlightenment began to slowly dawn on Dee as he watched Rabbit try to grasp what was being said. The knacker's frustration and anger was understandable though. It was an account to which his activities had greatly contributed. Contrary to press comments, little had come from kidnap ransoms. That was a risky business depending on too many variables. It was difficult enough finding non-Irish victims whose wealth could be readily translated into cash. And multi-national corporations were even tougher than many governments. They certainly didn't like to be seen as soft targets for any young hothead with a gun. Besides, police tactics, intelligence and electronic sophistication were becoming so effective that kidnap was now a high-risk occupation for the perpetrators. Too much could go wrong. Only the gun-happy, naïve, and expendable were directed on such missions.

Nowadays, kidnaps were only necessary to make the threat real. And that threat was used as the real money-spinner:

protection. Companies that would not pay millions to meet ransom demands were more ready to pay the odd thousand here and the odd thousand there if it meant a guarantee that they could continue earning their millions. North and South of the border. It was almost a legitimate business expense.

It was so easy, Dee realised that. Only if a company collapsed suddenly might the money be found unaccounted for.

But it was not just the industrial giants who paid. Everyone did, if not to avoid kidnap, then just to avoid trouble. Construction companies, drinking-clubs; they all paid their dues. Dee saw nothing wrong in that. They were all capitalists who would normally donate nothing to The Cause, damn their black hearts. It was all quite amusing really.

Unlike bank and post office robberies. Dee knew The Man didn't like those. He and the other 'doves' amongst the IRA godfathers had been putting a stop to them lately. It stank of lawlessness and earned them a bad name. Several of those who had refused to stop were dead now. Or in wheelchairs.

Besides, as Dee knew, there were other ways to milk banks.

At last Tom Rabbit spoke again. His voice faltered – it may have been suppressed anger or just uncertainty. 'Why – why should we be left alone? And, besides, what happens to me share?'

This time they could all hear The Man's soft chuckle. 'Ah, Bunny, now the truth is out. Your cut. Don't worry, your cut is safe.'

'How do I know that?'

'Because I know, if you were not paid, you could not be trusted.'

Dee almost laughed aloud. That told the knacker bastard. No messing.

'And regards being left alone,' The Man continued, 'the Dublin and British governments are at this moment believing that we are all wringing our hands in despair. Like you. Just read the papers: "Another death blow to the IRA". On its knees. Finished.'

'But *who* told them?' Rabbit persisted. 'Those bastards in Boston again, I suppose?'

Dee immediately knew who he meant. Rabbit had no love for the 'Irish Mafia' as they were called. Based in the Irish-predominated neighbourhoods of Boston, the gang had orignally been formed to protect the immigrants from the local Italian Mafia. It was a task they had achieved successfully. Nowadays, they were left alone to run their empire by fixing horse-races, controlling illegal gambling and extortion rackets throughout New England. They also formed the American arm of the Provisional IRA.

'Yes,' The Man replied calmly. 'They alerted the authorities. Not directly, of course. But it nevertheless came on *our* instruction.'

Tom Rabbit was lost, and it showed as he anxiously fingered one of his long sideburns. 'Just what the hell are y' people playing at?'

Patiently The Man told him: 'The Brits are now under the impression that our funds have been greatly diminished. They will rest on their laurels and the heat will be off for a while. To achieve that, a pawn may have to be sacrificed. Sometimes a bigger piece.'

'And what about that *Marita Ann* last year?' Rabbit demanded. 'Sure, everyone knows that tip-off came from a gang informer. I suppose that was another of y' bloody pawns?'

The Man did not reply. But the silence appeared to convince Tom Rabbit. 'I may not share y' great belief in a united Ireland, but I do have a belief in loyalty. Loyalty to men in t' same business as me. Men whose trust I can count on.' His eyes glowed fiercely in the dimly-lit room. 'Three of y' men – our men – were taken from the *Marita Ann*. One of them from y' own Army Council. Did he volunteer to sacrifice himself to The Cause, or did someone want him out of the way . . . ?'

Dee smiled to himself; Tom Rabbit was just beginning to understand. Although even now it was unlikely that the knacker realised how close he was to the truth.

In a way, the gypsy reminded Dee of himself three years ago when he, as a trusted member of Provo GHQ staff, had first been appointed to the Special Finance Committee. The difference was that Tom Rabbit had never been fully trusted and had therefore never been privy to the secrets of the inner caucus. He had been grafted on as a useful extension to the Committee's activities – for as long as he served a purpose.

On the other hand, Dee had been exposed to the wisdom and foresight of The Man. And, for one, had no doubt that the shadowy figure before him, whose name was scarcely breathed by a few of its fellow members, was the most powerful man on the Army Council. The power and influence behind the throne.

If Dee ever had any doubts about that, they had quickly been shattered three years ago when he first joined the Committee. He had been appointed by the 'hawks' to look after their interests, in the same way that Eamon Molloy pushed the cause of the 'doves' who believed in the infamous 'Armalite and ballot-box' policy of Sinn Fein. But it soon became clear to Dee that The Man was wiser and smarter than all the young firebrands and revolutionary socialists whose interests he had been sent to protect.

Divide and rule. The old maxim that history proved worked. That was The Man's strategy.

Yes, Dee thought, the *Marita Ann*'s capture had been no accident. It had provided The Man with the ideal excuse not to deliver 160 Armalite rifles, carbines, shotguns, machine-guns and rockets to the hawks. Such an armoury in their hands would have been tantamount to bringing open civil war to the streets of Belfast, and maybe even Dublin.

The violent reaction of the Brits, the RUC and the Garda hardly need be imagined.

No, instead The Man allowed the few so desperate to be martyrs to struggle on, sharing weapons and making do. Just enough to keep the pot simmering and The Cause alive.

Meanwhile The Man controlled a weapon more powerful than guns, and mightier than any pen. The most powerful weapon known to the arsenal of mankind. Money.

In a rare moment of open honesty, The Man had explained to Dee that the nation of Israel had been established on proceeds from the American Mafia. Without that vast and secret investment of laundered money from their empire of gambling, extortion and vice, that country would never have got up off its knees. It was, The Man patiently explained, the only way that the 'United Ireland' he craved would ever be born.

And, although he never knew the details, Dee had become totally convinced of the unlimited extent of The Man's power and influence. He had witnessed it at work both sides of the border. In all walks of civilian life the tentacles snaked out until Dee was sure that few were untouched. It was both sinister and chilling, but also quite awe-inspiring.

Tom Rabbit was visibly trembling as he lit himself a fresh cigarette. 'There is also a rumour tha' the *Marita Ann* arms deal was paid for by drugs money.' He was on dangerous ground and he knew it.

Eamon Molloy sat more upright in his chair.

Instinctively, Dee's muscles tightened.

A grin spread over Rabbit's face. 'Hit a raw spot, have I?'

Quietly The Man said: 'Such matters are not of your concern, Bunny.'

Rabbit's grin slowly transformed into a sneer. 'But it concerns my friends in Sicily. They aren't happy to hear these stories. For the past few years we've organised your supplies of heroin. To you and to the families in America and Canada.' Perspiration glistened on Rabbit's upper lip. 'They say you have been supplying across the Atlantic. And you got those supplies from *another* source. That makes them very angry!'

The gauntlet was well and truly down this time. Molloy shifted awkwardly in his chair. Dee was motionless, but he could feel the adrenalin start to course through his body. Only The Man seemed unmoved, implacable.

The low voice drifted through the pall of tobacco smoke. 'You may tell your friends, Bunny, that the Provisional IRA deals with whom *it* chooses. And when *it* chooses.'

It was too much for Rabbit. To contain his growing impatience, he climbed to his feet and paced behind his chair, waving an accusing finger in the direction of The Man. 'There'll be trouble! They set up your deals. Tied arrangements in with the Australians. You had a good thing going. Now you are tryin' to cut them out! They know what's going on! You forget Italy has strong ties with Libya. Nothing goes on without them hearin' about it in Sicily.' Now venom was pouring out of Rabbit. Dee could almost see it oozing from his swarthy pores. Smell the fetid hatred the knacker had always felt when being forced to kneel before the IRA godfathers. 'What was the Australian doing in Dublin when he was caught? It wasn't just for medical treatment. He deals with Sicily, not you direct.'

The sudden silence was stunning. Everyone in the room knew why Robert Trimbole had come to Eire. Everyone except Tom Rabbit. The gangster described in the press as 'Australia's most wanted man' – a drugs baron, multiple murderer, and second-in-command of the Australian Mafia – had been arrested following the granting of a special extradition order by the Dublin Government. That had been last October. Now, just six weeks into the new year, Trimbole had been released on a technicality following a High Court ruling that he had been illegally arrested. Before the Attorney-General's office could appeal the decision, Trimbole had disappeared.

'And now he's in Spain!' Tom Rabbit accused. 'Tying up with the American families to get cocaine into Britain. Where does that leave Sicily?'

His voice had reached screaming pitch, and his question echoed around the silent mansion.

'Sicily,' The Man replied after a moment, 'is finished. It is a spent force, Bunny. Get wise to that. The *Cosa Nostra* have been too busy putting the finger on each other, telling stories, and fighting amongst themselves. And I shall tell you something. They have got too clever and sophisticated. Always one or two removed from the action. Dealing only in laundered money. They have ...' he paused for effect, letting the words soak in '... they – have – lost – control – of – things. Fighting over less and less business. Then they break *omerta*. Over 400 arrested by the police and it's even started spreading to America. No, Bunny, get wise. There are *other* organisations in the world – newer, smarter, leaner, harder – who do not mind getting their hands dirty. And it is they who will fill the vacuum as your relatives in Palermo go down the lavatory pan.'

To Dee it was like a vision. It had happened before when The Man spoke. Like a sighting at Lourdes. A momentary flash of enlightenment when a glimpse of the future is revealed. Crystal clear, logical. Inevitable.

Tom Rabbit gulped. Perhaps he too had seen it. 'Vacuum? Take over? Organisations like who . . . like you?' He had obviously meant his voice to sound derisory; he couldn't quite manage it. 'I'll tell you what. Palermo is far from finished. They have said that if you just think about cutting them out of the heroin trade, they will deal instead with the Protestants in the North!'

Eamon Molloy's lower lip protruded a further half-inch as he glared up at the gypsy.

'Sit down, Bunny.' The Man's voice had hardly risen an octave yet it struck with the uncompromising authority of an unsheathed knife.

Rabbit's look of triumph evaporated rapidly as he fumbled back to his place.

'Palermo can do what it will, Bunny,' The Man said. 'They know no more about us and our power than do the Brits. You talk about deals with the Protestants. Well, I shall tell you something. You may not believe it; that doesn't matter. Everyone else in this room *knows* it is the truth.' He paused. 'We're giving money to Protestant extremists every week.'

Tom Rabbit blinked his eyes like white marbles. 'Yeah, of course.' Uncertain.

'Every time they murder anyone in the North, we win a thousand converts to The Cause.'

Tom Rabbit didn't know whether to believe it or not. He blinked again.

The Man continued: 'When we first made one of them the offer, he said he would not change his views one iota. Fine, we said. When he was asked about the morality of a leading Protestant taking handouts from the IRA, do you know what he said? *Do You?* He said: "I will sup with the Devil with a long enough spoon." He does not care where the money comes from, as long as it comes.'

Tom Rabbit's mouth moved silently for a moment, and then his lips compressed into a small tight line.

Eamon Molloy spoke for the first time. 'Listen to The Man, Rabbit, and learn. *We* control the heroin supplies up into Ulster. If the Proddies try to muscle-in, they'll be massacred. Your friends in Palermo know *nothing* about us. But now you know a little. It is time for you to decide. You are with us or against us. There is no half-way house.' His voice sounded wet and slurping as though he was chewing an orange. Nevertheless it was filled with menace. 'Tell them never, ever to threaten us. That is the message. Understood?'

Tom Rabbit nodded. This time he really did understand.

'You had better go now,' The Man said. 'I must talk to the others. They will join you shortly by the car.'

The knacker was dismissed. Defiantly, he swigged the last of his drink before leaving the drawing-room without a backward glance. Somewhere from the darkened hall came the sound of a heavy door closing.

The Man said: 'I have two attaché cases here, gentlemen. Filled with unused dollar bills for distribution to the members of the Army Council in the usual way. It is to cover their out-of-pocket expenses. No receipts need be issued. Claimed expenses will be dealt with separately. Understood?'

Dee smiled knowingly. He understood. The Man was distributing his favours. No member of the Army Council would go short whilst he played along with The Man. Each would have his own considerable private nest-egg tucked away somewhere. More money than he would ever accumulate as a legitimate politician in the Shangri-la dream of the new United Ireland.

'And, Tommy,' The Man said.

Dee looked up.

'I want to speak to you about Tom Rabbit. Privately.'

Five

Friday night at the Czar public-house in Peckham was only marginally less frenetic than Saturday night.

By eight-thirty the air was already thick with smoke and laughing Irish voices as jokes and stories were swapped. Things would really start to hum, though, when the folk band began at nine. Then the singing would follow, joining in the chorus to ballads and Republican songs. By the inevitably belated closing-time there wouldn't be a dry eye in the house.

As soon as Billy Robson pushed open the door and let Sandy in, he felt like a fish out of water. An alien in a strange land. The hubbub of distinct Dublin and Ulster accents rushed at him all at once.

It was like stepping back into a nightmare: late patrol in Belfast; rain-slicked streets; the surprise raid on a *shebeen* drinking club. As the Marines burst in a deafening silence would fall as though the sound-track had suddenly been cut with a knife. All faces would turn in slow motion. A sea of white, blank, hostile faces. You could feel the hatred, smell it.

But tonight the chatter burbled on. The smiling faces stayed smiling. No one seemed to notice them.

Sandy whispered: 'They're all Irish. 'You sure this is the right pub, Billy?'

Robson gave her a reassuring hug. 'It's owned by Frankie Lewis's mother-in-law. Well, his mother-in-law *if* he was married. I get the idea Bernadette is his common-law wife. But I do know she's from Dublin, so it stands to reason her mother would run . . .'

Sandy nodded. '. . . An *Irish* pub. Well, he could have warned you. I just hope he's already here. I don't fancy hanging around by ourselves.'

Robson guided her through the crowd.

'Over here, Billy!'

Frank Lewis waved from a corner seat at the long bar, a Bacardi at his elbow. He looked as dapper as the last time they had met, dressed now in a pale blue lightweight suit with hand-stitched lapels that might as well have had its Savile Row label on the outside. A gold stud pierced the lemon knitted tie at mid-chest, matched by equally heavy cufflinks at each wrist.

He slipped from the stool and took Robson's hand in a vigorous shake.

'Nice t'see you again, Billy.' Then the sharp blue eyes passed to Sandy. 'And this must be the lovely Mrs Robson . . .'

'Er, yes, this is Sandy. Sandy, this is Frank.'

Lewis's eyes devoured her as he held her gaze whilst lifting her hand to his lips with exaggerated charm. 'Delighted, Sandy. You never said what a smashing lookin' missus you had, Billy.'

Sandy felt her face flush, and she could sense the nervous pink rash glowing across her chest as their host's gaze lingered for a few moments too long. Instantly she regretted her choice of the tight-fitting maroon dress with the neck cut a little too low.

'You never asked me,' Robson quipped and all three laughed awkwardly, the tension relieved.

A plump, middle-aged woman with a dyed-blonde beehive hair-do leaned over from the other side of the bar. 'You flirtin' again, Frankie? What are we goin' to do with you? I don't know how poor Bernadette puts up with it.'

'My mum-in-law,' Lewis introduced with mock apology. 'Mary makes my life a misery. Owns the pub and we always drink here. Bad idea that.'

'Aren't you goin' to buy your friends a drink?' Mary goaded. 'Give the moths an airing and get your wallet out!'

'Nag, nag!' Lewis groaned, and winked at Sandy. 'What'll it be?'

A few minutes later it seemed that half the patrons in the pub had been bought a drink by Lewis. Men raised their glasses to him and their women smiled knowingly.

'It was very good of you to offer to take Billy and me to Malta,' Sandy said. 'I mean, I could hardly believe it when he came home and said this stranger had made him an offer. I couldn't believe our luck. I thought there must be a catch.'

That wasn't exactly how I remember it, Robson thought ruefully. She had used every possible excuse not to go to Malta. From having nothing to wear, to feeling unwell, to hating going away with strangers. Like the rest of her recent odd behaviour, he had put it down to her bad nerves.

'Well, love,' Lewis said, 'you're right that there's a catch. I've got some business over there and your hubby knows the ropes. Besides, you'll be company for Bernie.' He glanced at his watch. A watch that Robson once remembered seeing in a Bond Street window. A Patek Phillipe Moonphase with a £4,000 price tag. 'Talkin' of which, I'm sorry she's late. She's been down at the Irish Board of Trade. Love 'er down there, they do. Usually carry 'er off for drinks after the office closes.'

Robson said: 'What line of business is involved in Malta, Frankie? I know you said you were in building and contract cleaning—'

'And catering supply,' Lewis completed the list for him. 'That's big business if you've got the right connections. It's my newest business area and going like a bomb.'

'Obviously you've got the right connections then,' Sandy suggested helpfully.

Frank Lewis grinned and patted her knee. 'Luckily, sweetheart, I married the right connections—' Then he leaned forward conspiratorially '—well, not *actually* married to tell the truth. Bernie and I are partners in business and well, in . . .'

Sandy returned his contagious smile. 'Life?'

'Actually, I was going to say bed! What a clever and discreet woman you are, Sandy. Anyway, Bernie's got lots of family connections with the cattle trade in Ireland. Actually, her old man used to run one of the biggest spreads out there.'

Robson frowned. 'I didn't know the Maltese were great meat importers. It's only a small population.'

Lewis appeared mildly irritated. 'No, Billy, the deal's with Libya, not Malta. It's just that the Libyans like doing business in Malta. It's the last bastion of civilisation before you hit the deserts of North Africa, and those countries are dry in *every* bloody sense.'

'Ah, Moslem,' Robson recalled.

Lewis downed his Bacardi and beckoned for a fresh round. 'That's right. And them little Arab buggers can't wait to get out of Allah's sight and start drinkin' themselves senseless – not to mention screwing every white woman they can – oh, sorry, Sandy, I didn't think.'

She smiled and shook her head to indicate that she'd taken no offence.

'Don't Moslems have special meat?' Robson asked.

'That's right. Bled, blessed, and specially prepared. We've got the plants in Eire and ship the stuff out frozen. A lot of the Arab states, as well as Iran – though I'm told that's not strictly Arab.' He handed Sandy a fresh vodka martini and Robson another lager. 'In fact, Libya is Eire's biggest customer for halal meat. Trouble is old Gadaffi keeps trying to use it as a political weapon. There was a bit of a scare last December when he threatened to stop the trade unless the Irish bought Libyan oil in return.

'The Fianna Gael Government were uptight about it, but old Charlie Haughey of Fianna Fail – that's the Opposition – leapt in to make mileage out of it. He gets on okay with Gadaffi. Anyway it seems all right now. My deal's going through, and that's what matters.'

There was a sudden commotion near the entrance of the pub. Voices cheered and laughed as a new couple entered, weaving their way through the press of hard-drinking Irishmen and women.

Lewis grinned widely. 'Looks like Her Ladyship's arrived.'

Both Robson and Sandy turned. There was no doubt who the warm welcome was for. Certainly it was not intended for the stout, grey-suited man with grey hair and a seemingly grey complexion.

The enthusiasm was for the girl on his arm. Robson guessed she was about five foot six. But the patent navy stilettos and matching two-piece business suit, with a pencil skirt that flared stunningly at her hips, added to her height. A froth of white lace and a small black necktie set off the smiling freckled face. A tumbling muddle of soft chestnut hair completed the framing effect.

As she came closer Robson found himself drawn to her eyes. Laughing green eyes with tiny brilliant gold flecks. And the single dimple to the left of her mouth which gave her smile a charmingly lop-sided look.

Lewis whispered: 'That's Liam with her. He's something at the Irish Embassy. Fancies Bernie rotten, he does.'

Bernadette pecked her husband briefly on the cheek, then turned immediately to Sandy. 'You must be Mrs Robson. Sure, it's lovely to see you. I'm just so sorry I'm late. It's unforgiveable, I know, but business comes first – that's what Frankie always says.'

'Of course, I understand,' Sandy muttered, a little overwhelmed by the ingenuous warmth of the welcome. More than ever she wished she had chosen a more modest dress.

'And this is Billy, who I was telling you about,' Lewis said.

Bernadette turned and shook his hand. 'It's lovely to meet you, Billy. Both of you. I'm sure we're going to have a grand time together.' Warmth radiated from her like some internal beacon. 'Billy, you must tell us what to expect in Malta.'

Robson considered for a moment. 'Well, I haven't been there for a few years, so there've undoubtedly been changes. But it's a small island. About thirteen miles long and seven wide. You can tour it in a day or two by car, no problem. Sicily is only sixty miles to the north and Libya just over two hundred to the south. So there's a strange mix of Italian and Arabic influence, especially with the language. Oh, and British influence of course.'

'Wasn't it a colony?' Lewis asked.

Robson nodded. 'Yes, after the Napoleonic Wars up until Independence in – er – 1964, I think. So they nearly all speak perfect English, which makes for a good holiday. Not much sand, though. In fact, apart from the buildings, it's not that attractive. Odd place really. They say you love or you hate it.'

Bernadette leaned forward, intrigued. 'And what about you, Billy, did you love it or hate it?'

He laughed awkwardly. 'That's hardly a question to ask a Royal Marine.'

Bernadette looked puzzled.

However, Sandy explained sourly: 'Whether they like a place or not depends on the beer and crumpet.'

'*So*, Billy?' the Irish girl pressed mischievously.

'Personally I liked it.'

'*Really!*' Bernadette studied his eyes closely.

Suddenly Sandy felt shut out of the conversation. An invisible screen had descended between them. She was only vaguely aware of her husband chuntering on about how good the people were, how interesting the food, and how many British people retired out there . . .

The four musicians arrived and began tuning their instruments. The discordant notes jarred against the rolling hubbub of chatter and laughter. Everyone was pressing in around her. Sweat and smoky breath filled her nostrils. The place was airless. Perhaps the drink was going to her head; she felt a little giddy. Alternate hot and cold flushes rippled through her body. The damp patch of perspiration on her back suddenly seemed to freeze over, then melt again.

She tugged at Robson's arm. 'I don't feel too good, Billy. I feel dizzy. Is it all right if we go?'

Before he could reply, Bernadette was at her side. 'Would you like some water, love? It's pretty close in here.'

Sandy drew back. 'No, no. I'll be all right. If I can just get out.'

Robson glanced across at Lewis and shrugged helplessly. Both men knew they still had business to discuss.

Lewis said: 'Take her upstairs, Bernie, while Billy and I talk things over. She'll be better up there.'

Sandy pushed the helping hands away and climbed awkwardly from her stool. 'I'd rather go. You stay, Billy. I'm sorry everyone, really. I must get home.'

'If you're sure, Sand . . .' Robson began.

Lewis plucked a twenty-pound note from his wallet and handed it to Bernadette. 'Get Mrs Robson a taxi, Bernie, door-to-door.'

'I'm sorry everyone . . .' Sandy's voice trailed off as Bernadette helped her walk unsteadily towards the door.

Robson watched them disappear into the crowd with a growing feeling of helplessness and desperation. He had never known his wife like this before. Totally unpredictable and in a permanent state of nervous exhaustion. It was impossible to reason with her about anything, let alone her state of health. She insisted that the course of tablets she was on was helping, but the doctor had told her there was nothing more to be done until her natural resistance improved. It was all so frustrating.

Frank Lewis nudged him. 'C'mon, Billy, let's go upstairs. We can talk things over.'

He led the way up the staircase and along a passage. It was refreshingly cool in the games-room. A pool of yellow light spread across the green baize of the snooker table from the overhead canopy which trembled to the muffled bass of the band below them.

'That's better,' Lewis said. 'Peace and quiet. Sometimes I wouldn't mind drinking somewhere else. Especially on a Friday night when I'm knackered. But Mary would be mortally offended.'

'Look, Frankie,' Robson began, 'I ought to tell you straight away that I think I've hit a snag.'

Lewis's blue eyes clouded, but the even white smile remained. 'So soon? Don't tell me you're backing out.'

Robson shook his head. 'No, not me, Frankie. This is a welcome start for me. God knows I'm grateful, but well, you know I'm still on probation?'

'Sure.'

'Well, I phoned my officer this afternoon to tell him about Malta.' He was finding this humiliating. 'You know we have to get permission before we leave the country – or take a job?'

'Sure, Billy, it's a sod, I know.' He grinned reassuringly. 'I did a spell in Borstal as a nipper, so I know the difficulties.'

Robson took a cigarette pack from his pocket. 'Well, I've just been given this right bastard called Vance. Really got it in for me, he has.'

'And?'

'He reckons it's fishy. Says strangers don't just come up to you and offer you a free holiday and business deal out of the blue.'

'I see,' Lewis said thoughtfully as he accepted one of Robson's cigarettes. 'You didn't tell him *where* we met? At Rich Abbott's?'

'Christ, no, Frankie, I'm not stupid. I just said in a pub. But he reckoned he'd have to check you out first, says he knows everyone in our area. But he wasn't hopeful and he'd have to check it out with his chief.' Robson sent an exasperated cloud of smoke tumbling over the snooker table. 'The sickening thing is I got on well with his predecessor, but this bastard . . .'

'So you've good reports until recently?'

'As far as I know.'

'So if his chief made the decision based on your record, you'd be in with a chance?'

Robson grimaced. 'But not while Vance has got his ear.'

Frank Lewis placed a consoling arm around the other man's shoulder. 'Don't worry, old son. I'll put a call into Vance first thing Monday. Maybe even get Bernie to charm the bugger. I've got a respectable international business, so he can check us out until he's blue in the arse.'

'That's a hell of an imposition—'

Lewis raised a finger to his lips. 'No more to be said. Just be sure to give me Vance's number before you go tonight. Now, let's get down to details.'

Not convinced that he shared Lewis's optimism, Robson seated himself on the edge of the snooker table and took a small notebook and pen from his pocket.

Lewis laughed. 'My, my, we are efficient.'

Robson began to share the other man's humour. The confident way Lewis tackled problems reminded him of the attitude of so many old friends back in his Marine days. 'You said a "briefing", Frankie. Old military habits die hard. So, when do I start?'

'Tomorrow.' The change in Lewis's tone took Robson aback. Suddenly this *was* business. 'Tomorrow I want you to book a package week for the four of us. Go through a reputable agent. I suggest Maltese Max in Old Compton Street, Medtravel Ltd. We always use him. What's a good hotel there?'

Robson frowned. 'The Phoenicia used to be good. All Victorian splendour and high ceilings.'

'Not my style.'

Robson tried to visualise Frank Lewis in all the hotels he could recall. 'The Hilton?'

A smile spread over Lewis's face. 'That's my boy! Great. Book us in and also a car through Hertz. Something a bit smart, you know my style by now.'

Robson scribbled rapidly into his book.

'Start the booking a week from today – next Friday – is there a good choice of flights?'

'No problem, especially this time of year.'

'Good. Then I want you alone to take a flight out on Tuesday—'

Billy Robson's pen came to an abrupt halt. 'Tuesday? Alone?'

Lewis's smile had a hint of sarcasm. 'Don't Marines like flying alone? Yes, Billy, Tuesday and alone. When you arrive get one of your Maltese contacts to find another hotel, good but not too flash, and duplicate the whole booking in there. But don't you stay there until you join us on the Friday at the airport – what's it called—?'

'Luqa,' Robson replied absently as he added to his notes. This was ridiculous; it didn't make sense.

'You got a reliable man there who can keep his mouth shut?'

'I was thinking of a woman.'

Lewis grinned. 'Typical Marine, eh? That's all right, maybe better. She can be trusted?'

'Implicitly, *if* I can still trace her. I'll try phoning—'

'NO!' Frank Lewis's raised voice even surprised himself. He blinked, then smiled apologetically. 'Sorry, Billy, but *no* international telephone calls and all arrangements to be made face to-face with the people concerned. And no discussing my business with anyone. Get it?'

Robson said slowly: 'What am I getting into, Frankie? All this is – is – well, it's odd to say the least.'

Slowly Lewis crossed the floor and plucked a cue from the rack. 'Ever dealt with the Libyans, Billy?'

'I've met a few. Never dealt with them. No business or anything.'

Lewis smiled. 'That's what I thought.' He began chalking the tip of the cue. 'They're a curious bunch of bastards. They set a lot of conditions and like to see the white man jump when they pull the strings. Their minds work in a funny way – if they work at all. Half of them are up to no good. Those I deal with work at the People's Bureau, or embassy, or for some diplomatic mission or other. They're all trying to feather their own nests, or else, when they've finished dealing with me, they'll be off to have another go at blowing up the nearest Israeli Ambassador. In fact they literally had a go at the one in Malta last year, I'm told.'

Lewis sauntered back towards the table. 'It's like handling a barrel of nitroglycerin. Unstable and potentially danger-ous. Add to that the Yanks and the Yids are always bugging their phones and generally poking their noses into any busi-ness deal the Libyans are involved in. And, if you ask me, not without good cause.'

'I see,' Robson said. Suddenly the upstairs snooker room seemed very chill indeed. Later he was to recall the feeling.

'That's why,' Lewis continued, 'I don't want the slightest risk to either of us, or the girls. We'll show up at the Hilton and have a meal. Make ourselves known. A few large, well-placed tips. All easily traceable, like the Hertz car. But, when the real business starts, to all intents and purposes we'll operate from our reserve hotel. Just to be on the safe side. So if anyone's got any funny ideas, we'll be gone before they have a chance to find us.'

Robson was still unsure. 'I didn't know the meat business could be so exciting.'

Frank Lewis lined up a black and potted it with an accurate full-length diagonal stroke. The clack of porcelain sounded like a pistol shot in the cold silence of the room. 'You'd be surprised, Billy. Lots of people don't like us doing business with Libya.'

Robson went to put away his notebook.

'Just a couple more things, Billy.'

'Yes?'

'Get two other hired cars lined up. Not from Hertz, but good motors. At least two-litre jobs. Choose them like you would a getaway car.'

Robson's eyes glared.

'Sorry, no offence. You know what I mean. And a motorcycle. Same criteria.'

'Anything else?'

Lewis nodded. 'An apartment or villa that's a bit secluded. Preferably with its own courtyard or garage with gates that lock. Book that in the name of O'Casey. Sean O'Casey.'

Robson looked up.

Frank Lewis was suddenly his usual smiling, charming self again. 'Right, let's join the merry men downstairs and celebrate. Especially celebrate the two thousand fee I'm going to pay you in advance for your few days' work.'

An involuntary smile broke over Robson's face. Four thousand in just a week. Things were really looking up.

He hardly heard as Lewis was saying: 'We might even find Maltese Max in tonight. He often pays us a visit. We might persuade him to take us to one of the night spots he runs. He's got some really kinky private clubs. Very private. Ever heard of The Dominatrix?'

'I can't say I have.'

As Lewis opened the door they were met with the throb of guitars and accordion from downstairs.

'Oh, then you haven't lived, old son. You haven't lived!'

'How do you feel?' Bella's voice was deep with concern.

Sandy Robson stirred on the sette and opened one eye. The dim glow from the standard lamp felt like an interrogation light.

Her eye closed again and she sighed. 'I'm okay, Bell. Floating. I'm okay. That was good shit.'

Bella's own sigh of relief matched her friend's. 'I haven't sold that crap stuff since you passed out in here. That scared the daylights out of me.'

Sandy renewed her effort to surface and opened her eyes again.

'There's some coffee,' Bella said. 'Black.'

'You're sweet.'

Bella snorted and ran thin white fingers through her dark hair. 'You mean I'm soft. After last time I vowed never to let anyone shoot up in here again. Not least you.' She glanced towards the curtains. 'Did you know the fuzz are watching these blocks again?'

Sandy squinted in an attempt to focus on the coffee mug she tried to raise to her lips. The liquid slopped onto the settee. Bella didn't seem to notice. Another stain would just add to the random pattern of spilt blood, alcohol and coffee already there. 'The police? Oh God, I didn't know.'

Bella lit her fiftieth cigarette of the day. 'Yep. The little blue men from the Drug Squad have got themselves a hide up on the roof of the block to the south. So they can keep this estate under surveillance. Funny thing is in the flat immediately beneath them live a couple of hardened junkies and the cops have no idea. Everyone else knows about it.'

'Everyone except me, it seems.' Sandy managed to get the coffee mug to make contact with her lips. The hot strong liquid tasted good.

Bella laughed. 'You'd better keep your eyes open then, love. Otherwise you're going to walk into a lot of unnecessary trouble.' She reached out and touched her friend's hand. 'And I don't just mean the Bill.'

'What?'

'Well, this do at the pub you were at tonight, for instance.'

Sandy wrinkled her nose. 'Oh, God, that was awful. The place was filled with bloody Irishmen, and then this couple we're supposed to be going to Malta with. Money coming out of their ears, and *don't* they just know it!' She thought for a moment. 'Well, *he* was all right. Quite good-looking really. But his wife or girlfriend or whatever . . . shit . . . a proper little smarty-pants. You could tell she thought she was someone special. All the men drooling over her. Billy as well. He couldn't keep his eyes off her. It was sickening.'

Bella's large dark eyes were gimlet hard in her emaciated white face. 'For God's sake, Sand, wake up, love. It was your first night out with Billy since his release, and you blew it. That's the truth. *And* you might have blown this free holiday.'

Sandy huddled over the coffee mug which she held in both hands, and drew up her knees. 'I don't want to go.'

'Why?'

'I told you. I don't like them.'

'*Why?*' Bella persisted.

Sandy flashed her an angry glance. 'All right, if you're so clever, *you* tell me why I don't want to go?'

'Because, Sand, you're scared Billy and your new friends will find out. You can barely afford one fix at a time and in Malta, you won't know where to get the cash. Or where to go to score.'

Sandy pouted. 'Maybe there won't even *be* a place to score.'

Bella sneered. 'You can score anywhere nowadays. Just ask around.'

'Give us a cig, Bell.'

The younger woman tossed over the packet and watched her friend fumble to get out a cigarette with trembling hands.

'How bad's the money problem, love?'

For a moment Sandy was tempted to snap back that it was none of her business. 'I'm skint, Bell. Bloody skint. But Billy got some money this week. A sort of whip-round from Rich Abbott. We've got a joint account, so maybe I can . . .'

'Jesus!' Bella exploded. 'Don't be so fucking stupid! Billy's all you've got. He's a nice, decent bloke. Don't chuck that away!'

Tears began to trickle down Sandy's cheeks. Bella quickly put a comforting arm around her shoulder. 'Don't cry, Sand. Just *think* your way out. Get a job until you can kick the habit. Use your brains.'

Sandy's words were almost incomprehensible between her sobs. 'Like your club, I suppose. Christ, I couldn't do anything like that.'

'It's better than whoring,' Bella replied testily. 'Because that's what you'll end up doing, believe me. Then how will you feel when you give your old man a dose of the clap?'

'But your club, it's kinky, isn't it?' The tears had subsided into a miserable snuffle.

Bella smiled gently. 'With a name like The Dominatrix, it's got to be. But once you get into it, it's not bad. And the pay's good. Two hundred a night, plus tips.'

'What's it like?'

Bella shrugged. 'Like I've said. It's a private club. This posh house in the North London suburbs at the moment. But they move the venue frequently. Strictly vetted membership. No plaque or name outside. The punters watch, or some participate.'

'Participate in what?'

Bella half-smiled. 'Discipline and duty they call it. Or domination. You know, bondage and that sort of thing. Sex-slaves.'

'Christ, Bella, how could you suggest such a thing?' Sandy looked shocked as if suddenly seeing a vision of the dark future that lay ahead of her. 'What do you do there?'

'Mostly bar work. Serving drinks. Then sometimes you get called on by a master or mistress to be subjected. Sometimes the punters take the role of a master or mistress. Or slave. Blokes as well sometimes.'

'Subjected to what?' Sandy was as intrigued as she was horrified.

Bella appeared a little embarrassed. She snuffed out her cigarette and lit another one. 'Well, there's the bondage. Nothing heavy like controlled breathing and rubber stuff. But you're probably tied up. Then they might bind your tits. And use nipple clamps. Like bulldog clips or clothes pegs . . .'

'Bella! I don't want to hear any more!'

The younger woman laughed. 'It's not what you think, Sand. It's painful, sure, but a sort of exquisite, sexual pain. It heightens the pleasure . . .'

Sandy was incredulous. 'You mean you *like* it?'

Bella sucked in a deep lungful of smoke. 'Well, maybe I've just got used to it. But it's not vicious; no one ever draws blood. It's all done for sexual pleasure, that's the idea.'

'It's disgusting.'

Bella didn't seem to hear her. She was studying her glowing cigarette butt with intensity. 'Max, the man who owns it – he's Maltese, by the way – reckons all women are masochistic to some degree or another. That's why women put up with being beaten. Or are attracted by blokes who treat them mean. He says he's never yet met a woman who didn't enjoy being spanked. Some men get kinky about it, too.'

Sandy looked at her friend curiously. 'I suppose that goes on as well at this place?'

'Oh yes, and more. Maybe it's my Catholic upbringing, but sometimes it gives me a buzz. It's like accepting punishment for everything bad I've ever done and got away with.' Bella pulled a tight smile and turned to face Sandy directly. 'So now you know all about my guilty secret. Max calls me "Poppy" – that's what I'm known as. His idea of a joke. I get my stuff through someone he knows.'

Sandy shook her head in disbelief. 'I just don't know how you can let people do that to you.'

This time Bella laughed aloud. 'I get my own back, Sand. On Thursday nights, I'm *Mistress* Poppy. Then I can give as good as I get.'

Swinging her legs from the settee, Sandy said: 'Do *you* honestly think *I* could get involved with something like that?'

Bella shrugged. 'Max doesn't mind if his girls wear masks. I know one girl who's the daughter of some lord, a debutante. Another's the wife of an MP, I think. It's all terribly discreet and no one ever knows. Max is adamant about that.'

Unsteadily, Sandy climbed to her feet. 'Thanks, Bell, but I'm not interested. I'll sort things out my own way. And not like that.'

Bella showed her to the door. 'Okay, love. I just wanted you to know your options. It's better than a lot of others.'

Bella kissed her quickly on the lips, then the door closed behind her.

It was raining now, a steady persistent drizzle that had already formed puddles on the uneven pavement slabs that wound towards the dominating sentinel of Newey House. Even from where she stood, she could hear the wind moaning around it. An empty beer can clattered against concrete somewhere in the shadows.

Flicking up her raincoat collar, Sandy began walking through the estate. It was slow progress, partly because her steps were unsteady, and partly because most of the street lamps were out, long since smashed by vandals.

The rain became heavier, drifting in sheets before the gusting wind. In seconds, her hair was sodden and droplets of water ran down her face. But she didn't care. She could no longer tell the difference between the tears and the rain. At least it was cooling, soothing. A wet balm that allowed her mind to float.

She thought of that awful club where Bella worked. God, did people really do things like that? She imagined herself prostrate, maybe manacled. A whip descending. She could almost feel the kiss of the soft leather.

Jesus, she thought savagely, I must stop thinking like this! And then she imagined the peace of mind at being able to pay for her addiction. For a split second she understood how Bella felt about it all. The virtually self-inflicted punishment for the self-inflicted sin of being a junkie. Crime and punishment all neatly taken care of.

It suddenly occurred to her that she was feeling randy for the first time since Billy had come home.

She quickened her pace, glancing at her watch. Just gone ten-thirty. It was possible that he was already home, but she doubted it.

If he stayed until closing time, she would have time to make the bed and clear things up. Billy had bought her a cheap but pretty nightdress as a present the day before. All see-through nylon lace. She'd planned to sell it. But perhaps she'd be wearing it when he came home tonight.

'Hi, Mrs Robson.' Spiro, the West Indian, was coming out of the lift as she approached. 'How's the old man settlin' in? Enjoying 'is freedom, eh?'

She smiled; his was the most cheerful face in the block. 'Fine, Spiro, thanks.'

'I'm just out to a party,' he explained. 'Want me to escort you up before I go?'

'You're sweet. But isn't the lift working?'

He laughed and showed a huge, white smile. 'Fer once, Mrs R., you're in luck.'

'Then that's all right. Thanks for the offer.'

'No problem!' he replied cheerfully, and sauntered into the night, tuned in to the headset of his personal stereo-set.

She smiled to herself: Spiro was perpetually wired to sound.

The graffiti-splattered aluminium doors groaned to a close, shutting in the smell of litter and stale urine. As if grunting at the effort of yet another ascent, the lift creaked slowly upwards.

As always, Sandy began the slow count. It took a whole three minutes to get to the top. Tonight it would be longer, because someone had thought it would be fun to press all the buttons. On one floor, she heard the echoing laugh of teenagers as they ran down the steps, and guessed it must have been them.

She rummaged in her handbag for her keys as the lift jolted to a stop. There was a pause as the doors decided whether to open or throw another tantrum and jam.

But tonight they were in good humour and opened slowly to show a black void. The landing light was out. Only the faint glow from inside her own front door threw a bar of illumination across the concrete floor.

Behind her the doors closed. She fumbled to get the right key between her thumb and forefinger.

'Hallo, sweetheart!'

The quiet voice hit her like an electric shock from the darkness behind her. The keys hit the floor with a loud clink.

'God, you gave me a . . . ! Who's there?'

'You don't know us, sweetheart. But we know you. Sandy, isn't it? Sandy Robson.'

Her heart tried to pound its way out of her chest bone. '*Us?*'

'Yes, sweetheart, us.'

For one crazy moment, she thought it was Billy playing tricks. The voice sounded vaguely Irish. An association of ideas formed in her mind: The Czar, the Irish . . . and Billy. But this accent was harsher than those she'd heard earlier that night. Harsher and uglier.

Nervously Sandy backed towards the front-door, glancing over her shoulder. Then she saw the second man. A silhouette outlined against the light.

'We didn't think you were coming back tonight.' A faint chuckle. 'Dirty little stop-out.'

'What do you mean?' Her voice had faded to a croaking whisper. 'What do you . . . ?'

'Want, sweetheart? What do we *want*?' Another chuckle. 'Not you, sweetheart. Certainly not a festering little junkie like you. Not a poisoned slag like you.'

This time the man behind her laughed too.

'Then *what* do you *want*?' It was a hysterical scream of a plea, but it came out like a whimper. 'My handbag? Is that what you want? Take it.' She held it out at arm's length.

'Is there money in it?'

She hesitated. 'Some.'

'How much?'

'Christ, I don't know. Ten pounds?'

The first man laughed somewhere in the darkness. 'That's not much good. Not much good when you owe a friend of ours three hundred. Now is it?'

'A friend?'

This time it was the voice behind her, closer now. She could feel his breath against her neck. 'You know him as Harry. The greasy little toad you score your smack from. You remember greasy little Harry, sweetheart? You ought to. Seeing how he reckons you used to let him feel your tits.'

God, it was a nightmare. The handbag slipped from her hands. It landed on the keys with a sharp crack.

'And feel down your knickers,' the man in front added.

'That's all very well, sweetheart,' continued the man behind. 'What you do with greasy Harry is your business. But now Harry's three hundred quid short on what he owes us. So we thought we'd call direct to collect. And we're not interested in what's inside your knickers. Certainly not after greasy Harry's been down them.'

They both laughed. But it was thin laughter without humour. Then the man in front stepped forward and Sandy got the vague impression of a square, clean-shaven face belonging to a man in his thirties. He wore a dark overcoat, and she noticed the carefully knotted tie against a very white shirt.

'We called on your boyfriend first. The one who runs the E-type, seeing as how Harry says you get the money from him. But it seems the VAT man got there first. So, sweetheart, we just had to trouble you personal.'

'But we're glad we did,' said the man behind.

'Oh, yes, sweetheart, I'd forgotten. Yes, we're glad. Because we've learned that, not only do you owe Harry, or us three hundred, but you've also been scoring your smack from someone else lately. That's not very nice.'

'Not nice at all.'

Sandy was flustered. 'I – I . . .' There was no way she could tell them she'd been buying from Bella since the street dealer known as Harry had cancelled her slate.

'Who, sweetheart?'

'*Who?*' persisted the other.

'No one!' she croaked. 'I've kicked it!'

The square-faced man grinned and shook his head slowly, rubbing one black-gloved fist into the palm of his other hand. 'No, sweetheart, we do the only kicking around here.'

She hadn't expected the first blow to come from behind. The rabbit punch to her kidneys was short, hard and vicious. A gasp of air escaped from her mouth as she lurched forward, grasping at the lapels of the square-faced man's coat. She clung on for a second with her eyes closed, trying to steady herself.

'Take your hands off me, slag.' He spat the words contemptuously.

Then his knee came up into her groin. She almost blacked out with the pain as she slithered down his body to fall in a crumpled heap on the floor. Her mind was swimming, her head full of the smell of wet concrete and the distinct aroma of polished leather.

Dimly, she focused on the pair of smart shoes inches from her face.

The voice echoed around her brain, indistinct and overlapping like a double-tracking tape: 'We're reasonable men, sweetheart. We know you're hard up. So shall we say a hundred a week. Starting a week today. Give it to Harry. He'll be able to count it. He still has one good eye left.'

Her voice was almost inaudible as she mumbled between panting breaths: 'I don't know ... where to get ... any money ...'

The other man said: 'Your friend's E-type needs a respray. We had an accident with some acid, see? My friend's always having accidents with acid. Clumsy fellow. Getting angry makes him clumsy. So you see, you've got an incentive to find the hundred.'

The wet rubber sole of the black shoe lifted and pressed down on her cheekbone, scrunching her face into the rough concrete surface until she could feel her teeth scraping on the stuff.

'Maybe, sweetheart, you can find some other mug punter to go down your knickers,' said the voice above her. 'Someone with poor eyesight. Just make sure it's not Harry this time.'

As the shoe ground her face like a cigarette butt, she felt the skin tear.

'Now, just to show us there's no hard feelings, tell us who's been supplying you, eh?'

The rubber sole lifted from her cheek. She gasped for breath. 'Just ... just a man I met in a pub ... never seen him before ... AAGH!'

This time the man behind her head struck, the hard cap of his shoe snapping into her ribcage without a second's hesitation. The power of the blow sent her rolling over onto her back, her legs flailing, as she tried to suppress the pain.

'Talk, sweetheart, before the next boot breaks your front teeth.' By now, Sandy couldn't register which of the two men was talking. And she didn't care.

Her eyes were tight shut in terror as she muttered a name through torn lips.

'Who?'

She began to blub. 'Bell . . . Bella . . . Oh God, Bella!'

'Where does this Bella live?'

Sandy told them between sobs.

Then she was suddenly aware that the two men had stopped talking. They were alert, agitated. There was another noise. A pounding. It echoed through the concrete floor close to her ear.

She heard one of the men say: 'Get the lift.'

'Push the fuckin' button!'

Then she recognised the sound. Footsteps. The fast footsteps of someone running up the stairs.

'The lift's here! It's all right.'

As the lift doors opened, the sound of stamping feet grew louder. She could hear someone's laboured breathing.

The lift doors groaned shut and she heard the whine of the cables.

The landing door burst open and the footsteps scraped to a halt. Someone was gasping for breath. A flashlight played over the landing. It stopped on her face, momentarily blinding her.

'Christ! Sand!'

Her heart leapt and she burst into tears.

Andy Sutcliff hugged her to him, pressing his rain-wet beard against her face. 'Oh God, Sand, I'm sorry! I got here

as soon as I could. The bastards gave me a right pasting. I
didn't have any cash in the house. None. Then they turned
over the car. Acid over the bonnet and slashed the tyres.
Then I couldn't find a cab . . . God, what have they done to
you?'

Gradually, she was regaining her composure. She held his
head close and kissed him. 'I'm all right, Andy love, honest. I
think it's only bruising.'

'We'd better get you inside. They can thank their lucky
stars Billy didn't hear the row. He'd have taken them apart.'

'Billy's out. Just Gran Jacobs is in looking after Danny.
And she's as deaf as a post.'

'Oh God!'

'What is it, Andy?' Her eyes followed his to the lift. It was
coming back up.

'Quick, get inside.'

Sandy shrieked. 'My keys! I can't find my keys! They're
here somewhere. Shine the torch.'

'Oh sod it, they've gone.'

'In the corner, Andy. They got kicked.'

The lift groaned to a halt. Too late. Andy Sutcliff's mouth
was dry as he braced himself ready to use the torch as a
weapon.

With a squeak, the doors parted. 'God! What's going on?
Turn that torch off!'

Sandy gasped. 'Billy?'

'It's Billy,' Sutcliff confirmed.

Billy Robson stepped out of the lift. 'What the hell's
happened?'

Sutcliff hesitated. 'Er . . . there's been an accident.'

'So I see.'

Sandy said quickly: 'It was muggers. A couple of yobs.'

Their friend fell in quickly. 'Yeah, Billy, I was just coming over to see you and bumped into Sand in the lift. Then these two guys jumped us. You might even have passed them in the lift.'

Robson shook his head. 'No, just a couple of business-men. Respectable-looking, even said good night. Sounded like Ulstermen.'

Sandy shook some of the dirt from her hair. 'No, Billy, that wasn't them. The kids must have gone down the stairs.'

He peered at her face, tracing a finger gently over the lesion on her cheek. 'Are you hurt bad?'

'No, just bruises.'

'Me too,' Sutcliff added. 'And they didn't get anything.'

Robson grinned with relief. 'Thank God you were with her, Andy. C'mon, let's get inside and get a brew on. We'll have something strong in it. Expect you could do with that.'

For most of the night that followed, Sandy lay awake thinking and worrying about Bella. But she couldn't tell her husband for there was no way she would risk him finding out the truth about her.

It was to be the next morning before she found out that Bella was perfectly safe. The evil duo had indeed called and asked questions. Seeing that they meant business, Bella had simply given them the answers they wanted. Her supplier of heroin was Maltese Max.

Her reply had interested the pair. Apparently they had supplied Max until a few months earlier when he had told them he was pulling out of heroin distribution.

The men were not very amused. But they rewarded her information with two twenty-pound notes and the promise to rearrange her face if she ever bought smack from Maltese Max again.

They recommended a man called Harry.

Six

On Saturday morning, Robson awoke in sunshine. It was, he decided, an omen. From now on, everything was going to be different.

He bounced out of the bed with an exuberance he hadn't felt since his days in the Corps. There was a chill in the flat despite the mild sunshine, but he was oblivious to it. He threw on his dressing-gown and tiptoed out of the room, leaving Sandy asleep. Nowadays, she rarely rose before ten and this morning she was dead to the world.

While the kettle boiled, he shaved, and while the tea brewed in the pot, he showered and changed into jeans, a T-shirt and a corduroy bomber jacket. Five years ago he'd owned a couple of suits but now they were nowhere to be found. It was a pity because he thought a business-like approach would be good, as it was the way he intended to continue.

He took a cup of tea into Danny and another into the living-room. 'Wakey, wakey, Andy. Hands off cocks, on with socks. Tea's up.'

The huge foetus stirred under the blanket on the sofa. A dishevelled mass of hair appeared at one end, a screwed-up face hidden somewhere in the middle of it.

'Jesus, what time is it?'

'Eight o'clock,' Robson replied breezily. 'How're the wounds this morning?'

Sutcliff sat up and rubbed the sleep from his eyes. 'Ask me in an hour when I'm awake.'

Robson laughed. 'In an hour, I hope we'll be well on our way to Soho.'

'Soho?'

'I've got some work to do for my new boss. I was hoping you could give me a lift. The tube's useless on Saturdays.'

Two hairy legs appeared and two large feet planted themselves on the carpet. Two trembling hands held the mug of tea as though life itself depended on the stuff. 'Sure. It's the least I can do after you putting me up here.'

'Great.' Robson grinned. There was something to be said for thinking positive. He'd always told his platoon that in the old days.

'Shit!'

'What is it?'

Sutcliff looked up apologetically. 'I forgot for a minute, Billy, my E-type's off the road.'

'Oh.' Robson shrugged, then grinned again. 'You really ought to get yourself a *decent* motor.'

His friend glared at his mug of tea. 'I think I'll have to.'

'Anyhow, I'm putting some breakfast on. Eggs and beans on toast suit?'

The mop of hair shook in disgust. 'I'll pass, Billy. I'd rather take another ten minutes' nap. But I'll walk down to the station with you. It's on my way.'

Robson sauntered into the kitchen and started cooking the breakfast with a flourish, whistling as he worked.

'Nosh up, Danny!' he called a few minutes later. 'Rise and shine!'

But he was halfway through his own meal before the kitchen door edged open and the pyjama-clad figure shuffled sleepily in.

'Mornin', son. How's it going? More tea or orange?'

Dan squinted sideways at his father. The world was still too bright. 'Orange juice, please, Dad.'

'No early morning football practice then?'

His son smiled sheepishly as he climbed onto the stool. 'No, Dad, not today.'

They both knew that they understood each other now. Robson was relieved. The way his son had been avoiding him at every opportunity during the week had been getting to him. At least things were looking up.

'Dad?'

'Yes.'

'Why was Uncle Andy sleeping here last night?'

Robson took the last mouthful from his plate. 'I'm afraid he and your mum were mugged last night. Right outside the door here.'

Dan wrinkled his nose. 'I didn't hear nothing.'

'You were asleep. It was late.'

'I thought you and Mum was out together last night?'

'Were,' he corrected.

'What?'

'We *were* out, not *was*. We were out but your mum felt ill and came home early, and met up with your Uncle Andy in the lift.'

For a few moments, Dan sipped thoughtfully at his orange. 'Mum's always ill. I get fcd-up with it sometimes.'

Robson could scarcely prevent a smile; the callousness of youth. 'It's not much fun for her either, is it, Dan? We've had a hard time and it's not her fault. Or yours. It's down to me and I'm going to put things right. We'll just have to be patient with your mum.'

The boy nodded and began playing at his breakfast with a fork. He didn't seem hungry. 'Dad?'

'Yes.'

'Why was Mum and Uncle Andy cuddling on the sofa last night?'

Robson sipped absently at his tea. 'When?'

'In the middle of the night when you was asleep. I got up for a widdle and saw them.'

'Yes?' He replaced the cup on his saucer. 'I don't know, Dan. But they were both hurt so maybe they couldn't sleep. If Mum was upset, probably Uncle Andy was consoling her. Nothing to worry about.'

'Dad?'

'Yes, son.'

'I don't think I like Uncle Andy.'

Robson couldn't bring himself to challenge Sutcliff while the two of them walked the first part of the way. On the chill but sunny morning, his son's concern seemed totally out of place. His own explanation, or something similar, had to be the only rational one.

By the time he reached Old Compton Street, the incident had gone from his mind.

Outside the Medtravel office a youth was sweeping the remnants of the plate-glass window into the gutter. Lengths of planking stacked beside the door suggested that it was about to be boarded up.

'Sorry, mate, we're not open today.' The youth had an accent that Robson recognised as Maltese.

'What happened?'

'I don't know. Some bloody vandals wrecked the place in the early hours. Now the glaziers say they can't come till Monday. No wonder this country's in a mess.'

'Is Max in?'

The youth leaned on his broom. 'I told you, mate, we're not open. Come back Monday. Max don't wanna see no one.'

Robson was irritated. 'It's on business with Mr Lewis.'

'I don't care . . . Who? Lewis?'

'Mr Frankie Lewis.'

The youth looked thoughtful. 'Ah, well, maybe Max *would* like to see you. He's been trying to get hold of Mr Lewis all morning.'

Robson was led through the doorway into the shop area, although it could hardly be recognised as such. Someone had done a thorough job. The counter had been overturned and the brochure racks ripped from their mountings. Holiday literature carpeted the floor and a mound of charred paper suggested that an attempt had been made to set fire to the lot.

The youth opened the door to the rear office which had received similar treatment.

Behind the desk sat a stout middle-aged man with a swarthy complexion and slicked-back curly black hair. The blue jowls twitched irritably as the man looked up from nursing a very black eye.

'Louie, I said no one . . .' he began.

'This bloke says he's from Frankie Lewis.'

Max glared at Robson with his one good eye. 'Then perhaps you can tell me where your boss is? I've been ringing him since first thing.' He sounded very disgruntled.

'I was with Mr Lewis last night. I think he was going away to a house-party with friends for the weekend.'

Max grunted and replaced his thick tortoiseshell spectacles. One lens was cracked. 'Know where?'

'Sorry, I don't.'

'Well, if you hear from him, get him to ring me pronto.' Max was obviously used to giving orders.

'I will,' Robson promised. 'Is it about this?'

Max's good eye blinked at him. 'You've got a long nose, son. You'll get it caught in a door one day.'

Robson wasn't in the mood to be put down. 'The same one that caught you in the eye?' He intoned enough humour to make the travel agent see he was just standing his ground.

Max didn't quite manage a smile. 'You weren't with Frankie at my club last night? I didn't see you.'

'No, I had to leave early.' In truth, he hadn't liked the sound of it, a view evidently shared by Bernadette who also left early to pack for their weekend away. Besides, he had been concerned about Sandy. But for good measure he added: 'I'm sorry I missed it.'

That just earned a grunt. 'Well, what does Frankie want?'

Robson told him. A package deal for four to Malta. He had been half expecting the man to tell him to clear off. The commission on it wasn't going to contribute much to the replacement window.

However Max's immediate reaction was to draw a sheet of paper and the telephone to him, and fish in his desk for a couple of brochures.

'Another beef deal, is it?' He sounded interested.

'I believe so.'

Max grunted again and went to work with a vengeance. Twenty minutes later, everything had been arranged: Malta by Club Class, a suite at the Hilton for the Lewises and a double for Sandy and himself. And a smart Capri, courtesy of Hertz.

Robson took out the envelope of fifties that Lewis had given him the previous night, and peeled off the full amount. Cash.

He grinned to himself. That was the way to do it. It might not be his money, but he still felt good spending it.

'Don't forget, Robson. I need to speak to Mr Lewis urgent. Right?'

'Right.'

Robson then traversed the bustling Soho neighbourhood until he reached the British Airways office in Regent Street. After a heart-stopping moment when the computer decided that there were no more seats available, the attractive receptionist finally managed to persuade it to fit in one more passenger on Tuesday's 2100 hours Air Malta flight from Heathrow. Again, he settled in cash, then hailed a passing cab right outside.

Thirty minutes later, he was dropped outside his own bank in Mile End Road, which fortunately opened on Saturdays. The request for fifty pounds Maltese currency and a thick wad of dollar Travellers' Cheques for Tuesday morning brought a pained expression, but a reluctant promise that it would be done.

He stepped out onto the pavement feeling like a millionaire. It was all done. It was really happening. His first small business assignment and a holiday to Malta. For the first time, he allowed himself to think about Emy.

For the last seven years, she had seemed a million miles and a lifetime away. Now she seemed a lot closer.

But maybe not. Despite his elation, he realised it would still depend on Frankie's telephone call on Monday morning. To a certain Mr Vance of the Probation Office.

To hell with it, he thought savagely. Think positive. It was twelve-thirty and the Crystal Tavern was on his way home.

*   *   *

Peter Vance was still smarting when he left the Probation Office on Monday evening.

It had been the first telephone call he had received that day, but it was still niggling him. Just who the hell did this Frank Lewis think he was? Telephoning out of the blue like that, insisting that one of his 'clients' should be given permission to leave the country the next day.

That was certainly not the way to get Vance to agree to anything. He was his own man. No one was going to browbeat him into a decision that he believed was fundamentally unwise. This Frank Lewis might claim to be a legitimate and respectable businessman, but he just sounded like some flash whizz-kid to Vance. Local boy made good, judging by the accent. Probably got rich quick by a bit of smart wheeler-dealing in dodgy goods.

Vance, dressed in his grey tracksuit and carrying his casual 'office wear' in a sports holdall, arrived at the car park at the same time as he arrived at a definite decision. Billy Robson was not going to Malta.

That morning, he had told Frank Lewis he would think about it and let him know for sure the next morning, Tuesday. Well, he had thought about it. And he didn't like being told that the tickets were already purchased and that it was a *fait accompli*.

He reached the railings at the far end of the car park where his drop-handled sports bicycle was chained, and wondered whether to call in on Robson on his way home. Put a flea in his ear. Tell him in no uncertain terms that he wasn't one to bow to pressure. Bloody cheek.

'Sod!' The word was scarcely audible as Vance realised that the front tyre was flat. It was a new tyre as well. They just didn't make them like they used to.

He bent to examine the valve and noticed the piece of matchstick jammed inside. Some vandals' idea of a prank.

Instinctively, he glanced around the car park. But there was no sign of anyone. No teenagers were loitering around the only two remaining cars on the deserted stretch of tarmac. By the entrance to the road sat a battered red Avenger with its exhaust burbling evil blue contamination into the chill air. Its occupants, two scruffy men in their thirties or forties, were engrossed in conversation. Vaguely he wondered why they were waiting, then he turned his attention back to the bicycle.

Luckily, he always took his pump with him when he parked in the mornings, so it would only take a few moments to repair the damage. However, the incident had turned his mood even more sour than it already was. He decided not to call on Robson. The man was due to visit the office the next morning anyway, for his regular report, so he could stew in his own juice until then. Mr Frank Lewis would just have to lose his holiday deposit, and Billy Robson would realise that he wasn't yet a free man to come and go as he wanted, unless it was at Her Majesty's pleasure. Arrogant bastard.

As he stooped over the wheel and cleared away the matchstick, Vance became aware that the exhaust of the Avenger had changed tone. The vehicle was moving slowly.

He pulled the pump from his sportsbag, extracted the extension tube, and screwed it into position. The noise of the exhaust had softened to an even purr. It was nearer than it had been.

He fitted the pump tube to the valve and settled down to inflate it with a steady rhythmic action. As he did so, it vaguely occurred to him that there was no exit to the road down here by the railings. So perhaps someone in the Avenger was having a driving lesson in the deserted carpark. He didn't remember seeing L-plates.

The exhaust sounded very near now. Its pitch changed suddenly and angrily.

Peter Vance's head turned just in time to see the Avenger's bonnet leap towards him like a living thing. Loose stones spewed from the thrashing tyres into the blossoming trail of blue exhaust. He just glimpsed two smirking faces through the dirt-smeared windscreen before he instinctively brought up his hand to protect his head.

There were no passers-by to hear the sickening squelch of yielding flesh as the chromium bumper ground Vance's legs and his bicycle into the railings. The smell of burning rubber wafted from the rear wheels as they spun at a standstill.

The man was unconscious before the driver's foot was lifted from the accelerator pedal, and reverse was engaged. As the Avenger backed up with a slow sucking sound, the torso of the victim fell against the bonnet. Then, as the car edged away, the body collapsed onto the ground.

The driver peered forward to get a better view. In the messy pulp that remained of Peter Vance's legs, his bicycle frame and the railings were indistinguishable.

Satisfied, the driver reversed right up, changed gear and took a wide circle towards the exit.

In ten minutes the Avenger, which had been stolen that lunchtime, had an appointment with the crusher-machine at a nearby breakers' yard. Then the two labourers would return home; the next morning they would be back at work on the site, each £250 better-off.

'Oh, goodness, Mr Robson, there's been a terrible accident, I'm afraid.' The woman with the purple rinse was quite distraught.

'Accident?'

There were tears in the eyes behind the ornate plastic-framed glasses. 'Yes, dear, it's Mr Vance. It happened in the car park round the corner after work. It seems a car ran into him. Hit and run the police say.'

Immediately Robson saw the chances of his Malta visit disappearing fast.

The woman was nattering on: 'They think someone hit him in the dark, then panicked and drove off.'

'How is he?' Robson tried to sound concerned, but he knew that Vance's welfare was the least thing he was worried about.

'Intensive care, dear. They're doing their best, but they don't think he'll ever walk again.' She took a deep breath and forced a brave, feeble smile. 'Still, our doctors are wonderful, aren't they? Things they can do nowadays.'

Robson nodded. 'So, who's going to see me this morning?'

The answer, it transpired, was the Chief Probation Officer. Short and bearded, he had the air of a man who was perpetually in a state of being overwhelmed by events. It looked as though Peter Vance's accident had very nearly succeeded in doing it.

'Well, Mr Robson, I had a call this morning from a Mr Frank Lewis. Apparently our Mr Vance was going to confirm the question of a visit abroad for you and your wife. I gather a holiday but also the possibility of future employment if things work out . . .'

'I'm hopeful,' Robson confirmed.

'Vance hadn't yet raised the matter with me – that's necessary you understand – but I found a note on his desk which was evidently going to be sent to me today. It didn't appear favourable.'

Robson's heart sank.

'However, there was no explanation as to why he didn't like the idea. I certainly found Mr Lewis to be quite charming, and I was permitted to speak to his bank manager for reference. He confirmed Mr Lewis's background and sound character. So I took the liberty of phoning your previous Probation Officer, Mr Heathers, at Richmond, for his advice. He seemed to think it an excellent opportunity for you.'

Robson couldn't believe his ears. 'So it's on?'

The Chief Probation Officer smiled widely; he liked to please. 'Unless you can give me a reason why it shouldn't be . . .'

As the Air Malta flight rose into the rainy night sky over Heathrow, Billy Robson felt like a bird set free from its cage.

It was impossible to believe that, just over a week ago, he was sharing a sweaty, smelly cell with two other men. His prospects had been virtually zero, and he could almost hear his marriage creaking under the strain.

Now he was off to the sun with no financial worries for the next week and the prospect of a job if he came up to expectations.

That was the promise Frank Lewis had made only an hour before in the airport bar. In fact, the call over the Tannoy and the man's sudden appearance had quite taken him by surprise.

Robson glanced down at the black attaché-case on the spare seat beside him. That had been the last-minute item of luggage that Lewis had brought.

'Don't worry, old son,' he had laughed. 'There's no gems sewn into the lining. Just some papers. They'll want them at the Libyan Embassy – sorry, People's Bureau. I've put the telephone number on the envelope. Make an appointment with a bloke called Sher Gallal. Don't mention my name. Just say you want to make arrangements to ship *halal* meats.'

Robson believed he understood Lewis's over-elaborate precautions. If you paid any attention to the hysterical headlines of the popular press, you would imagine that *all* Libyans were terrorists! After all, they were entitled to eat meat like anyone else.

He settled down to enjoy the flight. Previously, all his flying had been done courtesy of the Royal Air Force and the luxury of hostess-service was the best part of the novelty. He took a small bottle of red wine with the light mini-meal on the plastic tray. It definitely put the Forces' 'In Flight/ Transit Meal' ration-pack in the shade. Afterwards, he slept fitfully until he was woken by the urgent ding-dong call of the warning lights as they approached Luqa Airport.

As he adjusted his seatbelt, he realised he had been dreaming about her. The lyrical singsong Italian accent still rang in his ears. Her voice soft and husky with passion.

Emilea Graziani. 'Emy'.

After seven long years, she was just a short taxi ride away. He felt his loins stir.

The tatty cab took him through the darkened countryside to the outskirts of the capital, Valletta, and then through the maze of narrow streets to the Sa Maison. It was a nondescript hotel, and indistinguishable from the other buildings in the terraced row overlooking the small inlet which operated as a ferry terminal. It was just how Robson remembered it when it had been used on occasion by members of the Corps in transit, or when wives or girlfriends came to visit. Friendly, inexpensive and discreet, it was just what he wanted.

On impulse, Robson booked a double room overlooking the inlet and was immediately glad that he had. He threw off his clothes and spread himself out diagonally, making full use of the extra space. It had been a long day and the new dawn was only a few hours away.

It was to be nine before he woke. Instantly, he was aware of the warm air and the noise of the traffic as it rattled past below his window. He peered out to where the sleek hull of the Gozo ferry gleamed brilliant white in the soft winter sunshine. A light breeze flicked white tops off the lapping waves of the inlet. It was a far cry from the view from Newey House.

After a quick shave and shower, he put through a call to the Libyan People's Bureau. The man who answered was irritable and suspicious. It wasn't helped by the fact that he spoke no English. Robson's little Arabic came in useful and, after a long delay, he was put through to the man called Sher Gallal.

Thankfully, the man's English, spoken in a soft, liquid voice, was good and he gave the impression that he had been expecting Robson's call. An appointment was fixed for that afternoon at four.

Hanging up, Robson set out to find some good maps and guide-books. Afterwards, he dropped in at one of the harbourside cafés for croissants and coffee, and pored over his purchases to refamiliarise himself with the island.

Its historical, cultural and commercial centre was Valletta – a walled fortress city, built in the sixteenth century on a ridged peninsula between two harbours. Bastions and stone curtains formed sheer and impregnable walls down to the sea, while within them the intricate criss-cross pattern of narrow sloping streets had changed little since the days when they had first been built. Even the savage blitz by Italian and German bombers during the Second World War – which earned the island the George Cross – had done little to change its character when the rebuilding was complete.

Robson traced his forefinger along the main street from the City Gate, visualising it in his mind. Kingsway it had been called until Dom Mintoff had become Prime Minister in 1971 and begun a long-running dispute with the British Government. A couple of years later, it was to be renamed Republic Street.

That's where he would find Emy. The Maltese were creatures of habit and, unless something drastic had happened to her circumstances, that's where she would be at lunchtime.

He could visualise the pâtisserie, but the name escaped him. It was overlooking a square dominated by a statue of a stern-looking Queen Victoria. He compared two maps, a new one and a much older issue. Ah, that was it! 'Queen's Square' was now 'Republic Square'. Another Dom Mintoff change, no doubt.

Although his stroll back to Sa Maison was leisurely, his pulse was racing. Memories of his times with Emy had begun as a vague trickle, her face and her mannerisms faded by time, like an old photograph. But now the recollections were starting to come thick and fast, turning into a flood. The picnics they had enjoyed on remote beaches, evenings spent dining and dancing, or the stolen weekends on the nearby island of Gozo. It was there that Emy had felt happy that no malicious gossip would reach her family. In particular, her sharp-tongued elderly mother.

Robson smiled to himself as he changed into a light-weight blue suit, courtesy of Lewis's expense account.

Mama Graziani had been approaching seventy the last time he'd seen her, so maybe she'd passed on. But somehow he doubted it. Longevity had always run in the family.

Of course Emy might have married, but he couldn't imagine her doing that if it meant leaving her mother to her own devices. And certainly no husband with any sense was likely to welcome such a cantankerous old dragon into the family nest.

No. He felt sure Emilea Graziani would be in Republic Square. It was almost a certainty.

But, by the time he paid off the cab just inside the City Gate, he began to have doubts. Filled with trepidation, he set off down the hill along Republic Street. It was closed to vehicles, but was bustling with people going about their lunchtime shopping. Even in his suit, he was perspiring slightly in the mild sunshine. Yet most of the Maltese were still wearing overcoats.

It was strange walking down this street again. Little had changed: a mixture of grocery stores, antique shops and souvenir parlours huddled together beneath the crumbling stucco façades of the narrow street.

On his left he passed the National Museum of Archaeology and then the Law Courts overshadowing Great Siege Square. A few moments later he'd arrived. Republic Square. It was like stepping back in time. As though he had never been away . . .

His heart was pounding as he took a seat beneath the sun umbrella at one of the scattering of metal tables directly under Queen Victoria's unamused gaze. There was a strange echoing unreality in the small square, created by the high walls of the National Library surrounding it, as though the whole scene was indoors in a giant film set.

He ordered a local Hopleaf beer from the waiter and focused his attention on the pâtisserie across the street. Cordina's. That was it, the spotless gleaming windows filled with white, loaf-like carnival cakes, and the exotic fancy pastries that he recalled Emy had found irresistible.

Five to one. Uneasily, he waited, watching as the office workers streamed in through the doorway opposite to have a snack or buy a treat for the family tea.

From where he sat he could see directly across to Palace Square which was filled with cars. The large building behind it was adorned with Arabic hieroglyphics. The Libyan Arab Cultural Centre. He grimaced. Something about the mix of Libyans and the Maltese was incongruous. Unsettling almost.

His eyes switched back to Cordina's. Still there was no sign of her. It occurred to him that his mission would become decidedly more difficult without her help.

He stared back up Republic Street at a fresh wave of bobbing heads moving towards him.

Then, suddenly, he knew it was Emy. It was just a glimpse. A diminutive figure in a grey spring coat. Long hair swinging as he saw her pass behind two tall men and disappear from view. It was something about the way she moved. Then again he saw her as she slipped into Cordina's.

For a second his courage ebbed. How would she react? He just couldn't be sure.

Slowly, he crossed to the pâtisserie and stepped into the cool interior. It was packed with customers, anxious to be served at the glass-fronted cake counter. Others were eating at rows of tables in the snack bar area.

He glanced back and forth, taking each face at a time. She was nowhere to be seen.

Then the girl standing at one of the chromium bar tables right in front of him lowered the newspaper she had been reading as she drank her coffee. Two smoky brown eyes peered at him through a pair of large, owl-like spectacles. And blinked. A heavy Latin frown fractured the fine eyebrows. Just as he remembered.

He glanced down at the two small fancy cakes on her plate. Trying not to smile, he said: 'I suppose you couldn't spare one of those for an old friend?'

Emy's eyes blinked again, and her mouth opened.

'Holy Mother . . .' It was scarcely a whisper.

Her eyebrows arched in surprise and her nostrils flared. Then her face transformed instantly, her eyes wide and dancing with happiness. 'Billy!' she shrieked.

Everywhere heads turned. A waitress jumped and dropped a coffee cup. Somewhere a baby began crying as it was woken.

'Billy! Billy, Billy!' Tears began to roll down her cheeks as she stared up to him, still not believing what she saw. He clasped her small hands in his. 'Oh, Billy, it is really you?'

His grin was in danger of splitting his face in half. 'I'm afraid so, Emy.'

'I always know you will come back!' She began to laugh. 'Ah, and you know how to find me always. With the cakes at lunchtime!'

'Nothing's changed. You look great.'

It was strange but he had forgotten how small she was. Just five feet tall with delicate fine boned features like a doll. 'Thank you, you flatter me. But when do you arrive in Malta? This morning?'

He nodded. 'Very early.'

'And you come straight to see me?'

'Who else? I couldn't wait.'

She reached up and kissed him on the lips. 'It's been a long time, Billy. A long, long time.'

Seven

After the cakes had been demolished, they went out to the open-air café in the square and ordered drinks. This was something to celebrate.

'Aren't you worried about the time?'

Emy snorted haughtily, part of her vast repertoire of sounds and expressions that could totally transform her appearance. 'It does not matter. I am always staying in my office, that is my way. Others are always chatting and laughing with their friends. I am by myself and work. So no one is sure when I come or go.'

'If you're sure?'

She reached out for his hand. 'I am sure. This is a special day. Besides, my boss is a pig, so it pleases me to stay out.' It sounded as though Emy's boss was in for a lot of trouble if he was intent on making an enemy of her. Over the years he had seen many dissolve under her quicksilver Latin temper. And usually it was no more than they deserved. Her frown melted into a smile. 'Did you know that I think of you only yesterday? Isn't that funny? Actually, nowadays I never think of you. Then yesterday, I think of you.'

'Great minds.'

She tossed back her shoulder-length henna-coloured hair. 'No, it is destiny, I think. I read in a magazine only last month. A horoscope. It says someone from your past will come back to you.'

'Pisces?' He couldn't be sure.

Her eyes twinkled. 'You remember. The fish, yes.'

'Very sensitive.'

'Very.' She held his gaze. 'We can tell these things, we Pisces.'

He laughed. 'Clever fish.'

Her eyes clouded with uncertainty. 'You are making fun of me?'

'No. I'm just remembering things that you said in the past. Destiny, fate. You always said we would meet again.'

Her eyes were serious. 'If God wills it.' She hesitated. 'You are still married . . . ?'

He nodded.

'To the same girl?'

'Yes.'

She was studying him closely. 'And your son, Daniel. How is he?'

Robson knew then that she had not forgiven him. Like many Marines stationed abroad, it was often convenient to reclaim temporary bachelordom; prospective lovers were often deterred by the thought of a faithful wife awaiting a husband's return. Especially in devout Catholic countries like Malta.

But Emy Graziani had seen it all before. Many times she had been misled and cheated in her early years. Holidaymakers and businessmen passing through, and foreigners on contract-work, were happy to make rash promises and tell lies knowing that they would eventually leave Emy and her island without any comeback. It was the penalty for living in such a place. It was the price that had to be paid, and it had left her wary of men.

Gently, after they had known each other for several weeks, she had let Robson know that it didn't matter if he was married. The way she felt about him it would make no difference; she would 'go against the word of God'. She just wanted to know.

He had told her, confirmed what she already suspected. And, if anything, their relationship became closer as a result.

But it had only been at their last meeting, some seven years ago, that he had mentioned his young son Danny.

My God, Robson recalled, the emotional explosion that followed was like a nuclear blast that could have shattered the rocky island with its velocity. He witnessed the full brunt of Emy's Latin fury, her face contorted with anger, as her words had cut him like a knife. Their last farewell had been a brittle affair.

'So you are not coming to rescue me from my island prison?' Her words were light, but he could see the sadness in the smoky brown eyes.

'I'm afraid not, Emy. I'm here on business and pleasure. In fact my wife is coming out on Friday.'

Her eyes widened. 'You are going to suggest that I meet her?'

Robson hadn't thought that far ahead. 'Would you like to?'

Emy's voice was suddenly colder. 'Is that what you want?' He didn't reply.

She said: 'You think perhaps that the past is the past. Now it is over, it is history. Now we can meet and be friends as though what once happened never happened?' Emy held his gaze and placed a slender hand on his knee beneath the table. 'But, Billy, it *did* happen and it isn't over.'

There was something about the way she said it that unnerved him. Because he knew she was right? He could already feel himself drawn to her as he had been a decade earlier. Like a moth fatally attracted to the glare of a lamp.

He said: 'There's something I ought to tell you, Emy. I have been in prison for the past five years.'

Her eyes clouded. 'In prison? In England? I don't understand.'

'I left the Corps and got mixed up with some bad people. I was driving a getaway car for a bank robbery and we got caught. I was only released a week ago.'

She laughed uncertainly. 'You, Billy? You in a bank hold-up? I do not believe it! You are joking with me. You make fun of me. Like you always used to . . .'

'It's true. Honestly, Emy. I wouldn't joke about it. Now a friend has given me the chance of a job. That's why I'm over here, to make some arrangements.' He paused. 'I thought you might agree to help me.'

It was as though she hadn't heard his last words. In her mind she was still trying to create an image of Billy Robson in jail. '*Five* years?' she whispered. 'Oh, my poor Billy.' She squeezed his hand in sympathy.

He tried to ignore the feelings stirring in him. 'Would you help me?'

She smiled softly. 'Do you have to ask? What do you want me to do actually?'

He explained and she listened patiently, interrupting only occasionally to clarify one or two small points. At the end he handed over an envelope which contained money that he had changed that morning.

'This is a lot,' she observed. 'I will start today and make the phone calls from my office. Make the bookings. And get a car for you by tonight.' She thought for a moment. 'Then tomorrow you can drive me around and we will pay over the money.'

'Aren't you working tomorrow?'

She smiled mischievously. 'I think I have a cold coming on. Before I go home tonight I will tell that pig of a boss of mine that I feel sick.'

'Shall I ring you at home tonight?'

'No,' she replied sharply.

'Ah,' Robson guessed. 'Your mother? How is she?'

Emy pouted. 'Still she makes my life a hell on earth! I feel like a prisoner. I am not free. If you phone, she will pick up the extension. She will ask questions and we will have a row. I hate it. If anyone writes, she opens my letters . . .'

Robson remembered it all from before. 'You're, what – thirty-nine, Emy. It's time you led your own life. Leave her.'

She shook her head vehemently. 'No, Billy, you know I cannot do that. Actually, I have even got our priest to talk to her, but it makes no difference. Still she is the same. I think she hates me.'

'I can't believe that.'

Emy shrugged. 'I think so. Actually, I will not say you are back. After you went I told her once you are married with a child.' She allowed herself a wry smile. 'I think now she would hate you even more than me. No, tell me where do you stay?'

'Sa Maison.'

'Then I will ring you.' She stood up from the table and drew the stylish spring coat with its beaded embroidery about her. 'Ciao, Billy.'

'Ciao.'

He watched her go with mixed emotions. He had believed that what they once had between them was dead.

Now he wasn't so sure.

Vaguely, he recalled the small, dog-eared book of John Turnbull verse that had passed around the Scrubs: '*That old flames somehow never die . . . They simply lose their spark.*'

As he swallowed the last of his beer, he became aware of someone watching him. It was that strange sixth sense that most people possess.

He glanced sideways at the man seated a couple of tables away. The newspaper the stranger was reading hid most of his head from view, apart from the well-trimmed wavy black hair. The hang of the navy blazer and pale grey slacks suggested the lean, athletic figure of a younger man. It was an English newspaper.

As the page was turned, Robson glimpsed a sunburnt aquiline face with distinctive black eyebrows that was somehow familiar.

Penetrating dark eyes flickered in his direction. Their gazes met and held. The man frowned, then smiled uncertainly.

On impulse, Robson asked: 'Don't we know each other?' Then he placed the face. 'Shard, isn't it? Kevin Shard?'

The eyes squinted in recall. 'Roberts. Sergeant Billy Roberts? Four-Two Commando.'

'Robson, actually.' He grinned. 'Billy Robson.'

'What a small world!'

'Join me for a quick jar?'

Kevin Shard glanced at his watch. 'Well, old lad, I have to go in a minute.' As he stood up, Robson realised he was a very tall man. Probably six-foot-three. They shook hands. 'Still, I'll finish this one with you.' He sat in the chair vacated by Emy. 'Anyway, thank God it's you. I thought someone was trying to pick me up for a minute. Malta attracts a lot of poofs, y'know, especially in the summer.'

Robson laughed. 'Well, you can rest easy on that count.'

Kevin Shard winked. 'I know. I saw you with your friend a few minutes ago. No chicken, but quite a tasty lady.'

'We go back a long way.'

'And so do we. Are you still in the Corps? I think you were L Company last time I met you.'

Robson offered a cigarette which Shard declined. 'I left about six years ago.'

'Really? Still look like a Marine though, Billy. The haircut and the old moustache.'

'Old habits.' As he spoke, Robson was recalling a little more about Shard. He had known him when he was in M Company – or 'The Mighty Munch', as it had later become known in the Falklands War. A quiet, slightly introspective sergeant who was dedicated to soldiering. If his memory served him correctly Shard had passed the gruelling Mountain Leader (ML2) course. Their paths had crossed briefly on several occasions. He remembered they once got drunk together in Hong Kong. 'Are you still in, Kevin? I guess not by the hair.'

Shard laughed. 'Giveaway, isn't it? No. I left – what – four years or more back.'

'So what are you doing in Malta? Holiday?'

'A spot of business.'

Robson was intrigued. What people did for a living had become a near-obsession with him lately, and to discover how an ex-RM had made it in Civvie Street was irresistible. 'What do you do?'

The other man looked embarrassed, and glanced at his watch. 'I do some diving for the Libyans. Some work on the single-point mooring buoys for tankers off the coast. And lately some ordnance-clearing supervision of the Turkish divers around Bengazi and Tripoli. They're a bunch of cowboys and the Libyans reckoned my background might help.'

Robson's enthusiasm was dampened. He'd never taken up diving. 'Are the Libyans diving in Malta then?'

Shard laughed. 'No way.' Then he lowered his voice. 'To tell the truth, I'm doing a sort of "minder" job over here for a visiting delegation.'

'What?' Robson was incredulous. 'The Libyans trust a Brit to bodyguard them!'

'Well, they sure as hell don't trust their own.' He swallowed the remainder of his drink. 'When Colonel Gadaffi goes anywhere, he takes a hundred male bodyguards, *and* a hundred gun-girls to shoot the blokes if they step out of line. Well, something like that.'

'They sound an odd bunch,' Robson reflected. 'I just hope my boss has no trouble with them. He's doing some business deal or other. This is a sort of recce. Rather like you, I'll be looking after him.'

Shard looked surprised. 'Business with Libyans, eh? Oh well, no doubt he knows what he's doing. But you be a bit wary, Billy. Keep a low profile and don't upset them. And keep eyes in the back of your head.' Again he lowered his voice. 'Generally speaking, Billy, I don't mind Arabs. Strange coves, some of them, but they're okay. But Libyans – at least those in power – are evil bastards. Animals. Just a word from one who knows. So watch yourself, all right?' Aware that he was beginning to sound too serious, he grinned. 'Still, it pays the old mortgage.'

At that moment, a bleeping sound came from Shard's pocket. Apologising for the interruption, he extracted a small RT transceiver and listened for a moment before replying: 'I'm on my way. Out.'

They shook hands. 'Nice to see you again, Kevin,' Robson said.

And with that, Shard mingled with the crowds moving towards Palace Square, and Robson watched until he lost sight of the towering figure near the entrance of the Libyan Arab Cultural Centre.

Robson shivered, realising suddenly that the sun had gone in and there was now a chill to the wind eddying up Republic Street from the sea.

He looked at his watch. Forty minutes to go. He realised then that he wasn't looking forward to his meeting at four.

Once out through the City Gate, the main route north follows the coast around several built-up creeks until it reaches the heavily residential area of Sliema. There, the maze of backstreets are hemmed in by modern hotels, bars and restaurants which overlook the long promenades.

It was the route that Robson's taxi took to the Libyan People's Bureau, which is a large villa set back in grounds between a row of shops in Tower Road.

He paid off the cab and studied the building for a moment from the opposite side of the road. Beyond the low cream wall with its green railings, he could determine the two-storey, green-shuttered embassy building set back behind some trees.

A group of scruffy-looking civilians with mops of curly black hair were standing inside the iron gates. They talked and gesticulated earnestly as they shared cigarettes together.

Hostile stares focused on him as he crossed the road and approached the gate.

'Excuse me,' Robson began. 'I have an appointment with Mr Gallal. Mr Sher Gallal.'

'Who are you?' one of the Libyans demanded suspiciously. His breath stank and Robson thought he could detect traces of whisky.

'My name is Robson. Bill Robson. Mr Gallal *is* expecting me.'

The man smiled sarcastically. His eyes were dark and wild, and Kevin Shard's earlier description seemed chillingly apt. 'He expects you, eh? You got passport?'

Robson hesitated.

The Libyan fumbled for the word. 'Ident-f'cation. Passport for ident-f'cation, uh?'

'I see.' Dutifully, he handed it through the gates and wondered dimly if he'd ever see it again.

It was ten minutes before he did. Eventually he was escorted in by four Libyans. At the lobby he was thoroughly frisked and his wallet checked. From the corner of his eye he glimpsed one or two large denomination notes slip surreptitiously into convenient jacket pockets.

He was led down a tiled corridor sparsely decorated with Libyan flags and a faded colour print of Colonel Gadaffi. The place had a strange air about it, empty and hollow, as though it was a temporary residence. It also smelled unclean, reminding Robson vaguely of a lavatory on a British Rail station back home.

The room into which he was ushered comprised simply of a utilitarian teak desk and a red plastic chair with tubular steel legs.

An anxious-faced young man in a crumpled beige suit and open-throated shirt was pacing up and down. He had the same unkempt hair as his colleagues and evidently had had no time to shave. The black sunken eyes suggested that he had spent a particularly heavy night – maybe several in a row. Tossing his cigarette butt to the floor, he turned to Robson and shook his hand perfunctorily.

'Sit, please. I am Sher Gallal.' There was no smile.

'Billy Robson,' his visitor offered politely.

Gallal sat on the edge of the table and lit another cigarette. He didn't offer one. 'I know. I read your passport. We
Libyans can read, you know.'

Robson forced the most genuine-looking smile he had
ever managed. 'Of course. I've come from Mr Lewis.'

'I know this. You should have documents.'

'Yes.' Robson placed the black attaché-case on the table,
opened it and handed over the sealed envelope.

Gallal squinted at the outside. 'What is this?'

Robson stood up and peered at the writing. 'Er, oh, it's
your telephone number.'

The Libyan's eyes darted at him with the speed of an
angry snake. The narrow black pupils bored into him. Then,
apparently satisfied, the Libyan ripped the envelope open
and tossed the wrapping on the floor.

Quickly, Gallal flicked through five pages of neatly written
Arabic script. Then he picked up a note that had been pinned to
it. Robson guessed it was a covering letter from Frankie Lewis.

The man frowned, clearly having difficulty in understanding it.

'May I?' Robson offered, adding: 'Mr Lewis's handwrit-
ing is bad.'

Gallal eyed Robson uncertainly, as though unsure
whether or not he had just been insulted. Apparently the
Libyan decided he had not.

Grudgingly, he handed it to Robson who read it slowly:

My dear Mr Gallal,

*I bring you greetings from your brothers in Eire. Your
friends and my friends in Dublin have gone over the
attached document together and I am assured it is correct
in every detail.*

Appendix A lists the requests for my forthcoming visit when I look forward to meeting you.

Meanwhile the man who brings this letter, Mr Robson, may be fully trusted. Do use him as a courier with any written message – but keep our business confidential ...

Robson slowed at this point, unsure if Frank Lewis didn't really want him to be trusted with anything important at all. Still, he reasoned, that was scarcely his concern. Then his eyes moved over the next paragraph:

I should appreciate it if you could furnish Mr Robson with the two items agreed with your colleagues in Ireland, just in case they prove necessary.

Yours sincerely,

Frank Lewis

Robson looked up to meet Gallal's wide smile. 'That is good, my friend.' The Arab reached out and shook his hand again, although Robson noticed that his eyes were still watchful and humourless. 'Now we work together. When does your man Lewis come?'

'Friday.'

Gallal's smile persisted. 'Good. You contact me then.' He turned and called towards the door. 'Ali! Ali!'

A tall man with stooped shoulders shambled in. His hair was straight and straggly, falling in an untidy fringe over a gormless face.

The open mouth moved slackly around broken teeth as he exchanged words with Gallal before shuffling out. Neanderthal man, Robson thought grimly, and again remembered Shard's prophetic words.

An awkward silence settled over the room. Gallal was back to his usual impatient self, pacing the room again and adding to the pile of cigarette butts on the floor.

He turned sharply. 'Hey, tonight, my friend, you come with us to the Casino, eh? Up at Dragonara.'

Robson hesitated. 'That's very kind of you, Mr Gallal, but I already have an appointment tonight.'

A slow, knowing grin spread over Gallal's face, showing a row of crooked yellow teeth. 'With a woman, heh?'

Instantly Robson felt resentful. 'A friend. A lady.'

Gallal laughed. 'You choose good, I hope. Firm thighs and big . . .' He searched for the words as he cupped his hands to his chest. Then he frowned. 'She is Maltese?'

'Yes.'

Gallal looked glum. 'Then it is no good. They don't allow Maltese at the Casino. Mr Mintoff says no.' He chuckled. 'That is a pity. The place not so good without them. Once I have four Maltese women. I teach them good. But now they do not go with us. They think they are too higher and mighty.' He stared out of the window. 'But soon it is summer and the English girls they come. They are easy.'

Robson felt his bile rising and was pleased for the interruption when Ali returned carrying two oilskin packages.

The man unravelled the smaller of them first and the contents clattered loudly onto the desk.

'Jesus,' Robson breathed.

It was an obsolete 7.62mm Tula Tokarev automatic pistol. A star and the letters CCCP were embossed on the grip.

The second package contained another, larger weapon that Robson couldn't identify.

Gallal obliged: 'A machine-pistol. The Czech Skorpion. Very small. Very useful.'

Robson's mind was reeling. 'You're joking. I don't want these . . .'

'It is what your boss requests. They will fit in your attaché-case. Just for protection. You cannot fly with these into Malta on the airlines, but we have our ways.'

'I still don't understand.'

A mocking ghost of a smile passed over the Libyan's face. 'Perhaps, my friend, you are not as trusted by your boss as you think.'

Billy Robson sat on the end of the hotel bed, his chin supported by his hands, and stared at the two weapons he had placed on the dressing-table.

What in God's name had he got himself into?

No wonder Frankie Lewis had been interested that he was a Royal Marine when they'd met back at Rich Abbott's spieler. Not only did he have a thorough knowledge of Malta and contacts, but he would be familiar with firearms.

He reached out and picked up the Tokarev. Certainly he knew enough about firearms to know that this ancient pre-War specimen had had a lot of use in its time. From the state of it, though, not recently. There was a lot of grit in the barrel and the greased areas were studded with fluff. Tiny rust spots marred the plain gunmetal finish.

The chances of hitting a target with it, he reasoned, were remote. In its present condition, the user would be in more danger from it than its intended victim.

In a way, that made him feel happier. Perhaps Libyans were in the habit of handing out old weapons for the protection of friends, never expecting them to be used. Certainly those he'd met at the People's Bureau were a suspicious and restive lot. He could well imagine paranoia being endemic amongst them.

His eyes shifted to the Skorpion machine-pistol. That, however, was a different matter. It was immaculate and well-maintained. A short, stubby barrel protruded from the main body of the weapon which housed the magazine, chamber and pistol-grip. The steel wire stock was hinged so that it doubled the length of the weapon when it was used as a sub-machine gun. Alternatively – when folded-back over the weapon – it would fit into the chamois leather shoulder holster also supplied by the Libyans, along with a silencer and four ten-round magazines. It was a 7.65mm calibre weapon which Robson guessed would give it a useful range of about a hundred metres. Probably more if you weren't expecting to hit anything specific.

Yes, that Skorpion was a different matter.

No doubt it could all be explained quite simply. Although he couldn't for the life of him see how. Try as he might he couldn't visualise Israeli Mossad agents or CIA operators running around Malta trying to sabotage meat deals with Eire.

Perhaps, though, the Libyans just thought they might.

The sudden trilling of the bedside telephone made him jump. He grinned to himself as he reached over to answer it. This pantomime was making him nervous.

It was reception. 'A young lady to see you, Mr Robson. A Miss Graziani.'

'Fine. Would you ask her to come up? Thanks.'

He replaced the receiver and returned to the dressing-table. Hastily, he repackaged the two weapons in their oilskin wrappings.

Just as he finished, there was a knock at the door. Quickly, he crossed to the bed and shoved one package under each pillow and smoothed the bedspread over them.

He opened the door. 'Hallo, Emy, how did it go?'

'It's all done, except for the apartment,' she replied as she stepped inside. 'There is a choice of three and I think perhaps you should look at them and decide tomorrow.'

She was brilliant, Robson decided. 'And the hotels?'

'Actually, I have booked you in at the Preluna in Sliema. Ten years ago it was one of the most favourite. Now it is quieter, but still the standard is good. Just not so fashionable.'

'It sounds ideal,' he replied as he took her coat. Beneath it she wore a simple blue sleeveless trousersuit with baggy legs and a cut-away back; over her shoulders she'd draped a white silk scarf against the evening chill that only she felt. Her hair was swept up and back now, and the owl-like spectacles had vanished. No doubt the contact lenses were in. Another famous Emy transformation complete.

He laughed. 'Do I gather you're going somewhere?'

She nudged him playfully. 'I think perhaps you will want to take me somewhere to celebrate.'

'You do, do you?'

But she didn't rise to the bait, she was fast remembering his constant mockery of her seriousness. No one had ever made her laugh at the world as Billy had.

'Maybe you'd like to eat some good food – after all that bread and water in prison.'

He put his arm around her slender shoulder. 'Where would you like to go?'

'I don't mind. You must decide.'

'You still eat like a pigeon?'

Emy laughed. 'If I don't I cannot have my cakes. But tonight I eat more – just for you.'

'I'm flattered. And, after the food, what then?'

Her smoky brown eyes looked at him steadily. 'Perhaps we dance, yes? The Falcon Bar at the Hilton is good. Nice music.'

It was settled. A short taxi ride took them to a small back-street garage where a slightly battered white Granada awaited them. In ten minutes, the formalities were over and they were driving along the winding sea-front road towards Paceville, a bulging promontory of land which was dominated by the Hilton complex.

Emy suggested a small Italian restaurant that Robson didn't remember from previous times. It was almost empty when they arrived at La Famiglia. They sat in candlelight by one of the half-moon windows looking out over Spinola Bay where the waterfront lights cast their reflections on the lacquered surface.

Having interrogated the waiter on the freshness of the fish, Emy settled for grilled red mullet with tomato and green pepper sauce to follow the *minestra* soup. Robson decided to celebrate his changing good fortunes with a lobster thermidor which Emy defiantly pronounced as 'not fresh' when she sampled it.

In no time they were into their second bottle of Marsovin Special Reserve. 'You are trying to get me drunk?' she challenged over the rim of her glass.

'Never!' he protested.

Her eyes narrowed appraisingly. 'I remember, Mr Robson, how you took advantage of me the first time. We met at the Pegasus Bar at the Phoenicia, you remember?'

Suddenly her eyes clouded; her voice sounded distant. 'Actually, sometimes I wish that I could forget that we ever met. Not to spend my life thinking one day you will come back again.'

'I'm here,' he said softly.

Her smile was bitter. 'No, Billy, not like this. This is not what I have prayed for all these years.' She reached across the table and held his hand. 'I have even wished that your marriage would break up so I could have you, do you know that? I have confessed it so many times to the priest that he is getting sick of hearing it.' She anticipated his response. 'No one has ever made me laugh like you do. When I think of the days we enjoyed together, it is like looking at family snapshots.'

'There must be good days sometimes.'

Her face contorted, her deep frown breaking the fine lines of her eyebrows. 'Not any more. Life is different now. Since you go I have only two boyfriends. One is serious, but it turns out he, like you, is married. It was a long time before he told me. And my mother makes it all so difficult. I am not free. Not as a person, and not as a Maltese.'

He'd forgotten, over the years, how strongly political Emy was, like all Maltese. She was a staunch Nationalist opposed to the radical socialist regime of Dom Mintoff's Labour Party. 'Things are bad?' he asked.

'Not just bad, Billy. Things are very bad. They fix the last two elections. Move boundaries during voting and rig the ballot. Even the police are involved. Last time 5,000 voting papers are washed ashore in Valletta harbour.

'There is nothing in the shops nowadays,' she continued. 'And we are not allowed to go to Italy because the Government has some row with them.' Robson knew how that would upset Emy who used to enjoy frequent trips to Naples in search of chic fashions. 'They fight with the Church and try to stop private education, and if you are not a Party member . . . pooh! . . . things can be made difficult . . .'

'Emy?'

Her eyes widened. 'Yes?'

'Stop it,' he said gently. 'Don't upset yourself over these things. We've only got a short time together, let's enjoy it.'

'You mean until your wife arrives on Friday?' She said it lightly, but there was an edge of sarcasm to her voice.

Robson said: 'I'm not trying to pick up where we left off, Emy. I just want to be with you and enjoy your company. As old, good friends.' He hesitated. 'I don't know how you feel about meeting my wife?'

She was puzzled. 'Is that what you want? Why is that? To prove to me that I no longer matter?'

He shook his head and poured more wine. 'No, it's just that I have to put the past behind me. I've got to start again. I should like you to be a friend, not a past lover who must be hidden away. And, as Sandy and my boss's wife will want to tour the island, I thought you would be ideal – if you like the idea. And, of course, you would be paid.' He smiled to show her what a good idea it all was. 'I'm sure you and Sandy would get on well together.'

Slowly she picked up the fresh glass of wine and sipped at it. 'If that's what you want, Billy, I expect I can take some days' holiday.' Suddenly her smoky eyes seemed fathomless as he found himself staring into them. 'If it means that I shall be closer to you.'

They never did get to the Hilton.

Looking back, Billy Robson was sure that, although neither of them had said anything, they both knew what was going to happen.

He lay on one elbow, looking down at her as Emy

stretched out with catlike contentment on the hotel bed. She was naked except for a pair of simple white G-string pants which emphasised the fading tan that she nurtured with such care every year.

Nothing about her that he could remember had changed. Even the passing years had done nothing to destroy the firm lines of her small, delicate body. As he traced his finger around the perfect tight orb of her right breast, he realised that she was as familiar to him as Sandy – even after all this time.

He felt her small brown nipple stiffen to his touch, and heard her faint gasp of surprise. Perhaps, too, it was coming back to her now.

'Why am I lying like this with you?' Her hushed whisper was almost to herself. 'It must be the drink.'

'The drink?'

He looked along the line of her breasts to the slender throat and he saw that her eyes were closed. And as she laughed with even white teeth, he could see more lines now than he remembered.

'No,' she was saying, 'of course, it is not the drink, Billy, it is you. Why I am here. Why I will always be here.'

Gently, he pressed his mouth against hers. And, as he slid his hand across the flat hard plain of her belly, he felt the sharp bite of her teeth on his lips. She was rousing. Rousing as she always had, as though from sleep. A gentle tremor shook her body as her loins began to stir.

Her lips closed around his tongue, sucking with a hard, demanding urgency for him. Thin scratch trails etched across his muscled shoulders in the wake of her nails.

And then it came to him. His erection surged with life and wanting. It was a feeling he thought might never return after his years in jail. Being together again with Emy had broken a spell.

She kicked away her pants hurriedly, leaving them still caught around one ankle as she arched her back and drew him into her. She was soft and ready. As though she had just been waiting for this moment since the last time they'd parted.

To his surprise, it was not all over in seconds, but seemed to go on and on for ever in a growing up-beat rhythm which reached a crescendo with the blood pounding in his ears.

The explosions were almost simultaneous, and not singular, but multiple. A small series of detonations that ebbed and flowed between them, with Emy trailing and gasping, a few moments behind him.

For the first time he could remember, Emy had cried out without restraint.

He opened his eyes. She lay beneath him, her breasts glistening with perspiration as she heaved to catch her breath. Slowly, very slowly, the rate of her breathing subsided.

Then their eyes met.

She smiled and turned her head slowly from side-to-side. 'Please, Billy,' she murmured. 'Don't say anything.'

After a few minutes, she raised herself onto one elbow and consulted the watch she had strewn on the bedside table. 'It's late.'

'Your mother?'

She looked helpless, almost ashamed. 'If I am late, there will be a terrible row. She will wait up. I don't want that. It will spoil a beautiful evening.'

As she swung her legs off the bed, she turned and felt the pillow behind her. 'I wonder what is so uncomfortable? A parcel.'

Carelessly, she held it up and the oilskin unravelled. The Tokarev bounced solidly onto the bedspread.

The Man watched with faint amusement as Eamon Molloy mopped his brow. Perspiration was flowing down his fat face, soaking the collar of his shirt as he watched the girl bend to serve the teas on the low table.

Pale sunlight shafted into the panelled room, side-lighting the small breasts that hung clearly within the deep neckline of her wrap-round blouse. She wore no brassière, Molloy realised, as his bulging eyes feasted on the pink points of her nipples.

'Thank you, Kathy,' The Man said quietly.

She peered up from beneath a soft fringe of auburn hair. And she smiled with pleasure and amusement at seeing their reactions to her body.

'My pleasure, master.' Her small bobbing curtsy reminded Molloy of a genuflection.

As she turned and left them alone, Molloy began to regain his composure. 'Where in God's name do you get them?'

The Man eased his slight frame into an armchair. 'Wherever, Eamon. There are people who know what I want. What I am looking for in my housegirls.'

'Housegirls!' Molloy thought jealously. That wouldn't be how he'd describe them. But then, as far as he knew, they weren't whores. Usually they were in their teens. Always beautiful, and always timid and submissive. They would never speak unless they were spoken to, and they would hang on The Man's every word. Their adoration for him showed in their eyes.

How in the hell did he do it? Molloy knew for a fact that The Man was pushing seventy. Churlishly he put it down to wealth, but inside he knew it was more than that. He himself was no pauper, but he could never command such blind obedience and devotion from a woman. Not from a whore, a society groupie, or even his fat-thighed wife. No, The Man had charisma and charm, but there had to be something else. There were never less than two of them to be seen around the mansion.

'To business.' The Man was getting bored with his initial amusement at watching Eamon Molloy gawp. 'You got my message?'

'About Maltese Max?' Molloy's mind was elsewhere, and his plump lips spluttered awkwardly over the alliteration, sending a fine spray over the bone china tea service. 'I don't like the sound of it.'

'Nor do I. We've had run-ins with the Proddie drug-runners before, and it's bad for business. Max runs our main distribution network through Scotland. More than twenty kilos a month. So, if they're allowed to put the pressure on, we could lose a big slice of business.'

Molloy smirked. 'Max knows what'll happen if he tries to go back to doing business with the Proddies.'

The Man's face was deadpan; not infrequently Molloy spoke like a fool. 'That won't solve anything. Sure he'll be scared shitless and stop distributing anything. Besides, he *trusts* us. That's why he contacted Frankie Lewis for help.' He allowed himself a faint smile. 'Also I have a small personal arrangement on the side with Max.'

Molloy realised his blunder. Opening his big mouth again and doing his best to stick both feet in it. It really aggravated him how stupid he always made himself seem in front of the Special Finance Committee chief.

He tried a more positive approach. 'You want they should be terminated?'

'At least deterred, don't you think?'

Molloy nodded thoughtfully. 'Dee's tied up. And Cavan's not back yet. Perhaps there's an Active Service Unit on the mainland?'

The Man reached forward and poured out two cups of sweet Darjeeling tea. 'I wouldn't waste class on those bastards, Eamon. Besides, the Army Council won't sanction a unit being put in jeopardy for such a task – there's a big campaign in preparation for hitting mainland holiday resorts this summer.'

Molloy shrugged. 'What then?'

'We've plenty of young firebrands. Just fill them up with Guinness and patriotic songs, tell 'em they're doing it for The Cause, and point them at the target.'

Molloy twitched uncomfortably. Violence didn't sit well with him; he preferred to leave such matters in Dee's hands. 'There is another way. More subtle.'

The Man raised his eyebrows and steepled his fingers together. Molloy using his brains. This would be interesting.

'Our contacts in Pakistan could help us. Most Proddie gangs deal direct, or buy straight off the importer. For the price of a couple of back-handers we can find out what they're up to. Then we can have their courier intercepted.'

'Tip off the police?' The idea amused The Man. 'That would certainly slow them up. But make sure they know it's the *Provos* who've dropped them in it. Tell them it's a shot across their bows if they want to continue in peaceful co-existence.'

Molloy grinned hugely, basking in the unspoken praise of having his idea accepted. Quickly he gulped down the last of his tea. He knew he must move fast to be effective. He would call from his office as soon as he got back, using their usual open-line code that would raise no suspicions with any eavesdropper.

The Man watched Eamon Molloy go, then reached for the small brass handbell on the table. It rang out two sharp, bright notes.

He had always known that one day there would be open warfare between Ulster loyalist gangs and the Provisional IRA over the drugs market. It was inevitable and he knew that the prospects haunted the British and Irish security services. Maybe this was the opening shot?

'You rang, master?'

Kathy stepped into the sombre room and moved to where his finger pointed. She stood still and hung her head like a chastised schoolgirl.

The Man smiled to himself. She was the best one he had had in the last twenty years since he had first learned the dark secrets of sexual domination.

Kathy was just the latest in a long line of housegirls. At first it had been tricky, selecting those who would recognise and submit to their own latent masochistic tendencies. But The Man's charm, warmth, kindness and generosity persuaded most to stay. Those from from deprived social backgrounds were easiest, he found. From the rundown Dublin suburbs of Crumlin or Dun Laoghaire. They valued the protection and security he offered, and a beautiful home that was theirs for as long as they played their part. And the in-built sense of guilt that their Catholic upbringing had bestowed on them made it easy for The Man to twist it into a psychological desire for self-punishment.

Only sometimes he regretted that his thin penis would no longer rise unless he was inflicting degradation on the girl of his choice. Lately his pleasures had become more bizarre

and his interest deeper. He had even visited the notorious
Doma Club in Amsterdam and spent a weekend at El Chalet
in a remote village near Malaga. But he was an intensely
private, almost reclusive man by nature and preferred to
experiment in the closely guarded confines of the mansion.

'This afternoon, Kathy, did you flaunt yourself before my
friend?'

She would not look up unless commanded. 'Yes, master.'
A whisper.

'Deliberately?'

She nodded.

'What should I do with you, Kathy?'

Inaudible.

'I beg your pardon?'

She cleared her throat. 'Punish me, master.'

The Man didn't smile. He enjoyed this game, and he
knew she did, too. 'How, Kathy? How do you want me to
punish you? The crop?'

'No, master. The soft leather strap.'

'Why?'

Again a mumble.

'I can't hear you.'

'Because it turns me on, master.'

Eight

'Just what the hell is the meaning of those guns, Frankie?' Robson demanded as he swung the Hertz-rented Capri out of the grounds of the Hilton Hotel.

Frank Lewis, in his pale lemon tropical suit from Hornes, relaxed in the passenger seat and adjusted the collar of his open-necked shirt. 'Oh, those. Nothing to worry about, Billy.'

Robson slowed to turn left into St George's Road, which wound around the seafront towards Sliema and the Libyan People's Bureau. 'Well, I *do* worry, Frankie. If I'm caught with those bloody things, I'll be in it up to my neck. With my record, it'll look brilliant! They'll probably think I'm here to turn over a branch of the Mid-Med Bank. If I go inside here, they'll throw away the key.'

Lewis settled an expensive pair of gold-rimmed Zeiss sunglasses on his nose. 'C'mon, Billy, one of the reasons I chose you for this was because Rich Abbott said you'd got bottle. Shit, as an ex-Marine you ought to have. And you know all about guns.'

'There's only one thing you need to know about guns,' Robson replied as he swung around the Spinola Bay bend and into Grenfell Street. 'They kill people. There's no other point in having them. So who do you plan to kill?'

'I'll forget you said that, Billy,' Lewis murmured darkly. He wound down the window to let the slipstream ruffle through his crop of fair hair. 'Look, believe me, I'm no happier about it than you. The simple fact is that the Libyans insist on it. And I don't intend to risk upsetting their delicate Arab sensibilities by refusing, and perhaps jeopardising the deal.' He glanced out at the shimmering Mediterranean beyond the promenade. 'Besides, you only need keep the small one with you. The pistol.'

Robson still wasn't happy. 'Who's the other one for?'

'For the same man who'll be using the apartment you've rented.'

'And the motor-cycle?'

Lewis nodded. His jaw was set firm.

'Who is this mystery man?'

'It's not really your business, Billy, but in fact he represents the people who are selling the cattle in Ireland. He likes to remain anonymous.'

Robson shook his head in disbelief, then tooted loudly as a Maltese car came careering straight out of Birkirka Road in front of him.

'The man also sells kosher meat to the Israelis,' Lewis continued evenly. 'So you can see why he doesn't want to be seen also dealing with Libya.'

With a sudden burst of acceleration, Robson overtook the offending Maltese vehicle. 'And he's pretty handy with a Skorpion sub-machine gun . . .'

Lewis was losing patience. 'Stow it, Billy. I'm very impressed with what you've done out here in the short time available. And hiring that Emy woman to show the girls around was a masterstroke. They all get on well together – like three cackling hens! So don't go and spoil it all.' He hesitated for a moment, then added: 'I was going to wait until we got back to England to talk more about this. But I need someone to head up my new transport firm. International haulage. It could be right up your street.'

Robson was so surprised that he almost missed the faded road-markings at the pedestrian crossing. He fired a rapid warning toot and saved an elderly British holidaymaker from instant death. 'It certainly could.'

'It would mean a directorship,' Lewis confirmed. 'And that's a business where you *have* to bend a few rules in order to survive. You get my drift?'

Robson saw it all right. Bribing Customs officials at remote borders, false documentation . . . there were a million-and-one tiny ways around day-to-day difficulties. Suddenly his alarm over being asked to pack a gun for the protection of his boss seemed ill-judged.

He lapsed into thoughtful silence, unsure if it was wise to push Lewis further. If the Libyans insisted he and his boss should carry firearms for their own protection, then perhaps they knew best. Like everyone else he'd heard that they were a strange bunch, and they certainly had plenty of enemies. So, although he wasn't happy about it, it could be a sensible precaution.

After all, he was new to this game and he hadn't been hired for his looks. Lewis knew his way around and had wanted him because he was an ex-Royal Marine who wouldn't baulk at the faintest hint of trouble. He had little doubt that if he let his own paranoia get the better of him, Lewis wouldn't hesitate to give him his marching orders. And then all his dreams of building a new future for his family would walk right out of the door. It would be the next flight back and straight down the Job Centre to sign on. No, he decided, he daren't risk rocking the boat.

It was difficult to park near the People's Bureau, so Robson pulled in on the Tower Road amidst a row of stationary vehicles.

'It's just a short walk up the hill,' he explained, opening the door. 'On the left.'

'I'll find my way,' Lewis replied. 'You can wait here.'

Robson shook his head and eyed his boss over the Capri's roof. 'If I'm going to bodyguard you, we'll do it right.'

Lewis was surprised. 'You're tooled up now?'

Robson nodded. 'I'll escort you to the gates.'

Lewis grinned. 'I'm beginning to like this VIP treatment.'

Dee watched from the corner of the room with the cold eyes of a cobra.

The man seated on the red plastic chair at the desk opposite Sher Gallal, was squirming. But Dee wasn't concerned. He didn't like Frank Lewis anyway.

'They want to deliver the shipment on Tuesday,' the Libyan was saying. 'Their man will come in on the ferry from Gozo. He arrives at Marfa Bay and will drive south to Mellieha.'

Dee rubbed a hand thoughtfully through his curly brown hair. 'That's the rendezvous? At Mellieha?'

Gallal showed his nicotine-stained teeth. 'There is a church there, high on a hill. At midday there will be no one there. Inside, the deal is made. Below there is a courtyard. A good place for exchange.'

'I don't like it,' Frank Lewis said.

'You haven't seen the place,' Dee retorted with quiet contempt.

'I mean the whole damn business. I make it a policy never to be in the same country as a consignment.'

Yes, Dee decided, Lewis was definitely edgy. 'What's the matter? Is Mr Twenty-Five Per Cent afraid of getting his hands dirty?'

Lewis's eyes hardened. 'Look, I run a legitimate business. That's the only reason this operation is working so well for you. If I had any sort of record, my outfit would be useless to you. And you won't find many straight businessmen that would co-operate with you.'

Dee smirked. 'My heart bleeds. But I'll remind you that your business is no longer as legitimate as it was. Perhaps it's time you took some of the risk.' He laughed. 'Don't worry. You're in no danger from the authorities here. They're all in it up to their pretty little Maltese necks anyway. The island's got a big heroin problem now. It works well for the Government here. It keeps the powerful in fancy villas and yachts, and it's eroding the bourgeoisie that opposes them.'

'I'm not interested in politics,' Lewis snapped.

'No, you're not, are you?' Dee replied coldly. Then abruptly he flicked his lighter and started a cigarette. 'Anyway, there's no danger to you. Even so, it is mere coincidence that a delivery is being made while you are here. But perhaps it's fortuitous.'

Lewis looked up. 'How so?'

Dee blew a circle of smoke into the centre of the room. 'It's to be the last one from our Sicilian friends in Palermo.'

'Why?'

'It's getting risky dealing with them. The Italian police are closing in. The Mafia are under constant surveillance. As their laboratories are getting raided and consignments seized, they're starting to fight between themselves like cats and dogs.' Dee paused to let the words sink in. 'They feel cornered. They are getting greedy and they are trying to lay down conditions on us. My friends in Ireland don't like that.'

Frank Lewis stared at his hand-stitched doeskin moccasins. 'But what do we do without them?'

Dee nodded towards the Libyan. 'Our friend Gallal here has already set up the new Iran route. That is now working well?'

Lewis confirmed it. 'Our fourth consignment should be nearing the Channel by now.'

'Good. Then we repeat a similar operation direct from Libya, using the same method.'

'The cattle shuttle?'

'The same. Only now Gallal has set up a direct route across North Africa. Smuggled across the Persian Gulf to North Yemen via Arabia. Then by ship to Tripoli. That's when you take over as before. But this time without the risk of the police picking us up along with the Sicilians.' Dee raised an eyebrow. 'And cutting them out of the operation boosts our profits by around 25 per cent.'

Lewis still looked concerned. 'Do they know it's their last delivery?'

Dee smiled thinly. 'Let's say they've got the general drift. There are no more deals in the pipeline.'

'Then there could be trouble.' Lewis was emphatic. 'They can get pretty mean.'

'That's why I'm here,' Dee replied without emotion.

'And the reason for all the precautions, I suppose?'

Dee didn't reply.

Now Lewis was looking very agitated. 'Why me, for God's sake? Why do I have to speak to them?'

Dee dragged heavily on his cigarette butt before replying. 'Because you're our front-man, Frankie. You set it all up at our behest. Now you tell them it's finished. You know our people won't allow us to deal direct with the Mafia. Common criminals.' The contempt with which he uttered the words left Lewis in no doubt the same opinion applied to him.

'They're not fools. They know who's behind it in Ireland.'

The cobra eyes had returned. 'They can guess. They can think. But they can't *know*. That's why our people insist we never front-up when dealing with them. Criminals can get vindictive. You forget we've a lot of experience of supergrasses.'

Reluctantly, Lewis accepted his fate. 'Well, thank God I've got a minder, then.'

Dee's eyes flashed darkly. 'Just make sure that fucken cabbage-hat keeps well away on the exchange. I wasn't too pleased to hear you'd rented a fucken Royal Marine bastard. Not pleased at all.'

It was Lewis's turn to smile. If his choice of Billy Robson made this Provo hardman smart, then he was well-pleased. '*I* run my business, and *I* do the hiring and firing. He's just doing a legit minding job for a legit firm. He knows nothing else. Besides, he's been out for around six years, and he has a record. He'll be ideal, and you've nothing to worry about, just as long as you keep away from me.'

'Is that a threat, Frankie?' Dee's voice was very soft. 'Or just your idea of a joke. Because you ought to know that I'd just love the excuse to blow the brains out of a cabbage-hat. Six years out or not, I owe those bastards.' The smile returned, but without a hint of warmth. 'So just don't give me that excuse.'

Sandy Robson's cold turkey had lasted four days.

It had begun on the Saturday morning after the visit by the Ulstermen. As she had lain in bed that night, nursing the tender bruised flesh of her groin, she vowed that she would never touch heroin again. Now she had a real incentive.

Not only did she at last have a chance to rebuild her marriage, but she would have to get through the coming week in Malta with total strangers and not give anything away. In addition there was no way she could lay her hands on three hundred pounds to pay off her debt to Harry the dealer, let alone raise money to score.

On the Thursday after her husband had left for Malta, she awoke at seven in the morning. For the first time in months she felt fresh, clean and rested. It was as though the previous weeks of degradation and self-disgust had only been a bad dream after all.

Once dressed, she actually made herself a light breakfast. As she washed it down with strong black coffee, she resolved to do what had to be done. Somehow she had to pay Harry before she left for Malta. Otherwise she might never even reach the airport.

Taking the bus to the West End, she spent the morning in a succession of ladies' lavatories in the big department stores.

The first time was the worst. A grossly overweight woman in a fox wrap had waddled into the centre cubicle and bolted the door. Sandy dabbed a lipstick at her mouth as she watched in the mirror until the occupants of the other cubicles had gone.

As the last one left, Sandy crouched down until she could see under the last occupied cubicle. Thick brown support tights were wrinkled in an unappetising sausage around stout ankles. Beside them was a large crocodile handbag.

Sandy took a deep breath and edged nearer, all the time glancing over her shoulder at the entrance door. No one came.

Now she was right beside the cubicle, her hand starting to reach with fingertips outstretched. She felt the sweat gather in the small of her back.

There was a loud crash behind her. Startled, Sandy stood bolt upright as the desperate young woman burst in and hurried past to a vacant cubicle.

'Gawd! Thought I wasn't going to make it!' the woman laughed. Sandy turned her head away until she heard the bolt crash home.

Tissue-paper rattled out of its holder in the fat woman's stall.

Well, Sandy told herself, it's now or never.

Without further hesitation, she dropped to her knees and, in one quick movement, swept her hand under the door. Her fingers caught around the long strap and began hauling the weighty handbag towards her.

The sudden stunned silence behind the door gave way to a shriek of protest. Sandy heaved with both hands. The gold clasp jammed under the door and stuck fast.

'Sod!'

At once, she felt the woman pulling back on the other strap. Sandy hauled again, her knees sliding on the damp tiled floor. She felt her tights ladder and the flooring burn into her skin as she slipped. Her arm muscles began to ache.

The absurd tug-o'-war seemed to last an eternity before Sandy finally pulled the bag free, forcing it through the narrow gap by sheer brute strength, driven by panic.

To screams of 'Help! Thief! My handbag!' Sandy had staggered out of the lavatories in a cold sweat, her heart pumping and her legs trembling. She careered blindly towards the escalator with the offending handbag, crashing helplessly against fellow shoppers as she tried to hurry without running. Every face seemed to turn towards her. She even imagined she could still hear the fat woman's screams in her ears.

Only when she hit the icy blast of the north-easterly swirling along Oxford Street did she realise that she had actually got away with it.

The crocodile handbag had yielded seventy-five pounds and a plastic concertina of credit cards.

Sandy had to repeat the procedure twice more at different stores before she accumulated the necessary £300.

That afternoon, Harry the dealer had been a very relieved man.

'You look a million miles away, gorgeous.'

Frank Lewis's words jolted her back to the present: Winston's, the plush, mahogany-panelled fish restaurant in Sliema, where Emy Graziani had insisted that the men take the girls.

It had been a good choice, although strangely, Emy herself had not come with them. Having spent the day giving directions to Bernadette's hectic driving as they toured the south of the island, she had announced that she had to stay in to wash her hair.

'I'm sorry, Frankie, I was back in England for a moment there,' Sandy replied. 'It must be all this wine after a tiring day. Bernie must be *exhausted*!'

From the table, Bernadette chuckled softly: 'Sure, driving over here is a bit o' a hazard. Especially as Emy doesn't know the road signs – what there are of them! So she'd say go left, or right, and *I'd* have to decide if we *could*!'

'Twice we went the wrong way up a one-way street,' Sandy recalled.

'Ssh!' Bernadette scolded. 'I'll never hear the end of it. We girls should keep our little secrets.'

Lewis roared with good humour. 'It's a shame she couldn't join us tonight, don't you think, Billy?'

Robson pulled a tight smile. 'Yes, I suppose it is.'

'C'mon, Billy, the girl's a gem! Quite a find. She's really made the trip for the women; given us the chance to get on with business without being nagged for not being around. And she's good company. Knew her when you were out with the Marines, I suppose?'

Robson nodded.

Lewis laughed. 'Don't tell me she's an old flame?'

Sandy's eyes flashed as though a sudden doubt crossed her mind.

Robson's laugh was a little brittle. 'No Frankie, nothing like that. As they say, we were just good friends.'

Lewis beckoned the waiter to bring the bill. 'Well, Emy or not, we'd better call it a day. It's Tuesday tomorrow and Billy and me's got a lot on. Early start.' He hesitated. 'Also, girls, I want you up bright and early. As soon as we've gone, I want you to take the Capri and go down to the Preluna Hotel. It's on the front at Sliema. Just book in and wait until we arrive.'

Bernadette's chestnut hair floated around her freckled face as she shook her head. 'I half expected you were joking about these crazy arrangements, Frankie. You really *mean* it?'

He leaned across the table and kissed her. 'I know it's crazy, love, but these crazy A-rabs insist on security. Trust me, eh?'

Bernadette nodded uncertainly.

That night Robson and Sandy made love like in the old days. For once she was both relaxed and impassioned.

Afterwards, she said: 'You seem very distant tonight, Billy.'

'I'm sorry. I've a lot on my mind.'

Her voice sounded very small in the darkened bedroom. 'What Frankie was saying about Emy. About her being an old flame. It's not true is it?'

'No, of course it's not. Just Frankie's idea of a joke. Winding us up.'

'So there was never anything between you?'

'No, nothing.' And as he spoke them the words twisted like a knife in his gut.

Detective-Sergeant Dick Spicer was not amused.

He was just about to dive off round the corner for a pie and a pint at the Albert with WPC Gifford when the call came through. With the clerks at lunch, he had no option but to take it.

The pie and pint was a small sacrifice, but he'd been chasing WPC Gifford hard ever since she had flashed the green light at the Christmas party. She evidently fancied the lean young detective with the wire-rimmed glasses that gave him a sternly handsome Teutonic look. Nevertheless, she had found it necessary to field the usual run of excuses to avoid a date. 'Sorry I'm on early shift tomorrow', 'I'm washing my hair', 'I've got a previous date – with the Chief Super'.

At last he had her pinned down. Or so he thought. He glared at the mouthpiece of the telephone hatefully.

'Yes? Drug Squad, Detective-Sergeant Spicer.'

The Irish voice at the other end told him to shut up and listen. He did, instinctively reaching for the tape-recorder.

Immediately colleagues talking, or poking awkwardly at typewriters on the bench-like rows of desks in the Squad-Room, sensed that something was up. Heads turned.

Spicer beckoned them. He placed his hand over the mouthpiece. 'Quick, see if the Chief Super's in. And get a trace on this call.'

'Tip-off?' one asked.

The detective nodded, and resumed his intense concentration on the caller. 'Flight from Karachi? This afternoon?'

Again he listened. Pakistan Airways Flight PIA 781. Arriving Heathrow 1535 hours. Passenger by the name of Balu. Mrs Naima Balu. Acting as courier bringing in heroin. Quantity unknown.

Spicer's pen raced across his notepad as he strained to catch every word of the fast Irish dialect. 'May I ask your name, sir?'

The sharp click was followed by a discordant continuous burr. Spicer looked angrily down at the mouthpiece and swore silently.

Before he had time to replace the receiver, Detective Chief Superintendent Ray Pilger rushed through the door as though it wasn't there. He slid to a halt, the half-eaten sandwich that was sufficing for lunch, still in his hand.

Spicer shook his head. 'Sorry, sir. Someone grassing, but he wasn't going to hang about. And I doubt there was even time for a trace.'

Pilger took it with reasonable grace. 'Where?'

'Heathrow from Karachi. A woman.'

The detective nodded. It was the usual formula. The poor buggers were queuing up in Pakistan to act as couriers. To them it was the one chance to make the only money they'd ever have, courtesy of the big drugs barons. What they didn't realise was that many of them were considered to be expendable pawns. To be sacrificed for a few grams of heroin to create a diversion whilst the queen sailed through with the main consignment.

'Anything on the informer?' Pilger asked.

Spicer was uncertain. 'He was definitely Irish. I may have had him before. I'll check the voice-print.'

'IRA?'

'No, Chief. No recognition code, anyway. In fact, he sounded like an Ulsterman to me. Doing an Ian Paisley impression.'

Pilger pulled a wry grin, just as Spicer's phone rang again. It was the telephone supervisor. 'Wonders of modern science, Chief, they got a trace.' He shook his head. 'A public box in Kilburn.'

'Okay, let's get things moving right away. Check everything out with the Intelligence Unit and see if they can throw any additional light. A passenger list would also be useful. And see if we can persuade Customs to let this woman run.'

Leaving Detective-Sergeant Spicer to smoulder over his lost date with WPC Gifford, Pilger strolled thoughtfully back into the corridor, still munching his canteen sandwich.

Although there was an obliging Customs liaison officer attached to the Yard's Central Drugs Intelligence and Immigration Unit – to give it its full unwieldy name – Pilger still doubted he would get the particular co-operation he wanted. His request would have to be sanctioned by the Customs' Drugs Section chief because Heathrow was their domain. The cantankerous Fred Roxan didn't like to allow 'runners' at the best of times, and Pilger knew the man had just started another in his perpetual cycle of head colds. That always put him in a bad mood.

His own phone was ringing as he reached his private office. It was his direct line. Unhurriedly he picked up the receiver.

'Pilger!' hissed the voice immediately. The tone was so harsh that it took the detective aback for a second.

'Yes. Who's that?'

'Never mind, just listen. Flight 781 from Karachi. It's either today or tomorrow. Name of Yasim Shah, a businessman. Sure it'll be in your interest to take a look.' The phone went dead.

Ray Pilger replaced the receiver and stared at it hatefully. Tracing a short call on a direct line was almost impossible.

Tip-offs often came out of the blue like this, but not usually two in the same day. And certainly not both with Irish accents. This one, if he was not mistaken, had a distinctive Dublin brogue.

An hour later Spicer entered his office, carrying a roll sheet of computer print-out.

The young detective-sergeant was grinning. 'This Mrs Balu is on the passenger list, Chief. Looks like a hot one.'

Pilger looked up. 'I'm also after another name. Yasim Shah. Maybe today, or tomorrow. Take it through to the end of the week.'

The sergeant peered over the top of his spectacles. 'No need, Chief. Unless it's a coincidence there's a Yasim Shah on the same flight as Mrs Balu.'

A slow, wicked grin spread over Pilger's face. Unless he was very much mistaken, someone, somewhere out there, was double-crossing. There was a smell of vengeance in the air. And, in the usually hermetically-sealed secrecy of the drug-trafficking world, that could lead to a rare chink in the usual armour of silence.

Pilger snatched up the telephone. 'I'd like to put a call through to Fred Roxan at King's Beam House. It's urgent.'

Dee had been waiting for an hour. He was not a man to leave anything to chance.

Only now the ferry was due to arrive from Gozo. It would berth at the long, surf-tossed jetty at Marfa on the flat coastal plain around Paradise Bay, where the spume was carried several hundred yards by the wind. If the ferry was on time, it would take the Alfa Romeo barely three minutes to follow the pitted ribbon of tarmac road southward to the hilltop of Mellieha where he now stood.

He became aware of his tension rising as the time for the exchange approached. Mentally, he checked his heartbeat: steady and quiet, just slightly faster than usual. No shakes, or trembling. Just a slight tightening of the intestines. Mind clear, sharp as a bell.

Yes, it paid to be in good time.

He had parked the 250cc Honda motorcycle on the upper village road which led to the towering peach-coloured façade of Mellieha Church. From between its twin square bell-towers, the stone figures of Christ and the prophets had gazed down as he approached. He smiled to himself. Did he sense a look of disapproval on the impassive carved faces? Probably.

Along the eastern flank of the approach road ran a waist-high parapet. It formed the top of a stone curtain that fell away steeply to a secluded courtyard some twenty-five feet below. That was where the exchange would take place. To reach it from the church necessitated the descent of a steep flight of steps and approaching through an archway.

The other side of the courtyard opened onto the tree-lined lower street of Mellieha, and the main road to the south. There were a few shops, a garage, a bar, and, to Dee's amusement, a sleepy police-post.

It was outside the building that the battered Granada, rented from a backstreet garage, had just been parked. From the gateway to the courtyard, Dee watched as Frank Lewis and the man called Robson emerged.

The Irishman felt his bile rising while the ex-Royal Marine leant against the car's roof as he exchanged words with his boss. There was something about the natural arrogance of Robson's stance, and an alert inclination of the head that made it easy for Dee to imagine the powerful frame camouflaged in battle fatigues. As Robson glanced up the sloping road to the courtyard gateway, Dee could clearly distinguish the black moustache. Virtually the hallmark of the Brit forces.

Dee stepped back into the shadows and waited until Frank Lewis arrived alone.

'Does your man know what to do?'

The Irishman's voice caught the other unawares. 'God, Dee, you gave me a fright!'

'Does your man know what to do?' Dee repeated tersely.

Lewis looked disparaging. 'Of *course* he does. Just stay put with the engine running.'

'Outside the police-post?'

Lewis smiled slyly. 'My idea. It's likely to discourage the Sicilians from trying anything. Not right outside a cop shop.'

Dee said nothing but led Lewis through the shade of the pine and olive trees to the arch. From it, there was a magnificent panoramic view to the north.

'Is that the road they'll come along?' Lewis asked.

The wind tugged at Dee's hair. 'Yes. It could be any time from now. We'll exchange here. By the shrine.'

Lewis peered back into the courtyard at the white Madonna and Child statuette encircled by white iron railings. 'Where will you be?'

The Irishman jabbed a finger upwards to the parapet overlooking the courtyard. 'It'll give me a clear field of fire.'

Lewis looked anxious, sweat glistening on his brow. 'For God's sake, don't start anything stupid. I suppose you've brought that bloody machine-gun thing.'

'I'm not likely to have forgotten it.' He patted the front of his black motorcycle jerkin. The bulge in the leather was hardly noticeable. He smiled gently at Frank Lewis' obvious distress. 'Don't worry, I'll not do anything stupid. Now go through this arch and up the side of the church. Use the small door. It's open. I slipped the caretaker a few notes. Just go in and take a pew at the front.' His smile broadened. 'And pray.'

That, Lewis decided as he panted up the stone steps, was one thing he needed no encouragement to do. He'd already started. This whole thing was turning into a nightmare. He just hoped that Dee was as professional as his cool exterior suggested. Not for the first time he wished he could take Billy Robson fully into his confidence. While Dee was around, he felt he needed an ally.

Dee had been right. The door to the Mellieha Church was unlocked. Before entering, Lewis looked nervously behind him. From the pavement opposite, an old man waved him in. No doubt the caretaker.

Lewis stepped inside. It was more like a cathedral than a church. High walls in local pink limestone and a high vaulted ceiling supported by square pillars that ran either side of the pine pews in the centre.

His moccasins squeaked eerily on the floor of Maltese marble as he moved towards the high altar. He passed several magnificent carved wooden statues decorated in gold leaf that were used for the annual carnival processions. But he hardly noticed them.

The place was so quiet that it made him uneasy. Serene and hallowed, with the wind outside moaning plaintively around the domed roof above the altar. Lost souls trying to gain sanctuary and failing to find a way in.

He manoeuvred awkwardly into a front pew and glanced back towards the door. He didn't have long to wait.

Minutes later he heard a car labouring up the hillside road alongside the church. It came to a halt and the engine died. Slow footsteps scraped on the steps and he heard the door creak. A sudden gust of wind whistled through the nave. Somewhere he heard papers scatter.

Lewis kept his eyes fixed dead ahead until the footsteps reached the top of the aisle and turned towards him.

Carmelo was a short man. His distinguished silver hair was brushed straight back off the swarthy face with its fleshy hooked nose. Years of good living and his wife's generous pasta dishes had long ago swollen the flat belly of his youth. But in the immaculately-cut suit, he merely looked portly.

As he sat beside Lewis, the Sicilian's toothbrush moustache curved around a smile of teeth that were too perfect for a man of his years. The eyes, brown and fluid, seemed friendly enough, but deep and fathomless. As he had thought the first time they met, Lewis decided the man's eyes never hinted at what was going on in the mind behind them.

Carmelo crossed himself briefly, then turned to the Londoner. 'Hello, Frankie. It has been a long, long time since we meet. What is it? A year? Two maybe?'

Lewis inclined his head. 'Too long.'

The Sicilian nodded with the sad expression of a pensioner recalling his childhood days. 'That was when we set up our arrangement. Since then it is always Sher Gallal we deal with on your behalf.' Momentarily the eyes hardened. 'Libyan pig! He forgets the days that Italy runs his country. When all he eats is rice and lives in a tent, and shits in the street. Now his country has oil he thinks he is a prince. Why does God always see fit to give the richest countries to the least deserving people? To the scum of the earth? Penance, I suppose, as we look forward to a better life hereafter.'

Lewis shrugged. If Carmelo thought he was on the side of the angels, that was his business.

'Where do you stay in Malta?' the Sicilian asked casually.

Lewis found his voice, but it was hoarse. 'The Hilton.'

Carmelo nodded. It was what he expected. 'It is a good choice. Malta is going to the dogs nowadays, so it isn't easy to get a good hotel. No one comes anymore. There is no money for investment. The Government is stupid . . .' He smiled . . . 'But it serves our purpose, eh, my friend?'

'You have the consignment?'

'But, of course. It is in the car. Fifteen kilos.'

'Good,' Lewis replied. 'I have the cash. Let's get down to the courtyard and exchange.'

He went to stand but the thick fingers of Carmelo's right hand restrained him. Lewis could sense the steel strength of them biting into his flesh.

'There is one thing, Mr Lewis.'

Lewis's face paled. 'Yes?'

'Should we not discuss the next delivery?'

The Londoner found himself mesmerised by the movement of the toothbrush moustache as Carmelo talked; he shifted uncomfortably. 'I'm sure Sher Gallal will be in touch.'

There was no let-up of the pressure on his arm. 'But *you* make the decisions, Mr Lewis. As you know, we have a man with your friends in Dublin. A liaison man, I think you call it? A Mr Tom Rabbit. He is outside now. He seems to think that this might be the last consignment. That you have made plans to buy the product direct from source. Through that Libyan pig Sher Gallal.'

Lewis swallowed heavily. He tried to avoid them as Carmelo's eyes burned into his. He fumbled for the right words: '. . . Er, the situation is under review . . . There are no plans at present . . .'

'Because,' Carmelo continued with velvet menace, 'we should be very *unpleased* if Tom Rabbit's report is true. So, I should like you to confirm to me . . .'

The front door suddenly blew open. Its crashing noise echoed like a shout around the ceiling. A dark figure stood silhouetted in the entrance.

'I think, gentlemen, it is time we got on.' Dee's voice was quite distinct.

It was the first time Lewis had ever seen Carmelo angry. The barely-contained outrage coloured his cheeks and his eyes bulged with indignation.

Lewis seized the opportunity and stood up. His heart was thudding as he retreated down the aisle, with Carmelo following behind.

Dee ushered the Sicilian through the door first. 'Drive down to the courtyard. Mr Lewis will meet you there.'

Carmelo stared hard into the Irishman's face. 'So the little sewer rats from Dublin show their faces at last.' His eyes travelled down to the leather jerkin. 'No need to ask if you back your orders with guns, I suppose?'

Dee's mouth remained firmly closed, but there could have been a hint of humour in the eyes.

'Liggio will not be pleased,' the Sicilian hissed.

No doubt, Dee thought, the *capo di tutti capi* of the multi-million Mafia drugs empire would not. But he let it pass, and

watched as Carmelo climbed into the front seat of the Alfa
Romeo. At the wheel was Tom Rabbit.

'Just the two of them?' Lewis whispered his question
nervously out of the corner of his mouth.

'Here, yes,' Dee replied. 'But there's a second car parked
below on the main street near your Granada. It arrived a
minute after Carmelo. A red Citroën GT. His eyes followed
the Alfa as it circled around in front of the church and began
back down the road that led to the courtyard arch. 'My guess
is they'll try and get you on the road before you can get the
stuff back to the Libyan Bureau.'

'Not at the exchange?'

Dee smiled gently. 'Not with me standing up here. So I
just hope your cabbage-hat knows his stuff.'

Lewis ran a nervous hand through his hair. 'Are you sure
there'll be trouble?'

'The man driving the Alfa is Tom Rabbit. Half-Irish, half-
Sicilian. A man of divided loyalties. This was the time for
him to make a decision. From Carmelo's reaction, I think
he has.'

'Chosen?'

Dee nodded. 'The wrong side.' He took Lewis by the
forearm. 'When you've finished your deal, stand well clear
of Carmelo and Rabbit, and at no time position yourself
between them and me. Otherwise it could give them the
chance to try something on. Got it?'

Lewis's mouth was dry; he nodded.

'Go on then. Down the steps. Go and meet them.'

Dee watched coldly as the Londoner walked slowly away
to the top of the stone steps in the lee of the church. The
man was quietly shitting himself, there was little doubt about
that. He'd probably even forgotten momentarily that the

attaché-case he held was crammed to bursting with untraceable US dollars.

From his vantage point at the parapet, Dee could see directly into the open courtyard. As Lewis stepped through the arch, the Irishman unzipped the leather jerkin so that he could slide his right hand around the butt of the Skorpion machine-pistol.

The sound of the Alfa was scarcely discernible above the buffeting of the wind. Dee waited patiently for Carmelo and Tom Rabbit to appear through the archway with the package.

Wrapped in brown paper, it looked harmless enough.

Inside it was fifteen kilos of fine white powder. Ninety per cent pure. This batch would have started life on the remote hillsides of Pakistan, Afghanistan or Iran. It was impossible for Dee to know which. Thick, latex-like substance would have oozed from the series of vertical cuts made by the farmers in each pod in the poppy field. *Papaver somniferum*. The poppy that bears sleep.

It would have been dried and then boiled with other chemicals, notably vinegar-like acetic anhydride. That may have been done at one of Carmelo's secret 'laboratories' in Sicily, but it was unlikely. The smell was a giveaway and the police were forever closing in nowadays ... No, Dee reasoned, it had most likely been refined at source by one of the local Pathan chemists. Refined to become diacetylmorphine. Heroin. Producing mind-blowing euphoria, but followed rapidly by a numbing depression.

Dee was now familiar with Carmelo's favoured routes. This package would have been smuggled out of Iran, north of the war-zone with Iraq, over the border into Turkey. That trade had been going on for years amongst the mountain men, but it had never been as profitable as it was today.

A lot of heroin, Dee knew, went north through Sofia where the Bulgarian KGB demanded, and usually got, their cut.

But that was not Carmelo's route. His supplies swung south from Istanbul and into Greece. Onward shipments, not destined to feed the blossoming infestation of Greek addicts, would be broken down for couriers to take on the internal ferry to the holiday island of Corfu. From the ancient city of Corfu Town the couriers would take a second three-hour ferry trip, this time south to the tiny island of Paxos.

Arriving at the quayside capital of Gaios, the courier would meet the representative of a select group of islanders, some of them prominent and most of them capable of at least a few sentences in Italian. The packets would be handed over for stockpiling until the winter months.

An appalling, pot-holed road links Gaios in the south with the picturesque mini-port of Lakka at the opposite end of the island. In the summer it is a haven for yachtsmen and holiday-makers who prefer a quieter time. In winter it is a ghost town. Few inhabitants. No tourists. Also no police or customs officers.

So, the arrival of the occasional yacht on a dark November evening goes unnoticed. If anyone does notice, they don't say anything. Lakka is a poor town.

Carmelo's yachts made the trip regularly, quietly collecting an unspecified cargo, then slipping out again on the morning tide. During the four-hundred mile journey in international waters, the consignment for Dee would have been checked, tested for purity, and repackaged.

In the same way that it left Greece, it arrived in Malta – one stop removed. The consignment would go ashore from the yacht at a remote bay on the west coast of the Maltese satellite island of Gozo. There, the Alfa would have been waiting to drive to Mgärr at the other end of the island. Then straight onto the car ferry for the short journey to Marfa on the northern tip of Malta.

Tom Rabbit was the first to appear through the archway. There was no mistaking him: long black hair curling over the collar of his jacket, his scimitar sideburns and the jut of the unshaven chin. For ever the gypsy 'knacker'.

Suspicious black eyes took in Frank Lewis who stood the other side of the Madonna and Child statuette. Satisfied, Rabbit surveyed the parapet twenty-five feet above the courtyard and, momentarily, he met and held Dee's unblinking gaze. Even from that distance each man could feel the other's hatred. Then Rabbit stepped back and, with an evil grin, held wide his jacket with both hands.

Look, no weapons.

Dee allowed himself a wry smile. Everyone knew Rabbit carried a pistol tucked in the back waistband of his trousers, retained in a small clip-on leather holster.

The joke over, the gypsy beckoned Carmelo to come out of the shadows and into the arena. He was struggling with the weight of the package. Rabbit stepped forward and took it from him, then carried it easily into the centre of the courtyard. Contemptuously he tossed it to the ground. The impact exploded a cloud of dust which spiralled away in the breeze.

Slowly, he backed off some fifteen feet and waited.

Frank Lewis glanced up to the parapet for reassurance; Dee nodded gently. Then, clutching the attaché-case, the Londoner edged forward until he stood over the package. He was filled with the sudden urge to grab the stuff and run. But he checked the impulse. There was no guarantee that Carmelo hadn't tried something. Maybe substitution. A mixture of milk, sugar and the Italian laxative Mannitol was favourite.

Quickly he took the switchblade from his pocket and, stooping, ran its razor edge along the top of the parcel. He peered inside. As usual, the goods were packed in individual kilo packets. That was the way Carmelo always did things. Neat, precise. No room to argue. Like buying the stuff off a supermarket shelf.

He selected five of the polythene packs at random, split them, and added an eye-dropper of nitric acid to the powder. The colour quickly deepened from yellow to a rich blue. Excellent. Undoubtedly ninety per cent purity.

Lewis hastily stuffed the bags back into the torn parcel, scooped his arms around it, and shuffled awkwardly back towards the gate. There he waited whilst Carmelo and Rabbit advanced to where he'd left the attaché-case, bathed in sunlight in the centre of the courtyard.

Three minutes later, they were satisfied. Unsmiling, Carmelo's dark eyes searched and found Dee on the parapet. He nodded.

It was then that a scudding cloud crossed the sun. Accompanied by a sudden eddy of chill wind, a shadow passed over the courtyard. Everyone was on edge, and Dee noticed the figures below stiffen involuntarily. And it was in that frozen moment that Dee's eye caught the surreptitious movement in the shadow of the arch.

Dee's thought processes hummed like a computer. If the Mafia was going to try it on, his commanding position on the parapet demanded that he would have to be taken out first.

He spun round towards the front of the church. For a second, he could not believe his own prediction. The man in the dark raincoat moving casually towards him looked harmless enough. An innocent passer-by.

It was the man's eyes which gave him away. Although his path was taking him almost directly towards Dee, his gaze was averted. As though the Irishman didn't exist. A second later he wouldn't have.

The front of the dark raincoat parted like curtains, the black muzzle protruding like the misshapen penis of some grotesque flasher. Its seed giving death, not life.

Dee's reactions were hair-triggered. The Skorpion machine-pistol shook like a mad thing in his hands, trying to escape his grasp. He'd had scarcely a split second to aim before the other man's bullets were kicking holes out of the parapet all around him.

Dee thought he must be dead. But Carmelo's gunman had been equally taken by surprise at the speed of Dee's response. It was as though someone had kicked the man's legs from under him as he collapsed onto the church steps. He rolled raggedly down them until he sprawled in an ungainly heap at Dee's feet. The gun clattered from his crooked white fingers onto the stone.

The entire sequence was over in the click of a camera eye, yet Dee was certain disaster had already struck in the courtyard. As he dived back to the parapet, the sun came out.

But below no one had moved. No one except the man in the shadow of the arch. He could tell that Lewis had seen him now, but the Londoner was petrified, frozen. His eyes appealed upwards for help.

It came. Ten rounds of spitting lead venom flashing from the silenced barrel of the Skorpion, as Dee aimed into the arch with a crazed hosing motion. He was aware of a gasp or cry of pain from someone. But he had no time to wait. He swung around the Skorpion with a double-handed grip until the pip of the gunsight covered Tom Rabbit's heart.

The gypsy had his revolver only halfway levelled when the Skorpion jerked and Rabbit was blasted off his feet.

Momentarily, the sun glinted on Carmelo's silver hair before Dee's aim shifted and the Sicilian's body collapsed in the dust like a deflated balloon. The firing-pin of the Skorpion clicked against an empty chamber.

Dee's breath escaped in a hiss of relief. Below Frank Lewis was clumsily attempting to pick up the dollar notes that had been tossed around the courtyard like confetti.

'LEAVE IT!' Dee bawled. 'LET THEM KNOW *WE* HAVE HONOUR! GET OUT, FAST!'

Frank Lewis needed no second bidding. Clutching the awkward parcel to his chest, he turned and ran towards the gate. His trembling legs took him unsteadily down the sloping, tree-lined road to where the Granada was parked.

He threw himself into the passenger seat, dumping the parcel in the rear.

'How did it go . . . ?' Robson began.

'Don't talk!' Lewis snapped. 'Just get out of here. Fast.'

Robson blinked in disbelief. His boss was obviously panic-stricken.

'Come on!' Lewis's voice was almost a shriek. He visibly relaxed a little as Robson let out the clutch. 'Have you seen a red Citroën GT?'

Robson shook his head as they pulled out. 'No. But then I haven't been looking.' He straightened out. 'Is that it? On the right?'

Lewis's head turned abruptly. He just caught a glimpse of two faces through the dust-smeared windows. They looked sallow and mean. 'Oh my God . . .' he breathed.

The Granada reached the bottom of the slope and joined the main road towards St Paul's Bay. 'What on earth happened back there, Frankie?'

'Just drive, for God's sake!' Lewis hissed, turning around in his seat to look back. 'Someone tried to kill us.'

'What? You're joking . . .'

Lewis sounded angry now. 'I don't joke about things like that. It happened, I tell you. They tried to kill us.'

'Who's *us*?'

Lewis hesitated. 'Me and the man I was meeting. They fired shots at us.'

'Was the man all right?'

'Yes, yes,' Lewis replied irritably. 'But those bastards are following us now.'

Robson glanced up to the mirror. 'That Citroën?'

'Is it following?'

'Yes. And closing. But what in heaven's name are they up to? Are they after that parcel?'

Lewis took a deep breath and tried to bring together the fragments of his cover-story in his mind. 'That *must* be what they want. It's full of cash. It's the way the Libyans insist on doing business, but it breaks every currency regulation in the book. Someone must have got wind of it. Local gangsters, I suppose.'

Robson's jaw set in a firm line. His new boss's earlier words rang loudly in his mind. In international business, it was necessary to bend a few rules. It wasn't a crime, just a matter of survival.

'Don't worry, Frankie. They won't get your money.'

Nine

At the next bend Robson changed down to third and accelerated hard out off the left-handed curve. The powerful 2.3 litre engine hummed with a surge of energy that sent the rear wheels biting into the worn tarmac.

Glancing in his mirror he saw the Citroën fall back into the billowing trail of dust.

'How are we doing?' Lewis enquired anxiously.

Robson smiled with satisfaction. 'Holding our own.'

But they weren't for long. As the Citroën slithered through the next bend on the sharp run down to St Paul's Bay, it had made up the lost distance.

'Frankie, grab a look at the map, will you,' Robson said. 'I think we'll make a cross-country detour.'

Lewis responded instantly. 'Where are we?'

'St Paul's Bay. Pwales Beach.'

'Got it!'

'I think there's a road coming up that would take us across the island. On the right. To Ghajn Tuffieha.'

'*Where?*' Lewis glared at the map. 'Yes, yes, I've got it. Not this one . . . the next!'

Robson swung into the Pwales Valley road in a four-wheel drift. A stench of burning rubber came up through the floor and a screen of dust arced in their wake. An unsuspecting local panicked and drove his car straight into a roadsign. Robson glimpsed the fountain of steam rising from the shattered radiator before they slid into the next bend.

The Granada began to take flight along the badly pitted road. On either side a patchwork of small fields growing tomatoes, beans and grapes stretched out across the flat valley. They were interspersed with fig and olive groves and the occasional windpump.

Now the road was comparatively straight and Robson was able to open the car right up until the needle was nudging one hundred mph. But the vehicle was becoming impossible to handle, the wheel kicking in his grasp as they bounced from one pothole to the next. An astounded group of peasant farmers tending a field of young marrows gawped as the car rocketed past.

Lewis looked over his shoulder and grinned. 'Fangio eat yer heart out. That Citroën's slipping back.'

They hurtled into the next bend, and near disaster.

The open-backed Toyota truck was chugging along, straddling the centre of the narrow road. Robson hit the brake with his full weight. Nothing happened. Instinctively, he pumped. At last the brakes locked in an ear-splitting screech. He spun the wheel to compensate as the Granada fishtailed. Dip the clutch, change down, let up. Like the reverse thrust of a jetliner the force pulled the car up short, its front bumper almost nudging the truck's rear.

Robson blasted the horn. Again and again. Stubbornly, the Toyota driver refused to pull over. On both sides a dry stone wall said 'no way'.

In the mirror, the sleek red bonnet of the Citroën began to swell in size.

Spinning the wheel left and right, Robson tried to see past

the Toyota. Left again. Nothing. Right again. Nothing. The
Citroën was a hundred yards away and closing.

Suddenly a low and ancient stone farm building appeared
ahead to the left. Its recessed courtyard was tiny, where a dog
sprawled contentedly at the feet of an old crone as she sat,
clicking away with her lace bobbins.

He'd have to chance it. He swung the car out, at the same
time blasting hard on the horn. The dog sprang to its feet and
barked in protest. Sparks flew as the Granada's tail grazed the
corner of the building. Then they were in the courtyard, the
car accelerating alongside the Toyota like a thing possessed.
Engine pounding at fever pitch, tyres squealing in protest.

There was a dull squelch and the dog vanished beneath
the swerving bonnet as Robson threw the vehicle into the
narrowing gap between the front of the Toyota and the next
building.

'Oh shit . . . !' Lewis breathed and closed his eyes.

The sour sound of crashing cymbals shook the entire car
as the truck's wing tried to trap the Granada's boot against
the wall. For a second the Granada was stunned, held back.
It heaved. The rev needle went off the dial. Then, to the
sickening noise of wrenched metal, it pulled free, leaving its
entire bumper behind in the dust.

'Jesus Christ!' Lewis gasped. 'You've got to be the luckiest
sonofabitch on the island.'

But Robson wasn't listening. His ear was tuned to the
engine and he didn't like what he heard. It was starting to
heave like a man with one lung. It didn't sound right. The
power had faded. Outside, something was clanking beneath
them in the road.

'We're not out of this yet, Frankie,' Robson muttered. 'If
we stay on this road, it's just a matter of time before they

overtake us. Is there a road we can take to Mgärr? On the left?'

Lewis consulted the map. 'Sure, the next one, unless we've passed it. But it's just a track.'

Robson grinned without humour. 'Any port in a storm. Maybe we can hide up and let them pass us.'

But it wasn't to be. Just as the Granada swung left into the track by a clump of fleshy cacti, the Citroën reappeared in the mirror.

'Let me have the gun,' Lewis hissed.

'Forget it,' Robson returned. 'You'll only shoot yourself in the foot.'

'For God's sake!' his boss pleaded. 'They're right on top of us!'

As the Granada laboured on, the Citroën began creeping along the offside. Robson glimpsed the determined expression on the driver's face as the man nudged his vehicle inward.

The rear door crumpled to the ugly sound of metal grinding against metal. A shower of sparks spat out from the point of contact. The Granada edged into the embankment, branches from the wayside bushes whipping in at Lewis's open window.

Then the hedgerow gave way to a long, improvised wall of oil drums. *Crump!* The Citroën's dented front wing tore into Robson's door, buckling it instantly inward. Instinctively he leaned away as the window frosted and a mosaic of glass crystals fell into his lap.

With a resounding metallic boom, the Granada took the hollow oil drums like a row of skittles. They flew left and right, some bouncing up over the bonnet and onto the Citroën; others spun into the fields.

Robson then swerved violently back onto the road, this

time hitting the Citroën in the front wheel arch. Momentarily, he gained half a length distance. Then the engine started to expire, groaning in its death throes. The temperature gauge was on red. No doubt damage caused by the dog. And then the oil warning light blinked on.

In a sudden surge of power, the Citroën regained its ground, surging past as they approached a blind left-hand bend.

The front bumper, torn and twisted, suddenly became enmeshed, locking the cars together like two steel stags. They slewed around the bend, side-by-side, trailing a vast plume of dust.

Robson saw the bright yellow bulldozer first. It seemed to fill the entire windscreen as it bore down on them. He stood on the brakes. The Citroën continued at maximum revs, tearing itself free.

Spinning the wheel, Robson took the Granada up the embankment like a wall-of-death rider, accelerating as hard as he could. Lewis screamed. The bulldozer driver froze in disbelief as the vehicle flashed past him, somehow clinging to the near-vertical slope.

The Citroën driver, seeing the bulldozer a fraction later, had swerved right. It burst through the low stone wall with the velocity of a bazooka rocket, wheels spinning in mid-air before it dropped ten feet into the field below.

It hit the hard, rocky ground like a dropped brick. Stopping dead on impact, it burst open at the seams. Doors blasted out in opposite directions. The bonnet flew up, detaching itself from its hinges. A wheel sauntered away across a field of young onions.

The Granada fishtailed to a halt fifty yards beyond the bulldozer. Already the workman had climbed down and was running towards the wreck of the Citroën.

'Good God, Billy!' Frank Lewis breathed.

'We'd better go back.'

Lewis regained some composure. 'Forget them. They'll not want to mention us to the police. Let's just get out of here before that peasant gets a good look at us.'

Robson found himself grinning inanely. He hadn't enjoyed himself so much in years.

'We make a good team, Billy,' Lewis said.

Under a whine of protest, the stalled engine finally spluttered into something resembling life and ground noisily off down the road.

Naima Balu was a small, slender beautiful creature.

She walked with a quiet natural dignity through the vast unfamiliar corridors and lobbies of Heathrow Airport. Only the way that she clutched the silk headpiece of her sari suggested that she was nervous. That and the wideness of the stunning doe-like eyes set in her exquisite almond-shaped face.

Her apprehension was understandable. Certainly the stern official at Passport Control had understood it. The poor girl had never been abroad before. Nor had she seen her husband for three years, ever since he had left his homeland to work at his brothers' restaurant in Paddington. Naturally she was concerned that he may have changed.

After a string of questions, the official's face had relaxed its hard expression and smiled reassuringly.

He watched momentarily as the tiny figure moved away, dwarfed by the impersonal immensity of the building.

His smile melted. He knew she would have been more nervous still if she had known that at that very moment the Customs rummage crews with their sniffer-dogs were going over the Air India jet with a fine tooth-comb. Every inch of both passenger compartment and luggage holds were under intense scrutiny. Even the airliner's crew were having their flight boxes examined.

He also knew there would be an extra long wait at the luggage carousel because the Customs men were also investigating all the passengers' cases in the Baggage Loading Area. Naima Balu's would be of particular interest.

As the next immigrant presented his documents for inspection, the official glanced towards the plain-clothes man standing opposite, and nodded.

It was half-an-hour later before Naima Balu finally managed to lift her large suitcase from the rubber reclaim conveyor belt onto a luggage trolley. Manfully she fought to steer it towards the 'Green' Customs clearance area for passengers who had nothing to declare.

There was a series of low inspection benches set at an angle, and a uniformed Customs officer stood behind at least half of them. Each bench seemed to beckon her. They were set in such a way that you had to deliberately walk past each in turn to reach the exit.

She began to feel sick, physically sick, as she felt the eyes of each officer on her in turn. Their faces were blank, unsmiling. Their eyes seemed to bore right inside her head until she was sure they could read her mind. Should she look at them? Smile perhaps? No, they would think her too friendly. Instead, her gaze remained frozen on the exit sign.

By now, several of her fellow passengers had been politely stopped at random. She shivered and pushed on.

'Excuse me, may I examine your case, please?'

The shock stabbed straight into her heart, and for a second she thought she would pass out.

But the young man with ginger hair was pleasant enough. He seemed only interested in her hand luggage and the thin nylon bag with its meagre contents of vanity case and paperback book took only seconds to inspect. He looked at her curiously, then nodded for her to proceed.

As she passed a large and indignant Pakistani businessman who had been stopped at the next bench, relief ebbed through her. She could feel the sweat in the small of her back, and the dull ache of fear in her kidneys.

Then suddenly it was all over. She was around the last partition and into the roped-off-area where a forest of Asians jostled for a sight of their newly arrived relatives.

She recognised no one in the sea of bobbing brown faces. Then she saw her own name. BALU. It took her by surprise. And there beneath the placard was her husband, Assal. He was smaller than she remembered, but even more handsome.

Theirs was a heartfelt but brief embrace before Naima's husband picked up her case and led her out to the waiting Maestro car in the Short Stay Car Park.

As it emerged to begin the journey to the East End of London, a red surveillance car fell into line some three vehicles behind it. At the wheel was Detective Sergeant Dick Spicer. He was accompanied by a local CID police officer and both men were netted by radio to the team of surveillance cars and crews which would take it in turn to follow the suspect vehicle.

Meanwhile, back at a small room off the Customs Hall at Heathrow, the businessman who had been stopped in front of Naima, had identified himself as Mr Yasim Shah. A cursory visual search of his luggage revealed nothing. But, due to the earlier work of the sniffer dogs behind the scenes, the Customs officials knew the search was worth pursuing. Forty minutes later, separate quantities of 92 per cent pure heroin were found ingeniously hidden in various toiletry items: hairspray, talcum powder and shampoo bottles with false compartments. Added together, the consignment amounted to just over five kilos. Its street value was some £125,000 sterling.

Ray Pilger glanced across at Fred Roxan. His arch-rival was dabbing at his bulbous nose with a frayed handkerchief as he stared absently up at some point beyond the fluorescent strip-lighting. There was no mistaking the smug satisfaction on his face.

You have the luck of the very devil, thought Pilger with grudging admiration. The Central Drug Squad boss had wanted to let both suspect couriers pass. Roxan had insisted that only one should be allowed through – he was fond of reminding the police that his role was that of protector of the public interest, not hunting criminals. It was a fine line that he trod with relish.

In addition, he'd insisted that even the one they would allow to pass – Mrs Balu – would first be searched. If drugs were found, they would have been discreetly substituted whilst the woman underwent a strip-search.

As it was, they found nothing. That meant that either the tip-off was a hoax, or the woman was carrying internally.

Pilger had prayed that Roxan would arrest the decoy. There was no way of knowing which was which, but the amount of heroin found on Yasim Shah made it a certainly he was the main carrier.

As a throwaway decoy, the chances were that Mrs Balu's London contacts would now steer well clear of her, abandoning her to her fate.

Angrily, Pilger ground out the butt of his cigar underfoot. All for bloody nothing!

Twenty-five minutes after delivering the parcel to the Libyan People's Bureau, Robson and Lewis entered the large, gloomy reception area of the Preluna Hotel on the Silema seafront.

The car-hire people had been grossly upset at the state in which their splendid Granada had been returned. However, there was little they could do but accept the unlikely explanation of how the accident had occurred, involving no other vehicle.

Lewis paid over the insurance excess cheerfully. After all he was still alive, and the product had been delivered safely. That night he knew a light aircraft would touch down at the disused wartime airfield at Ta'Qali and spirit the consignment away to Libya. In six weeks' time it would arrive in Ireland aboard a ship of the General National Maritime Company of Libya, secreted in the returning empty meat containers from Tripoli. Within a further few days, it would be back in his hands in the UK.

Sandy and Bernadette were sitting in the lobby armchairs, both wearing tracksuits.

'Hi, boys,' Bernadette called.

'You're looking athletic,' Lewis quipped. 'Been doin' a spot of weight-lifting?'

'Weight-*training*,' the Irish girl corrected. 'This place isn't so bad. There's a gym upstairs and a sauna. It's lovely.'

Lewis turned to Robson. 'Didn't tell you Bernie was a fitness freak, did I?'

Robson shook his head. 'I certainly didn't know *you* were, Sand.'

His wife looked pleased with herself. 'I took a lot of persuading, didn't I, Bern? But it wasn't too bad once I tried! Bet my muscles will ache tomorrow.'

Bernadette laughed and looked up. 'And how was your morning, boys?'

Lewis grinned. 'Eventful. Yes, Billy?'

Robson nodded. 'You could say that.'

At that moment he noticed the familiar small figure enter through the revolving glass door.

'Over here, Emy!' Sandy called aloud.

Emilea Graziani waved as she approached. Today, she wore her hair up with glasses perched on the crown of her head, Italian-style.

She smiled in greeting, but Robson could read her face instantly. Trouble.

Lewis put an arm around her waist. 'Hallo, darling, and 'ow is our little Maltesa today? Comin' with us to the Casino tonight?'

Emy wasn't completely immune to Lewis' charm, and didn't attempt to escape his grasp. 'Actually, I am not allowed to go. The Government say no Maltese.'

'Really?' Sandy was incredulous. 'Not in your own country? That's awful.'

Lewis said: 'Old Sher will be disappointed. I'm sure he'd love you, sweetheart.'

Emy frowned. 'I do not understand?'

'Sher Gallal. 'E's a chum of mine up at the Libyan Embassy. Insists we go out tonight to celebrate our new deal.'

'Sher Gallal?' Emy looked perturbed. 'I will not miss it. To meet with Libyans. I am not so keen, you know.' She turned to Robson. 'Billy, can I talk with you?'

'Sure,' he replied expansively. 'Feel free.'

'In private.' Her tone was insistent.

Sandy looked irritated, but said nothing. Robson guessed the seed that Lewis had sown about some long-ago affair was still playing on her mind.

He took Emy through to the coffee shop overlooking the promenade and ordered two cappuccinos.

As soon as the waiter was out of earshot, Emy said: 'I come as soon as I hear, Billy. What happened?'

'Heard what?'

She looked angry. 'Please don't tell me lies. In the name of Our Father, don't lie about this. It is all over Valletta.'

Robson suddenly felt cold. 'What is?'

'You and your friend Lewis went to Mellieha this morning?'

He nodded. 'You know that.'

'And this morning two men are shot dead there in the grounds of the church.'

'*What?*' He couldn't believe his ears. 'Are you *sure*?'

She stared into his eyes, desperately seeking the truth. 'I work in a Government office, Billy. We hear things first.' She reached across the table and clasped his hand. 'Billy, *you* have a gun.'

'Good God, Emy, you don't think I ... ?' He glanced around to check nobody could hear them. 'I wasn't even at the church. I waited in the car – *with* the gun.'

His mind was racing. This was suddenly developing into a nightmare. First that Citroën determined to run them off the road, and now this. Lewis had said an attempt had been made on his life. But Lewis couldn't have done it; Robson knew damned well he didn't even have a gun.

He said: 'It must have happened after we left, Emy. It was a secret deal. A transaction. There was a lot of money involved. Perhaps some local villains decided to muscle-in.'

'Villains?'

'Criminals, gangsters.'

She shrugged and didn't look at all happy. After the waiter delivered the coffees, Robson began to understand why. 'Billy, there is a friend of mine in the Nationalist Party. He is very high-up and knows what goes on in Malta. I ask him about this Libyan. This Sher Gallal.'

'That was confidential, Emy! You shouldn't have discussed it with anyone.'

Her eyes suddenly pleaded for understand and her hands twisted around his wrist in anguish. 'I have to, Billy. I am afraid for you. After I see that gun, I know something is not right. But my friend is okay, believe me. I trust him.'

Reluctantly he began to accept the situation. In a way, he was intrigued to know what she'd found out about the Libyan. 'Tell me.'

Emy stared at her coffee cup. 'My friend says Sher Gallal is no good. He has links with top ministers in the Government here and with the Soviet Embassy. He is involved with many bad things.'

'Like what?'

She shrugged. 'There is a rumour he is involved with drugs. That he brings them into Malta and distributes them. Places like Raffles' disco where the wealthy Maltese go. He does this for certain Government ministers . . .'

Robson exploded. 'For God's sake, Emy! That's a load of Nationalist political claptrap. I know the Government's dodgy, but that's ridiculous. You said yourself it's just a rumour . . .'

'I am sorry, Billy.' She looked uncomfortable. 'Maybe it is not true. My friend thinks it is so. I have to warn you.'

'Thanks,' Robson replied bitterly.

'And your friend. Frank Lewis. Maybe he does drugs deals with this man, Gallal?'

That really did it. Robson was furious but managed to contain his rage. When he spoke it was in one continuous hiss: 'Lewis is a respectable businessman. He's halfway to being a millionaire, so why in God's name should he *need* to be in drugs?'

Emy's eyes blazed back at him. 'Billy, please do not take Our Lord's name in vain.'

The meeting with Emy left Robson feeling profoundly perturbed.

He couldn't believe, and didn't want to believe, that Frank Lewis could in any way be involved with anything like drugs. It did occur to him that he hadn't actually seen inside the parcel Lewis had collected that morning. But, after all, it had been delivered to the Libyan People's Bureau. Lewis would hardly do that if he was trying to smuggle the stuff abroad. Anyway, the whole idea was preposterous.

One thought did niggle at the back of his mind, however.

Whilst that morning Lewis had been unarmed, Robson's had not been the only weapon circulated by the Libyans. There was the Skorpion, which had been left at the apartment for Lewis's mysterious acquaintance from Dublin.

When Robson re-entered the lobby of the Preluna, he found Lewis standing alone at the souvenir stand selecting some postcards.

Robson told him the news about the murders at the church. He omitted the rumours about Sher Gallal.

Lewis took the news with surprising calmness. 'That's a bit scary, Billy. Shows how lucky we were. Sounds like some sort of double-double-cross to me. Gang warfare. You know, some villain's after my money, then some other villain thinks he's got it and jumps *him*! There's no honour amongst thieves.' He held out one of the postcards. 'What d'you think of this view of the Blue Grotto? For Bernie's mum?'

'For God's sake, Frankie . . . !'

Lewis smiled reassuringly. 'Look, Billy, it was all very unfortunate. But it's nothing to do with us. And there's nothing to connect us.'

Robson said: 'We were parked outside that cop shop. It won't take a Sherlock Holmes to trace a rented car at the scene of a murder back to us. And, in case you'd forgotten, I'm still packing a big lump of hardware.'

Lewis frowned. 'But it ain't the murder weapon, old son, is it?'

Robson could hardly grasp the other man's attitude. 'I could spend months in prison while the Maltese authorities decide that. No, I'm sorry, Frankie, I'm going to take it back to the Libyans.'

Lewis blinked at the strength of Robson's outburst. Then he relaxed and grinned. 'You're right, of course. You must do what you think best. That business this morning has given me the jitters, that's all.'

Robson looked at him hard. Despite the cool reassurances, the car chase had left him with a strong and nagging suspicion that something was very wrong. But without some real evidence it was pointless to antagonise Lewis further. He tried to look confident. 'We'll just have to be extra vigilant. Okay?'

'Okay.'

Later that afternoon, Robson made his excuses to everyone and drove the Capri to the small apartment in Paceville.

It was in a dusty sidestreet no different from the many

others; straight rows of baroque façades in peach-coloured Maltese limestone, roofs topped with a myriad television aerials, like swarms of mosquitoes on sticks, and the obligatory holy shrine on each corner.

The wind had dropped and it was quite warm and still as he reached the double gate set in a high rendered wall. Apart from two mongrel dogs chasing each other in between the line of parked cars, it was deserted.

Robson put his weight against the gate. It creaked open, grating over the uneven earth of the small yard.

The motor-cycle was where he had last seen it. In the shade of the bougainvillaea climber that topped one side of the high-walled rectangle. Slowly, he went up to the machine and ran his finger over the enamel paint of the fuel tank. Spotless. Yet only the previous evening there had been a heavy rain. It had blown up from the south, laden with Sahara sand which left splotchy orange deposits over everything. It was a curse the Maltese still found hard to accept.

A dark ring of discoloured earth surrounded the motor-cycle. He picked up a handful of the stuff. Moist. Someone had doused the machine in water very recently.

He tiptoed up the steps to the balcony entrance on the first floor. The door gave at a push. Deserted. The two-room apartment was pristine, exactly as he had last seen it. Only the slightly crumpled bedspread and a few basic groceries on the kitchen table suggested that anyone had been staying there at all. No clothes, no luggage. Nothing.

Well, just one clue. At the bottom of the wardrobe was a cardboard box. Inside, Robson found the Skorpion machine-pistol.

He raised his eyebrows. Evidently it had been methodically stripped down and cleaned and oiled meticulously before being reassembled. If ever it had been fired that morning, no one would ever know.

Wrapping it carefully in its original oilskin, Robson carried it out and shut the door behind him. The sooner it was back at the Libyan People's Bureau, along with his own Tokarev pistol, the happier he would be.

After her lunchtime visit to the Preluna Hotel to warn Robson about the shoot-out at Mellieha, Emy Graziani was late back at the office.

Her boss was waiting. Their feud had dragged on for six months, ever since she had rejected his amorous advances, and warned the younger girls to do the same. Emy was not one to be intimidated by veiled threats of lost promotion chances.

He wasn't going to miss this opportunity and the argument that exploded between them echoed throughout the Department of Information building. Finally Emy stormed out and headed for home, leaving her hapless boss reeling at the tongue-lashing she had given him.

Fifteen minutes later she stepped off the snub-nosed green and white Thames single-decker at the end of her street. Already her mind was racing ahead to the inevitable interrogation she would get from her mother. The old lady would be throwing up her hands in horror at her daughter's rash behaviour. But for once Emy thought she might enjoy telling her all about it. At least it might give vent to her anger.

As she reached the little terraced house, she was surprised to find the heavy maroon-painted door ajar. In recent years, her mother had become careful to lock and bolt the house whenever she was alone. However, her forgetfulness was as frequent as her paranoia nowadays.

'Mama!' Emy shut the door and peered into the down-stairs living room. Not that she expected to find the old lady there: the next room, with its white distempered walls adorned with a giant crucifix and pictures of the Stations of the Cross, was strictly for weddings, funerals and special guests. The sideboard, chairs and table gleamed from their regular polishing.

No sound came from upstairs. Perhaps she had gone out to see a friend.

'Mama! 'Emy couldn't keep the edge of concern from her voice as she mounted the steps.

Her own room was empty except for the bed, an over-flowing wardrobe, and a small writing table. A faded picture of a smiling Billy Robson was taped in the corner of the mirror above it.

Dropping her coat on the bed, she crossed the small land-ing to the kitchen and pushed open the door.

Her white-haired mother stared at her from the armchair by the stove. Coal-black eyes gazed unflinchingly from the wrinkled walnut face. Her mouth gaped open in an expres-sion of frozen horror. She was motionless.

For one awful, heart-skidding moment, Emy thought she was dead. 'Mama!'

Then she saw the old woman blink. Her expression didn't change.

My God, thought Emy instantly, she's had a stroke.

She rushed forward, then stopped abruptly. There was something about her mother's eyes. They were trying desperately to tell her something.

'Mama, what is it?' She leaned forward.

The kitchen door slammed shut behind her. Emy started and twisted round.

Two men had been waiting behind the door. Both wore dark suits, dark ties and black leather driving gloves. They looked Italian. Or maybe Sicilian. They may have been brothers because they shared the same eyes. Black and lacklustre, like the eyes of a dead mullet on a fishmonger's marble slab.

'Miss Graziani?' one asked. His voice was oily smooth.

She was in shock. 'Yes.'

'Miss Emilea Graziani?' the other double-checked.

Suddenly her senses returned. 'Hey, who do you think you are, coming in here? You frighten my mother half to death . . .'

The black leather fist whipped across her face with a sharp crack. Her nose burned with pain. Instinctively she raised her hand to nurse it, stunned into sudden silence.

'Last week a Granada car is rented out in your name.' It was the first man again. The expression in his eyes hadn't changed.

She looked at her hand. It was wet and warm with blood. Slowly, the stuff dripped from her nose onto the soft cotton fabric of her blouse. It began forming a random pattern. Livid red star bursts.

'What do you want of me?' Her voice was a whisper.

The second man smiled. 'I think you know.' His eyes travelled across the kitchen to the old woman. She was hugging herself now, rocking gently back and forth in her chair. Her eyes were fixed at some point beyond the wall.

Emy could read the man's mind. 'What have you done to her?'

'Nothing.' A smile. 'It is what we are going to do if you do not tell us what we want to know.'

She looked again at the old woman. How she hated her. How she had often wished she was dead. Wished she was

free of her. And now, at this moment, the only thing she
wanted in the world was for Mama to be safe. Alive.

Involuntarily, two glistening salt droplets squeezed out
through the tear ducts of her eyes, and trickled very slowly
down her face.

James Robinson was trembling, physically trembling, as he
switched off the answerphone in his plush St John's Wood
flat.

His companion, Ian O'Rourke, sat in stunned silence on
the leather sofa as he nursed a drink. He was so shocked that
he couldn't bring himself to lift the glass to his lips.

At last he managed to put his thoughts into words. 'Do –
do you think it's *really* them?'

'What?' Robinson felt frightened. It was not an experience he was used to and it made him irritable.

His irritability was contagious. 'The fucken IRA. Do you
think it *is* the fucken Provos?'

Robinson turned his square chin towards the window
overlooking the park. It was rainswept, bleak and deserted.
'How the fuck should I know? You want me to play it again,
you've heard it five times . . . ?'

'Shit, no!' O'Rourke finally got the glass to his lips and
downed the neat whiskey in one. He hardly tasted it.

Robinson studied the rain trickling down the pane.
'Maybe it's someone just putting the frighteners on us.
Saying they're the Provos. Whoever the fuck they are, they
know all about us. They've got our phone number, so probably they know about this address . . .'

'Jesus.' O'Rourke felt someone walk over his grave. 'We've
certainly upset *someone*.'

The other man gave a snort of harsh laughter and turned

away from the window. 'We've upset a lot of people lately. The Turks are a mean bunch and we've been muscling in on their territory in Stoke Newington. And the Greek Cypriots in Camden, they're a heavy bunch. Not to mention those fucken Italians in King's Cross . . .'

'But how many of those speak with an Irish accent?' O'Rourke observed gloomily. He reached for the bottle.

Robinson rounded on him. 'For God's sake, Ian, leave the booze alone. We're going to have to keep a clear head. Whoever these bastards are, they mean business. If they know enough to shop Yasim Shah to the fuzz, then they know too much full stop . . .'

'We can't be sure they've shopped him.'

Robinson shook his head at his companion's naïvety. 'Well, he didn't fucken show at the rendezvous, did he? And we know he was on the fucken flight. And that message *said* they'd fucken shopped him. What more fucken proof do you want?'

Angrily, O'Rourke climbed to his feet. 'I'd like to kill the bastard that's responsible for this. But who? Who?'

'I can guess,' Robinson muttered. 'That Maltese bastard. Max. He threatened us when we smashed up his travel agency. Reckoned he had Irish friends who would sort us out. Remember?'

Realisation suddenly dawned on O'Rourke's face. 'I thought that was just big talk.' He took his place at his companion's side by the window. 'There's going to be fucken ructions in Belfast when our people find out about this. It'll be open fucken warfare.'

Robinson looked pained. What the hell did O'Rourke think had been going on between the Provos and the Protestant para-militaries since 1969?

Suddenly the telephone rang, shattering the brooding silence in the flat. Robinson hesitated for a moment, then decided to brass it out, and grabbed the handset.

It wasn't the IRA; it was 'Greasy' Harry. A nervous user-dealer who operated out of one of the bleak East End tower block districts.

'Why the hell are you phoning, Harry?' Robinson snapped angrily, cursing the earlier days of this operation when he'd trusted too many people with his telephone number. But he was stunned at what Harry told him next. 'No, you were quite right to let me know. We'll come over.' He replaced the receiver.

'What was that?' O'Rourke was anxious.

Robinson looked pale. 'I don't believe it. The stooge has turned up. The girl – what's her name? – Mrs Balu. Harry found her wandering around outside that derelict house. The address we gave her—'

'He didn't know about this . . . ?' O'Rourke protested.

The other man shook his head impatiently. 'No, but as the place is a local shooting-gallery for junkies, he thought we ought to know.'

'But for Christ's sake, Eamon, why wasn't she arrested at Heathrow after we phoned? They've let our decoy go and picked up the main courier.'

'How the fuck should I know? Maybe our Provo friends confused the issue with their tip-off. Anyway, be thankful for small mercies. At least she's carrying a quarter-kilo.'

O'Rourke shook his head vehemently. 'I don't like it. It's too risky. It smells of a set-up.'

Robinson smiled sweetly. 'We need the fucken money. We'll be careful.'

'I don't like it.'

'Then bring a fucken shooter with you.'

In the event, Robinson and O'Rourke found that it wasn't a set-up. 'Greasy' Harry had been absolutely right that there was no sign of police in the area.

Naima Balu's husband sat in his Maestro outside the derelict house while his wife went inside with Robinson. Mr Balu's mind was on how he would spend the money to save his ailing restaurant. He did not realise the indignity Naima suffered in the dilapidated lavatory as she tried to pass the three condoms filled with heroin that she had swallowed before leaving Karachi. While O'Rourke kept watch at the boarded-up window, his companion waited irritably outside the lavatory door for the massive dose of laxative to work on the unfortunate girl.

Two of the packets were retrieved when disaster struck. The final rubber sheath burst under the strain in the girl's bowel. Within minutes her heart went into spasm and she collapsed, dead from a massive overdose. It was the risk that all such couriers ran.

Robinson and O'Rourke slipped quietly out into the back-yard. There was no point in paying out the husband of the hapless girl. There was no one he could complain to without implicating himself.

As the two Ulstermen walked down the deserted wet streets to where they had left their car, there was no way they had of knowing that they were in the centre of a highly skilled, four-man surveillance 'box' backed up by two unmarked cars.

Perspiration glittered amid the blue stubble of Sher Gallal's chin as his hard black eyes followed the ball. It bounced and clattered against the spinning wheel at the roulette table.

A pink tongue darted quickly over his dry lips. His expression relaxed as the ball suddenly surrendered, plopping neatly into RED 7.

He turned and grinned widely at Robson who stood by his side. The Libyan had just played another successful *Cheval* on two adjoining numbers, giving him a return of seventeen times his original stake.

Robson had lost track of how much the Libyan had placed, lost or won. It had gone on non-stop now for three hours and the novelty was beginning to pall. He had long ago lost the two hundred Maltese pounds – worth almost double that in sterling – that Lewis had quietly passed to him as 'investment money'.

Both Sandy and Bernadette were looking decidedly bored, and even Lewis was glancing regularly at his watch. So it came as a welcome interruption when the penguin-suited doorman approached them.

'Yes?'

The man smiled an ingratiating smile. 'There is a lady to see you, sir. She says she needs to speak to you urgently. A Miss Graziani. As a Maltese she cannot come in, you understand?'

Robson's eyes lit up. He turned to the others. 'Will you excuse me for a minute?'

Sandy's eyes narrowed. 'It seems your Emy can't keep away from you.'

He pecked his wife on the cheek. 'Don't be silly, Sand. I expect it's something to do with all the arrangements she's been making.'

'I *expect* it is,' Sandy retorted bitterly. Lewis and Bernadette looked at each other and shrugged.

Robson found Emilea Graziani waiting on the verandah

between the giant Egyptian sculptures which guarded the Casino entrance. She was wearing her spring coat and a silk headscarf which threw her face into shadow.

She turned as he approached. 'Oh, Billy, thank God you are safe!'

The bright lights of the Casino fell across her face. It wasn't possible to miss the livid weal across her cheek and the patch of congealed blood beneath her nostrils. 'Emy! Have you been in an accident . . . ?'

She placed her hand on his forearm. 'No, Billy, it is not an accident. Listen to me. I get a visit from some men. Sicilians, I think. They want to know all about you and your friend Lewis.'

An icy chill ran down Robson's spine. 'A visit? At work?'

'At home. They threaten to beat up Mama.'

'Jesus.'

Emy's smoky eyes were wide with fear. 'First they punch me and knock me around, you know. Then they say where do you stay? Who are you?'

He hugged her to him, feeling her small body trembling against his. 'I'm sorry, Emy. I wouldn't have got you involved in this for the world.'

She pulled away, and looked up into his eyes beseechingly. 'What are you mixed up with, Billy? These men, they are evil. Really bad.'

The doorman was watching the couple with increasing interest. Robson took her by the arm. 'That guy's got big ears, Emy. Let's go down by the cars.'

She was unsteady on her feet as they descended the steps to the cars parked by the low balustrade overlooking St George's Bay. A perfect silver crescent from the moon floated on the oily black water. A breath of wind rustled the fronds of the yew trees that edged the car park.

He could sense her relaxing. 'What did you tell them, Emy?'

'Actually, I tell them you stay at the Hilton, but already they know you must be stopping somewhere else. I say I don't know. Then they threaten to pour scalding water from the kettle on Mama ...' He squeezed her tight again as he felt the pain in her words. 'So I tell them the Preluna. Oh, God, I am sorry, Billy ...' Her words broke up, swamped beneath a wracking sob that she could no longer hold back.

At last she regained her composure. 'When they go, I leave straightaway to warn you. I go to the Preluna. In there I see them again, but they do not see me. Then I remember today you say you will go to the Casino.'

This sounded bad. Robson recalled Lewis making enquiries about the Casino at reception before they left. The men who threatened to torture Emy's mother could already be on their way.

At that moment his eyes caught the twin beams of a car's headlights as it swung in through the distant entrance arch to the grounds. The light shafts straightened, illuminating the front of the Casino as the car began down the long, straight drive.

'Quick!' he hissed. 'We've got to warn Frankie and the others.' The Casino was at the end of a narrow isthmus that jutted into the Mediterranean. There was no escape from it excepting a very long swim.

Emy followed, panic suddenly returning. 'You think that car . ?'

'Maybe.' Already he was several paces ahead and nearing the steps as Lewis, Bernadette and Sandy appeared on the verandah.

Lewis laughed as Robson emerged from the shadows. 'Hey, my good man! Be so good as to fetch the motor, will you?'

Robson pounded up the steps. 'Frankie, we've got trouble!'

'I say!' Lewis continued his mock charade, encouraged by the obvious amusement of Sandy and Bernadette. 'That's no way for the chauffeur to talk . . .'

'Frankie!' Robson yelled. He was aware of the car's headlights drawing closer. The Casino's white façade began to gleam with growing intensity. He could hear wheels crunching on gravel.

It suddenly dawned on Lewis that Robson was not skylarking.

'Emy's had visitors,' Robson explained briefly. Lewis glanced down at the girl. His eyes registered the cuts and dried blood.

'They are after you, Mr Lewis,' she confirmed.

Robson glanced over his shoulder at the car. It had stopped, just fifty feet away. The brilliance of its headlights on full beam was blinding. Instinctively Robson no longer had any doubts about the identity of the new arrivals.

He began to shout a warning, but the words were shattered by the sudden stammering of an automatic weapon. An unseen force tore away at the stucco rendering of the Casino as a hail of bullets swept across the verandah. Robson dived up the steps, grabbing his wife by the ankles and toppling her into the cover of the balustrade. Chunks of plaster and shattered glass rained down on them.

Keeping his buttocks low, he snaked across to where Sandy crouched beside Lewis and Bernadette, all of them open-mouthed with shock.

'Billy, what's happening?' Sandy screamed.

He shook his head; he could think of nothing sensible to say.

Then another horror dawned on him. Emy wasn't here. She'd been behind him on the steps. He turned in panic, not believing what he saw. The body in the grey spring coat lay sprawled on the steps. Motionless.

'Emy?' he yelled above the crash of gunfire.

No response.

He edged forward from behind the balustrade and stretched out his arm until his fingertips reached hers. They felt cold to his touch. Tightening his grip on her hand, he pulled until his muscles screamed. Very gradually he managed to drag Emy's body out of the line-of-fire.

'Is she all right?' Sandy asked.

He didn't reply. Instead he turned Emy over in his arms. Her eyes were half-open and her breathing was shallow.

'I think I am,' she murmured.

Robson shook his head in disbelief. There was no sign of blood or any entry wound. 'Where, Emy? For Christ's sake, where?'

But before she could reply the crack of gunfire renewed with vigour.

Suddenly someone came rushing out of the Casino and crashed frantically through the debris of masonry and smashed glass. The man came skidding to a halt by Robson's side.

He could scarcely believe his eyes. 'Shard?'

The ex-Marine smiled without humour. 'The very same.' As he spoke, he drew a Browning automatic from a holster beneath his dinner jacket. Gripping the butt firmly in both hands, he steadied his aim and squeezed the trigger. Instantly one of the car's headlghts shattered. Calmly, Shard shifted his aim. Again he squeezed the trigger.

Immediately the front of the Casino was plunged into darkness as the bullet found its mark in the second head-lamp. The shooting stopped abruptly.

Shard grunted with satisfaction. 'That should give the buggers something to think about. Should be able to see them now.'

The relief sounded in Robson's voice. 'Am I glad to see you. My friend's been hit.'

'Is she bad?' Shard replied absently as his eyes scoured the darkness for a sign of movement.

'I don't know. She doesn't look too brilliant.'

Shard nodded grimly. 'Right. I'll take a look. First let's give these bastards something to think about. Mind your ears.'

He lifted the automatic and fired around the outline of the car four times in rapid succession. In the confinement of the terrace, the detonations were deafening. As the sound rang in everyone's ears there was a sudden scurry of activity down at the car park. An urgent shuffling of shoes on gravel was followed by the harsh thud of slamming doors.

The engine revved and the clutch shrieked as someone jammed the gear into reverse and stamped on the accelerator. In a series of jagged movements, the car completed a rapid three-point turn, then raced blindly towards the drive. There was a *crump* of metal and glass as the front wing struck a parked BMW before groping its way into the night.

With the danger past, the terrace was suddenly filled as onlookers crowded out of the Casino. Voices rose in excited chatter as they formed a circle around the wounded girl, and the two men tending her.

Robson said irritably: 'Will someone get me something to use as a pillow!'

Sandy immediately took the cardigan she was using as a shawl and wrapped it up to form a soft cushion.

'I'll see if I can get an ambulance,' Bernadette offered and disappeared into the throng of onlookers.

Seconds later, Shard discovered the bullet entry hole to the left of Emy's navel. He shook his head slowly.

'Will she live?' Robson asked.

Shard ignored the question. 'How's her pulse?'

Robson sighed. 'There isn't one to speak of. It's so weak I can hardly count. Maybe fifty.'

'Internal bleeding,' Shard muttered, mostly to himself. 'You can't tell how bad. This needs surgery.'

Robson said: 'Thank God you were here. Otherwise we might all be like this.'

The other man stared at him. 'I was discreetly minding a friend of your chum – Sher Gallal – who's been gambling away Libya's oil wealth as fast as he can. I seem to remember telling you to keep away from them.'

Robson went to speak, but decided against it. He still couldn't think what could have led to all this.

'Sure, the ambulance is on its way,' Bernadette announced as she returned from the Casino.

But when it arrived ten minutes later, Emilea Graziani was already dead.

The flight back to Britain was the most miserable journey Billy Robson could ever recall having made. He had to make a determined effort not to peer across the Luqa Airport tarmac to the terminal building. In the past Emy would always have been up on the crowded balcony, waving tearfully. If he looked now, he knew he would see her.

He shivered. It was an eternity before the aircraft completed its interminable taxi-ing and finally got airborne. When it did Robson knew he would never return again to Malta's tiny, magical and isolated world.

Next to him Sandy was still in a state of shock after Emy's death. Jittery and irritable, she spent the entire trip flicking through the in-flight magazine, but clearly didn't absorb a word of it.

Across the aisle Frank Lewis was a chastened man. Pale and grim-faced, he stared ahead, deep in thought. After Emy's death he had been visibly shaken and upset. More than any of his reassurances it was that which finally convinced Robson that they'd become innocently caught up in some feud that was none of their making.

Only Bernadette bore any resemblance to her normal self, but even she avoided Robson's eyes. Yet when their glances did meet, he could sense her sympathy. Somehow he felt that she was the only one who knew how things had really been between him and Emy.

But he was wrong. Whilst Bernadette could only guess at what had gone on before, Sandy *knew*. She had known from the very first moment she had set eyes on Emy Graziani and seen the expression on her husband's face when he looked at her.

Sandy was sure that Emy had sensed her growing jealousy and anger. That was why she had made fewer appearances the longer they had been in Malta.

And when Emy Graziani had died, Sandy had felt a massive sense of relief, as though some great burden had been lifted from her shoulders. That was until she looked into Billy's eyes. Then she knew that, even in death, Emy was closer to her husband than she would ever be.

The night after the killing Sandy had made her excuses to go out for a long walk. Robson had been very understanding. He assumed she wanted some time alone after the lengthy interview sessions with the Maltese police. He didn't even begin to guess at his wife's real motive.

Like a dog with a scent she had tracked down the place to go without difficulty. You can place a drug-addict in any city on God's earth and he or she will be drawn inexorably to the dealers' haunts. In the same way that an African deer will smell water across miles of parched savannah. An hour after leaving the hotel Sandy had wandered into the Raffles nightspot. Within another fifteen minutes she was shooting up in the ladies' lavatory with a borrowed syringe.

Ten

By the time they reached Heathrow their mood had lightened a little. The past was the past. Nevertheless the optimistic tone of their small talk had a distinctly forced ring to it.

There was a Daimler to meet them. It was driven by a tall, thin Rhodesian in his early forties.

'This is Blair Wallace,' Lewis introduced. 'He's my right-hand man. You'll be working a lot together in the future, Billy.'

The man's eyes were dark brown, and wary. As he shook Robson's hand, his grip lacked enthusiasm and the twist of a grin in the tanned face looked less than genuine.

'How's everything been while I was away, Blair?' Lewis asked.

Wallace glanced again at the strangers. 'It's okay, Frankie. Nothin' I couldn't handle. The Persian consignment's on schedule. Be in Holland in a couple of days.'

Lewis nodded. It was the first really good news he'd had all week. 'That'll be part of your remit, Billy, when you join us. Keeping tabs on transport.'

'I can't wait.' Robson grinned. He meant it.

'Then why should you.' Lewis laughed. 'Come to the office tomorrow morning. Nine sharp. You've got the address of our warehouse and office down in Deptford? Blair here will show you the ropes.'

The expression in the Rhodesian's face suggested that the only rope he'd like to show Robson would be noose-shaped. He was obviously not a man who took easily to strangers.

The next day, however, Robson was to find other members of Frank Lewis's staff far more congenial.

'Ali here is our financial wizard,' Lewis said.

The small shirt-sleeved Pakistani looked up from the calculator which was half-hidden beneath a sea of invoices, credit notes and dispatch documents. His bright black pupils shone with pleasure as he swept his chair backwards and sprang respectfully to his feet.

'Ali, this is Mr Robson whom I was telling you about,' Lewis introduced.

'Call me Billy.'

Ali's handshake was vigorous and warm. 'I am most pleased to be having you aboard, Mr Robson. You can see that our boss here runs a very tight ship. He treats us all very well, but he is also making us work extremely hard. Another pair of hands is most welcoming.'

Lewis laughed. 'There, Billy, can't say you haven't been warned. The work's hard and long hours, but I pay well. You can see Ali here thrives on it.'

The Pakistani grinned his confirmation. Robson smiled back. 'I'm not afraid of work.'

Lewis' eyes hardened a little. 'If I thought you were, you wouldn't be here.' He turned back to his financial wizard. 'Ali, I've told you all about our plans. Billy will be looking after all our transport arrangements on the international front. His job will be to keep all our imports and exports on the move, deal with all the documenta-tion, and generally iron out all the wrinkles. If something goes astray or doesn't arrive on time, it'll be his head on the block.'

Robson shifted uncomfortably; he just hoped he wasn't taking on more than he could handle.

However Lewis's next words helped to allay his fears. 'He's new to the transport business, but he's a fast learner. In the first month or so he'll need all the help you can give, Ali. Gradually pass your workload over to him and let him take up the reins.'

In the corner the Telex machine began chattering fiercely.

'I understand,' Ali said.

'Good,' Lewis replied. 'Then let's start as we intend to continue. First, Ali, get onto our accountant and get ourselves a nice little off-the-shelf company with a suitable name. The directors will be one Mr Robson, yourself and Blair. I'll hold 60 per cent, and everyone else 10 per cent. Then arrange for a bank facility.'

'For how much?' Ali asked.

Lewis turned to Robson. 'What d'you think?'

'I've done a few calculations. Probably a good fifteen thousand.'

For a moment Lewis considered the matter. 'Make it twenty-five thousand, no thirty. No point in strapping yourself with a cash-flow problem. Transfer the funds across from the building company. That'll give us additional buying power to fill up on any empty return trips.'

Robson was getting lost. 'How does that work?'

Lewis smiled. 'This new company's job will be to hire and organise transport for my other companies, especially catering. Mostly we use owner-drivers with their own container rigs. They're more reliable and have got an incentive to deliver on time. They charge around a grand for an average twelve-day trip. But each trip is two-way. So if we haven't got goods lined up for the return trip, you'll have to find your own cargo. Sometimes you'll find someone who's got produce to move. On other occasions you'll have to buy locally on your own behalf and then sell at the end of the round-trip to cover your expenses.'

Ali intervened. 'Like most of our business is taking Moslem halal meat out of Ireland to the Middle East or Asia. Like the one consignment we are having on the road back from Iran now. He took out meat but is returning with figs. These I sell off at Vienna which is being a main interchange point. He then picks up a cargo of cheeses for delivery to the big cheese markets in Holland. So for the last leg returning to Dublin our load is empty. In this case we will be buying frozen fish seconds in Grimsby and taking them across to Ireland. Fish is selling well there. Always the Irish are eating fish on Fridays.'

Robson nodded. 'I follow. But it sounds very complex.'

Ali laughed. 'You will be juggling with cargoes like I am juggling with figures on the balance sheet. But we have lists of all contacts, buyers and sellers in every country. So you are just picking up the telephone.'

At that moment the glass door of the partitioned office burst open as though a minor tornado had struck.

'Please, Max!' All heads turned at Bernadette's plea.

It took an instant for Robson to place the stout, middle-aged man with the tortoiseshell spectacles. The blue jowls were lightly pinked with anger.

If Maltese Max from Medtravel recognised Robson he showed no sign. All his attention was focused on Frank Lewis. 'I *need* to speak with you!'

Behind him Bernadette shrugged her shoulders beneath a blouse of fine pink shot silk. 'I'm sorry, Frankie . . .'

Lewis hid his irritation well. 'That's okay, love. It's always a pleasure to see Max.'

The Maltese snorted like a horse winded after a stee-plechase. 'You wouldn't think so. According to your switch-board you're always out. Never do return my calls.'

Lewis' smile was as disarming as always. 'I've been away in Malta, or had you forgotten?'

Max grunted and straightened his suit, his composure returning. 'I wouldn't normally come here . . .'

'I do remember our agreement . . .'

'It's those Irishmen again,' he said emphatically. 'The ones from Ulster.'

'Steps have been taken,' Lewis returned sharply. 'I got your message before I left for Malta. I'm sorry I didn't have time to get back to you. But I had words with Dublin. You'll get no more trouble.'

Max stood his ground. 'I've *had* more trouble. Whatever steps your people took, it just upset those Ulster bastards more. I got a phone call.'

'When?'

'Two hours ago. Take their product or I'm in big trouble.'

'Shit!' Lewis cursed beneath his breath. Then he glanced at Robson and grinned uneasily. 'A small distribution prob-lem, Billy. Nothing to concern you. Why don't you let Bernie finish showing you around.'

'Grand,' Bernadette replied. 'It'll be a pleasure.'

Robson moved to follow her.

'And tell him about the new plan, love, eh?'

'I'll do that.'

She closed the door and the heated conversation that ensued between Lewis and Maltese Max was reduced to a muted mumble.

'What was all that about?' Robson asked as he followed her along the upper level walkway of the warehouse.

She turned to look at him. 'I don't know, Billy. I'm a part-ner in this business and sort of company secretary cum Girl Friday to Frankie, but he doesn't tell me everything. He's always got a dozen deals on the go, plus another one or two he doesn't talk about.'

Her words made Robson nervous. 'You mean it's not all legit?'

She laughed; a musical sound. 'Frankie's an East Ender, born and bred. Sure, his dad was involved in the black market during and after the war, and all his brothers have done time. But nothing serious. They're all good people, it's just their way of life.' The single dimple deepened to create that irre-sistible lop-sided smile. 'Like them, Frankie can't resist a good deal. I don't know but I suspect one or two might stray over the border of what's legal and what isn't quite.'

Robson understood exactly what she meant. He had spent his entire upbringing in that environment. Some of his playmates at school had been the children of local, mostly small-time, villains. Afterwards, most of his friends had had something going on the side, like Andy. Few reached their twenties without a short spell inside or in reform school. None could resist the temptation of a good racket or goods offered secretly at knock-down prices.

With such a background he could feel no moral indigna-tion about it. It was their way of life. He had just wanted no part of it. Even as a youth he'd realised how easy it was to blur the distinction between a bit of shady dealing and real crime. Looking back he was only thankful that he'd joined the Marine Corps and left it all behind him.

Or so, he'd thought bitterly, he'd believed at the time.

'You're worried about your probation.' It was a state-ment, not a question, and as Bernadette said it she touched him reassuringly on the forearm. 'I can understand that after Malta. But don't worry. I've never known Frankie do anything that would get others into trouble. Never. Besides, he's got a genuine thriving business empire. Building, decorating, contract cleaning, catering . . . he doesn't need it. He and Max go back a long way. Frankie's probably doing him a favour. That would be typical.'

'Where did you meet Frankie?'

She looked surprised. 'In London. About five years ago. It was at one of those frightfully boring international trade food fairs. I was on the Irish stand with my brothers. They were looking for export markets for their meat products and Frankie was looking for a good business opportunity. They got on like a house on fire from the start.'

'And you?'

The yellow flecks in her green eyes glowed like tiny flames. 'We happened a little bit later.'

Suddenly Robson said: 'It's nearly one. Would Frankie mind if I took you to the pub for lunch?'

She laughed. 'Don't you mean would *I* mind?'

Her good humour was infectious. 'And would you?'

'Not at all. I can tell you about Frankie's new idea.' Then she tilted her head mischievously to one side. 'There's just one snag?'

'Yes?'

Bernadette glanced down at his feet. 'Luckily you're wearing trainers.'

The snag was that to spend a lunchtime with Bernadette meant jogging with her to the pub.

It came home to Robson with the force of a sledgehammer just how out of condition he was.

'I don't give much for Frankie's chances with you as his

minder, Billy.' She seemed to think it was all very amusing, as he bought her a gin and slimline tonic from the bar.

She frowned at the lager he gulped with relish. 'You should try a dry white wine. Or at least cider, it's half the calories.'

He laughed. 'You sound like my old Mum.'

'And I don't suppose you listened to her either.'

'Not really. I always had a stubborn streak. She didn't like the idea of me joining the Marines, but I went ahead anyway. Best decision I ever made.'

Although Bernadette smiled, he noticed that her eyes had little humour. 'I bet you looked good in uniform.'

'You don't approve?' he guessed.

'I wouldn't say that, Billy. It's just that my views, such as they are, are a little coloured. I come from a staunch Republican background. And we get fed a lot of horror stories from the North. Marines in riot gear banging their shields and marching in phalanxes like conquerors.'

'They stopped us doing that,' he told her. 'But it *did* work. Defeated the enemy psychologically.'

Her eyes narrowed. 'Is that how you see the Irish, Billy? The enemy?'

'No, of course not. But I've seen too much. Witnessed too many things. Let's just say I'm cautious. It's instinctive.'

'I'm pleased to hear it.' Her laugh was light. 'Because Frankie has a trip lined up.'

'For me?'

'The three of us,' she replied. 'That's the new plan he mentioned. He wants to bring in cattle-heads from Ireland. They're cheap, you see, but there's a good mark-up.'

Robson pulled a face, and she laughed again. 'What do you think they put in your sausages and burgers, Billy? It may be pure beef, but it sure isn't rump steak.'

It had never occurred to him before. 'I can see I've a lot to learn. When do we go?'

'Frankie says tomorrow.'

Robson shook his head slowly in amazement. 'Frankie doesn't believe in letting the grass grow, does he?'

Again that laugh. 'It's part of his charm. Now tell me, are you ready for the return run? There's a lot to do this afternoon.'

The bastard.

Sandy had scarcely heard what Andy Sutcliff was saying. Instead, she was glaring at Robson's photographs on the sideboard.

'You haven't listened to a word, Sand!'

'What?' She looked back at the irrepressible grin showing through the untidy beard.

Half-heartedly she returned the smile. 'Sorry, Andy, I'm still mad at Billy. We're back just one day and he's off again.'

Sutcliff tried to show sympathy that he didn't really feel. 'But it's a job, Sand. That's good news. Great! I was sure I'd find him here as well. Under those circumstances, I'm glad I haven't.'

Sandy wrung her hands together morosely. 'At this rate I'd have seen more of him when he was inside.'

'You have just spent a week together on holiday,' he pointed out.

'Huh!' she snorted. 'Holiday? A week with Frankie Lewis and that snotty girlfriend of his. Not to mention Billy's old flame.'

Sutcliff frowned. 'Old flame? In Malta?'

'Yes,' Sandy snarled. 'In bloody Malta. And don't tell me you don't know about her. I can't believe he never boasted about her to you.'

He shrugged. 'Never. Billy's always kept his own counsel, you know.'

'Well, it doesn't matter now anyway. She's dead.'

'Dead?'

Sandy stood up suddenly, clutching at her arms in an irritable huddle. 'You sound like a parrot. Yes, dead. There was this shoot-out. It was like something out of a western on TV. Some sort of gangsters, local Mafia – I don't know.'

Sutcliff didn't know how to take it. 'Was this anything to do with Billy? Or Frankie Lewis?'

She stared out of the window at an East End bathed in cool early spring sunshine. 'I don't know. No, not directly. Something to do with the Libyans. The people Lewis was dealing with. Apparently it was all a terrible mistake.'

'Sounds like it.' Sutcliff's eyes followed her as she began pacing the room. 'Was there any trouble with the police?'

Sandy shook her head. 'No. Everyone just said they knew nothing about it. Billy and Frankie just said we were on holiday. Told us girls to say the same. Finally the police accepted we were innocently caught up in events.'

'And the Libyans?'

'We said they were just casual friends we met in the Casino where it happened.'

'Jesus,' Sutcliff muttered and stared at the carpet. Something about the whole business didn't ring true. Suddenly he felt afraid for Robson, afraid of what his friend might be getting into.

'Andy?'

He looked up, aware that the tone of her voice had changed. 'What is it, Sand?'

She was smiling weakly. 'You couldn't lend me a couple of quid till the end of the week, could you?'

Instinctively he reached for his pocket. 'Sure.' And stopped. His eyes narrowed. 'What d'you mean, a couple?'

She shrugged. 'Well, say fifty . . .'

Sutcliff's eyes widened in sudden realisation. He should have been expecting it, but somehow it caught him off guard. 'Sand! For Christ's sake, you're not bloody back on smack—'

'NO!' she screamed back at him with a vehemence that jolted him. Momentarily, she shut her eyes and drew a deep breath. 'I'm sorry, Andy. No, I'm just a bit short, that's all.'

Slowly Sutcliff stood up and drew himself to his full height. 'You are a lying bloody – bloody stupid cow. What do you take me for? My business is down the drain thanks to you. Or my stupidity in feeding your bloody habit. I'm being taken to the cleaners by the tax and bloody VAT people. And you have the nerve to stand there and . . .' He blinked. 'Sand, what the hell are you doing?'

For a second he couldn't believe his eyes. He stood, stunned, as her fingers moved down the buttons of her blouse, plucking each one in turn. Roughly she pulled the material from the waistband of her skirt. She wore no brassiere. The sudden sight of her ivory white breasts in contrast to the dark aureolae of her nipples mesmerised him.

'I need you, Andy,' she said hoarsely. 'And I need that fifty quid.'

The sound of the slap as he drew his hand across her cheek was like a rifle shot. He couldn't bring himself to speak at first as she shrank from him, clutching the edges of her blouse together. At last he fumbled for words. 'Don't you *ever* do that to me, Sand! Not ever!'

'I'm sorry.' Her voice was a whisper as she averted her eyes.

'I've always cared for you, Sand. Always. But it was wrong we went so far. But we couldn't help ourselves. Now Billy's back and it's over. We agreed.'

She nodded in silence.

The doorbell rang. Sandy started in alarm.

'Don't panic,' Sutcliff said evenly. 'Just do yourself up. I'm leaving.'

He helped her as she fumbled with the buttons. 'I'm all to pieces,' she said, shaking.

'Don't be.' He kissed her quickly on the forehead. 'I'm not going to say anything to anyone. Just leave that filthy stuff alone from now on. Promise?'

She pulled a tight smile and nodded, as he started towards the front door.

Bella was standing outside. Her black blouse and slacks emphasising the deathly pallor of her skin.

As Sutcliff left, she stepped in. 'Hi, Sand, I thought you were back. How was Malta?'

Sandy let her in and closed the door. 'I don't want to talk about it.'

'I see. Like that was it?'

Bella's friend didn't respond; she evidently had something on her mind.

Suddenly Sandy came to a decision. 'That club of yours, what do they pay?'

Bella was surprised. 'That depends on what you do. Or rather what you let them do. From a hundred quid a night to about four for the really heavy stuff. But I wouldn't recommend that.'

Sandy swallowed hard, trying not to let her imagination have any rein. The mere thoughts of the business turned her stomach. 'Are you sure they'd have me?'

Bella smiled. 'I can't see why not, but you'd have to meet the boss. It would be his decision, nothing to do with me.'

For a second, Sandy closed her eyes and took a deep breath. 'Can you fix for me to see him?'

Bella raised a finely drawn eyebrow, and nodded. 'I can do that, sure. When?'

'As soon as possible. Today or tomorrow.'

A knowing smile crept over Bella's face. 'You mean before you get cold feet and change your mind?'

'No. Before I start another cold turkey.'

As Robson stepped onto the busy concourse at Dublin Airport with Frank Lewis and Bernadette, the place seemed different to how he remembered.

His one and only previous visit had been years before when he'd been serving in the Marines. He and an oppo had wanted to see if there was another side to Ireland. But at the height of the troubles, and with both sporting short military haircuts and moustaches, their welcome had been less than warm.

But this time he'd noticed no one staring at the sound of their English accents as they looked around for Bernadette's brothers. No one eyed him with hostility. Perhaps it was because he wore his hair slightly longer nowadays. But, he reasoned, it was more likely that his own perception had changed. A lot of water had passed under the bridge since his last visit.

Bernadette gave a sudden squeal of delight. 'If that's not yer man! Would you ever look at that motor car!'

They followed the line of her pointing finger, past the security check on the one open door, to a gleaming stretched Mercedes that was drawing up outside.

'That must be their new "Florida",' Lewis observed. Robson couldn't be sure if it was disapproval or envy in the tone.

Dermot Mulqueen stood six-foot-three in his scuffed Church brogues. The silver-blue two-piece suit had obviously been made expensively to measure. But with the Irishman's gangling body, overlong arms and permanent stoop, it would have looked better on a scarecrow.

A charmingly boyish grin beamed from the unattended blue stubble as his eyes settled on his sister.

Dermot Mulqueen scooped Bernadette in his arms and spun her round in a clumsy circle. One of her shoes went spinning into the gutter.

''Tis grand t'see you, sis! Real grand!'

'Fine words, dear brother,' Bernadette replied as she regained her balance. 'But you haven't even managed a haircut in my honour.'

Dermot roared at his sister's reproach. 'Ah, my sweet colleen, some things never change!' He turned to Lewis. 'Hasn't she been the bane of my life since we were wee nippers together? Tellin' me Mam when Padraig and I take a day off school t'go fishin'. Or when she saw us smokin' behind the bicycle sheds.'

'Padraig's the other brother,' Lewis explained to Robson. 'Used to be inseparable – like twins, I'm told.'

'And always up to mischief. The diabolical duo,' Bernadette added. 'If it hadn't been for their kid sister, sure both of them would have ended up in reform school, or worse.'

Dermot looked pleadingly at Robson. 'Now d'ya see what I mean?'

'This is Robson,' Bernadette introduced. 'Billy Robson.'

Again the slightly crooked teeth grinned through the stubble as he grasped Robson's hand. 'Ah, sure we've heard all about you from Frankie here, sir. Singing your praises he was. So welcome aboard, I'm sure we can do a lot of good business.'

Robson smiled, trying to gauge the sincerity of the Irishman's welcome.

'Thanks, I hope so.'

Frank Lewis was getting impatient. 'So, where *is* this inseparable brother of yours, Dermot?'

'Ah, well you see, we got separated! He was planning to meet me here, but your consignment from Iran was late. Seems they got a puncture just after leavin' the Dublin docks. So Padraig decided to hang on at the works for it to arrive.'

'The abattoir?' Robson asked.

Perhaps it was his imagination, but Dermot's expression appeared momentarily frosty. 'Sure, Mr Robson, at the abattoir.'

Robson turned up the warmth of his smile. 'Billy. Please call me Billy.'

'So what's the plan?' Lewis asked.

'Well, we've booked you into the Burlington. Padraig thought you'd prefer the high life of Leeson Street to the village pub at Roscrea.'

Bernadette frowned lightly. 'Sometimes, Dermot, I think you know more about my man than I do. All his dark secrets.'

Her brother chortled.

'I'd like to examine the shipment,' Lewis said sharply. 'As soon as possible.'

Dermot nodded. 'Padraig said you would. So we'll be getting you booked in at the Burlington, then go on to the works. Then back tonight, because there's a reception we're all going to.'

'What's that?' Bernadette asked.

'Sure, it's t'celebrate the openin' of a new canning factory. Sort o' publicity party. You know, business acquaintances and the press. There'll be a lot of important people there. Some society people and Government officials.'

'Sounds very boring,' Bernadette observed. 'Will we know anyone?'

'Sure! Yer man is Eamon Molloy. It's his factory and we'll be supplyin' him with meat products for his cans.'

Bernadette wrinkled her nose in distaste. 'That lecherous old slob isn't *actually* a *friend* of mine, Dermot.'

'But he *is* good for business,' Lewis replied, giving her a consoling hug. 'You only have to make a couple of polite noises, then move on. Circulate. I'll do the rest.'

Dermot grinned; all seemed satisfactory. 'We'd better go. There's a policeman on his way and we're not supposed to park here.'

'We'll drop Bernie and Billy off at the Burlington,' Lewis added, 'and I'll come on to the works with you.'

'Frankie!' Bernadette protested. 'I'd like to come too. We are supposed to be partners.'

'Yes, I know, love. But it's a long drive there and back. Tiring. And you'll want to be fresh for tonight.'

'But . . .'

'No buts, Bernie.' Lewis was adamant. Then, suddenly aware that he was sounding unreasonable, he added: 'Hey, Dermot, isn't there a meeting at Leopardstown this afternoon?'

The Irishman finished stowing their luggage in the boot. 'I believe so.'

'There you are, Bernie. Why don't you let Billy take you to the races. And you can show him what the Irish are really like.'

So Leopardstown it was. Several hours passed like only minutes in the crisp afternoon sunshine as Robson and Bernadette argued and laughed, in turns, as they decided how best to invest the three hundred punts Frank Lewis had casually handed them before leaving with Dermot Mulqueen.

After a couple of losing races, they hit a winning streak and were soon caught up in the good-humoured fervour of the crowd. Without realising it, Robson found himself forgetting the trauma of recent events. Over lunch they ate little and talked a lot and drank too much.

He began to feel that he had known her for years. Over a second bottle of wine she began asking him about his days in the Marines. Warming to his subject, Robson recounted almost-forgotten adventures and a host of amusing misadventures. Bernadette laughed easily and warmly, eager to know more.

Robson slowly realised that he hadn't talked like this for years. It occurred to him that Sandy had soon become bored with his tales when he returned from a tour. Naturally perhaps, she was more interested in the day-to-day tribulations of running the house and bringing up young Dan.

The last person he had known who wanted to know every facet about him and his life had been Emy. It was curious that things about him that Sandy hated, Emy had found endearing. Habits and mannerisms, the way he said things. At home, he was often quiet and introspective; in Malta, Emy had somehow drawn him out.

As he and Bernadette waited for the start of another race, she said quietly: 'Billy, do you mind if I ask you a question?'

'Go ahead.'

'It's a bit personal.'

He smiled. 'That's all right.'

Bernadette tossed her chestnut hair as she turned her head to look out across the swathe of emerald green turf. 'It's about Sandy.'

Irrationally, he resented his wife being brought into the conversation. It was as though the very mention of her name might break this carefree spell. But he said nothing.

Bernadette's green eyes narrowed as she frowned at the horses gathering farther down the track, their coats gleaming in the sun. The air smelled sweet with grass. 'I can't be sure, but I don't think Sandy is very well.'

Robson's eyes followed Bernadette's to the start line. 'You're right. Sand's been under a lot of strain. Largely due to me. You know I did a stretch inside?'

She didn't answer.

He smiled knowingly. 'Of course, silly of me. If you hadn't known, you'd have asked me what I did after I left the Corps.'

She turned back to face him. 'I wanted to know, Billy. But I didn't want to cause you any pain. Any more hurt. Frankie said you'd done five years. He didn't say what for, but for five, it must have been serious.'

'Bank robbery,' he said evenly. 'Getaway driver.'

'Oh.'

'Now you can see why Sand's a bit – a bit . . . Well, been living on her nerves.' He couldn't bring himself to look the Irish girl in the eyes.

He felt her hand touch his wrist; her fingertips were soft,

warm. 'Billy, I don't think it's just that. I don't know. I can't be sure.'

'What do you mean?' Bernadette looked awkward, her lop-sided smile uneasy. 'I've a nephew who lives in the large Dublin housing estate called St Theresa's Gardens. It's a pretty dilapidated place down there, and there's a big drugs problem. Heroin mostly, I think. Anyway, he got himself hooked on the stuff . . .' Her words trailed off as she tried to find a way of saying what was on her mind.

'You're not suggesting that Sand—'

'No, no, Billy! Nothing like that. It's just that Sandy's behaviour in Malta just – well, I suppose it reminded me of my nephew. You know, the erratic behaviour, irritability . . . I hope you don't mind me saying?'

He stared at her in disbelief. The very thought of it horrified him. Sandy on drugs? Well, it was possible the medication she was on might be making her drowsy, lethargic even. But what Bernadette was implying was unthinkable. She had stuck by him all through his time in the Marines, although she hadn't enjoyed the life. And when he was in prison she'd been a tower of strength to him. No way would she have gone through all that just to give in to something as stupid as that. Not Sandy.

He said: 'She's suffering the after-effects of glandular fever. Maybe the pills she's on are pulling her down.'

Bernadette looked sympathetic. 'I think that's possible.'

Robson looked back up the track. 'Under starter's orders,' he observed. Then, after a moment's hesitation, he added: 'I'll get her to visit the doc's again when I get back. Or have a word with him myself. See if he can't start to reduce whatever it is she's on.'

Again she touched his arm. 'I'm sorry I mentioned it.'

So am I, he thought. So am I.

And, even though their horse romped home by a head, the afternoon's magic spell was broken.

Royce carefully placed his feet on the edge of the desk and adjusted the knife crease in the trousers of his cream suit. Then he lay back in the padded leather swivel chair.

He was disturbingly handsome in his way. Probably in his mid-thirties. Long black hair slicked straight back from the steep brow of a strong Latin face. His nose was thin and slightly hooked, his clean-shaven chin jutting as he silently appraised the girl who stood before him.

Sandy shifted uncomfortably. She was already regretting having worn the unfashionably long pleated skirt and simple pink sweater. It was hardly likely to impress under the circumstances. Maybe, she wondered, it had been a last-minute act of reluctance. Perhaps she had even hoped that it would persuade Bella's boss that she wasn't suitable. A hopeless case.

Her eyes flickered nervously sideways to where Bella stood. That was the sort of thing she should have worn. Beneath her friend's open trenchcoat, she could see the tight leatherette mini-dress with the laced criss-cross front.

No, Sandy told herself, if he doesn't think I'm suitable, I won't mind at all. In fact I'll probably cry with joy and run all the way back to Newey House like a girl let out of school early.

But as the gnawing silence in the office continued, she became increasingly perturbed at the dark interest in Royce's deep-set eyes.

She was suddenly aware that she was perspiring and trembling slightly. Dammit! Not now. This wasn't the time to start withdrawal symptoms. Then she noticed the twinge of an ache in her kidneys. It was starting again. She felt angry with herself for having come. Angry with Bella for having let her.

When Royce spoke, it startled her.

'What did you say her name was, Bella?'

Her friend's big childlike eyes widened. 'Sandy, Mr Royce.'

Christ, thought Sandy, the bastard's talking about me as if I'm not even here!

'How old is she?'

'I'm twenty-nine!' Sandy snarled without thinking.

One of Royce's heavy eyebrows arched in surprise, and he turned his head slowly towards her.

For a moment, there was a brittle silence, then he said softly: 'Bella has told you something of The Dominatrix?'

Unconsciously, Sandy took a step back. 'Yes. Some.'

A thin smile flickered on his face. 'Not much, I think. You see – what is it? – Sandy, the whole point about this club is that you do what you are told. Nothing else. It sounds very easy. It is. But some girls find they can't. Just do what they are told. Without question. With total obedience.' The smile curled up fully, and Sandy realised that he really was handsome in a macabre sort of way. 'And that includes only talking when you are spoken to. Not something that comes easy to women in this country.'

Sandy wasn't sure of her ground. 'I'm sorry.'

'Master,' Royce said evenly.

She didn't understand. 'Pardon?'

Royce chuckled, but his eyes were unsmiling. 'You address me as 'Master' at all times. Understand?'

'Yes.'

'Try again.'

She exchanged a nervous glance with Bella. Her friend nodded encouragingly.

Sandy gulped, and shut her eyes. 'Yes, Master.'

Her eyes opened to find herself once again under Royce's unblinking gaze. 'Fine,' he said softly. 'Tell me, are you frightened?'

'A little.'

'What?'

She swallowed. 'A little frightened – Master.'

Royce smiled. 'You're learning. Like you'll learn not to be frightened but to enjoy what you do. After all, you'll be well-rewarded. And we make a point of you agreeing to the level to which you will be subjected *before* we start. A sort of grading system. It's up to you if you move on and earn more. Or not.'

Sandy looked dubious; Bella had given her enough of an idea of what might be involved.

'Do you find it difficult to believe that you might even get to like what I and your other Masters will do to you?'

Sandy shut her eyes involuntarily; she felt faint.

Royce chuckled softly. 'Let me show you something that may surprise you. It will also give you an idea about how to conduct yourself in the club. You have an excellent teacher in your friend here. One of our finest submissives.' In one fluid movement, he swung his feet from the desk and turned the chair to face Bella. When he spoke, his voice had dropped an octave until the soft flow became hard and uncompromising. 'Poppy, take your dress off.'

Sandy was shocked. Shocked by the quiet authority of his tone, and that he should even demand such a thing in front of her. Even his use of 'Poppy' – Bella's clubname – seemed to transport her straight into the nightmare world she was praying didn't really exist.

'Yes, Master.'

'Watch her!'

Sandy realised she'd closed her eyes and averted her head.

'Watch her,' Royce repeated.

Sandy didn't trust herself to speak. Numbly she looked across the room. Already Bella had dropped her trenchcoat and was now unlacing the front of her leatherette mini-dress. This wasn't Bella. Not the self-assured, hard-bitten drug addict who knew her way around. This woman was meek and submissive, a mere plaything. This was Poppy.

Sandy's mouth was dry as she watched. Even if she had been ordered to, she couldn't have dragged her eyes away. She was mesmerised with curiosity and disbelief as her friend obediently opened the laces and let the dress fall around her ankles. Carelessly Bella flicked it aside, and looked down to her feet in an attitude of hangdog subservience.

'You see,' Royce explained matter-of-factly, 'she is not permitted to look on her master unless she is told.'

But Sandy hardly registered his words. She didn't know what to expect when Bella stood before her wearing only a black silk G-string held in place by a narrow thong. The first thing that struck her was the whiteness of her friend's long body. And her thinness. Hardly any flesh covered the narrow shoulders and her bones were quite pronounced. Below the taut skin of her ribcage, her belly was shrunken and flat.

Bella's breasts were smaller than her own, and jutted with a natural tightness. The light from Royce's desklamp played on the small gold rings that pierced through the angry brown buds of her nipples.

A small gasp escaped Sandy's open mouth.

'Surprised?' Royce asked. He sounded amused at her reaction.

'Yes.' Sandy's voice was a whisper.

'Yes, *what*?'

'Yes, Master,' Sandy whispered.

Slowly Royce climbed out of his chair. She noticed how tall and muscular he was, and how he walked with the easy grace and menace of a tiger. 'It may surprise you to learn, Sandy, that we didn't ask Bella to have her nipples pierced. She did it herself. To intensify the exquisite pain that she experiences.' He rolled his tongue around the words with practised relish. 'Isn't that so, Bella?'

'Yes, Master.' Still Bella remained motionless, her legs slightly astride with her arms held tightly behind her back.

'Look at me, Bella.'

The wide mascarared eyes turned sharply up in instant obedience.

Sandy's attention was caught by the movement of Royce's right hand. Between his thumb and forefinger he held a small metal object. It was like the heavy key fob from a hotel with a catch clip on one end.

Sandy was hypnotised as Royce's long fingers unhurriedly attached the clip to the ring on Bella's left nipple.

Then he simply stepped back, allowing the fob to drop from his grasp. Sandy winced. She saw Bella blink at the sudden flash of pain as the fob bounced for a moment on her distended breast.

Bella still stood immobile except for the rapid clenching of her stomach muscles as she withstood the sparks of ebbing pain. She no longer blinked, but stared at Royce with a strange expression that looked almost like adoration.

Two grey trickles of mascara trailed down Bella's cheeks. Softly, she said: 'Thank you, Master.'

Royce smiled reassurance and, leaving Bella with the fob still hanging from her distorted breast, turned to stand before Sandy. Gently he placed a hand on each shoulder.

He looked down at her with very penetrating violet eyes. 'Sandy, I know what your problem is. Like Bella, you are a drug addict. You need money. To get it, you will turn to crime or prostitution. Eventually, either of those will ruin your life. Working here will not. You may even find, like Bella, that it opens a new dimension to your life. *If* you *let* it. You will be exceptionally well-paid.' His tone was almost hypnotic and Sandy felt herself swaying with the ebb and flow of his voice. 'But we stand no nonsense. Addicts are prone to be unreliable. If you are unreliable, you will be out. Right out, and will never be able to return. If you prove reliable, I shall pay you two hundred pounds a night. You may earn more by agreeing to more severe punishments. Or by taking part in videos. Or going privately with our members. You will also have the opportunity to travel to similar clubs abroad. Do you have any questions?'

Sandy wanted to scream 'How the hell do I get out of here?' Instead, she heard a small voice saying: 'What will I have to do?' She blinked suddenly at the violet eyes so close to hers. 'Master.'

She watched his mouth form round the words; his teeth were very even and white. 'Submit. That's all.'

Royce's words were now rushing around her ears like a waterfall, drowning out all sense and reasoning, all logic. Her head was spinning.

'Will you do something for me now, Sandy?'

It seemed like a long silence. 'Yes – Master.'

'Take off that pretty pink jumper.'

As she drew it over her head, she felt her small breasts bounce free. Her hair tangled around the neck and when she'd finished struggling, she was surprised to find him still watching her face.

'Your skirt.'

She didn't fumble. To her surprise, her fingers found the hook-and-eye easily. Without hesitating she just let it drop.

Then she adopted a stance like Bella's, with her legs slightly apart and her hands behind her back. She knew his eyes were on the scrap of white pants she wore.

'Are you damp?' His voice was almost mocking.

She mumbled.

'I didn't hear you.'

'Yes, Master.'

There was a pause and then Royce said: 'Get down onto your knees. Then you can start by kissing my shoes.'

Royce looked impassively down at the slender back at his feet. This one had been easy. A golden-haired angel. Slender and delicate. Unlike the ravaged beauty of Bella. But still she had *much* to learn.

'Get your arse in the air, Sandy. Spread your legs and arch your spine.'

The girl's obedience was instant. She was anxious to please. Anxious, he knew, for the money to get her next fix.

Eleven

By eight-thirty the reception at the opulent Burlington Hotel was in full swing.

Although not gregarious by nature, Billy Robson found that he was actually enjoying himself. To begin with, the three-hundred punt stake money with which he and Bernadette had started out at Leopardstown had swollen to nearly a thousand – half of which she had insisted he kept.

He was also keen to make his mark in the new world of opportunities that was opening up for him. He had a lot to learn, and this party would be a good place to start, with its wealth of useful contacts.

He was also aware that another reason for his high spirits was standing only a few feet to his left.

Bernadette was looking her usual ravishing self, laughing with a group of admirers who were fast gathering around her. She seemed not to notice the lascivious stares of some of them, especially a grossly overweight, sullen-looking man with jug-ears.

In fact, she took him by the wrist and led him across to where Robson stood.

'Billy, I'd like you to meet Mr Molloy,' she said. 'Eamon Molloy.'

The man was totally disinterested as he shook Robson's hand under sufferance.

'Mr Molloy owns the new canning factory we're here to celebrate,' she explained with a discreet wink.

'Billy Robson. Congratulations.' He recalled mention of the man when they had been met earlier by Dermot at the airport. Evidently it was Bernadette's idea for Robson to distract his drooling attentions.

Robson gave it a try. 'What'll you be canning at the new factory, Mr Molloy?'

The man dragged his lacklustre eyes away from the girl. 'Meat products mostly.'

Robson tried to show interest. 'Oh, really. What, Irish stew and that sort of thing?'

Molloy gave him a curious look. 'Haven't you read our press hand-out?'

'Not yet,' Robson apologised.

'Pet food,' Molloy grunted. 'Export to Canada and the United States. Low grade meat, see? But high profits.'

'Isn't that a smart idea?' Bernadette said brightly to Robson. 'Normally you can't export meat to North America for love nor money. Well, you wouldn't, would you? Not when they're overflowing with prime beef. But pet food . . . And the marvellous thing is that my brothers have got the contract to supply the product. Apparently it's always a problem to get rid of the offcuts and offal for a good price.'

That had never occurred to Robson before, but he could imagine the difficulty. No doubt this deal could increase the Mulqueens' profits considerably. 'You're obviously quite a businessman, Mr Molloy,' Robson observed.

Something that might have passed for humour showed in Molloy's dull eyes. 'We Irish aren't all as daft as we're painted over the water, you know.'

Robson smiled hesitantly. This one was a touchy bastard. 'I'm sure.'

Molloy's eyes narrowed. 'Would you be Frankie Lewis's new man? The ex-Marine?'

'Very ex-, I'm afraid. It was all a long time ago.'

'Served in Ulster, did you?'

Robson didn't like the underlying tone. 'A couple of tours. As I say, it was a long time ago.'

'They're still there, you know.' The slack lower lips jutted belligerently. 'You might not be, but the Marines are still there.'

Bernadette looked anxious, no doubt afraid that her brother's contract might suddenly be in jeopardy. 'Sure Mr Molloy is one of the best businessmen in Dublin, Billy,' she blurted. 'He even managed to get a grant to set up the factory. He's very well known in Government circles. There are at least three ministers I've seen at this reception. And MPs from the Opposition party.' She glanced quickly around the sea of faces. 'That's Charles Haughey over there. The Opposition leader. Last year Libya threatened to stop taking Irish beef unless Ireland took more of its oil. Charlie flew out and sorted things out. He's on good terms with Libya. Anyway, you can imagine it rather put the Government's nose out of joint, the Opposition leader resolving the problem.' She laughed. 'Still, my brothers were pleased. Libya's one of their biggest customers.'

'Haughey's all right,' Molloy agreed, successfully diverted from his mounting antagonism to Robson. 'He knows what's good for this country. People thought he was finished a few years back, but he's more popular now than ever. Charlie's all right.'

Suddenly Bernadette said: 'There's himself, at last!' She sounded very relieved as she raised her arm and waved towards Frank Lewis who had just entered through the double-doors. With him was Dermot and another man.

'Gawd, I'm parched!' Lewis announced, kissing Bernadette swiftly on the mouth. 'I'd forgotten what a long drive it is. *And* what Dublin traffic can be like! Hallo, Eamon.' He shook hands with Molloy. 'Where d'you keep the booze at this party then?'

As Molloy flagged down a passing waiter with a tray of drinks, Bernadette introduced her other brother Padraig.

Apart from the same head of black hair, although by contrast it was neatly trimmed, he was the complete opposite to the gangling, cheerful Dermot. Padraig Mulqueen was short and stocky, his muscular frame compact in a smart grey suit. His smile was less forthcoming than his brother's and his eyes more wary.

'*Never* call him Paddy,' Bernadette warned with mock seriousness. 'Only I'm allowed to call him that when he annoys me.'

Padraig gave her a brotherly peck on the cheek. 'My little sister hasn't changed at all, I see. As cheeky as ever and too much lip.' He turned to Robson and extended his hand. The grip was dry and firm. 'I've heard all about you, Billy. And that business in Malta. Sorry about that. God knows what it was all about. Funny buggers those Libyans and the people they get mixed up with.' His mouth took on the semblance of a smile. 'Still, you came out of it well. Frankie's been singing your praises all the way back from the works. Specially that car chase. Where d'you learn to drive like that?'

Robson shifted uneasily. He wasn't about to mention his past connection with the Marines again. Or the VIP bodyguard and driving courses he'd been on. 'Just something I picked up.'

Padraig nodded. 'Mmm. Anyway, I gather you're organising transport for Frankie's operation from now on?'

'He sure is,' Lewis interrupted, slapping Robson play-fully on the shoulder. 'And we can make a start with two container loads of offal for next week.'

Robson was surprised. 'Not cattle-heads?'

'No, it won't work,' Lewis said. 'Nice price at £3.50 a head. But we want to move 'em hot, and Padraig reckons they'll be off before we can get them to London. Offal's different though. We can move that frozen. Just tie up the details with Padraig later, will you? He's got all the gen.' Before Robson could respond, Lewis caught someone's eye, and beckoned the man over. Out of the side of his mouth he muttered: 'You gotta see this guy, Billy. This man holds the purse strings, so be on your best behaviour . . .'

His voice trailed off as a slim elderly man approached with a beautiful young woman at his side.

'Hallo, Mr McCrohan,' Lewis greeted. 'Didn't expect to see you here today. A very pleasant surprise.'

Immediately Robson was struck by the man's penetrating cornflower eyes. And his skin. Skin that looked well-scrubbed and clear, like a child's, the only blemish being a small colour-less mole on one cheek.

McCrohan must have been well into his sixties, but the figure beneath the chocolate-brown suit and thin, mustard-coloured rollneck suggested a man who had looked after himself. The short, silver hair was perfectly trimmed.

Those eyes could have been smiling as he shook hands with Lewis. It was hard to tell. 'Sure, I have to make the occasional appearance in public, Frankie. If only to stop the rumours that I'm dead. And to stop my executives fighting over my business before I'm actually buried. Despite stories to the contrary, I'm not the Irish Howard Hughes.'

Lewis laughed loudly. 'No one could say that, Mr McCrohan. If I had a lovely estate like yours, I'd be reluctant to leave it. Certainly not for the hurly-burly of commercial life. And certainly not with delightful companions like the young lady here.'

His attention had been so inexplicably riveted by McCrohan that Robson had hardly noticed the girl who clung to his arm as though seeking protection. He had assumed she was a daughter or niece. Lewis seemed to know otherwise.

'Forgive me,' McCrohan apologised. 'This is Kathy. A little shy, you see. Not used to the bright lights of Dublin.'

As she turned towards them and inclined her auburn head in acknowledgement, Robson was stunned. The expensive blue silk dress was slashed to the navel, the half-orbs of her small breasts clearly visible. Feeling absurdly embarrassed, he diverted his attention back to McCrohan. He found his eyes meeting the old Irishman's gaze. For a second they stared at each other. Was there a mocking humour there? It was almost as if he was saying 'Obscene, isn't it? An old man like me with a voluptuous young slip of a girl. That's what money can buy; something you'll never have.'

The moment passed. After a few minutes talking with Lewis and the Mulqueens, McCrohan and his girl drifted away with Eamon Molloy.

'How does that old bugger do it?' Lewis murmured, his eyes following the taut blue silk of Kathy's buttocks appreciatively. 'They say he doesn't let his girls wear drawers. It's true, y'know, I can't see the outline of her knickers, can you?'

'He gives me the creeps,' Bernadette muttered. 'Almost as bad as Molloy.'

Lewis turned to Robson. 'McCrohan lives in this bloody great mansion in the country. Runs this vast empire of his from there. Beef and dairy farms, horse studs, racing stables, and a big supermarket chain.' He sounded envious. 'It was him that got Bernie's brothers set up. Financed them from nothing. And me. I was in building to start with, then went into catering a few years back. Then the slump hit the construction industry and I found myself pretty much over-extended. That was about the time I met Bernie, the little love. She arranged a meet with McCrohan and – bingo! – my worries were over.'

Bernadette laughed. 'So you *do* admit I at least played a *small* part in building your business empire?'

Lewis hugged her. 'Of course I do, gorgeous. See, Billy, nowadays I treat McCrohan more like a merchant bank. When we set up our transport company the other day, it was largely with McCrohan's money. And this new canning factory. One of his companies owns half of it with Eamon Molloy.'

'I don't suppose it's true,' Bernadette wondered as she looked across the room at the girl by McCrohan's side.

'What?' Lewis asked.

'Those rumours. About McCrohan and his housegirls.'

Lewis chuckled. 'What, that they're his sex-slaves? Whippings and all that?'

She said softly: 'You know, seeing that girl Kathy, I could somehow believe it. She seems so young and vulnerable.'

Lewis downed his drink. 'So that's the way McCrohan does it, eh? Treats 'em mean, and keeps 'em keen.'

Bernadette looked up at him mischievously. 'Don't let that give you any ideas, Frankie. You're mean enough as it is.'

Lewis grinned and took one further glance back at McCrohan's latest housegirl. 'Still, wouldn't mind spanking that one's backside, eh, Billy?'

'Hello, Frankie.' The voice close in his ear made Lewis jump. 'Not having lustful thoughts I trust.'

He turned round sharply.

Dee stood two paces behind. There was an amused smile on his face as he casually swilled the drink of mineral water around his glass.

'What are you doing here?' Lewis asked nervously.

Bernadette sensed the tension between them. Despite his charming boyish smile, she felt instinctively uneasy about the newcomer.

Robson, too, took an instant and inexplicable dislike to him.

'Sorry to interrupt, folks,' Dee said evenly. 'A little job's cropped up for you.'

'What sort of job?' Lews asked.

'Business,' Dee replied. 'I want you to go up to Donegal. There's a gentleman who wants to do business with us.'

'Who?'

'An American cousin. From Boston. He's in the export business. He's got contacts in Columbia who've got product to shift.'

'Product?' Lewis repeated hesitantly. 'Oh, I see. No, I'm not interested.'

Dee peered steadily at Lewis as he drained his glass of mineral water. Unhurriedly, he licked his lips. 'You're interested.'

A simple statement. Robson blinked. Did he imagine it? He had never heard a more simple statement so overloaded with threat and menace.

Robson took a step to stand alongside Lewis, and looked unflinchingly at the Irishman. 'If I heard him correctly, Mr Lewis said he wasn't interested.'

His boss touched him lightly on the arm. 'It's all right, Billy. There's no problem. Maybe there is something in this.'

Dee eyed Robson dispassionately. 'So, this is your cabbage-hat, eh, Frankie?'

Lewis ignored the taunt. 'When's the meet? And where?'

'Buncrana. Tomorrow night.' Dee shifted his gaze back to Robson. 'Go alone.'

'If I go,' replied Lewis, 'it will be with Bernie. And with Billy.'

An amused smile played over Dee's lips. 'If it makes you happier, Frankie, sure. In fact it may be best, come to think of it. I'm having a drink in the piano bar. Come and join me and we'll talk it over.'

He winked at Bernadette and handed her his empty glass. Without thinking, she found herself accepting it, holding it lamely as Dee turned slowly and ambled away through the crowd.

'Who in God's name was that, Frankie?'

The Londoner looked pale. 'Just a business acquaintance. He's all right. A bit of a hard case, that's all.'

Robson watched until Dee disappeared from view. Donegal. The northernmost state of Eire, isolated from the rest on the north-west tip of Ireland. And, just a short trip across the border from terror-stricken Londonderry, the village of Buncrana had always been a refuge for members of the IRA on the run.

Although it rained incessantly, it was a pleasant drive north up the N2.

Robson was almost enjoying the journey. There had been no problem hiring the new red Rover 2000 and by eleven, the three of them were on their way. Despite the dire lack of signposting, Robson found it a treat to drive with so little traffic on the road.

Only the atmosphere in the vehicle prevented him from relaxing fully; an atmosphere of tension that had begun with the arrival of the stranger at Molloy's reception the night before.

Dee. That was his name. Robson had coaxed that much from a reluctant Frankie Lewis, but nothing more. His boss had clammed-up tight.

After that first meeting, Lewis had made his excuses just as Molloy's public relations man mounted the platform.

Robson had quietly slipped out after him, making his way to the piano bar with its dark wood panelling and brass lamps. It was seething with Dubliners and visiting hordes from the American Bar Association who were discovering their roots and a liking for Guinness.

By the time he'd been served, he'd lost sight of Lewis. Nursing a pint of Smethwicks, he worked his way around to the elaborate split-level lounge section at the rear. It was all marble art deco stairways and alcoves with a pianist tinkling out 'Killing Me Softly' on the ivories beneath giant Michaelangelo wall prints.

He paused on the upper level. Directly below him Frank Lewis was sitting with Dee. His boss did not look a happy man. He sat stiffly with his glass ignored whilst the Irishman spoke quickly in a voice too low for Robson to be able to hear more than the occasional word. 'Consignment'. 'States'. 'Buncrana' again. 'Expected'.

Lewis shook his head and said something. To Robson it was as infuriating as watching television with the sound turned down.

Dee took the other's arm and held it. The grip looked fierce. Lewis's shoulders slumped in resignation.

There was just one last sentence from the Irishman, then he stood up and walked away through the milling crowd without a backward glance.

It was three minutes before Lewis stirred, leaving his glass still untouched.

Robson met him at the top of the steps.

Lewis laughed. 'What's this, my guardian angel?' But there was an effort in the humour.

'Are you sure there's not a problem, Frankie?'

'Not at-arl at-arl!' Lewis grinned with a music-hall Irish accent. 'Just a change of plan. We drive to Donegal tomorrow. A bit of business.'

'With him?' Robson inclined his head towards the exit.

Lewis's smile faded. 'I grant you, he's a nasty piece of work, Billy. But business is business. And you can't always choose who you do it with.' The smile returned with a vengeance. 'Still, thanks for keepin' an eye on me. It's appreciated. Now – let's taste the delights of Dublin's fleshpots.'

During the evening Robson kept turning the incident over in his mind. Whatever was going on, he was sure it wasn't strictly legal. As his boss clearly didn't intend giving anything away he decided to try and find out more from Bernadette – should he get the chance.

As everyone seemed to think Lewis was as honest as the day was long, it was unlikely it was anything too serious. If it wasn't then he decided he'd go along with it. He'd mind his own business and ask no questions. As long as it didn't involve him directly, what Lewis did was his own affair. Sometimes ignorance really was bliss.

Frank Lewis managed to keep his forced *bonhomie* going until the early hours. It was only a short walk to the Leeson

Street clubland where basement wine-bar discos did a thriving trade from midnight until dawn.

By three in the morning, the crowds had thinned, and they found themselves two clubs later in Maxwell Plums, one of the more sophisticated wine-bars.

'I'm turning in,' Lewis announced as another ice-bucket of Moët et Chandon arrived.

'You idiot,' Bernadette scolded. 'You've just ordered this.'

Lewis looked strained. 'I know. Stupid. Didn't realise I was so knackered. You finish it off with Billy. Anyway, I've been hoggin' the dances all night. I'm sure he can't wait to get his hands on you.'

'Frankie!' She blushed and exchanged grins with Robson.

'He's got a lot on his mind,' Robson observed as Lewis stumbled towards the door, none too steady on his feet.

'It's the man he met earlier, I'm sure of it. You know we're charging up to Donegal tomorrow?'

'So I gather.' Robson poured out the champagne. 'What's it all about?'

Bernadette shrugged. 'It's one of Frankie's little secrets. Probably a shady deal.'

'How shady?'

She laughed, the candleglow picking out the dancing yellow flecks in her green eyes. 'Not *that* shady!' She patted his hand gently. 'I know Frankie's handled dodgy stock before now. Maybe that's what it is. It's quite a racket in the north.'

'What d'you mean?'

She lowered her voice. 'Well, if a shopkeeper's getting into a bad way with his finances, he gets the paramilitaries to burn the place down so he can get Government compensation. But first the best part of the stock is removed.'

'Paramilitaries?' Robson's expression hardened. 'You mean the IRA?'

She pouted at his disapproval. 'Well, I'm sure the other side does it, too. The Proddies. It's well-known. Anyway, the stock has to be shifted. Buncrana's just across the border from Derry.'

'I know.'

She blinked. 'Of course you do, I'm sorry.' Her smile returned. 'Let's dance.'

And as the Rover 2000 sped towards the outskirts of Monaghan, just south of the border, Robson could imagine it was still Bernadette's waist he was holding, and not the steering wheel. Drink had dulled his memory of the half-dozen slow dances they had had together. But he recalled he had held her too close. Close enough for the smell of her to fill his head. An intoxicating mix of fresh perspiration and an expensive musky perfume. And close enough to feel her pressing against his groin.

He also recalled how she'd laid her head against his shoulder and made no attempt to draw away.

The sight of the border-post came as a shock.

It was as though someone had doused him in icy water without warning.

As he slowed towards the brickwork enclosure that surrounded the road, he felt his heart start to beat faster. Strange that, he mused. It wasn't as though he hadn't been expecting it. He *knew* their route cut across Ulster to Donegal; the scenic route would have taken forever through Longford and Leitrim. He *knew* the terrorist war wasn't over. Yet it still came as a shock.

When he'd left it seven years ago, he never dreamed he would return of his own accord. Ulster had come to mean to him no more than it did to any other mainland Briton. One of those irritations like inflation and unemployment that just refused to go away, regardless of what any government tried to do.

The soldier approached slowly in his baggy DPM smock, his FN rifle pointing downward. Despite the polite smile, the eyes beneath the tam-o'-shanter were wary. One of the Scottish regiments.

No, Robson decided, it was more than an irritation to him. It was a nightmare that he had lived and breathed. So long ago now that he had thought it would never recur. How long had it been since he had woken up in a cold sweat in the middle of the night? Wide awake and wondering how he was going to cope with the weightless void on the bed where his legs had been. Torn mindlessly from his body by the culvert bomb. Then the slow realisation that it was just a dream, and the next day he would be back on patrol of the Derry streets. With both legs.

'May I see your driving licence, sir?' The voice was tersely polite; the accent lowland Scots. 'Long way from home, aren't we?'

Robson smiled. 'Touring holiday. I'm chauffeuring my boss.'

The trooper peered into the back seat. 'Afternoon, sir. Ma'am. Do you have any identification?'

Lewis passed over two more driving licences.

As he studied them, the trooper said: 'Hired car, is it?'

'Yes, in Dublin.'

'Where you staying in Ulster?'

'We're not. Going straight through to Donegal.'

The trooper nodded. 'That'll take you through – er – what's it? – Derry?' He sounded unsure.

Robson couldn't repress the grin; they were still using

the old tricks. 'Londonderry, yes.' No true Republican could bring himself to add the prefix without choking on it.

The trooper's eyes narrowed. 'What's so funny?'

'Nothing. I used to be in the Royal Marines. Four-two. I've done a tour or two here.'

The trooper gave a smirk of a smile. 'Then you did the right thing getting out.' He shrugged. 'This is the last place *I'd* choose for a holiday.'

He waved them on.

The improved road surface was immediately noticeable. 'Yield' notices were replaced by British 'Give Way' signs and the roadmarkings were more distinct and ordered. The changes were subtle but unmistakable.

It was curious and eerie driving through towns whose names were well-known in the subconscious minds of the British public, if not their locations. Omagh, Newtownstewart, Strabane. Everything looked normal enough, along the main roads and in the housing estates on either side. Only the yellow restricted parking signs hinted at the hidden menace. And the police stations. Barricaded fortresses with towering wire fences and closed-circuit TV cameras. Beleaguered outposts within their own communities.

He shivered.

They were stopped only once by a temporary VCP mounted by officers of the Royal Ulster Constabulary, immediately following a blind bend. The exchanges were polite and good-humoured.

In Londonderry, they came across another group of RUC men on traffic patrol on the junction beside the bridge: two controlling the vehicles, two others just watching for the surprise attack that may never come, or was just about to. All wore blue flak vests, all were armed. All looked nervous.

Lewis noticed it, too. 'Jesus, Billy, and to think this is just an ordinary day-to-day job for those buggers. No wonder so many of 'em top themselves.'

Bernadette said: 'I haven't been to the Six Counties since before the troubles. Most Irish keep away, scared. I can see why now.'

Robson smiled wryly. 'Nowadays, it's quiet enough. Mostly nothing ever happens. It's just when it does, you're somehow never expecting it.'

Yet before they'd left the outskirts, they heard a distant dull thud from somewhere in the city. They all knew what it was; no one said anything.

It was with a blessed sense of relief that they crossed back over the border into Donegal and turned off the winding road towards Buncrana.

In the evening light, the vast expanse of Lough Swilly had the dull sheen of gunmetal. There was not a breath of air to ruffle its surface, and the only sound was the lapping of the water along its muddy grey edges.

The intense stillness was shattered by the wheels of the Rover as they crackled over the gravel driveway to the Victorian red-brick hotel with its garish yellow window frames.

'It's beautiful,' Bernadette decided. 'So peaceful. Would you ever think it's barely ten miles from Derry.'

Lewis wasn't feeling romantic. 'I'd have been happier if we could have got in at the Lough Swilly Hotel. This is a glorified guest-house.'

Bernadette punched his arm playfully. 'Sure, you've no soul, Frankie Lewis. You're in Ireland's most beautiful county and all you want is the plastic comforts of a Holiday

Inn.' She turned to Robson. 'We used to holiday here when I was a wee girl. Stayed at this hotel, too, we did.'

'It's a place to relax all right,' Robson agreed as he unloaded their luggage. 'Tranquil.'

'Can't stand the stink of seaweed,' Lewis grumbled, and headed to the door.

The tatty lobby, with its heavy oak staircase and peeling gold flock wallpaper, was deserted. A smell of dampness rose from the faded red carpet and mingled with the smell of frying chips from the half-open kitchen door.

Lewis rang the bell irritably. It was several minutes before the proprietor emerged from the kitchen. His white chef's smock and chequered trousers were smeared with grease.

'Isn't me good lady wife here t'see you?' He sounded flustered as he stubbed out his cigarette in the ashtray.

'Apparently not,' Lewis returned coldly.

'Sorry to keep you,' the man said, without sounding as though he meant it. 'I was in the middle of doing a grill. Patty must be cleanin' the bedrooms. We've a girl, too, but she's off sick.'

'The name's Lewis. Mr and Mrs. And a Mr Robson for a single.' He wasn't in the mood for excuses.

The proprietor wiped his hands on his trousers before consulting the book. 'Ah, yes. Rooms five and thirteen. Now will you be wantin' supper?'

Lewis eyed him suspiciously. 'Will you be cooking it?'

The man grinned proudly. 'To be sure. This *is* a family hotel. Home cooking.'

'Can't wait,' Lewis muttered.

'Well, if you go through to the restaurant after you've taken your bags up. We've no porters, you see.'

'I see.'

'Ah!' The proprietor lifted a hand-written note from the book and squinted at it. 'A message for you. Patty's handwritin's terrible bad. From a Mr Dee? Be at the Mannix Green at 9 p.m.'

'Where's that?'

'Ah, it's a little lounge bar in Buncrana main street. Not so popular with tourists like yourselves. Mostly locals.'

That seemed to leave Lewis in deep, quiet thought. It was a mood that stayed with him all through the greasy mixed grill. No doubt the burnt chips were a tribute to their untimely arrival.

When Bernadette left the table for the ladies' room, Lewis said suddenly: 'Billy, I think you'd better come with me this evening.'

Robson sensed his boss's concern. 'What's worrying you?'

'This place, the bar in Buncrana. The way this hotel owner described it as *for locals*. That means tourists not welcome . . .' Lewis was obviously searching for the words.

'You mean it's a Provo bar?'

Lewis looked uncomfortable. 'I don't know. That sort of thing.'

'Is Dee one of them?'

The other man's laugh was brittle. 'I dunno, Billy, I've never asked him. Well, you don't, do you?'

Robson smiled grimly. 'I suppose not. But you're not going to be in danger if you're doing business with him, are you?'

Lewis fiddled with the pepper pot. 'No. But then I'm not sure I want to.'

'And he can be very persuasive?'

'You've met him.'

Robson bit his lower lip thoughtfully. 'If Dee is in with the IRA, does it mean that this business is really legit? Nothing to do with their terrorist activities. No gun-running or anything?'

Lewis looked mortified. 'Good God, no, Billy! What d'you take me for? It's just if I don't like the sound of the deal, I want to get out of that place with both my knee caps.'

'Understood.'

'Then you'll come?'

Robson hesitated for a moment. The very thought of having anything remotely to do with the IRA turned his stomach. But neither did he feel inclined to abandon the one person who'd offered him a chance at the very time he was most needed. A bond had grown between them over the past weeks. They'd shared some hairy moments together and Robson felt a growing sense of loyalty. Almost like comrades.

There was no doubt that the man Dee was a bastard of the first order. Provo scum. He was obviously putting frighteners on Lewis who was clearly reluctant to cooperate. Apply their usual vile intimidation methods which he'd witnessed so often in the past. And that made Robson's blood boil.

He said quietly: 'I'll come.'

Lewis grinned with relief and called for liqueurs.

Robson took the precaution of parking the Rover some distance from the Mannix Green, down a side street.

Then he and Lewis completed the journey on foot, walking past the line of shop fronts until they reached the engraved window of the lounge bar. The curtains were drawn.

Lewis looked nervously at Robson, took a deep breath, and pushed open the door into the unknown.

Immediately his throat caught on the thick fug of tobacco smoke that filled the small room. The excitable exchange of conversation died instantly as half-a-dozen scruffily dressed locals turned their faces in the direction of the door. At the sight of strangers, the benign expressions vanished; the hostility in their eyes was unmistakable.

The voice on the television set burbled on unintelligibly, heightening the sense of unwelcome interruption, as Lewis crossed the small sawdust-strewn floor to the wooden bar.

Robson followed, and nodded to the patrons. 'Evening. Getting cold outside now,' he said conversationally.

There was no response. Two old-timers in flat caps and collarless shirts returned to their game of cribbage. Another pair at the bar turned their backs and concentrated unblinkingly on the banal television game show.

Behind the bar, the middle-aged woman's smile lacked enthusiasm.

'What d'you want to drink?' Lewis asked Robson uneasily.

'When in Rome.'

Lewis indicated the Guinness tap. 'Two pints please, love.' He turned back to Robson. 'No sign of Dee.'

One of the men watching the television turned his head. 'Is it Tommy Dee you're wantin'?'

Lewis nodded. As usual, the Guinness wasn't in a mood to be rushed.

'Who'll be wantin' him?'

'The name's Lewis.'

'Oh, yes?' The look was appraising. 'An Englishman, are ya?'

Again Lewis nodded.

'D'ya have business with himself?'

Lewis took the first frothing pint. 'Yes, we're due to meet.'

The man jerked his head in the direction of the frosted-glass partition at the rear of the bar. 'You'll find himself in the Snug. He's waitin' for ya'.'

'Yes? Thanks.' Lewis exchanged glances with Robson and the two of them made a move towards the Snug. But the patron reached out and grabbed Lewis's forearm.

'Just you, Mr Lewis. Your friend waits here.'

Lewis hesitated. 'All right. You okay, Billy?'

'No problem, Frankie. I'll have a quiet pint with our friend here.' He smiled reassuringly. 'Just call if you want me.'

Reluctantly, Lewis pushed open the door. Just two men sat in the tiny back room. One was a man Lewis had never seen before: middle-aged with short iron-grey hair and dressed in a chequered lightweight jacket. Under it, he wore a blue slipover and tie. A picture of respectability.

The other was Dee.

Before them, on the round tile-topped table, lay a three-foot long lacquered cudgel, made of spiky blackthorn.

Lewis forced a smile. 'What's that?'

There was an amused look in Dee's eyes. 'A shillelagh.'

'Never seen one before.'

Behind him, the door shut. The man who had been watching television leaned against the jamb, and folded his arms.

Dee picked up the stick and weighed the heavy rounded end in his palm. 'Yes, Frankie, unlike leprechauns they do exist. No need to hit anyone. Just lay it against a man's cheek and let him walk away. The blackthorn will take away his flesh. Haven't you heard the old Irish expression?' A smile formed around his thin lips.

'What expression?'

'Carry a big stick and talk with a small voice.'

Lewis nodded. 'The unspoken threat, eh?'

Carefully, Dee replaced the shillelagh. 'Something like that. Now sit down and meet our friend from Boston.'

The man with the iron-grey hair showed a set of teeth that were too perfect to have been God's own work. 'How y' doin', Mr Lewis? Sean Brady.'

Lewis sat down and placed his Guinness on the table. 'Pleased to meet you.' His response was perfunctory; he wasn't at all pleased and it showed. Nervously he looked back at the man guarding the door. 'I thought this was going to be a private meeting.'

Dee looked up. 'Wait on the other side. No one comes in, right?' Grudgingly, the man shifted and went back to the main bar. The door closed but his shadow remained firmly outlined against the frosted glass.

'Sean looks after our interests in Boston,' Dee began, lowering his voice. 'They run virtually the entire south area of the city.'

'Run?' Lewis asked.

Brady's smile sparkled again. 'I'd have chosen the word "control", but who's arguing? Let's just say we look after the interests of the Irish community.'

'I hope Sean won't be offended if I refer to him as representing the Irish Mafia,' Dee added. 'Years ago they reached an understanding with the local Italian mobsters. Established each other's "sphere of operations", so to speak. Now they have a healthy respect for each other.'

Lewis was impatient. He couldn't see what this had to do with him, and he said so.

'Recently,' Dee obliged, 'Sean's people have been forging links with Colombian businessmen in Miami. As you're probably aware, they smuggle in cocaine across the Caribbean to Florida. Distribution is achieved with Italian Mafia links.'

'So what?' Lewis growled as he took a mouthful of Guinness.

'So it's been very successful,' Dee replied tartly. 'So much so that cocaine usage in the States has reached saturation level. They need new markets before there's a glut and the price drops.'

Brady interrupted. 'They're interested in Europe, see, Frank. And the UK especially. For the past couple of years they've tried setting up a system through Spain, and through the Italian Mafia. But the Mob ain't very well organised in the UK. Never did get established.'

Lewis nodded. This was all part of underworld history. The old-time British villains had kept the Mafia out, and only allowed limited operations in return for a cut of the profits. The police, too, had played their part. And in more recent years it was Dee and his kind who controlled organised crime. Lewis knew that the film *The Long Good Friday* had got closer to the truth than the public ever suspected.

'In short, it's been a balls-up,' Brady continued. 'And with the Mafia fallin' like ninepins in Italy and the States, the Colombians ain't too keen to continue their association.'

Lewis was sceptical. 'Listen, I don't believe for one moment the Mafia's finished. It's too deep-rooted. I've read in the papers they've taken a knock, but in a year or two they'll be back . . .'

'Unless someone else has taken their place,' Dee said icily.

'I'll tell you something, Frank,' Brady said, warming to his subject, 'the Reagan administration's really putting the boot in. The Kennedys were pussy cats by comparison. The word's gone out for the Mafia to drop its involvement with drugs or the Government'll hound their legit operations until their eyes water.' Brady's teeth sparkled. 'They got the message. In fact, I've heard the whisper that the Mafia has taken out a contract on the Philadelphia Godfather because he refuses to put his house in order.'

Dee said: 'Now perhaps you are beginning to see how you fit into this?'

Lewis sniffed heavily. 'Not really.'

'An exchange,' Brady said. 'Now we're moving heroin in the East Coast off our own bat. No Mafia in sight. The Colombians like that. They're impressed. Their offer is that we shift their coke into the UK through Dublin. Two-way street.'

Lewis stood up. 'I'm not interested.'

Dee didn't bat an eyelid. 'Not even for 20 per cent?'

Lewis sat down.

'The potential market for coke is even bigger than heroin,' Dee spoke slowly so that each word would sink in. 'You know, it's the stuff that Hollywood film stars use. Glamorous. All that crap.'

Lewis shifted uneasily on the wooden chair. 'I'm in deep enough as it is. It was all right in the beginning, just a business arrangement between me and the Mulqueens. But Malta changed all that. It's getting too close. Too dangerous. Too . . .' He fumbled for the word.

Dee helped him out. 'Political?'

Lewis exhaled heavily. 'Yes, I guess that's it.'

A hard smile formed on Dee's face. 'It always has been, Frankie. You just chose to pretend it wasn't. Offended your sensibilities, did it? Working with the Provos.' He almost spat the challenge. 'You make me sick. It was clear to anyone but a complete fool who the Mulqueens were involved with.'

Lewis opened his mouth, then shut it again.

'That's better,' said Dee. 'Now, I'll tell you what you're going to do. In a few weeks you'll fly to Boston and make contact with Sean there. Your connections with the Provos are unknown, so it'll make the entire operation secure. You'll ensure there's the agreed shipment aboard a fishing boat that'll be setting sail. It will rendezvous off the Irish coast in international waters with a dinghy which will bring the consignment of coke ashore here in Buncrana.'

'Christ!' Lewis gasped. 'This is getting worse! That sort of thing went out with bloody laces for a lady and brandy for the clerk. Are you askin' to get caught?'

'We're experts at it all along the west coast of Ireland.' Dee paused. 'Anyway, that won't be your immediate concern. Our lads here will deal with it. The first you'll see of the consignment is when it reaches the Mulqueens' abattoir. Then it'll just filter into your existing UK distribution system for smack.' The faint smile deepened. 'And with lots of opportunities to expand that into Europe.'

Lewis stared gloomily at his Guinness; suddenly he'd lost the taste for it.

After a moment's thought, he made up his mind. 'Look, Dee, I'll admit that the offer's tempting. Very tempting. But all the money in the world's not going to do me any good if I'm behind bars. Or dead.' He leaned forward to make his point. 'Look, we've a nice set-up developing. A secret, virtually foolproof import route for heroin into the UK and Eire. Now, equally foolproof, we're starting to export to the East Coast of the States. Let's not get greedy.'

Lewis found himself mesmerised by the way Dee formed his thin mouth around the slowly spoken words: 'This is purely a logical marketing operation, Frankie. You can't stand still. The demand for coke is growing. If we don't supply, someone else will. Someone else will muscle in. The Colombians, the Proddies, the Mafia ... it doesn't matter who, it will be trouble.'

Lewis was adamant. 'No, Dee, I'm not interested.'

The gentle smile on Dee's face became strangely fixed. Sean Brady was looking decidedly embarrassed. ' "The Man" says otherwise.'

Anger was starting to rise in Lewis. 'He doesn't *own* me. I can manage without him. I've got funds enough of my own now. You can tell him to stuff it.'

Dee's head shook sadly. 'I don't think you'd really want me to tell him that. He might think you ungrateful. After all, it was his money that got you started.'

With a sudden movement, Lewis thrust back his chair and stood up. 'He can take his money out of my business any time he wants! In fact, I'll have my solicitors draw up the papers as soon as I get back. I've told you, this whole business is starting to involve too many people. Dangerous people that I don't know. I'll continue as we are, but no more. Understand? If "The Man" doesn't like it, then he can forget the whole thing. I'll concentrate on the legitimate side of my business.'

'If you don't do what you're told, Frankie,' Dee replied coldly, 'then you won't have *any* business. Legitimate or otherwise. Now sit down.'

'To hell with you!' Lewis snarled, and moved towards the door.

Dee reached towards the shillelagh.

'BILLY!' Lewis screamed.

Dee hesitated. Beyond the glass partition, there was a sudden commotion. The shadow guarding the door was joined by another. An angry exchange of words was followed by a quick scuffling sound and someone's whelp of pain.

The glass top of the door exploded inwards like a star-burst. Lewis ducked as a shower of crystal flew in over the tiny room. The man who had been guarding the door came flying in backwards through the jagged hole in its glass. His back hit the floor with a bone-crushing thud, but the momentum carried him on over the debris.

Instinctively, Lewis side-stepped the sliding figure as it crashed ignominiously into the base of the table where Dee and Sean Brady sat. Beer glasses leapt from the top and crashed down around the hapless victim. The shillelagh rolled off the edge and bounced onto the floor.

Still in shock, it took Lewis a few seconds to realise that Robson was standing in the entrance where the door now hung precariously on one hinge.

'Oh, my God!' Lewis gasped.

'Out!' Robson snapped, his eyes quickly falling on Dee. He found his past Marines training taking command of the situation, instantly assessing the source and type of potential danger. He found it.

Robson's eyes followed Dee's to the fallen shillelagh. The Irishman was already moving. In a trice, he was out of his chair and reaching out for the weapon. His outstretched fingers, closing around the blackthorn cudgel, met with Robson's foot. The ex-Marine pressed hard with his heel, grinding the other man's fingers into the crushed glass on the floor.

Dee's oath came out as a high-pitched yelp as he winced.

'Forget it!' Robson hissed. He turned to Lewis. 'Get out, Frankie! Quick, before the others get themselves together!'

Lewis didn't need any coaxing, already he was moving through the shattered doorway and into the main bar. The patrons gawped in utter amazement at the speed of events.

As Robson released the pressure on Dee's fingers, the other man gasped with relief, springing back to sit nursing his bloodied hand.

He glared hatefully as Robson backed out after Lewis, and made a run for the deserted street.

Sean Brady was as stunned as the rest. 'B'Jesus, that's a mean sonofabitch. You okay?'

'I'll teach that fucken bastard,' Dee muttered savagely as he staggered to his feet. Clumsily, he tried to wrap a handkerchief around his right hand with his left.

The patrons began crowding around the door. One of them asked: 'You want us to get after them, Tommy?'

Dee looked down at the man on the floor who was starting to regain consciousness. Dee's immediate reaction was to distribute firearms and have Lewis and his friend cut down. Permanently. He took a deep breath and marshalled his thoughts. No, that wouldn't do at all. 'The Man' had demanded Frank Lewis's co-operation. And if 'The Man' wanted, 'The Man' got. It was as simple as that.

Dee said slowly: 'You know where they're staying, Timothy. Get a couple of your best lads down there. Give Lewis a good hiding. He's running scared already, so it shouldn't be difficult. Nothing too serious, just a few cuts and bruises to remember.'

'And the other one? The one who did all this?'

Dee massaged the fingers of his right hand. 'That fucken cabbage-hat?' Thoughtfully he bent down and picked up the shillelagh. 'I don't mind if that fucken cabbage-hat never walks again.'

Timothy, a scruffy individual in his mid-thirties, showed his missing teeth when he attempted something resembling a smile. 'Then I'll be wantin' that, sir.'

He reached out and took the shillelagh from Dee's grasp.

Twelve

Bernadette opened the door a fraction. From beneath a confusion of chestnut hair, a pair of green eyes peered out blearily.

'Quick, get packed!' Lewis snapped and pushed the door open.

She stepped back in amazement and shielded her eyes as Lewis threw the light switch. 'God, Frankie . . . !'

He stared angrily at the champagne-coloured silk pyjamas she wore. 'What you gone to bed for?'

Bernadette's surprise was turning to anger at the sudden intrusion. 'I was *tired*, Frankie. I wasn't going to hang around the bar whilst you and Billy were gallivanting around Buncrana . . .' Her mouth dropped . . . 'What the hell are you *doing*?'

He'd begun tossing her things into a suitcase. 'What does it look like? Now get dressed. Just throw something over your pyjamas.'

She stood gasping in disbelief as Lewis opened the wardrobe doors and began throwing the contents on the bed.

He looked up at her. 'I said *move* it!'

'Frankie, what *is* going on?' Her anger had now been replaced by an increasing sense of alarm. This wasn't the actual cool, jokey Lewis she had grown to know and love.

'I had a disagreement with Dee.'

She snatched a pair of jeans from Lewis's grasp as he went to stuff them into the suitcase. 'What sort of disagreement?'

'It doesn't matter,' Lewis replied testily. 'Just that there was a bit of a punch-up. Billy chucked this bloke through a window.'

Bernadette stopped with her jeans hauled halfway over her pyjama bottoms. 'Good God, are you hurt?'

He shook his head and slung a sweater across the bed to her.

'And Billy?'

Before Lewis could reply, a voice behind her said: 'I'm fine, thanks, Bernie. Bruised knuckles, that's all.'

She turned to Robson who was standing at the door with a holdall in his hand. 'Thank God for that. But surely no one's going to come after you?'

'Don't bet on it,' Lewis grated, and zippered up the matching Gucci luggage. 'Right, that's it. Let's go.'

Bernadette pulled the sweater over head. 'You've forgotten my cosmetics,' she protested.

'Fuck 'em,' Lewis replied, casting a glance at the dressing-table. 'You can buy some more.'

Robson crossed to the window and peered through the gap in the curtains. 'There are some car lights up on the main road.'

'Right, let's go,' Lewis said.

'What about the bill?' Bernadette asked.

'Stuff the bill,' Lewis retorted. 'I'll phone and explain tomorrow. Everyone in the hotel is dead to the world.'

He shuffled awkwardly with the suitcase into the hall after Robson. As usual when he was in a hurry, he found that all the fire-doors opened the wrong way. It was a struggle down the narrow passage and stairs, banging into walls and banisters in the darkness.

Robson was waiting for them in the lobby. 'I can't see the road from here, but those lights have gone.'

'You're probably panicking unnecessarily,' Bernadette ventured hopefully.

Lewis grunted as they stepped out into the welcome cool night air. It held the faint tang of seaweed and salty lough mud. The porch light threw a semi-circle of illumination around the drive, the sharp edge of shadow cutting the red Rover in two.

'All clear!' Lewis declared with relief.

Robson hesitated.

'What is it?' Bernadette breathed.

Lewis was already halfway down the steps when he came to an abrupt halt. His mouth went dry.

A shadowy shape was leaning against the boot of the Rover. As the head turned towards them, the light caught the man's face, throwing the features into deep, demonic relief. Lank black hair fell over the forehead, and there were two teeth missing in the evil smile.

Timothy was patiently patting the smooth head of the shillelagh against the palm of his left hand.

Lewis took two uncertain paces back up the steps.

'Sure, this is no time of day to go travelling, Mr Lewis . . .' The thick brogue crumbled away to a cackle of laughter.

'There's another one,' Robson warned out of the corner of his mouth. 'Behind him.'

Lewis dropped the cases silently at his side. 'Go inside, Bernie.'

'But . . . !'

'Go *inside*!' he hissed, refusing to take his eyes from the drive. He heard the movement of the door behind him as she obeyed.

The second man was visible now. A bearded giant in a

fisherman's sweater had come out of the shadows to stand alongside Timothy. Slowly they advanced together.

'Keep back,' Robson warned quietly. 'And strike if you get the chance.'

Lewis nodded, unable to find his voice.

Robson moved lightly down the steps into the pool of light. His eyes flickered between the two men, deciding which of them would attempt to make the first move. If he allowed them to take the initiative, he guessed the big bearded man would start. That would let the man he remembered as Timothy come in from behind with the shillelagh.

That thing *had* to go.

Without warning, Robson sprang towards Timothy. He moved with all the speed he could muster, attempting to get inside the reach of the shillelagh.

He almost succeeded. Parrying sideways with his left forearm, his skin made contact with the blackthorn just above the Irishman's wrist. He felt his flesh rip along its spiky black teeth as he deflected the blow. His right hand followed through instantly with a sideways swing at Timothy's chin. But it was fumbled due to lack of practice. Instead of taking the jaw out of its mountings, it merely stunned.

But it was enough. Stepping forward on his right leg, he swung his left hard in behind his opponent's, sweeping him off his feet. Timothy's back hit the driveway with the force of a felled tree. No one had ever taught him how to break fall.

'Behind you!' Lewis yelled.

Instantly Robson turned, seeking the bearded fisherman.

But it was too late. The giant of a man had grabbed Robson around the shoulders with the strength of a mad bear.

'Hit t'fucker! Hit t'fucker!' Robson could smell the foul breath behind him.

Who the hell was the calling to? Timothy was groaning on the ground. There must be another. Of course! More waiting behind the hotel.

Swaying his torso to the left, he piston-punched his elbow back into the giant's ribcage. He heard and smelled the escape of breath, and felt the bearhug loosen.

Jamming his right shoulder into the giant's armpit, he grabbed the right arm with both his own hands and dropped to one knee. With his own huge weight acting against him, there was nothing the other man could do but follow. His bulk pitched helplessly over Robson's shoulder, his head pile-driving into the gravel. His own sixteen-stone landed on top of it.

Gasping for breath, Robson turned around.

There were two of them. But sweat was stinging Robson's eyes and the figures were a blur. He squeezed his eyelids hard and tossed his head to clear his vision.

The two newcomers looked unsure. One held back. The other decided to strike while Robson looked winded and groggy.

As the heavily booted foot came hurtling towards his groin, Robson knew the man was finished. In a different situation he might have smiled.

He danced to the left, deflecting the kick sideways with the inside of his forearm. The momentum of the man's attack carried him around in a semi-circle until he staggered to regain his balance with his back to Robson.

The ex-Marine moved in hard. Shoulder into the man's backside and a hand grip around each of his ankles. Heave-ho, and up! There could be no resistance. With Robson grasping his ankles like the handles of a wheelbarrow, the ground raced up to meet his face. Robson distinctly heard the nose go, and maybe some teeth. Still holding on, he swung his own foot hard up into the man's unprotected testicles. The cry was a muffled blub.

Finally, Robson let go, shattering the man's kneecaps onto the hard ground.

He gave a smile of grim satisfaction, and looked up for the remaining attacker. All he could hear was the frantic scamper of rubber soles running away into the night.

His smile deepened.

Regular practice keeps you sharp. After years away from it, it is easy to forget a golden rule.

As Robson turned, he glimpsed the face contorted with pain and rage for a split second. Lank hair, missing teeth. From the corner of his eye, he saw the shillelagh descending.

Instinctively, he side-stepped, just as Lewis's cupped hands clapped simultaneously over Timothy's ears from behind. Robson winced at the force of it, almost feeling the Irishman's agony as his eardrums burst.

He felt the slipstream of the shillelagh as it whistled past his head and clattered onto the drive.

Frank Lewis was grinning widely. 'Me brother taught me that one.'

Clutching his ears and whimpering, the Irishman staggered away up the path like a drunkard.

Robson watched him dispassionately. 'I'm glad he did. I'm getting rusty.'

Lewis chuckled. 'You were brill, Billy. Brill. And it was all so bloody quick.'

Robson didn't share his boss's high spirits. 'We were lucky, that's all.'

Behind them, the door opened and Bernadette came quickly down the steps. 'I saw it all. God! Are you hurt?' She picked up Robson's left hand and examined the six inch gouge in his wrist. 'I thought so. Shillelaghs are wicked things.'

Robson pulled his hand away. 'It's only surface.'

Lewis picked up the suitcases and started towards the Rover. 'Let's get out of here before those two clowns come round . . .'

'NO!' Robson shouted his warning so loud it stopped Lewis in his tracks.

'What is it?'

Robson nodded towards the car. 'We'd better check it over. Carefully.'

'What?' Lewis looked blank.

'It may have been wired.'

'Wired?'

The meaning struck Lewis and Bernadette together. 'Oh, good God,' she breathed. 'A bomb?'

Robson reached down and picked up the shillelagh. He looked at it thoughtfully. 'We may have won the battle, Frankie, but not necessarily the war.'

Lewis stared at the Rover in disbelief.

Robson said quietly: 'How mad is the IRA with you?'

The other man hesitated. 'Very mad, I guess.'

'That's what I thought.'

'So?'

Robson said: 'So, whenever and wherever, you'll always be looking over your shoulder. A time and place of their choosing. A bomb in the car. Your home. Or maybe a bullet in the back of the head one night when you're leaving The Czar.'

Bernadette shivered, her eyes wide and moist.

Lewis's voice was a croak. 'Is that what you think?'

Robson raised an eyebrow.

'You're right.' It had been an easy decision for Lewis to come to. 'Of course, you're right. I'll phone Dee straight away. There's a public box in the lobby. I don't really have any option.'

Robson stared out towards the lough. A few stars had broken through the veil of high cloud and their reflections were like gems on the still black surface of the water.

'Thanks anyway, Billy.' Lewis seemed relieved at his own decision. He held out his hand. 'Thanks for saving my skin.'

Robson didn't take it. 'Don't thank me, Frankie. I've just resigned.'

'That's Max in the front,' Bella whispered. 'Sitting with the champagne and the two blonde dolly birds.'

Sandy peered nervously around the edge of the red velvet curtain. She didn't want to be seen. Not by Max, the club's owner, or by any of the obviously wealthy patrons. Despite the black cat mask she wore, she felt as though anyone would be able to recognise her if they ever saw her in the street.

It was stupid, of course. She knew that. Half the patrons, as well as the players, wore harlequin masks or hoods. No one would be able to recognise, let alone name, anyone else.

She knew it was just because she felt so incredibly exposed and vulnerable. And that was before she was humiliated in front of a mixed audience. An audience that would share every gasp of her intimate pain, and the inevitable infliction of ectasy that Royce assured her every slave must have at the end of the punishment.

Even before it began, the soft black leather bondage costume made her feel humiliated. Costume? That was a laugh. A bad joke. The thigh-length boots with the showgirl heels were the nearest things to an item of clothing, laced so tightly that even her thin flesh bulged over the tops.

The rest of the outfit comprised a body-harness of leather straps drawn painfully tight around her waist, encircling her naked breasts, and drawn in a thong between her legs. Studded wristlets and a dog-collar with chain lead completed the effect.

She tried to put from her mind the ordeal which lay before her, and concentrated on what Bella had been saying.

'Max looks ordinary enough,' Sandy observed.

Bella gave a brittle laugh. 'Yeah, he's ordinary enough for a Maltese pimp. He used to run a dozen sleazy strip-joints and a prostitution chain at one time. But there was a lot of police harassment. He moved up-market into the high-class call-girl racket operating out of the top London hotels. That's when he met Royce, who was heavily into S and M and reckoned that was the way to clean up. Now Max has got interests in clubs abroad as well as this one. And of course the videos and photos market.'

'Don't the police give him any trouble now?'

Bella shrugged. 'Not that I've ever heard. It's all so under-ground. All the slaves are brought here blindfolded.' Sandy nodded; it had been a frightening enough experience to start the evening. 'All I know is it's a private house in North London. And Max moves the location every few months. I'm told the patrons are only invited after having been regular customers on a fetish video list for at least a year. Everyone else has to be sponsored.'

Sandy's eyes darted around the curious mixture of customers who sat at the candlelit tables in the spacious drawing-room. Others stood at the small bar to be served by topless barmaids in bizarre leather and rubber costumes like her own. Many of the patrons, too, were similarly dressed. Men as well as women. There were quite a few foreign accents; she'd detected Dutch, German and Scandinavian, as well as some cut-glass British society voices.

On the spotlit stage area that resembled a medieval torture chamber, the previous punishments were coming to an end. A tall masked woman with straight-cut blonde hair was being unchained from the giant rotating cartwheel on the back wall.

Royce, his muscular frame in a black executioner's leotard and wearing a leather balaclava hood, helped her across the floor. Evidently the victim was dizzy and unsteady on her feet. Even in the dim light, Sandy could see the livid weal marks across her belly. She shivered.

Bella smiled at her reaction. 'That's Lady Someone-or-other. You'd never guess if you saw her shopping in Peter Jones, would you? She's always high on coke when she comes here. Volunteers herself for the most excruciating things. Her husband's out there in the audience somewhere. Apparently it does great things for him.' She gave a short laugh. 'Punishment for her overspending his money, he says.'

From another part of the stage, a leather-clad mistress was removing the manacles from another audience partici-pant, this time a man. He'd received a particularly vicious treatment from the woman, but judging from the state of his exposed genitals, he'd got his kicks.

Sandy shook her head. It was so degrading. More sad than sick.

Now Royce moved forward and picked up the micro-phone at the side of the stage.

He blew into the mesh bulb to check it. 'Er, ladies and gentlemen. Your attention please. To end this evening's activities, we present you with a newcomer to our little gatherings. A complete novice to S and M. One of the club's new girls whom we have named "Opium".'

He glanced sideways at Sandy and smiled. Her mouth twitched in response. She appreciated his reassurance, but it did nothing to quell the pounding in her chest and head. Her kidneys, too, were beginning to ache. Another hour or two and she'd be desperate for a fix. At least tonight she would have no problems about the money for it. Or for the next few days. And the comfort of that knowledge made the thought of what was coming bearable.

Suddenly she realised Royce was talking again. 'We will start gently with her, ladies and gentlemen, and teach her the pleasure of our art. I am sure you understand. She'll feel pain more intensely than some of us more experienced in these things. That should add to your pleasure. And, indeed, I am sure you will enjoy the delights of Opium's slender body for many evenings to come.'

Bella gave her a gentle push. 'Go on, love. Just relax. It's not that bad.'

Her legs were visibly trembling as Sandy took the first tentative steps onto the stage area. A low ripple of applause trickled through the audience. There were a few comments of appreciation.

She stopped a few feet in front of Royce, remembering to keep her head bowed in subservience as she had been told, her arms hanging limply by her side. She could feel all the eyes in the audience watching her, and suddenly she was sick with fear.

'Opium, look at me.' Royce's voice was guttural and demanding. Obediently she raised her head, her gaze

immediately transfixed by Royce's intense violet eyes which
burned out of the holes in his hood. She was close enough
to be aware of the animal smell of him, a muskiness that
blended with the tang of leather. He was sweating, she
noticed, from the exertion of the previous punishment, fine
trickles of sweat winding down the contours of his chest.

He reached out slowly and picked up the chain lead that
hung from the studded collar around her throat. Carefully,
he began to wrap it around his wrist, tugging her closer
to him in a series of short, jerking movements. Then the
hooded face was only inches from her own, filling her vision.
She could see every pore on the swarthy skin, the droplets of
perspiration, the fine black stubble of his strong chin.

But mostly it was his eyes that dominated her, burning
with a fierceness that frightened her.

'Why are you here, Opium?' His teeth were very white
and square.

For a moment, she was flustered, the words she'd been
taught lost in a moment of panic. As his eyes calmly main-
tained their hypnotic gaze, she found her breathing slow. The
pounding in her chest eased. In the audience, no one spoke.
They watched with an awe that she could feel.

'I am waiting, Opium.'

She swallowed. 'I am here to be punished, Master.'

'Have you done wrong, Opium?'

'Yes, Master.'

'You have sinned?'

She didn't feel foolish as she recited the words. Just scared.
'Yes, Master.'

'Are you a slut?'

She took a deep breath but her eyes did not leave Royce.
'Yes.'

His eyes bored into her head. 'Then tell me, Opium.'

'I am a slut, Master.'

Royce jiggled the lead tauntingly so that cold chain brushed against her exposed nipples. She felt them tighten in response. 'So what should I do, little slut?'

The stillness of the audience was intense. Someone clinked a glass. A voice scolded. Again the hush fell.

'Hurt me, Master.'

As she spoke the words, the eyes in her mask pleaded with those in the hood opposite. Pleaded for mercy, for understanding, for kindness. Royce's eyes were unblinking.

He backed away, pulling the chain so that she staggered after him, bent forward, hobbling awkwardly in the high-heeled boots into the very centre of the stage.

Quickly, she found his eyes again. In panic she knew if she just watched those eyes she could hypnotise herself into being somewhere else. She could raise her mind above her body. Let it suffer without her.

'We won't need this,' Royce said, waggling the thong handle of the lead. 'You won't run away, Opium, will you?'

She shook her head.

'Open your mouth.'

As she did so, he pushed the thong between her teeth. 'Good, that'll keep it out of the way. Drop it and you know the punishment?'

'Yes, Master,' she said, through clenched teeth. Her words sounded childish and pathetic. A further twist to Royce's spiralling system of humiliation.

As he began, she forced her mind back to earlier that evening. Desperately she tried to remind herself that this was the same Royce whom she had met at the West End rendezvous. The same severely handsome man who spoke with an intriguing mix of authority and charm.

Obediently, she stood astride as the anklets were placed around her boots and secured to the floor fixings.

Earlier she hadn't been expecting dinner. Especially not the devastatingly expensive French restaurant in Mayfair. In fact, she wouldn't have thought that she could have kept anything down.

The wristlets were clipped onto chain-pulleys fitted to the ceiling, slightly in front of her. As they were tightened she was stretched out by her wrists like a diver leaving the springboard. Suspended painfully in mid-flight.

Over the meal Royce's words had been soothing. The wine flowed and she had even eaten a little. She found herself fascinated by his looks. The strong sunburnt features and the long slicked-back hair. The magnetism she felt towards him frightened her.

The clasps were no more than clothes-pegs, painted gold for effect. She gasped as one was attached to each nipple, sending a shock-wave of pain sparking through her body, the nerve-tracks merging at her groin. Her stomach heaved involuntarily, drawing in tight, as she mastered and accustomed herself to the sensation.

Over dinner Royce had warned her how it would feel. How once she got used to it, it was a lingering exquisite pain that some people actually found addictive. He had explained to her much more besides, taking her into a strange world of which she knew nothing. It was Royce's contention that there was a little of the sadist and the masochist in everyone, to varying degrees. Psychologists would explain a woman's desire to hurt a man as vengeance for their dominance. Or a man's sadism as his resentment of his dependence on women from childhood, through puberty, to the grave. And a masochist's desire to be punished for misdeeds only they perceived, or to receive the chastisement they'd never had, but felt they deserved. They were long and convoluted explanations that she had only half begun to follow.

The first kiss of the soft leather whip across her buttocks made her start. A glowing sting that began to spread up through her loins as blow was added to blow in a steady exotic rhythm at which Royce was reputed to excel.

'Pain begets pleasure.' His voice over the cognac rang in her ears now. And she remembered how she had repeated the phrase silently to herself, the words swilling gently around her head like the amber liquid around the glass balloon she warmed in her hands. 'Pain begets pleasure.' And then Royce told her how the session would end. Two vibrators, not one. Teasing and tormenting her until she climaxed. That, he had insisted, was how it should always be.

And, as she hung suspended, her body slicked with sweat from her ecstatic convulsions, she knew that was exactly how it had been. Royce was indeed the master.

It was over. Royce bent and kissed the top of her head. A thank-you, a reassurance. It was not something she had seen him do to any of the other girls.

She had just managed to gasp the expected: 'Thank you, Master.' It occurred to her dimly that maybe she meant it.

Some of the audience started to clap their appreciation. Then abruptly it died away. Something was wrong.

Sandy was suddenly aware of a heavy crashing sound in the background. Penetrating, determined. A sound of timber giving under pressure.

She tried to open her eyes, but they still smarted with sweat. It was hard at first to make out the carpeted aisle in front of the stage that led to the short flight of steps to the double oak-panelled doors. A stunned silence had descended on the audience. All heads were turned towards the doors.

Beside her, Royce stood poised, motionless.

By the doors, a dinner-suited bouncer shrugged in a gesture of helplessness.

Maltese Max stood up. 'What is it? Police?'

The bouncer was starting to look scared. 'I don't think so, guvnor.'

Even as he answered, the head of the first sledgehammer pierced the panelling of the doors with ear-splitting power. The bouncer leapt back, just as a second hammer blow burst in, wrenching free one of the top hinges. With a sickening squeal, the door lurched inward. A woman in the audience screamed.

At that moment three figures appeared as silhouettes in the doorway. The first two were tall and smartly dressed in black overcoats. Overcoming his initial surprise, the bouncer rushed forward. His stomach met with the handle of a sledgehammer, jabbed hard into the soft tissue of his overweight stomach, ripping a hole in the frothy white front of his tuxedo. He let out an involuntary belch as he doubled over, only to be met with an upper cut to the jaw from the metal hammerhead.

He tumbled backwards and bumped ignominiously down the steps.

This time a dozen women screamed and the stunned audience burst into a frantic attempt to escape the intruders.

The detonation of the first barrel of the sawn-off shotgun merged with the noise from an avalanche of plaster descending from the ceiling.

'FREEZE!' The power in the man's voice demanded immediate compliance. All movement stopped instantly as a murmur of frightened voices ran through the gathering. 'Anyone who moves before they're told gets the second barrel, right?'

James Robinson looked slowly around to see if anyone was going to argue with him. No one was. A sickly smile began to spread across his face as his eyes fixed on the small stage and the suspended girl.

'My, my,' he said, his eyes glittering, 'what have we here? A gathering of perverts. How very interesting.' He lowered the shotgun, cradling it casually in the crook of his arm. 'Now everyone stays calm and no one gets hurt.'

Robinson edged slowly down the steps, circled the bouncer's body, and walked across to Max's table. The Maltese proprietor was visibly trembling, his cheeks purple with rage and fear.

'Hallo, Maxie,' Robinson goaded. 'I don't suppose you expected to see us again, did you?'

Behind the tortoiseshell glasses, Max's eyes blinked rapidly. 'What do you want?' The defiant tone was crumpled at the edges.

'A word, Maxie. Just a word.'

The Maltese swallowed. 'I did what you said.'

Robinson didn't seem to hear. He turned and called up to Ian O'Rourke who stood by the shattered doors, weighing the sledgehammer menacingly in his hands. 'Let the people go, shall we?' he called out mockingly. 'Let the perverts off lightly?'

Ian O'Rourke smirked. 'I don't think they'll cause any trouble. I'm sure they won't want the police to call and close this place down.'

Robinson tittered. 'Won't have anywhere to play their perverted little games, will they?' He called to the third man who remained a shadowy silhouette in the doorway. 'What do you think?'

The third man's accent was different from the other two. It wasn't the voice of an Ulsterman that replied impatiently: 'Let's just get on with it! Get rid of this filth!'

Once more Robinson looked around at his captive audience. 'Right, you heard the man. Leave real slow. Any rush and I'll blow you away. In five minutes I don't want to find one car left in the grounds. And if anyone calls the police, they'll find your friend Max here spread all over the wall like strawberry jam.' Again he smiled, before adding: 'And we'll come looking for *you*. Right, get *going*!'

There was a sudden shuffle of activity as everyone began moving towards the aisle.

Royce stepped forward. Robinson swung round and jabbed the barrel into his solar plexus. 'Not you! You stay put, you fucken pervert. And unstrap that fucken whore.'

Robinson stepped up onto the stage, and waved the gun at Royce as he unwound the wall winch, lowering Sandy's arms. Slowly, she went down onto all-fours, her feet still retained by the anklets.

'You!' Robinson snapped.

Bella stepped nervously forward from where she'd been hiding behind the side curtain.

'Jesus, another fucken pervert,' Robinson exclaimed as he saw the nipple-rings. 'Go on, undo your friend's legs.'

He watched as Bella went to work with trembling fingers. 'Don't we know you?'

She didn't reply.

'Oh, yes. You're the little junkie that told us about Max when we called.' He chuckled at the irony of it. 'So this is how you get your kicks?'

As the blood flowed back into her limbs, Sandy staggered to her feet. She'd started to shiver like a tuning-fork. Not from the draught from the open door, but in sheer terror. It had taken only a few moments for her to recognise the two men. Not by their faces, but their voices and the callous way they spoke. They were the two who had beaten her up outside her flat in Newey House when she'd got into debt with 'Greasy Harry'.

She cursed the stupid, provocative regalia she now stood in, naked and vulnerable. There was nothing she could do except stay quiet and hope she'd escape their attentions. Thank God she still wore the catmask.

As the last of the patrons fell over themselves to get out, she realised with a sinking heart that the Ulstermen had no intention of letting those on the stage go, too. When the crowd had finally dispersed and the noise of starting cars began outside, the third man came down the aisle.

He walked with the aid of a stick, she noticed, and had one arm in a sling. It was difficult to tell much more because he was still outside the stage spotlight when he sat down on a chair.

Robinson looked over to where Max still stood, stout and defiant. 'So you can't think why we've called, eh?'

'No, I did what you said,' Max replied grumpily.

'Stopped dealing with your friends from Dublin, have you?'

'That's what you told me to do.'

'Don't get smart with me,' Robinson sneered. 'You still haven't ordered supplies from us.'

Max was not one to be lightly intimidated. 'I told you, I'm getting out of this business. It's not worth all this hassle.'

Robinson leaned forward until his breath began to steam up the lenses of Max's spectacles. 'Not *worth* it! Now I *know* you're lying, you perverted pimp. With the amount of smack you're shiftin', it's always got to be *worth* it! What's a little aggravation against what you're stowing away?'

Robinson looked up at Royce and the two girls on the stage. He jabbed the barrel of the shotgun in Sandy's direction. 'You! Take off that bloody mask!'

He swung the weapon towards Royce. 'And you, you desecrator of women, take that stupid fucken leather head-dress off! I ought to whip your fucken bollocks for you.'

In one movement, Royce ripped off the leather helmet, his long black hair falling free. His violet eyes blazed with rage. 'You are such a brave man when you've got a gun to back you up. These girls have got more guts and courage than you'll ever have!' His words were venom. 'The world is so full of men like you. Only happy when you intimidate the helpless. To us, that sort of thing is a game, a fetish. To bullies and cowards like you, it is real!'

Robinson blinked for a moment, then appealed to O'Rourke. 'My God, am I hearing things? Did this pervert really say that?'

O'Rourke cackled. 'I do believe he did.'

With a sudden movement, Robinson swung back towards the stage, swiping the barrel of the shotgun hard up into Royce's groin. A grunt of agony escaped his lips, as he collapsed into a crouch on the floor, hugging himself against the pain.

O'Rourke laughed. 'Steady on. You've probably given the bugger a hard-on.'

Robinson turned back to Max. 'Now, listen, you. I'm just about sick of your smart-arse back-talk. It hadn't escaped our notice that just days after we put the pressure on you, your friends in Dublin tipped off the Customs to intercept our latest consignment. And we are *not* very amused.'

Max shrugged. 'I know nothing about it. It's nothing to do with me.'

'No?'

'No.'

A sickly smile crossed Robinson's face. 'I think it's very much to do with you. You told your friends in Dublin, and they've decided to frighten us off. Well, it hasn't worked. And, what's more, we want revenge. We want *their* next consignment and you're going to help. Understood?'

Max shook his head. 'They don't tell me anything.'

Robinson laughed bitterly. 'Well, they've got to tell you about *your* next delivery, haven't they? We'll make do with that. Call it quits. That way you can keep your precious club and all your perverted friends.'

Max stood his ground. 'Get stuffed.'

Robinson and O'Rourke exchanged glances and shrugged in mock helplessness. 'There's always an easy and a hard way of doing things.'

He looked back onto the stage, deciding the best way to persuade Maltese Max to co-operate. Royce, now bent double in a very private agony? The junkie with the nipplerings? The other girl, the one in the catmask? . . . He did a double take.

Without the mask she looked a mess. Like the other girl she had the sunken moon eyes and waxy pallor of a heroin addict. But beneath the sheen of sweat and dribbling mascara, she looked decidedly more attractive than Bella. Not hardbitten, but innocent and vulnerable. Her mouth was soft. He watched as she nervously wiped the damp hair that stuck to her forehead. Something about her was familiar.

O'Rourke got there first. It was the association with Bella that put the final piece in the jigsaw. 'That's the bird from Newey House, remember?'

A sudden smile of realisation spread over Robinson's face. 'The Robson woman.'

O'Rourke added: 'Her old man's been knocking around with Lewis for the last few weeks. They were in Malta together.'

'Small world,' Robinson muttered.

'Did you say Lewis?' It was the third man who spoke.

The other two turned as the man climbed unsteadily to his feet and limped into the glare of the stage lights with the aid of his stick.

Sandy's pulse began to race, her ribcage heaving against the restraining leather harness as the growing fear made her breathless.

Who was this strange man whose dark gypsy eyes glared at her with such malevolence? Why was there such hatred in that face with the sideburns that cut like scimitars across his high cheekbones?

'I'll get Max to co-operate,' he promised darkly. 'If this woman's husband was with Lewis in Malta, then it was probably him who did *this*!' He lifted up his bandaged arm. 'I owe that bastard.'

Sandy's mouth dropped open. She just didn't comprehend.

'You got a cigar?' he snapped at Max.

'Er, yes . . .' The Maltese suddenly realised what he was being asked. 'Oh, no-oo!'

Tom Rabbit snatched it from him. 'Bring that bastard Max closer. I want to see if he can stand the smell of a woman's burning flesh.'

★   ★   ★

'You won't regret your decision,' Frank Lewis said emphatically.

'I think I do already,' Robson replied bitterly, and swung the Rover towards the town centre.

Lewis laughed lightly. He was a man used to having his own way. Everyone had their price and he had just found out what Robson's was. Five thousand pounds, and cheap at the price.

'I promise you,' Lewis was saying, 'this'll be positively my last business deal with Dee. I had no idea he was involved with the Provos.'

Robson slowed to negotiate the high street traffic. 'It was as clear as the nose on your face.'

'To you perhaps.' Lewis was becoming tetchy. 'I just looked on it as business.'

Robson wasn't convincned. 'And if he puts pressure on you again?'

'It'll be different once I'm back in England. I'll be on home ground. Anyway, with you around he'll think twice about causing any trouble. He won't forget that carnage you caused in a hurry.'

'That's what I'm afraid of,' Robson replied. 'Besides, I've only agreed to be around, as you put it, until you get back from Boston. Then I quit.'

Lewis nodded. 'I understand.'

'I'm not sure you do,' Robson replied testily. 'I'm staying on against my better judgement. And I'm doing it just because that money will give me a chance to make a go of things. I trusted you, but I think you've been less than honest with me. Yet you knew the shit I'd be in if I'm caught in something dodgy.'

It was Lewis's turn to sound irritated. 'Exporting pet-food is hardly a criminal offence.'

Robson grimaced. 'If Dee's involved I wouldn't bank on it. There must be something in it for the Provos. It stinks.'

The other man shrugged. 'They probably want a cut for setting up the deal, that's all.'

'It's enough,' Robson retorted.

He didn't want to dwell on the thought that he was compromising his ideals. The idea had crossed his mind to report everything he knew about Dee to the authorities. Maybe even look up his old Commanding Officer and tell him in confidence.

But he was a realist. In fact he actually *knew* precious little. Mostly it was his own speculation. And how would that look when it inevitably got back to his Probation Officer? He was walking a knife-edge. Found mixing with company like that even old Heathers would have him thrown back in the slammer. He was sure of that.

Lewis jabbed a finger towards a discreet sign at the roadside. 'Right here.' Robson complied, slowing to turn down a narrow track beside a railway line. 'Anyway, Billy, I'm sure you'll change your mind about quitting at all when you have time to think it over.'

It had taken a lot of persuasive talk by Lewis to make him stay on at all. Apparently he didn't fully trust Blair Wallace to run things in his absence, and pointed out that Robson, at least, owed him some loyalty after giving him his first lucky break in five years. That appeal to his conscience had finally done it. He couldn't deny he was grateful.

He had little option but to accept that Lewis hadn't realised what he was getting into with Dee. But he wasn't so convinced that Lewis would be able to resist the obvious hold the man had over him. The Irish Sea was hardly a deterrent. Not when you considered that a passport wasn't even needed.

No, he'd just take Lewis's offer of five thousand pounds and run. Added to his earnings over the past few weeks since his release, he'd have enough money to buy a decent car and join a mini-cab firm. He knew a few friends who had done very nicely out of that.

'It's just up ahead,' Lewis warned.

Robson slowed the Rover around the last bend of the track as high wire gates came into view.

'Bigger than I thought,' he admitted. The perimeter fence topped with coils of rusted barbed wire disappeared into the trees on either side. At intervals, signs in bright red lettering warned of guard dogs on the loose. Beyond, the dark grey prefabricated building looked vast and, as he drew to a halt, he could see it was just part of a complex of several factories. Outside one of them a row of refrigerated trailers was backed up to the platform of a loading-bay.

'Give a couple of toots,' Lewis advised. 'The Mulqueens aren't small fry, Billy. This is one of the biggest meat operations in Eire. Apart from the abattoirs, there's meat-processing and packing plants as well. A couple of dozen trailers leave here every day for the Middle East. And now that new canning factory – the one owned by McCrohan and Molloy – has been built at the back.'

The noise of the hooter had disturbed Bernadette who'd been asleep on the back seat.

'Are we here?'

'Getting here was the easy part,' Lewis replied. 'Gettin' in is the tricky bit.'

'Security is a bit over-the-top,' Robson observed. 'I can't believe there's much crime in a small backwater like this.'

Bernadette laughed as she smoothed out her clothes. 'You'd be surprised what goes on in Ireland, Billy. Its very quietness attracts a lot of unscrupulous people.'

A uniformed security guard emerged from the main building, opened one of the gates, and checked the occupants suspiciously before allowing them in.

A black Audi with diplomatic plates was parked alongside the Mulqueens' opulent Mercedes Florida. Robson slid the Rover into an adjoining space. As he climbed out, he was stunned to recognise the driver.

'Small world, Billy.' Kevin Shard was immaculate in blazer, Marine Corps tie, and grey slacks.

'Good grief, what are you doing here?'

Shard smiled thinly. 'By the look of things, the same as you. A bit of chauffeuring.'

Robson turned to Lewis and Bernadette. 'You remember Kevin? The shoot-out at that casino in Malta.'

'Remember!' Lewis shook Shard's hand enthusiastically. 'I only wish I could forget! I reckon we all owe our lives to you. In fact, we looked around for you afterwards. The least I wanted to do was buy you a drink.'

Shard's smile was embarrassed. 'I thought it best not to hang about with the police asking awkward questions.'

'There were no problems afterwards?' Robson asked.

'No. There might have been if the police had got hold of me. As it was, the Libyans contacted the Maltese Government and smoothed everything over. No problem.' He hesitated. 'I'm sorry about the girl. What was her name?'

'Emy. Emy Graziani.'

'Oh yes, I gather she was a particularly close friend.'

Robson suddenly sensed that Shard knew more than

might have been expected. 'Yes. Her death was a devastating blow. Tragic.'

'Even more so for her.' Shard's eyes followed Lewis and Bernadette as they walked towards the office door. 'I warned you about mixing with the Libyans.'

Robson wasn't sure how to take it. 'We don't all have a choice, Kevin.'

Shard seemed angry. 'We all have a choice, Billy, and it's not worth it. Get out while you can.'

At that moment, the door to the office swung open and three men with distinctive Arabic features emerged. Robson recognised one of them as the Libyan he had met in Malta, Sher Gallal.

Kevin Shard straightened his back. 'We'll be off now, Billy. Just remember what I said.'

Thoughtfully, Robson walked towards the office, passing Gallal who was too busy in conversation to notice him.

Shard's words had left him feeling profoundly uneasy. No, not so much his exact words as the implication behind them. As though he wanted to say more but couldn't.

But at the same time Robson resented his interference. Men like Shard always fell on their feet, he thought bitterly. He'd got to the top of his military career hardly without trying, and he'd evidently made a smooth transition to civilian life. Like a duck to water. Lucky bastard.

'Like to see your first consignment?'

The boyish, crooked-toothed grin of Dermot Mulqueen greeted him at the door.

'Pardon?'

Dermot laughed and extended his gangling arm in the direction of the abattoir. 'This way. Thought you'd like to see the fruits of the first business deal of your new company. It's being loaded now.'

'The offal for London?'

'Indeed! Indeed!' Dermot returned gaily, and led the way into the tall clinical shed of the abattoir where row after row of beef carcasses rattled automatically on hooks along gleaming aluminium rails. Robson never realised that death could be so automated.

Without thinking, he said: 'It's likely to be my first and last deal.'

'Really?' Dermot seemed surprised.

'I'm quitting.'

'Oh,' the Irishman replied thoughtfully, and led the way across a steel gantry that crossed above the clanking train of red meat. 'Frankie seemed to think you'd been given a good deal. Directorship and all.'

'Just not my scene,' Robson replied cagily.

Again Dermot laughed. 'It's a bit gory, isn't it? But you get used to it. You'll change your mind once your first business deal comes off, and you see the profits totting up in your bank account.'

Dermot Mulqueen had a point. Robson couldn't deny a thrill when he saw the bright aluminium caskets of offal being loaded onto the freezer trailer. Lewis and Bernadette were already there.

'Look at that!' Lewis enthused. 'In a few days that'll be in store with some catfood manufacturer in London. And we'll have added a few more noughts to our bank balance. Gives you a good feeling, doesn't it?'

Robson gave a wry grin. It was the first time he'd ever been in business. He had to admit it did give him a good feeling. Independence.

Lewis saw his opportunity. 'Don't quit, Billy. I know we'll make a great team. Put the past behind us. After Boston I promise you I'll have nothing more to do with Dee. Never again. In a year or two you'd be set up for life. Financially independent. What's that Marine expression of yours? Go for it?'

After a pause, Robson said: 'Do you really mean that, Frankie?'

'Promise. I just wish I'd never met the bastard in the first place.'

Robson smiled. 'Then let's give it a try.'

Andy Sutcliff fumbled for the bedside light.

The heavy night's drinking at Rich Abbott's spieler had been worth it. He'd chanced the entire proceeds from the unexpected car sale on a game of poker. And he'd come up smiling with three kings. It was a result that meant he'd be able to buy off the VAT-man for a few months while he got himself on his feet again.

Only now he wished he hadn't celebrated his windfall *quite* so enthusiastically. His thumping head was the penalty.

But, as the dim glow from the lampshade scorched his eyeballs, he realised that the distant banging wasn't all in his head. Someone was at the front door. Christ!

He stumbled out of bed and threw the well-worn tartan dressing-gown over his naked body before padding to the door.

The urgent thud of the lion's-head knocker grew in volume as he negotiated the stairs to the passage.

'Okay, I'm coming,' he croaked. Half-asleep, he threw open the door.

'Thank God you're in!'

Sutcliff blinked. 'Christ, Sand. What the hell . . . ? Do you know what time it is?'

Sandy Robson's face was as white as a sheet. 'Yes, Andy, I know. I'm sorry.' She turned to another figure whom he hadn't noticed in the darkness behind her. Vandals had knocked the street lamps out again. 'This is a friend of mine. Bella.'

Sutcliff squinted at the drawn white face huddled in the collar of an expensive fur coat. 'Charmed, I'm sure. At any *other* time, but . . .'

'Andy, *please* can we come in? It's important.'

He stood back. 'I guess it must be. Sure, come on in. You're just in time for breakfast. Go on through.'

He followed them into the rear living-room, and watched as they sat down on the settee. Sandy was clearly trembling.

'I just hope this isn't about what I think it is,' he warned. 'I've no cash in the house, so you're out of luck.'

Sandy shook her head vehemently. 'No, Andy. I'm all right for money. It's about Billy.'

Suddenly Sutcliff felt horribly awake. 'Christ, what's happened to him? An accident?'

She shook her head. 'No. Nothing like that. He's still away in Ireland. But somehow he's got himself involved in a drugs racket –'

'Billy?' Sutcliff was incredulous. 'God, Sand, are you high? Having hallucinations or something? Not Billy. No way.'

Tears began to seep from her eyes. 'It's true, Andy.'

'I thought he was working with Frankie Lewis.'

'He is!' Sandy retorted. 'But Lewis is all part of it.'

Sutcliff was confused. He scratched at the tangled mane of fair hair at his chin. 'This is crazy. Everyone knows Lewis is as straight as they come.'

'Apparently not.' Bella spoke for the first time.

Sutcliff eyed her suspiciously. 'Who told you this?'

'It doesn't matter who,' Sandy said quickly.

He went to retort, then decided against it. He crossed the room uneasily and flopped onto the spare armchair. This was all a bad dream; he must still be asleep. It didn't make sense. He looked up. 'Sand, this is preposterous. I don't believe it for a minute. And even if it was true, what the hell do you expect me to do about it? Certainly not at – what? – four in the bloody morning. I mean, Christ, couldn't it have waited a few more hours?'

Bella said: 'Tell him. Tell him all of it.'

Sandy looked horrified. 'Bella, please . . .'

'What the hell is going on?' Sutcliff demanded. He was starting to sound very angry.

'Tell him,' Bella repeated.

Sandy's tear-slicked face turned to Sutcliff. She had to sniff heavily before she was able to continue. 'I came straight here as soon as I found out because I was scared. We both were.'

'Scared of what? Where were you?'

'At a club,' she replied evasively. 'While we were there those two Irishmen came in and bust things up.'

'What Irishmen?'

'Jesus, Andy. The two that called here and knocked you about, and poured acid over your car.'

Sutcliff paled. 'Oh my God, *those* bastards?'

She nodded. 'The same two who beat me up. They forced their way into the club. Obviously they had some sort of feud with the owner over drugs. A Maltese bloke called Max. Anyway, they recognised Bella and me. They knew Billy was my husband and they knew he worked for Lewis. Another bloke said he thought Billy had beaten him up or shot him or something, in Malta . . .'

Sutcliff raised his hands in protest. 'Hey, slow down! You're losing me. You mean this is something to do with that business in Malta?'

She shrugged. 'That's what they claimed.'

'Well, there was certainly something odd about all that,' Sutcliff muttered, and stared at his fingers for a moment, flexing them thoughtfully. Then he looked up. 'How do you know this is all about drugs? Those two Irish bastards could be into all sorts of things.'

Sandy shook her head. 'Max is a dealer. Bella gets her smack from him and—' She looked sheepish, '—and so do I now. It's obvious the Irishmen wanted Max to buy off them but he won't. All I can think is that he's getting the stuff off Frankie Lewis.'

Sutcliff smacked his forehead with his palm. 'I had no idea Lewis was into anything like that . . . ! I don't think anyone else is. Even Rich Abbott swore blind he was the straightest bloke he knew.'

'It's not the sort of business people advertise,' Bella interjected.

Sutcliff grimaced. 'No, of course not. Anyway, what happened when those Irish blokes recognised you? They didn't do anything . . . ?'

'I don't want to talk about it,' Sandy snapped.

Bella stood up. 'Show him, Sand.'

'No, I can't.'

With a quick movement, Bella caught her friend's wrist and twisted it against the joint. 'Get up!'

'Leave her!' Sutcliff protested.

Sandy gasped for breath as she tried to hold her balance. She exchanged a long hateful look with Bella, then nodded, resigned. With trembling fingers she unbuttoned her rain-coat and let it fall open.

It took a full two seconds for Sutcliff to comprehend what he saw. The first thing that registered and shocked him was the bondage harness she wore. A complex criss-cross of leather straps and nothing else. Then he saw the circular weals on her belly and thighs. They were still wet and weeping, the surrounding skin tinged with scorch marks.

Aghast, he looked at her, waiting for some kind of explanation.

'A cigar,' Sandy said. 'They wanted to find things out from Max. After they did that a few times, he agreed to talk.'

'They went into the office,' Bella added. 'That's when we managed to slip away. We grabbed our coats; there was no way we could risk trying to get our clothes.'

Sutcliff shook his head in disbelief. 'Is this what it's come to, Sandy? Prostitution?'

'It's not what you think,' she pleaded.

He looked disgusted. 'What am I supposed to think? All the kinky gear.'

Bella said: 'Max's club is an S and M place.'

'What?'

'S and M. Sado-Masochism. It's not prostitution.'

Again Sutcliff's mouth dropped. 'God, I don't believe this. I need a drink.' He shuffled across the room to the drinks cabinet and poured a measure of Scotch into a tumbler. He had second thoughts and added another slug. 'You two?'

The women declined, and he turned back to face them.

'I don't know what to say. I really don't. God, is this really the level you've sunk to? I mean, I mean, Christ, it's a sewer, a . . .'

Bella was getting angry. 'You don't *have* to say anything. Just *help* her. She's got no one else to turn to.'

Sutcliff downed the drink in two quick gulps. 'I'm through

with her. Before, it was heroin. Now this as well. Sod it, I've had enough.'

'You were happy enough to screw her when it suited you,' Bella snarled.

Sutcliff's eyes blazed at Sandy. 'Bella's my friend,' she said lamely.

He poured another drink; this time he was shaking too. 'I don't see what I can do.'

Bella crossed the floor and pulled at his shoulder, twisting him round to face her. 'The least you can bloody do is look after her until Billy gets back. She's scared witless those Irishmen will come back. They know where she lives.'

A thought occurred to him. 'Is Danny at the flat?'

Sandy nodded, biting her lower lip.

'Christ. Alone?'

'He is nine . . .'

Andy Sutcliff was suddenly galvanised into action, heading towards the door. 'I'll drive over right away and bring him back here. I'd better bring some of your clothes as well. When is Billy due back?'

'The day after tomorrow.'

'Well, you can stay until then. There's a lot of sorting out to be done.' He glanced at Bella. 'What about you?'

Bella replied sweetly, 'They're not interested in me. Perhaps you could drop me off at my place on the way.'

'Sure.' He turned back to Sandy. 'You be all right on your own for half-an-hour?'

'Yes.'

He went to leave, but Sandy clung onto his arm. 'Thank you, Andy. I don't know what I'd do without you.' Her eyes were moist.

Sutcliff bit his tongue. He had no doubt she'd always want the needle as her real friend when things got too much.

He gently prised away her grip. He said: 'Bella was right. It's the least I can do.'

Thirteen

'Marvellous things, computers,' Major Bill 'Boyo' Harper decided aloud.

He peered over his half-moon spectacles at the gathering around the table in the spartan New Scotland Yard conference room.

'Personally, I don't understand the bloody things,' Fred Roxan of Customs and Excise muttered.

Across the table Detective Chief Superintendent Ray Pilger allowed himself a faint smile. If anyone was going to disagree with anyone, it was Fred. It was a matter of principle.

'Well, like 'em, understand 'em, or not,' Harper rejoined, 'we wouldn't have progressed this fast without them.'

'I'm not sure that we have anything that definite yet, Bill,' Pilger interrupted. He didn't want to give the impression of a breakthrough, just to allow Fred Roxan the satisfaction of crowing when it all came to nothing.

'Not at all,' Harper replied. 'That's the whole point. It's the computer that's been able to link together one and one to make three.'

Roxan's florid face turned belligerently towards the major. 'What I *do* understand about computers is that they can only say one and one equals one and one,' he said sourly.

Harper grinned. 'Point taken. Basic binary, eh? I'm not trying to read more into this than there is. But we've been able to link up some quite separate incidents and a sort of pattern seems to be emerging.'

He turned to Pilger. 'Would you like to bring us up to date with how it began, Ray?'

Pilger lit a cigar and consulted the file on his desk. 'It all started about a week after our first meeting here. When we briefed you about the whole heroin scene. Out of the blue we got a tip-off by telephone to the Squad Room. An Irish accent, but no IRA code. Then, within minutes, I got a second call on my direct line.'

'Another tip-off?' Harper checked.

'Yes. Same flight from Karachi, but another name. And the speaker was also Irish, but this time with a definite Southern accent.' He glanced across at Roxan. 'That, of course, was Customs jurisdiction so we passed the information over.

'In short, the main courier was apprehended. He couldn't tell us much, but by checking with Fred's agent in Pakistan it seemed pretty clear it was set up by one of the Protestant para-military outfits from Ulster. Probably the UDA. Apparently someone from the organisation was reported recently as having been seen making enquiries in Landi Katal.'

'Ah, yes!' Harper exclaimed, consulting his notebook. 'That's a mountain village in the Khyber Pass right on the Afghan border. A medieval bazaar where the trade is in arms and heroin. A virtual no-go area for the Pakistan authorities.'

'My, my, we have been doing our homework,' Roxan muttered. His sarcasm hid a growing respect for the major.

Pilger continued: 'We put a tail on the decoy courier: a Pakistani woman. Eventually she had a rendezvous with a couple of Irishmen at a derelict house by an East End hous-ing estate. We now know them to be a James Robinson and an Ian O'Rourke. Special Branch have confirmed they are believed to have connections with the UDA. Nothing conclusive, but Robinson's got some previous for carrying a firearm without a licence. That was Belfast in '74. Nothing since but he's a known hardcase. In 1980 we had his name linked to a cannabis racket, buying from Jaffras in Lebanon. But he was always in the background.

'His partner O'Rourke is a bit of a clown, but a mean bastard all the same. Anyway, the two of them met this Paki woman, which was a surprise, I admit, as she was only the decoy. It suggests they were desperate for a consignment. In the event, they didn't even get all of that. The poor cow had swallowed the stuff in condoms, and one of them burst.'

Harper grimaced. 'She died?'

Pilger sniffed distastefully at the glowing tip of his cigar. 'Massive overdose. Nasty way to go, but quick enough. At least she connected us with Robinson and O'Rourke. We trailed them back to their flat in St John's Wood.'

'Can't beat the old basic policework, eh?' Harper chimed encouragingly

Roxan grunted.

'We were able to get a Telecom man in to repair their phone the next day and put a tap on. And that's when everything started to click.'

Harper raised his hand. 'Before you lose me, Ray, let's go back to this strange double tip-off. Are you saying the one was from someone with Eire connections, and the second from an Ulsterman?'

Pilger looked uncomfortable. 'I'm afraid it's jumping to conclusions. But for our purposes, we might *assume* that the IRA's somehow involved. I think Robinson tipped us off about his own decoy, to let his main courier slip through. Then *someone else* – with the Dublin accent – told us about the main courier.'

Harper pursed his lips. 'So what did you learn from the tap?'

'Firstly, that the Protestant Irishmen were putting the pressure on a distributor known as Maltese Max,' Pilger replied. 'He used to be one of the Soho porn kings. Clubs and prostitution. Now he appears to run a respectable travel agency – although his client list is a right rogues' gallery. Organises a lot of trips to Spain, Amsterdam, and that sort of thing. But his main income now must be from heroin – most of it directed north to Scotland.'

'So what sort of pressure were O'Rourke and Robinson putting on Max?' Harper asked.

'To buy from them.'

'Ah, trying to muscle in, eh? So who was this Max buying from? Is that where this chap Lewis comes in?'

Pilger nodded and stubbed out his cigar butt in the ashtray. 'As well as the telephone tap we also put a watch on Max's travel agency where he operates. He made a whole series of phone calls to a man called Frank Lewis. He sounded desperate, but he kept getting one of those blank-wall receptionists. Lewis was playing hard to get. Eventually, he paid a visit to Lewis. Unfortunately, there's no way of knowing what they discussed.'

'And there's nothing at that stage to connect this Frank Lewis specifically with drugs?' Harper asked.

Pilger shook his head. 'None at all. Apart from a few misdemeanours in his youth, Lewis is as clean as a whistle. Bit of an entrepreneur. Built up a little business empire. Catering supplies, building, contract cleaners.'

'And the IRA?' Harper pressed.

Pulling an awkward smile, Pilger said: 'A lot more possibilities there. His common-law wife is an Irish girl called Bernadette Mulqueen. Her mother runs a staunch Republican pub called the Czar in South London. Her brothers run a big meat-processing plant in Eire. They're well-connected, and it's since Lewis became involved with the Mulqueen girl that his empire has really expanded. His building business involves a lot of Irish labour. *And* he buys the Mulqueens' meat to sell in the Middle East. His main customers appear to be Libya and Iran.'

'And that made you suspicious?' Harper asked.

'That's when I handed over a copy of the file to your TIGER people,' Pilger confirmed. 'It struck me that, of all the Middle East countries, he was doing business with two of the most notoriously difficult to deal with. You have to have *very* good contacts by all accounts.

'Also, Iran used to be an important source of heroin, although Ayatollah Khomeini is reputed to have clamped down on it. And, of course, Gadaffi of Libya is known to have flirted with the IRA from time to time.'

For once even Fred Roxan seemed impressed with his arch-adversary's powers of deduction.

'Well, I'm glad you brought it to my attention, Ray,' Harper said. 'Our computer access tied-up Lewis to an SIS report of a recent incident in Malta. The High Commissioner filed an account of the murder of a well-known Sicilian Mafia drug dealer called Carmelo. There was an ambush at a church during an apparent drugs exchange. With him was an Irish fellow called Tom Rabbit. He's a well-known Dublin gangster with Provo connections. He was wounded in the incident, but there was no evidence of a charge on which the Maltese police could hold him.'

'Where did Lewis fit in?' Pilger asked.

'Frank Lewis was in Malta at that time. He was tying up some sort of deal with the Libyans, ostensibly about meat. In fact, his meeting coincided with a visit of a top Libyan diplomat who is Gadaffi's key liaison man with Iran.'

'How d'you know that?' Pilger was intrigued.

Harper grinned and tapped his nose. 'God and Her Majesty's secret services move in mysterious ways.'

'Is that so?' Roxan growled. His indigestion was playing up and he was anxious for the meeting to be over.

Harper read the message. 'At that time there was a lot of radio traffic between the Libyan People's Bureau in Malta, Teheran, and Moscow. Intercepted by our GCHQ listening-post at Larnaka, Cyprus. Mostly, it was low-grade, uncoded material about meat shipments, and other imports and exports. I say "uncoded", but then that isn't to say there aren't key words. I mean "lamb chops' could stand for heroin, if you get my meaning.'

'You said Moscow?' Roxan queried. 'Are you linking the Russians in with this business?'

Major Harper smiled faintly. 'They were certainly party to this particular piece of communications traffic, apparently concerned with Frank Lewis. Probably he'd be totally unaware of the link. In fact, though, the Soviets have recognised the use of widespread drug abuse as a possible political weapon since the sixties at the height of flower-power.

'Since our last talk I've been making a lot of inquiries. Apparently, there was a meeting of Warsaw Pact intelligence services in 1967 to discuss the possibilities of using drugs against the West. As a result of that, a three-year plan was started in 1970 through the Bulgarian state KINTEX enterprise, which you gentlemen will know all about. It exchanged arms for drugs with any terrorist or insurgency movement that could supply them. It started channelling the drugs into Europe through existing terrorist and criminal networks. Not only did it give the Warsaw Pact much-needed hard currency, it was also starting to erode the fabric of Western society. In Latin America, Cuba started doing the same sort of thing with cocaine to the United States.'

Pilger and Roxan nodded in agreement. Bulgarian and Cuban involvement had long been recognised but was rarely possible to pin-point.

'What you gentlemen may not appreciate is how large the Soviets' original low-key operation has become. The oil crisis of the 70s and the resulting recession played right into their hands. By the end of the decade Europe was awash with disaffected youth. No jobs, no future, and the propaganda of a nuclear holocaust hanging over their heads. They began turning to drugs in their thousands. And just at that time the Soviets found themselves in Afghanistan – the current heartland of heroin country.' He paused and removed his half-moon spectacles. 'Now I'm not saying they've engineered the current heroin plague. But since 1980 they've been riding the dragon for all it's worth.

'The CIA started it, encouraging the *mohahajeen* to grow the stuff for arms. Then the Soviets adopted the same policy as part of the "hearts-and-minds" campaign for Afghans in areas of their control. That village we talked about earlier – Landi Katal – is rife with KGB men overseeing the selling of the stuff. Our intelligence sources also suggest that, as pressure mounts on the Pakistanis to stop the trade, they are moving it west as well, over their border into Iran.'

'Hold on a minute,' Pilger interrupted. 'I thought Russia backed Iran in the Gulf War. Surely they're not going to do a deal with the Ayatollah.'

Harper's laugh was genuine. 'I'm sorry, Ray. When you've been in my game for as long, you'll see the funny side of that comment.' He leaned forward in earnest. 'Listen. The Soviets deal with anyone if its suits them. Besides, it might not be with the Ayatollah's inner circle. There are plenty of greedy little mullahs trying to build their own little empires. Maybe the Soviets even see it as a way of financing a new clique into power – one which supports them.

'And, besides, that lunatic Gadaffi is supplying Iran with Soviet arms for the war. Moscow doesn't like it, but it doesn't stop them supplying Gadaffi. It's all swings and roundabouts.'

'So if I read you right, Bill,' Pilger said, 'you think Frank Lewis's heroin is being supplied from Afghanistan – or in fact the Russians? It's being routed through Iran and Tripoli, and the whole thing is being orchestrated by the Libyans – who've direct connections with both Iran and the IRA?'

Harper smiled a fat cat smile. 'It's a possibility.'

One thing puzzled Roxan. 'Then what about the murder in Malta? The Sicilian drugs-runner Carmelo who was killed?'

'The word from Malta,' Harper replied, 'is that the IRA are trying to cut out the Mafia.'

'Oh my God,' Pilger gasped. Whether his reaction was to the sheer monumental significance of the revelation, or the thought of the bloody gang war it could herald, he himself wasn't quite sure.

'After Carmelo's murder in Malta,' Harper added, 'gunmen tried to kill Frank Lewis and his oppo. An ex-Royal Marine called Robson. Billy Robson. It was almost certainly the Sicilian Mafia trying to take revenge. At any rate, they failed. Just some woman bystander got killed.'

'We know about this Robson character,' Pilger confirmed. 'Only teamed up with Lewis recently. He's still on parole for a bank job.'

Roxan grunted. 'Some people never learn.'

'I don't like to see ex-Servicemen involved in this sort of thing,' Harper admitted. 'Involved with drugs and possibly the IRA. As a military man, it always leaves me with a nasty taste.'

'We still have no definite connection with the IRA,' Pilger reminded. 'Just that Frank Lewis has a lot of Irish connections. In itself, that isn't a crime.'

Harper said: 'I think we may have something a little more positive shortly.'

'Yes?' Pilger was surprised.

At that moment there was a tap on the door and Derek Dillinger, the quiet, dark-haired detective inspector from the Anti-Terrorist Squad, appeared.

'Spot-on cue, DD,' Harper laughed.

'Sorry I'm late, gents,' Dillinger apologised as he took a seat and opened his attaché-case on the table. 'I've been over at the Irish Embassy doing a bit of homework on the major's behalf.' He waved a buff envelope triumphantly. 'This is what we've been looking for. The direct link between Frank Lewis and the IRA.'

Harper said: 'Lewis turned up in Ulster the other day. He was passing through from the south on his way to Buncrana. We picked him up on a standard computer check on all people passing through our checkpoints. His wife was with him. And Robson was driving.'

Dillinger took over. 'Bill asked me to check up with Irish Special Branch. To see if they had anything on Lewis's visit.'

'And did they?' Roxan pressed.

Dillinger plucked a sheaf of five large glossy prints from the envelope and spread them on the table. Everyone craned forward to see.

The photographs were fuzzy, but clearly showed two men entering a bar. Behind them the engraved legend on the window read 'Mannix Green Hotel'.

'Taken with an image-intensifier night-lens. The bar is a known Provo haunt. The Irish Special Branch keep it under routine observation,' Dillinger explained. 'Half-an-hour later, they left in a hurry.'

He jabbed a finger at a second picture. It was of the same two men, but was badly blurred. 'A few minutes later, they drove down the street – fast. The picture shows the number-plate clearly. Lewis's hired car.'

There were three more prints. 'These are blow-ups of the two. You can see clearly. That's Lewis. And that's his chum Billy Robson.'

'And the third?' Harper asked.

Dillinger smiled with satisfaction. 'That's the man they went to see. Tommy Dee. He's suspected of being very near the top of the IRA hierarchy.'

'Well done, DD,' Harper congratulated.

Dillinger grinned. 'It cost me a crate of Guinness.'

'And worth every bottle,' the major laughed. 'It's our missing link. Well, gentlemen, I think you'll all agree, we are onto something big. Very big.'

'Hey, man, no problem! Hop aboard!'

Spiro hadn't hesitated at Robson's request for a lift. With his usual good humour, the West Indian had offered the pillion of his Yamaha.

It was a slightly chilly ride through the early morning

sunshine. But Robson was glad to be away from Frank Lewis for a while and to put his own thoughts into some sort of order.

He'd been surprised, but not unduly alarmed, at finding the flat empty. He was back a day early after all. Danny could have left early for some football practice before school, although it was unusual for Sandy not to be there. Lately she found it difficult to rise much before noon.

It was very much on impulse that he decided to visit Andy Sutcliff. He couldn't remember the last time they'd had a heart-to-heart, and he would welcome the chance to talk over the Lewis business. Sutcliff was never one to pull his punches, and Robson appreciated his advice – even if he rarely took it.

The raucous burble of the Yamaha shattered the stillness of the narrow sidestreet as Spiro swept away, leaving Robson on the pavement outside No. 36.

The curtains were still drawn, he noticed. Andy Sutcliff never had been an early bird.

The door opened just as his fingers reached the lion's-head knocker.

'Dad!'

Robson blinked. 'Danny? Good grief, son, what are you doing here?'

His son looked uncertain, his face wearing a crumpled expression that suggested he was near to tears.

Robson knelt down. 'What is it, Danny? What's wrong, tell me?'

Danny averted his eyes. 'I dunno, Dad. Mum's gone funny. She went out last night and left me in the flat. I gone to bed and the next thing I know is Uncle Andy's in me room. He says not to worry but there's been some bother. He wants me to come over here with Mum and spend the night.'

'What sort of bother?'

'I dunno, Dad, they wouldn't say. Just said it wasn't nothing to worry about.'

He stood up and put his arm around Danny's shoulders, hugging him roughly. 'Don't worry, son, we'll sort it out. If Mum says there's nothing to worry about, I'm sure there isn't.' His tone belied his true feelings; he could feel his skin crawling with alarm. 'Mum and Andy are in now I take it?'

'Upstairs.' As Robson moved forwards, Danny grabbed his arm. 'No, Dad.'

'What is it?'

Danny fumbled for the words. 'Something's wrong, Dad. I *know* it is. Mum's sick, in the bathroom . . .'

'What?'

His son's face finally disintegrated as he burst into tears.

Robson's eyes moved to the stairs. 'All right, little soldier. Don't you worry about a thing. I'll sort it out.'

'Oh-oh-okay.' Danny sniffed hard and wiped his hand roughly across his nose.

'Were you leaving for school when I arrived?'

Danny nodded.

'You know the way from here?'

'Course, Dad.' Independent.

Robson grinned despite himself. He was proud the way his son seemed to have coped with the family's recent traumas. 'Stupid of me. Now look, I'll pick you up from school this afternoon. We'll go and have a Macdonald's, eh? Special treat. Just the two of us.'

That seemed to do the trick; the tears were finally staunched.

He watched as his son set off sullenly down the road, the battered sports bag swinging from his shoulder.

After quietly closing the door, Robson climbed the stairs, careful to avoid any creaking timbers. On the landing, the bathroom door stood slightly ajar. Something his son had said came back to him. On impulse, Robson pushed the door.

It creaked slowly open onto a scene that momentarily turned his stomach. A shaft of sunshine played like a spotlight on the dribbles of bright red blood glistening against the white porcelain of the wash-basin. Splashes of it had dried on the peeling wallpaper below the mirror.

Immediately he *knew* what it was. But for some reason, his mind by-passed what Danny had said. Christ! Andy Sutcliff on drugs!

Perhaps subconsciously Robson didn't want to accept the truth. But, as his gaze travelled along the blood-trail to the base of the lavatory bowl, he could not ignore the open floral sponge-bag on the floor.

It was Sandy's.

His blood turned to ice. Slowly he knelt down and gingerly picked up the syringe that protruded carelessly from the zipper. Disbelief throbbed in his head. And quite distinctly he heard Bernadette's voice gently warning him at the Leopardstown race-course. This time her words were trapped inside his skull, reverberating round and round and round.

As he opened up the bag, his hands were trembling, his palms sticky with cold sweat. He tipped it up and the whole revolting paraphernalia clattered onto the linoleum. A foil paper package. A dirty teaspoon. A box of matches. A plastic Jif lemon. A length of pyjama cord. A razor blade. There were two plastic pillboxes, too. He could just discern the chemist's scrawl on the label. Valium. The label had peeled from the other, and he prised off the lid. Inside there was a bright assortment of different coloured tablets and capsules.

Sweet Jesus! Slowly he replaced the lid, then stuffed everything back inside the bag. He slid the zipper shut and stayed kneeling, staring blindly at the lavatory bowl, for several long minutes.

'What the fuck do you think you're doing?'

Sandy's words stung his ears.

As though trying to put off the dreaded moment he got up slowly, and turned to face her. She stood in the bathroom doorway, her thin face pinched with anger. Her pupils were like pinpricks, burning out of eyes sunken with exhaustion. Her hair was a stringly mess, hanging on the shoulders of a dressing-gown that was several sizes too large for her. Behind her, the door to Andy Sutcliff's bedroom was open.

'Sandy?' Robson's voice pleaded for some rational explanation.

'What the fuck are you doing with my bag?'

'I'm back a day early.'

'I can see that!' she retorted. 'Let me have my bag.'

'What's all this, Sand?' He nodded towards the bloody mess in the basin.

She was irritable. 'I don't know. Probably Andy cut himself shaving. Now give me the sponge-bag.'

He handed it over, and she snatched it from him. 'I know it's you, Sand.'

'Know what's me, for Christ's sake?'

He took a deep breath. 'I know what's in the bag.'

'That's private . . . !' Her eyes blazed.

'How long has it been going on, Sand?'

Her head began to shake, her eyes turning from side to side as though seeking an escape. 'I don't know what you mean . . .'

'Too long, Billy.'

Andy Sutcliff emerged from the bedroom wearing just a pair of pyjama bottoms.

'Yes?' Robson asked, fighting hard to contain his rising fury.

'It's been going on *too* long,' Sutcliff repeated. 'Sand's been hooked on the stuff for at least two years. Heroin.'

'You BASTARD!' she screamed, flailing a badly-aimed blow which Sutcliff evaded, restraining her with one hand. Giving up, she buried her head against his chest and began to cry.

'And screwing my wife, how long has that been going on?' Robson spat out the accusation.

Sutcliff shook his head. 'It's not what you think, Billy. She came here because she was scared.'

Robson said tersely: 'I thought it was customary for guests to sleep on the sofa?'

'Be your age!' Sutcliff snapped back.

Suddenly Sandy pulled away, tears glistening on the waxy texture of her skin. 'Tell him, Andy! He knows everything else! Tell him!'

'Shut up!' Sutcliff hissed.

'Tell me what?'

Sandy turned up her chin defiantly. 'Andy and I have been having it off for *years*! An affair. An on-going affair. He's got more balls than you'll ever have. How else do you think I managed to keep going?'

Sutcliff was shaking his head. 'It wasn't like that, Billy. Honest.'

'LIAR!' Sandy screamed. She was on the verge of total hysteria.

'Well?' Robson demanded.

Sutcliff shrugged in resignation. 'Oh, Christ, well, yes we did. But not like you think. I was just looking after her. Keeping an eye on her – for a—' He hesitated – 'for a mate. You know. Nothing much happened – well, just a couple of times, before Sand got onto drugs. She needed help. Comfort and understanding. You know?'

'I've got to be hearing things,' Robson said quietly.

Sutcliff sighed. 'Anyway, it all stopped. It all finished before you came out.'

Robson shook his head in disbelief. 'That was bloody decent of you.' He glanced towards the bedroom door. 'And last night?'

Sutcliff looked sheepish. 'It was a mistake . . .'

Sandy glared defiantly. 'If you must know I was scared. Scared and randy. And specially randy for Andy.' She gave a brittle laugh. 'Isn't that funny?'

'God help me!' Robson was seething. 'And with Danny in the next room . . . ?'

'We're suddenly very concerned about our son,' Sandy hissed. 'I suppose we are talking about the same one? The one you didn't want to see you in prison? The one you were happy to leave in England while you went humping your little tart in Malta—'

Robson's knuckles rapped hard against his wife's cheek, stopping her in mid-flow. She fell back against the door jamb.

'Leave it out,' Sutcliff warned.

Robson screwed his eyes tight. 'I'm sorry. I shouldn't have done that.' He opened his eyes again and looked at Sandy. The pathetic huddled figure sobbing in the doorway was no one he knew.

Sutcliff said: 'Billy, we've got to talk.'

Robson nodded.

His friend indicated Sandy. 'She'll need to be in the bath-room for a bit. Let's go downstairs.'

Robson looked at the sponge-bag clutched against her stomach. 'You mean she needs a fix?'

'Yeah. To shoot up.' Patient. 'She *needs* it, Billy. It's not a choice. Her body demands it. We'll be able to talk better then. She'll be calmer. Believe me.'

Reluctantly Robson stepped aside as Sandy pushed past. He had scarcely cleared the door when it slammed shut and the bolt clacked home.

'I'm sorry you came back to that mess in the bathroom,' Sutcliff said, leading the way down the stairs.

Robson's reply was spontaneous. 'It's better this way. Now it's in the open.'

'It's still not a pretty sight. She was in a right state last night. She must have shot up after I went to sleep. I had no idea she'd left the bathroom in such a mess.'

'I should fucking kill you,' Robson said.

Sutcliff paused at the bottom of the stairs. 'I don't blame you. I'd feel the same. But remember, we *all* go back a long way, Billy. Back in our schooldays I fancied her, too, y'know. Along with dozens of others.'

Robson held his gaze. 'That's no excuse.'

Sutcliff shook his head. 'You don't understand. I'm saying that I've always been fond of her. Like you've always been a mate. If she hadn't been a woman, it would have stayed platonic. But I've always *cared* for her. Always. And when she started getting screwed-up while you were inside. Hell, it started with me just being nice to her. You must believe that.'

'And ended up with you screwing her,' Robson reminded coldly.

Sutcliff went to answer, then changed his mind. He could hardly deny the accusation. Instead, he said: 'I'll put some coffee on.'

From upstairs, Robson heard the sound of Sandy being sick. For a moment he hesitated, then followed Sutcliff into the kitchen.

'You said Sand has been on heroin for a couple of years. What started it?'

Sutcliff filled the electric kettle and plugged it in. 'I think you know that, Billy.'

'When I went inside?'

His friend pulled a tight smile. 'You're an insular bastard sometimes, aren't you? It goes back long before that. To when you were in the Marines. Of course, I didn't see so much of either of you when you were based down in Devon. But she used to confide in me then how she hated it. I guess she was never cut out to be a Services wife. All that time left alone. She felt pretty useless, keeping home for a husband who was never there. Even then I had to keep an eye on her – No, not like that! – On one or two occasions I had to tell her to keep off the booze. Used to tuck it away sometimes. Anyway, it got better after Danny was born. I think she felt fulfilled. Useful.'

Robson found himself studying the kettle as it began to rattle towards the boil. It was strange hearing Sutcliff talk like this. As though his friend knew more about his wife than he did. Perhaps it was true.

'Then she got depressed again,' Sutcliff continued, 'because she realised nothing had really changed. She blamed it on – what is it? – post-natal depression. But I reckon it was because she was still living half a life. Well, as she saw it, anyway. It was about that time she started smoking the odd joint or two. One of the Marine wives down at the disco had a ready source.'

The kettle began to boil, and Sutcliff poured three mugs. 'Still black and sweet?'

'Just black. I'm trying to give up sugar.'

Sutcliff pulled a wry smile. 'That's the difference between you and Sand. You've the iron self-discipline, she hasn't. I don't think you could ever sympathise with someone on drugs.'

'And you can?'

Sutcliff added milk to his own. 'In Sandy's case, yes. When you left the Marines, it seemed to her that everything was coming right for the first time. By then, you even had a home of your own, a kid, and she had a full-time husband.'

'Then I went and blew it.' Robson sipped at his coffee.

'You said it, mate,' Sutcliff replied lightly. He'd understood his friend's dilemma at the time, as much as he had Sandy's. 'That's what I was saying. You acted positive when you couldn't get a job – you go and rob a sodding bank . . . !'

For a moment, they shared an ironic chuckle. Sutcliff said: 'You sure you wouldn't like some sugar?'

Robson grimaced. 'It does taste foul without it.' He accepted the sugar bowl and added a single spoonful. Compromise.

'Anyway, Billy, I think that's what did it for Sand. When you went down it was like you signing on with the Marines for another five. Then losing the house and being stuck in that sod-awful tower-block. I know she was on pills from the doctor for a while. Then some neighbours gave her some tabs. What is it? Uppers? I don't know who got her onto smack. I think it was a friend of Bella's. Sand used to snort the stuff. You know, "chasin' the dragon" is the in-expression.

I warned her about it, but she pooh-poohed the idea that she was hooked. It just gave her a buzz. Said it was under control. Promised she'd never ever spike herself. I believed it.' He stared morosely at his coffee mug. 'And so did she at the time.'

'You should have told me.'

Sutcliff's laugh was brittle. 'And what would you have done? Broken out to rescue her? Besides, if the Probation Office had ever found out, that would have been your parole up the Swanee.'

Robson's eyes hardened. 'So what did you do about it? Bugger-all except decide that going with her was some kind of therapy . . .'

'That's not fair!' Sandy's voice from the passage jolted him.

Robson turned. 'Sorry, I didn't hear you.'

She was leaning unsteadily against the staircase, clutching Sutcliff's dressing-gown tightly around her middle.

Her skin had regained some of its colour. Although the look of acute tension had gone from her face, she still held Robson with an accusing stare. 'Just don't try and blame Andy for all this. It was you who fucked up my life. *You.* Andy always stood by me. Always there when I needed support.'

'So I gather,' Robson said.

Her lips curled in a sneer. 'I don't mean *that!*' She turned to Sutcliff. 'Have you told him what you did for me?'

Sutcliff looked embarrassed.

'The money?' she pressed.

'It's not the time . . .' Sutcliff protested.

She turned back to Robson. 'Two years ago, Andy had two garages jam-packed with bloody cars. Nearly all one-owners. He was even negotiating a new high-street site with a Ford franchise.' She paused to let it sink in. 'And then he spent it all on *me*! ME! Twice for an expensive clinic, and in between he paid so I could score.' She turned back to him. 'Now he can't even scrape together a couple of old bangers and he's got a tax bill bigger than the National Debt.'

'I didn't realise,' Robson said lamely.

'You never bloody have!' Sandy retorted.

Sutcliff shuffled uncomfortably. 'Here, there's a coffee for you, Sand.'

She took the offered mug with a trembling hand. 'And you needn't think Andy's responsible for keeping me in money to score. He knew if he didn't, I'd get it some other way. I'd already sold all the furniture, clothes, your suits . . .'

The penny dropped. 'That's right,' Robson recalled, 'I was looking for those . . .'

Sandy seemed to think that was deliriously funny. 'Did you? Did you really . . . ?' She started laughing until her mirth gave way to a choking cough.

Sutcliff said quietly: 'Let's go in the living-room. Sit down and talk it over.'

Robson was still too stunned to argue. Half-an-hour earlier he had unwittingly stepped into a nightmare. It was as though the whole of their lives was passing before his eyes. But had it really been like that? This nightmare account in no way resembled the life with Sandy he recalled.

Insular bastard, Andy had called him. So wrapped up in his own problems, he hadn't even seen the world crumbling around his ears.

He found himself desperately searching for something positive. 'We must get you to a clinic, Sand . . . Get you to someone, somewhere where they can help. We've got a few grand now . . .'

Beside him on the sofa, Sandy suddenly reached for his hand, squeezing it with her own. 'Billy. Stop it. Look, love, you really don't understand. It's not that simple.'

'What d'you mean?'

She took a deep breath. 'For a start, you don't have as much money as you thought.'

Robson frowned. 'Our account . . .'

For the first time that morning, Sandy looked sympathetic. 'Our *joint* account, Billy. I have access to it—'

'You mean . . . ?'

She nodded sadly. 'I'm afraid so.'

'Get that changed,' Sutcliff advised.

Robson said: 'That won't be necessary. Not now. It'll be all right.'

'It *won't!*' Sandy almost shrieked.

Sutcliff explained slowly. 'She can't *help* herself, Billy. Change it. She'll bleed you dry like a fuckin' vampire. I know.'

Sandy looked wretchedly down at the floor.

'Okay,' Robson said at length. 'But we must still get you treatment.'

'It's failed twice before,' Sutcliff pointed out.

Robson was getting angry. 'Then we'll try *again!*' He looked thoughtfully at his coffee mug. 'At least I've got a job. At the moment I'm still working for Frank Lewis. At least he pays well. I had thought of jacking it in . . .'

Sutcliff raised an eyebrow. 'So you *do* know?'

'Know what?'

'Know what business he's in?'

Robson was becoming impatient. 'Of course I bloody do. I'm handling transport and catering supplies. Trouble is he's got some shady friends over in Ireland. They could be connected with the IRA.'

'Oh, my God,' Sutcliff breathed. 'That as well?'

'As well as what?'

Sutcliff nodded soberly. 'So you *don't* know. I thought you didn't somehow.' He stood up. 'I'll pour you a drink. A real one. You're going to need it.'

'Why, for Christ's sake?'

Sutcliff took his time pouring out the three tumblers of Scotch; subconsciously he wanted time to think how best to put it. He decided there was no easy way. 'Frankie Lewis is a drugs trafficker.'

Robson nearly missed the proffered glass. 'What?'

'You heard.'

'That's bloody ridiculous. If he was, I'd know about it.'

'Would you?' Sutcliff held his gaze unblinkingly. 'Like you noticed Sandy was a junkie? Look, Billy, if he's involved with the IRA, he could be involved with *anything*. Perhaps the two are even connected.'

Robson shook his head in disbelief. Sutcliff had been right about the drink. Right now, he could do with the whole bottle.

'It's even possible,' Sutcliff went on, 'that he's the importer of the stuff that Sand's been using.'

'C'mon!' Robson protested.

'Billy, it's true.' There was no lack of conviction in Sandy's quiet statement.

Robson frowned. 'How do you know?'

She told him. Quietly and calmly she recounted the story of the two Ulstermen who had beaten her up outside the flat. The two who had visited the club where she and Bella had been that night. She spared him the details of the type of club and why she was there. Robson seemed to assume that they had just gone out for a quiet drink; all girls together. She did nothing to shatter his illusions.

'Are you sure Maltese Max is a distributor?' he asked.

'Absolutely,' she confirmed. 'The Irishmen said Frankie Lewis is the main supplier. They know you, too. There was another man there as well. Someone I didn't know. He seemed to think you'd shot him in Malta.'

'What?' That made no sense at all to Robson. It had to be something to do with the incident at the church, or that car-chase afterwards. But he couldn't for the life of him work out what.

'So you *do* know this Max bloke?' Sutcliff asked.

Robson nodded thoughtfully. 'It's true he's a friend of Frankie Lewis. Or a business contact, anyway. God, I still can't believe it.'

'Well, those Irishmen did,' Sandy said with feeling. 'Bella and I got away after Max agreed to talk. That's why I couldn't go back home. They know where I live.'

'And they didn't hurt you too badly?' Robson asked again.

'No,' she lied. 'Just knocked me about a bit.'

'Bastards.'

'It could be bad for you if you're involved with drugs,' Sutcliff pointed out unnecessarily.

Robson glared at him. 'Don't I know it! Lewis, the bastard! Christ, if I went down for that, they may as well chuck away the key.'

Sandy opened her mouth in horror. 'Oh, don't!'

Robson stared at the drink in his hands. Suddenly it all became so transparently clear. He had been used. Duped. Taken for the sucker he was. A desperate man clutching at straws. Lewis had offered the helping hand and he'd grabbed it in desperate gratitude.

He'd blindly accepted every explanation that had been offered to him. That crazy business in Malta. Whatever had been going on, he was now certain it had nothing to do with meat.

Meat! That was a joke. Or was it? Meat. Meat was the lowest common denominator. Meat in Malta. Meat deals with the Libyans. Meat in Ireland. That important consignment of meat from Iran Lewis was so eager to check in Ireland.

The thought suddenly struck him. 'Oh, my God!'

'What is it?' Sutcliff asked.

Robson shook his head, then finished his drink in one gulp. 'Nothing.' He stood up. 'I've got to go out.'

'Billy!' Sandy pleaded.

He bent and kissed the top of her head reassuringly. 'I have to go and see Lewis.'

'Don't,' Sutcliff warned. 'That's not a good idea. The drugs business can be pretty nasty.'

'I know. Without realising, it looks like I'm already in it,' he replied icily. 'Don't worry, I'll take care. Can Sand stay with you here?'

Sutcliff blushed. 'Sure.'

Robson realised what his friend was thinking. 'At least Sand's safe with you. Can I borrow your car?'

'If you don't mind the state of the paintwork.'

He tossed the keys across which Robson snatched out of the air. 'It's got to be an improvement over what it was.'

With that, Robson was out into the passage, through the front door and crossing the pavement to the acid-scarred E-type.

As he gunned it into life, his worries about his wife's addiction and her affair with his friend were swamped out by a new fear. The prospect of another long stretch inside. Somewhere on the road or sea between Dublin and London was a container trailer laden with offal.

All the paperwork and documentation was down to one name. One signature. His.

Fourteen

It was ten-thirty when Billy Robson swung the E-type into the drive of Frank Lewis's home in Blackheath.

Difficult to find, the big mock-Georgian house was set well back from the main road in pine-studded grounds. It was fronted by a large, manicured lawn, dotted with orna-mental trees. To one side, evergreen creepers almost hid the private tennis court from view.

The dozen shuttered windows in tasteful dove grey and the treble garage, suggested that Frank Lewis had a rates bill heavy enough to make a millionaire's eyes water. A British Telecom van was parked outside a low flight of steps that led to a pair of panelled oak doors.

Robson parked the E-type beneath a decorative iron street lamp that someone had uprooted from its original site in a Chelsea backstreet. As he passed the open up-and-over doors of the garage, he could see only a yellow Metro. There was no sign of Lewis's Daimler.

He tugged the brass bell pull, and heard it chime some-where within the building.

Whoever he had been expecting to answer the door, it certainly wasn't the tall, thin figure of Blair Wallace.

The dark brown eyes glared suspiciously out of the Rhodesian's tanned face. 'What the fuck are you doing here, Robson?'

'That's not very friendly,' Robson replied evenly.

'I'm not paid to be friendly.' Wallace's chin jutted defiance. 'Mr Lewis doesn't like people calling here on business. You know the rules. So, what d'you want?'

'I've come to see Frankie. It's important.'

'Tough shit.' With his boss out of sight, Wallace saw no need to hide his resentment. 'He's away. Only Mrs L. is in.'

'When's he due back?'

'Didn't say,' Wallace sneered, starting to close the door.

'Then I'll wait.'

'Over my dead body . . .'

At that moment, an overalled British Telecom engineer appeared behind Wallace, tapping him on the shoulder. 'Okay, mate, I'm off. Should find the phone's all right now.'

Thrown for a second, Wallace backed up against the door to let the engineer pass. As he did, Robson stepped to one side and quickly slid his hand under the Rhodesian's arm, catching him behind the neck with his fingers. He pressed the armlock home against Wallace's elbow joint. He'd forced the helpless man through the open door before the engineer had a chance to realise what had happened behind him.

Robson slammed the door shut with his foot. 'Right, you obnoxious tow-rag, we'll have no more back-chat from you. No wonder Lewis doesn't trust you when he's away. Now are you going to answer my questions or am I going to have to send you and your arm out the front door separately?'

'F-fuck o-off!' Wallace gasped as Robson tightened the armlock. Then the Rhodesian's legs started to buckle under the strain. He tried to say he'd had enough but the words came out in a gargle.

Robson pushed him back into an antique Queen Anne chair, where the man heaved to regain his breath as he hugged the wrenched ligaments of his arm.

'Want to talk?' Robson invited. 'Or do we start again?'

Wallace gave him a withering look. 'Talk about what?'

Robson's smile was all sweetness. 'Let's try the heroin for starters.'

'What about it?'

'Does Frankie supply Maltese Max?'

Wallace scowled, regaining his breath. 'What's it to you?'

Robson's knuckles swiped hard across the Rhodesian's face.

The man's lip had split and he dabbed at it nervously with his hand. 'What's got into you, you bastard?'

'Just talk,' Robson demanded.

Wallace spat out a chip of broken tooth. He hesitated. 'Frankie supplies Max, sure.' He wasn't offering more.

'And others?'

Wallace sneered. 'Well, you aren't going to get rich on one dealer, are you?'

'Don't get smart,' Robson warned. 'Now tell me how he brings the stuff in.'

Wallace managed a painful smile. 'He doesn't tell me how he gets it in. And I don't ask. You're the new transport man – if anyone knows, you ought to.'

Robson's smile was equally sarcastic. 'Well, like you, it seems Frankie doesn't tell me everything either.'

Wallace struggled into a more dignified position on the chair. 'What are you anyway? Police?'

Robson's eyes narrowed. 'Let's just say I'm an injured party.'

The Rhodesian started looking like a worried man. 'Lewis will cripple me for talking to you. And God knows what he'll do to you. He's got some nasty friends.'

Ignoring the threat, Robson said: 'Where's Mrs Lewis?'

'She's around. Probably in the gym at this time.'

Robson hauled Wallace roughly to his feet, and quickly searched him. Apart from a wallet, cigarettes and loose change, it revealed a spring-loaded switchblade knife which he pocketed.

'Someone should have told you they're illegal,' Robson said. 'Now let's pay Mrs Lewis a visit. Any trouble from you and you're an invalid. And I don't need a weapon.'

Wallace looked at him steadily. 'I know, Frankie told me you can handle yourself. Look, Billy, I know I didn't welcome your arrival with open arms, but let's pax, eh?'

'Get up the stairs, Wallace.'

The Rhodesian shrugged and led the way up the ostentatious staircase. A crystal chandelier dominated the upper landing which ran to three sides of a square with a succession of doors opening onto the inner balcony.

Sounds of exertion and the clank of equipment came from the far end.

Wallace nodded. 'The gym goes off the master bedroom.'

'This one?'

'That's the dressing-room.'

Robson felt his disgust rising. 'Our Frankie's certainly done all right for himself.'

He opened the gym door, and pushed Wallace through first.

'Blair? What is it . . . ?' Bernadette's breathless voice called above the thud of a Dire Straits number booming from a portable cassette player on the window sill.

She was riding the cycle machine, dressed in just a pair of pink silk shorts and a matching singlet. The sweat stains suggested she'd just been travelling hard on an uphill straight.

'Billy! What on earth . . . ?' The swinging momentum of her breasts beneath the singlet slowed as she stopped pedalling. 'What's going on?'

'I need to talk,' Robson said flatly.

She climbed down, pulling the Terry towelling sweatband from her head so that her hair tumbled free. 'Of course, but what is it? What's wrong?'

'You and Frankie, that's what's wrong.'

'Sorry?'

'Setting me up.'

Bernadette still didn't understand. 'I know we set you up. In business, you mean . . . ? I'm sorry?'

Wallace smirked. Robson's foot caught him behind the knee, hard, and he dropped involuntarily to the floor. 'Sit down, Wallace. And keep your face shut.'

The girl looked horrified. 'What are doing to him? Billy, what's come over you?'

Robson's eyes blazed hostility. How could she feign such innocence? Play the sweet 'butter-wouldn't-melt' colleen? Play him for a sucker? He said accusingly: 'No wonder you knew about Sandy.'

'Knew *what*, Billy?' Bernadette pleaded for him to make sense.

'That she's a heroin addict.'

Her mouth dropped. 'What? Oh my God, are you sure?'

Robson was sorely tempted to strike her. 'Seeing that you and Frankie are the suppliers, you know bloody well that I'm sure.'

She fell back against the cycle-machine as though winded. 'Are you off your head? Frankie and me supplying heroin? It's downright ridiculous.' She seemed to regain her composure. 'Look, Billy, I'm sorry, truly sorry if Sandy's an addict.

And I know you must be shocked. But to come in here accusing Frankie and I of . . .'

Then, as though a thought suddenly struck her, her words petered away.

Robson prodded Wallace who was still down on his knees. 'Tell the lady what you just told me.'

Wallace wriggled uncomfortably.

'Tell her!' Robson hissed.

'Frankie's into heroin. Importing and distribution in a big way.' He mumbled the words from the corner of his mouth as though he hoped no one would hear.

She looked suddenly pale, unsteady on her feet. 'It can't be true. Frankie would never . . .'

'When do you expect him back?' Robson demanded.

Even before he'd finished asking the question, they all heard the slamming of the car door in the forecourt below.

'That sounds like him,' Bernadette whispered. 'He's been over at Max's getting a ticket for Boston. You can ask him yourself.'

'I intend to,' Robson grated.

Downstairs, the key sounded in the lock and the door brushed over the mat.

'Bernie? It's lover-boy!'

Robson gave Bernadette a warning glance. She swallowed and called out in a fractured voice: 'I'm in the gym, Frankie! Can you come up?' Robson placed his hand over her mouth so she could add nothing more. Her eyes stared widely at him in fear.

It was several minutes before Lewis bowled into the gym waving his airline ticket. 'Old Max is a gem. You know the price he got my flight for—?' Surprise chopped his sentence off like a guillotine.

'Come in, Frankie,' Robson invited menacingly.

Lewis was stunned. 'Hey, Billy – What's the meaning of all this?'

'Don't you start!' Robson snapped. 'And I'll ask you the same question. What's the meaning of setting me up as a front to import bloody heroin?'

The composure of Lewis's face began to disintegrate like a schoolboy's caught in the act of daubing graffiti. 'What's Wallace been saying?' he demanded.

'Only what I *forced* out of him,' Robson replied acidly. 'So you can cut the pretence. Just tell me why?'

Lewis fidgeted uneasily with the lapels of his expensive suit. 'It's not like you think, Billy. Really it isn't.' He glanced sideways at Bernadette and then at Wallace on the floor. 'Let's talk in private.'

Slowly Robson nodded. 'All right.'

Lewis prodded Wallace in the side with his foot. 'Get downstairs and wait. I'll talk to you later.' Obediently, the Rhodesian climbed to his feet and walked painfully to the door. Lewis turned his attention to Bernadette.

She stood her ground. 'I'm not going, Frankie. I want to hear this, too.'

'Get downstairs, woman!' Lewis snarled.

Robson made a decision. 'She can stay. *If* she knows nothing about this, then you're putting her in as much danger as me.'

'*Is* it true?' Bernadette asked, trying to get Lewis to look at her straight.

He appeared to have regained his self-control. 'I'm afraid it is. But,' he added quickly, 'it isn't how it seems, believe me. It was just a one-off. That bastard Dee put the squeeze on me. You know who he's mixed up with.'

Bernadette shook her head in disgust. 'I wonder *how much* of a squeeze he had to put on you?'

'Meaning what?' Lewis sneered. '*You* needn't be so bloody self-righteous about it all. You want all the fancy trappings like this house. Your bloody private gym. Your fur coats.'

'From a *legitimate* business we've *both* worked hard to build,' she retorted angrily. '*Not* from drugs.'

'All this *has* been earned, Bernie. I told you the drugs business was a one-off.'

Robson said: 'From what I've heard you've been at it a while. I suppose that's what it was all about in Malta?'

'Yes,' Lewis conceded, deliberately averting his eyes from Robson. 'That's where it was set up.'

'Oh, dear God, I don't think I want to hear this,' Bernadette muttered.

Robson saw the anguish in her face, and guessed that there was worse to come, and suddenly felt very sorry for her. He said: 'I think you ought to hear this, Bernie. Because, as I see it, your brothers have got to be involved.'

'Never!' Her eyes widened in horror. 'Dermot and Padraig? They never would.'

Robson watched Lewis closely. 'I don't know much about heroin. But I do know some of it comes from western Asia. Afghanistan – and Iran. The same place Frankie here sells the bulk of your brothers' meat exports. I've seen the list. There's a permanent fleet of trucks shuttling to and from Teheran. How many of those come back with a load of heroin on board?'

'I told you,' Lewis insisted, 'just the odd one or two consignments.'

Bernadette looked physically shaken. 'And to think I trusted you! And, as for my brothers, I still can't . . .'

Robson interrupted. 'The offal consignment that's coming over here, I suppose that's how you're doing it?'

Lewis shrugged. 'The Customs boys don't want all the trouble of defrosting meat products. Besides it would get contaminated, so it acts as an effective deterrent.'

'Christ!' snorted Robson, 'I don't want a bloody lesson, Frankie! I just wanted to be sure what sort of bastard I was dealing with. That's *my* name on all that documentation, not yours. You've just set me up as the fall-guy if anything goes wrong.'

'It won't go wrong,' Lewis replied tersely. 'Not if you act sensibly.'

Robson could see it all now. 'And if it did go wrong, you wouldn't even be here. You'd have been nicely out of it in Boston.'

'Look, Billy, that's just the way things are done. You're never in the same country at the same time as the delivery, that's all. It's common sense because then it's virtually impossible for the police to nail you. For God's sake, you don't think I *want* the consignment to get picked up, do you?'

Robson was astounded at Lewis's matter-of-fact attitude. 'So you're happy to take the money and to hell with the poor sods whose lives are ruined because of that filthy stuff?'

Lewis shrugged. 'If it wasn't me, it would be someone else. There's dozens of outfits importing it now.'

Robson's fist struck without warning. It caught Lewis full on the nose and sent him reeling backwards onto the floor. For a moment he lay stunned, groaning as he fought back the unconsciousness that threatened to overwhelm him.

A restraining hand touched Robson's forearm. 'Don't, Billy, please. I know how you feel, but it won't help anything.'

Through clenched teeth, Robson said: 'Well, it *helped* me feel better.'

Bernadette knelt beside Lewis. She handed him a clean hankerchief. 'You're a fool, Frankie. Sure, Billy's just found out that his wife is hooked on heroin. Sandy is a junkie. And he says it's the stuff you've brought in.'

Lewis dabbed at the trickle of blood from his nose. He looked up at Robson with an expression that could have been taken for genuine remorse. 'You can't be sure.'

'I'm sure,' Robson spat. He wasn't going to go into details.

Sniffing painfully, Lewis said: 'God, Billy, I'm sorry. Really I am. I like you and Sandy a lot. You know that. If I'd had any idea . . .'

'Don't say any more,' Robson advised.

Lewis ignored it. 'If I can help in any way . . . ?'

A bitter smile creased Robson's lips. 'Yes, you can help. You can write a letter now, stating how you duped me into being responsible for this current consignment. And how I was totally unaware of your involvement in drugs trafficking.'

Lewis stared in amazement. 'You're joking.'

'Listen,' Robson snarled. 'I'm on probation right now. If this thing blows up, I'll have to serve another two years on the robbery automatically. That's *before* they throw a drugs trafficking charge at me.'

Lewis staggered to his feet, rejecting Bernadette's help. 'We'll do a deal.'

'No deal.'

'So what do you think you'll do? Take your precious piece of paper to the local nick and plead Queen's Evidence?' Lewis sneered.

The vein in Robson's temple began to pulse.

'Well, it ain't that simple,' Lewis continued. 'You know how Dee reacts if people don't co-operate with him. He'd have my bloody kneecaps off as soon as look at me. So how d'you think you're going to get anywhere with what you know? You cause ructions and you're a dead man.'

'Is that a threat?'

Lewis's laugh was brittle. 'That's a *fact*, Billy-boy. Not a threat. You remember that bit of trouble you had with your probation officer? What was his name – Vance? That accident he had was *no* accident. I wanted you and told Dee I had a problem. True, he didn't know you were an ex-Marine then. But it was good enough for him that Vance was in the way.'

Robson's mouth dropped.

The other man arched an eyebrow. 'See what I mean? Dee's organisation has got men everywhere. Inside the nick as well as outside. So if you try to bug out, how far d'you think you'd get? Dee could get you, Sandy – or that son of yours – any time he wanted. If I step out of line, I get my legs broken, or Bernie's.'

'Who the hell *is* that man?' Bernadette demanded angrily.

'He's IRA,' Robson said. 'A Provo.'

She sat down on the window sill, drained. 'How in God's name did you get involved with those people, Frankie?'

'Through your damn brothers,' Lewis replied testily.

'Is that so?' Bernadette clearly didn't believe him. 'Then they'll have me to answer to.'

Lewis looked incredulous. 'Don't be so bloody stupid, woman. Haven't you been listening to a word I've been saying? Just keep your mouth shut and play the innocent little sister you are. There are dark forces at work that even your brothers can't control.' He turned back to Robson. 'You may not want a deal, Billy, and I don't blame you for that. But it's the only sensible option you've got open to you. If you rock the boat, we're all dead. Play along and perhaps we can wean ourselves away from these bastards.'

'We?' Robson pressed.

'Look, Billy, even I'm deeper into this than I wanted to be.' He sounded as though he meant it. 'I admit I was tempted by the profits, but things in Malta and Buncrana have changed all that. I want out, too.'

'So what are you suggesting?' Robson asked suspiciously.

'For a start, keep your cool. Dee wants me to set up a deal in Boston. I'll do it, but let him know that's positively my last work for him. If I can persuade Bernie's brothers I can be trusted, I might just get away with it. Meanwhile, you see that the consignment of smack coming over in the offal containers gets safely distributed . . .'

'No way!'

Lewis took his arm. 'Listen, it's in *your* interests to make sure it doesn't fall into the wrong hands. It wouldn't be the first time some Smart Alec has pulled a double-cross. With the money we're talking about, the temptation's always there. And I wouldn't trust Wallace to walk an old lady across the road – I hired him for his brawn, not his brains.'

'And if the police are on to this?' Robson pushed.

Lewis grinned reassurance. 'That's the *least* of our worries. One thing I've learned about this business is that old plod isn't in with a chance. Everyone involved is too busy shooting up – sorry – or else wallowing in the fattest of profits. No one's got the incentive to inform. Only the user-dealers ever get nicked. I'm always at least five removed down the chain, and I've no record. So you've no problems there, my old son.'

Robson pulled a packet of cigarettes from his jacket and lit one thoughtfully. 'I'm afraid I'm just not interested, Frankie.

I'd be happier if you just chucked the lot in the Thames, and kissed your profits goodbye for once.'

'I agree,' Bernadette added with feeling.

'Not so easy. You see, I'm only on 25 per cent of the cut. When I sell, our friend Dee wants the other 75.'

'Oh for God's sake, Frankie!' Bernadette was exasperated. 'Can't you just give it to him out of the business? He wouldn't know.'

Lewis held up his hand. 'Just *think* for a minute. I've got a hundred-kilo consignment. That's worth £2½ million on the London streets. I'll sell to a middle-man for around £2 million. That means Dee will be expecting a £1½ million payoff.'

Bernadette blanched. 'Maybe that wasn't such a good idea,' she murmured.

'Quite,' Lewis said. 'You can see the problem. But if we hold on, we can still extradite ourselves from this mess.'

'It's *your* mess,' Robson said. He was starting to feel trapped in a maze he didn't begin to understand. 'I'm the innocent party. I'd rather go to the police, and take my chances with your Irish friends.'

Lewis blinked. 'That is *dangerous* talk! Never talk about the fuzz, even if you're joking. Christ, do you want me to go down?'

Robson eyed him coldly. 'I don't give a fuck.'

'Then, just in case you've any doubts, Billy, let me tell you, if I go down, I'll bloody take you with me. That's a promise!'

'Frankie!' Bernadette protested.

Ignoring her, Lewis made a final impassioned plea: 'There's another good reason to hold on, Billy – apart from protecting yourself and your family. And that's *your* cut of the profits.'

'Blood money?' Robson was incensed. 'Piss off!'

'Fifty thousand.'

Robson gaped in disbelief. He couldn't even visualise that much money.

'A hundred thousand,' Lewis bartered. 'A hundred thousand if you stay with it until Dee agrees on a break. A few weeks at the most.'

Robson found himself wondering reluctantly just what could be done with that much money. Lewis saw his opportunity and stoked the fire. 'For a start, it would pay for the best possible clinic for Sandy. And those places cost a packet.' He paused. 'There'd be nothing wrong in that, would there? Money from heroin to get your wife off. Sort of ironic that. A perverse justice.'

Robson's mind was in a turmoil. How in God's name could anyone be expected to decide on such a thing? He said: 'I'll have to think about it.'

'No.' Lewis shook his head. 'There's no time. I leave for Boston in a couple of days, and that's when the consignment arrives. Besides, you *know* you don't have a choice.' He thought for a moment. 'Agree now and you can make a call immediately to get Sandy into the best private clinic. With money, you can jump the queue. Without it, she may be dead by the time her turn comes.'

Bernadette glared at him. But despite her anger at his insensitivity, she knew he was right.

Robson drew heavily on his cigarette. 'It seems I don't have a choice.'

Relief broke like sunshine on Lewis's face. 'I knew you'd see sense, Billy. That's great. You won't be sorry.'

Robson said nothing as Lewis continued: 'I'll be in the office this afternoon, Billy. I'll speak to you and Blair then. Sort out what needs to be done.'

Robson sighed resignedly and nodded. He was shattered. Never in his life had he felt so drained of self-respect. In silence, he turned and walked slowly out of the door.

Lewis watched and waited until he heard the front door slam. Only then did he allow his relief to show. As he turned he was surprised to find Bernadette gone.

Deep in his own thoughts, he followed her through the adjoining door to the master bedroom. He smiled at the sight of her stripped to her pink shorts, her breasts and stomach gently muscled from her regular hard exercise regime.

'You're looking good, Bernie. Really fancy you dressed like that.'

She glared at him across the king-sized bed. 'Don't even *talk* to me, Frankie! You *disgust* me!'

He went to protest when he suddenly realised she was in the middle of packing clothes into a suitcase. 'What do you think you're doing?'

'What does it look like?' Her green eyes were as hard and beautiful as emerald stones. 'I'm leaving.'

After the trauma with Robson, now this. 'You're being stupid, Bernie. We can talk this over.'

Her face contorted with anger. 'Talk it over? Talk over what? The fact that you're a bloody drugs-trafficker? My God, I still don't believe it. You, of all people. And you've betrayed me.'

'Rubbish! It's bought you all *this*!'

Bernadette's smile was bitter. 'Well, I don't *want* it. You might con Billy, but I realise now how you've got all this in just four years. No *wonder* you won't let me near the accounts. Because I'd have smelled a rat. YOU!'

Lewis was losing his patience. 'Okay, so it's been more regular than I let on. But I meant what I said, Bernie, I want out.'

'Well, SO DO I!' she screamed. Her breasts heaved as she regained her composure. 'It's like Billy said, you've put me as much at risk as you have him. And no doubt you'd also make sure I went down, too, if anything happened to you.'

He tried to make light of it. 'I didn't mean that.'

'No?' Her eyes glittered. 'Well, I know you well enough to know when you mean something. As far as I'm concerned, anything that was ever between us is finished. I'm going over to The Czar to stay with my mother.'

Lewis stared at the ceiling in suppressed fury. 'The same applies to you as Robson. If you try to get out, the IRA will take a contract out on the lot of us.'

She smiled sickly. 'I know that. Don't worry, I realise I'm trapped. Just like Billy. But it doesn't mean to say I have to sleep with you. In fact, the thought of that turns my stomach.' Deliberately she turned her back on him, depriving him of the sight of her body as she pulled on her tracksuit. Pleased by his stunned silence, she added: 'I'm not giving you the satisfaction of just disappearing out of your life. I may not be your wife on paper, but I am a co-director in the companies. I'll be in the office tomorrow, and I'll be going through the books with a fine-tooth comb – and my lawyer.'

The threat whipped at Lewis's senses like a razor. 'Like hell you will!'

She turned. 'As a director, I have rights. Legal rights.'

'Just you try . . .'

Bernadette gave a deep-freeze smile. 'Well, if you don't like the idea, you'd better think about buying me *out*!'

Lewis glared at her. 'I should fucking kill Robson for all this.'

'No, Frankie, he should kill you.' She slammed shut the lid of her case, and picked it up. 'He's one of the kindest,

most considerate men I've met. And he's more loyalty, guts
and courage in his little finger than you've *ever* had. It's a real
shame he's had such a terrible bad run of luck. And even
worse luck to have met *you* just when he needed help most.
That is almost the most despicable thing of all about you.'
She moved towards the door.

'If you leave here, you needn't bother coming back.'

'Don't worry, I won't.' The door slammed, with Bernadette
on the other side of it.

Lewis stood motionless for a long three minutes until he
was sure it was her yellow Metro racing away down the drive.

He slumped down on the edge of the bed. Damn! He
knew Bernadette well enough. She was stubborn and determined as only the Irish can be when she made up her mind.
And he had never seen her with her mind so made up. She
wouldn't be coming back.

He reached out across the satin bedspread, his fingers
curling around her discarded pink singlet. Slowly he lifted
it to his cheek. It was still damp and full of the smell of her.

Angrily, he threw it against the wall.

'Sod you, Billy Robson. Sod you and damn your fucking
eyes!'

'Tom Rabbit alive?'

The Man's words had a hollow ring to them, as he stared
down the overgrown grassy embankment to the sluggish
green waters of the Liffey.

Dutifully, Eamon Molloy and Dee had stopped behind
him on the footpath, conscious that the news would not go
down well.

Suddenly, The Man shivered and turned up the collar of
his camel coat against the biting north-easterly wind. It was

uncommonly cold for the time of year, and a dull ceiling of cloud pressed down on the centre of Dublin. A threat of rain was in the air.

At last he made his pronouncement. 'I am afraid the Army Council will have to be informed.' As he turned to face his two comrades on the IRA Special Finance Committee, they could see that his cheeks were pinched with cold. The cornflower-blue eyes watered in the face of the stiff breeze that rippled across the river below. 'How was it able to happen?'

Molloy looked pointedly at Dee; this was not his baby and he intended to keep well clear of the flak that would surely fly.

There was no hint of apology in Dee's manner, despite his sombre expression. 'It was one of those things we Irish are supposed to be famous for. Murphy's Law.' He hadn't expected the others to laugh, and he was right. 'I gather since that I hit him three times. In the chest, a leg and an arm. Reports in Malta were of two men dead. Only one of them wasn't Rabbit. A freak ricochet killed one of Carmelo's other men. I had no idea at the time. Apparently he was in intensive care for a few days, then discharged himself. He was picked up by members of Carmelo's family.'

'And now he's in London?' The cornflower eyes were unblinking.

'He was. But I have word that he's gone to Boston.'

'This gets worse.' The Man looked directly into Dee's eyes. 'Tom Rabbit wants vengeance, I know it. And he knows enough to wreak havoc.'

Molloy's bloodhound expression looked even more morose than usual. 'He knows about the petfood export operation. And the plans with the Colombians.' His spittle carried on the wind. 'I never wanted the knacker on the Committee. I always said it was a mistake.'

'The Army Council will have to be told,' The Man repeated softly, almost like an incantation, scarcely audible above the buffeting wind. 'The men from the Six Counties will not be pleased. Not at all pleased.'

Dee's mouth was set in a grim line. He knew all too well the truth of The Man's words.

The men from the north, from the battlefields of Ulster, would not welcome the setback. They were struggling to maintain their grip of power over the Provisional IRA. Struggling to promote their 'Armalite and ballot box' policy that had served them so well. A policy taught in the Kremlin's secret schools for subversion that had enabled them to actually elect politicians. A blood-stained cloak of respectability that gave them the democratic right to be heard and contemptuously manipulate the free media with gentle weasel words of reason. Terrorist leaders portrayed as family men with soft tweed jackets, playing with their children, and smoking pipes. God-fearing men who did not drink, who 'deeply regretted' the loss of all life caused by the British 'occupation'.

It was clever stuff. Effective. But the subtlety was lost on the old-guard Provos in Dublin who wanted a return to all-out bloody war.

Not that the men from the Six Counties had renounced violence and murder. When it was deemed necessary, they weren't averse to blowing the legs off some unfortunate. Nearly always a soft target nowadays. Unsuspecting and vulnerable.

But, more recently, their moves were carefully controlled. The sudden acts of vicious violence were just enough to satisfy the young firebrands, and helped stifle those Provo diehards in Dublin. And more than ever they would have to be spectacular. Like the Brighton bombing that had come so close to wiping out the entire British Cabinet.

But Dee knew that such acts were just an elaborate smoke-screen for what the men from the north really had in mind. As The Man had patiently explained to him, they had come to realise that they could never take the Six Counties against the bigoted Protestant majority in the immediate future. But time was on their side. For the Orangemen's natural numerical superiority was gradually eroding, their numbers waning, as the Catholic population grew inexorably.

Meanwhile, there was another, softer target. Every bit as important. Eire itself.

For several years now, the Provisionals' masterplan had been under way. Using long-proven Trotskyist methods, Sinn Fein supporters had begun infiltrating the large Fianna Fail party in opposition. It was a carbon-copy of the long-term infiltration of the British Labour Party by extremists of shadowy far-left groups. Even some well-known Sinn Fein politicians had blatantly changed their colours without a murmur of protest being heard from the Provisionals. And, against all predictions, Fianna Fail was now enjoying a resurgence of popularity carried along on a new tide of anti-British feeling.

The Dublin Government was reduced to fighting a desperate rear-guard action. A hopeless national debt left them unable to diffuse the political time-bomb ticking away on its streets: thousands of unemployed and disaffected youth. With many drip-fed on the seemingly unstoppable supply of heroin, they rode a rising wave of crime and violence that was shaking Irish society to its roots.

The men from the north were well-pleased. Their tentacles were spreading up unseen throughout the political apparatus of the party that would soon be elected to the Dáil.

It was not only the politicians and councillors who were being slowly spun into the web of intrigue, but civil servants, police, the legal system, the church, and commerce. In a country where discreet bribery and the exchange of favours had been a way of life for centuries, it had not been difficult.

But such ambitious, all-embracing plans for power cost money.

Money to fuel the greed of those who needed to be bought. And, as The Man had long ago discovered, every man had his price.

Some took a little longer to justify the bribery to themselves – even if some needed a little physical persuasion.

All that demanded an income far in excess of the £2 million a year the media estimated it cost the Provos to run their organisation. The long-term political masterplan cost far more. And Dee knew that drugs were the only commodity that could provide the huge sums necessary fast enough – and with little risk to those involved.

Now they were suddenly faced with the prospect of a renegade Provo creating havoc with their carefully laid plans with the Colombians. Not only that, but he had the active support of a Mafia faction that owed them a grudge – *and* of some Ulster loyalist paramilitaries.

Dee knew that within the next twenty-four hours, Tom Rabbit would be at the top of the Army Council's list of most wanted men. And if he wasn't careful, very careful, his name could be the next.

He said: 'You can tell the Army Council that I've mobilised every resource on the British mainland to track down

Robinson and O'Rourke. They've gone to ground, but they won't get far.'

'I hope not.' The Man's voice was as chill as the gathering wind. 'And Rabbit?'

'I've sent word to our friends in Boston. If Rabbit so much as breathes too heavily over there, Sean Brady will hear about it. He knows what to do.'

Eamon Molloy sniffed heavily, his nose starting to run in the chill air. 'What about the Libyans? They'll be no happier than the Army Council.'

Sod you, Dee thought. Trust you to shit on a man when he's down. But he said nothing.

The Man was thoughtful. 'We'll give ourselves more time before we tell them. They're too unpredictable. That bastard Sher Gallal could throw a tantrum and call the whole thing off.'

'Would our friends in Moscow *allow* that?' Molloy queried.

The Man chuckled at his friend's naïvety. 'The Libyans do what the hell they please. Sometimes that works for Moscow, sometimes not.' He thrust his hands deeper into his pockets. 'No, we'll tell the Libyans later – if there's still a problem. Wait until they're too deeply committed to pull out.'

Molloy nodded sagely as though that was exactly what he'd worked out for himself.

Dee said: 'I'll keep you informed.'

They parted then, without shaking hands. Dee sauntered away along the footpath towards Dublin centre.

Eamon Molloy followed The Man respectfully to the white Rolls-Royce parked up at the roadside; he knew he wouldn't be offered a ride.

As the door, with its tinted window, was opened by the chauffeur for The Man to climb in, Molloy caught a glimpse of the girl in her fur coat.

He stood watching enviously as the vehicle purred away. There was no doubt in his mind that she would be wearing nothing underneath.

'Billy, I think I'm going to die. I'm scared.'

Sandy's words haunted Billy Robson throughout the long drive to the Fatton Place drug-dependence unit in Epping.

She had said it just before they left. Sutcliff had called at Newey House to pick them up in one of his tarted-up showroom saloons just after nine that morning. His overt cheerfulness had been to no effect. Sandy had been through a bad night, tossing and turning, and gradually becoming more irritable until it was obvious that she would have to have a fix. Come morning, she was jittery and deathly pale.

As Sutcliff stood in the doorway, she had looked at herself in the hall mirror with vacant eyes. For a full minute, she hadn't moved. Then slowly, she traced the trembling fingers of one hand around the hollow dark skin beneath her eyes. Both Robson and Sutcliff guessed what she was thinking. The face in the mirror was a stranger's face. Even to Sandy.

She spoke softly to her reflection. 'I don't feel anything. It's my body, but I don't feel anything at all.' It was then she turned slowly to Robson and murmured the words. 'Billy, I think I'm going to die. I'm scared.'

He had hugged her then, squeezed her hard with all the love and comfort he could muster. He tried desperately for something consoling to say, but all he could think about was how thin she felt beneath his hands. Emaciated and wasted.

His spirits had only lifted marginally by the time they

reached Epping. Fatton Place was everything the brochure had promised. A Gothic mansion sanctuary set in several acres of ornamental parkland. Inside its wrought-iron gates, the drive wound through undulating lawns and sombre shadows cast by the ancient Scots pines.

The matron was out to meet them before the car had fully come to a halt.

She greeted Sandy with severe formality that verged on the curt, and showed them the way in through an oak-timbered porch.

'You didn't stop at a pub for lunch I trust?' she asked Robson. The smart grey uniform, he noticed, couldn't quite disguise the stout figure, and the lace cap failed to add the intended touch of femininity.

He smiled. 'We'd planned to, but ran late.'

'That's as well. If you've touched a drop, we cannot let you in. Our clients come here for a number of unwanted dependencies, including alcohol-abuse. As you may imagine, they become particularly sensitive to the tainted breath of visitors. Or indeed, the slightest slurring of words.'

'So no booze for the patients, eh?' Sutcliff mused.

'Certainly not,' she replied, leading them across the parquet-floored hallway to a spartan waiting-room. 'Or the staff. We can't have our clients substituting one prop for another now, can we?'

'Wouldn't do me at all,' Sutcliff muttered beneath his breath.

The matron gestured towards the leather seats. 'If you'd like to make yourselves comfortable while the doctor examines your wife, Mr Robson, and has a chat with her. It'll take a little while, I'm afraid. Perhaps I can get you both a coffee?'

It was two hours and several cups of coffee later before Dr Arnold Swinburne was ready to see them. He was much younger than Robson had been expecting, in fact around Robson's own age, with short, curly black hair, and moist dark eyes. He offered the two men seats before parking himself casually on the edge of the desk top. His tweed hacking jacket seemed at home with the rows of leather-bound volumes in the bookcase behind him.

He smiled briefly, as though life didn't allow him much time for niceties. 'Are you sure you want your friend here, Mr Robson?'

'That's fine. We've both known Sandy since we were at school together.'

'Ah, I see.' Again the briefest of smiles, and Robson was left wondering if Swinburne really had seen something in the throwaway explanation. 'Well, I've had a little chat with Mrs Robson – or Sandy, we don't have too much personal formality here – and I'm afraid I don't know if we can help.'

Robson's heart sank. 'No?'

Swinburne wrung his hands together as he picked his words carefully. 'You see, you cannot help a person with drug-dependence unless they want to help themselves. And I'm not sure Sandy's ready yet.'

Robson shook his head in disbelief; he felt angry and frustrated. 'Only this morning she said she thought she was going to die. How scared she was.'

The smile. 'Let me explain. The pattern of addiction goes through several phases. First, of course, the start. Maybe out of curiosity, or for kicks. No worse than kids smoking their first cigarette at a party. Or having the first drink too many. Then the move to dependence.' He spoke his words in the same clipped manner as he smiled. 'That's the tricky bit. The root cause. Usually to escape. A feeling of hopelessness. A feeling that the world doesn't understand you, and you can do nothing about it.'

'I know the feeling,' Robson said.

'We all do,' Swinburne replied easily. 'But most of us struggle on. People like Sandy slip by the wayside, and the pattern continues. Denial. He or she will deny they take drugs. They will swear blind to their nearest and dearest. Even to themselves. Until they are caught out or something happens to make them accept the fact. An overdose usually. Or someone catching them red-handed.

'From there they develop a fierce anger as to why it should happen to them. Why *me*? They also become furious with everyone else involved in their lives. They argue with themselves as to whether or not they should try to come off. Inevitably, at this stage, they will go for the soft option.'

'Why?' Sutcliff interrupted.

'Simply because it is so hard. Do you smoke?' Both men nodded. 'Then you know how hard that is. Imagine it ten times worse. Or being in a kitchen having not eaten for two days and the place smelling of freshly baked bread. Could you resist the offered slice?'

Neither man had ever quite thought of it like that before.

'Having taken the soft option,' Swinburne continued, 'they fall into deep, mind-numbing depression. Then finally they accept their lot. They see themselves as tragic heroes, trapped by life and forces they cannot fight against. That, in my opinion, is the stage Sandy is at.'

'I see,' Robson murmured.

Swinburne spared a slightly longer smile. 'She is starting to get desperate for help, but only just. It's starting to occur to her that she will die. If we de-toxify her now, she may persuade herself that she's in control again. That she can handle the odd fix.'

Robson cleared his throat. 'Are you saying you won't take her?'

This time the smile lasted a full second; reassurance. 'No. Normally, I might. But in view of your generous donation to our trust, above our normal fees, I'm obliged to give your wife the benefit of my doubt.'

Robson shifted uncomfortably in his chair. The 'donation' had been Lewis's idea.

'But you must understand that she may not be ready,' Swinburn continued. 'You must be prepared for the possibility that the treatment she is about to begin may be a complete waste of time. She may have to make several return stays. Until a client is *totally committed* to coming off heroin, we are all wasting our time.'

'What form does the treatment take?' Robson asked.

Swinburne was beginning to look bored; he'd been through this so many times before. 'I'll be frank with you, it's a tough regime. Most of our wardens are ex-addicts. Even Matron is a reformed alcoholic.

'They understand, you see. Especially the deceit. Addicts are the worst liars in the world. Our people can see straight through them. You have to be tougher and more resourceful than they are. Kindly but tough. We even had one outpatient whose mother took our advice quite literally – she actually handcuffed her son to the bed for six months.' Again the brief flash of teeth. 'It worked. We, however, are a little more civilised. We work on the Minnesota Method evolved by the Hazeldon Foundation. That's to say the principle that drug-addiction is a disease of a person's biochemical make-up which can develop a dependence on anything from alcohol to heroin, and all the stops in between.

'We run a highly structured day here at Fatton. After initial detoxification, the client finds every minute of the day accounted for in half-hour segments. That includes communal duties, cooking, cleaning and maintenance. Then, there are the group therapy sessions. That can be very traumatic for some, but also very helpful. Especially if we can make them laugh at themselves – addicts do take themselves much too seriously.'

Robson nodded. 'That all makes sense.'

Swinburne stood up and walked briskly around the desk to his chair. 'There's one thing of which you should be aware, Mr Robson.'

'What's that?'

The doctor picked his words carefully. 'Our treatment eventually brings the patient face-to-face with the problems in life he or she has been trying to escape. It teaches them to confront those problems with determination and self-confidence. Close relatives do not always like the results.'

Robson shook his head. 'It all sounds sensible to me. What worries me is if you're right about Sandy not being ready. If she leaves here, how long would it be before she would actually *want* to come back herself?'

Swinburne shrugged. 'It depends on the individual. Perhaps another six months.'

Robson looked aghast. 'God, she could be dead by then.'

'That is, I regret to say, a strong possibility.'

Fifteen

The tension in the Squad-Room was like electricity in the air.

Major Bill Harper felt it as soon as he stepped through the door. In one corner a gathering of shirt-sleeved detectives were talking earnestly. Sharp, brittle humour. Adrenalin flowing and nerves jangling. He could sense it a mile away. And it did him the world of good.

It was six months now, almost to the day, since they'd finally managed to prise him away from the intelligence unit of the Special Air Service Regiment at Hereford. If it hadn't been for the intriguing nature of the job at the newly set up TIGER outfit, they would probably have had to throw him out bodily.

As it was he went with a good pension and the biggest booze-up they'd seen at Bradbury Lines since the end of the Falklands War. And his memories. That was something the sour-faced pen-pushers at the MOD wouldn't be able to take away from him. Even they couldn't find rules and regulations to cover those – provided you didn't try to publish them.

Memories that spanned half the world. From the deserts of Oman to the jungle hell of Malaysia. From counter-revolutions in Africa to secretly snatching a British hostage from Iran after the fall of the Shah. Even now he could see the faces of the men he'd worked with passing before his eyes.

Like fading prints in an old photograph album: Ducane, Forbes, Turnball, Hawksby, Penaia, McDermid, Mather ... Some dead now, or medically discharged. Some still in the SAS, others gone. Out there somewhere, trying to hack it through the boredom of civilian life.

But to a man, they'd have appreciated the atmosphere into which he had just walked. They would have smelled it, too.

'Thank God you made it, Bill.' It was Detective Chief Superintendent Ray Pilger. For once the policeman didn't look his usual dapper self: his face was haggard and unshaven, his shirt crumpled and lightly soiled around the collar where his tie hung loosely. 'Sorry to have interrupted your meeting.'

'Not at all, old man.' The Welshman's voice was as buoyant with good humour as ever. 'Damn welcome to tell you the truth. These Ministerial chin-wags can be a pain in the proverbial arse.'

'Coffee?' Pilger beckoned WPC Gifford to do the honours. 'You sound very concerned.'

Pilger pulled a pained expression. 'It's a tricky one, Bill. You remember our friend Frankie Lewis? Clean East End wideboy made good. Well, we managed to get a tap in a couple of days ago. Nothing significant at first, then this morning – Bingo! A conversation with Maltese Max. Setting up a meet to deliver a consignment of heroin.'

Harper raised a quizzical eyebrow. 'He did this on an open line?'

'The pillock thinks he's Jesus Christ.' Pilger grinned. 'Obviously hasn't a clue that he's in the slightest risk. Not that he actually mentioned drugs. His exact reference was to 'fancy tea-cakes'. Nobody talks like that to someone on the phone. Not 'fancy tea-cakes' every time. Evidently thought his code language was a huge joke. Anyway, if you've ever seen one of Maltese Max's establishments you'd realise just how improbable that was.'

'So when is this exchange?'

'Tonight. That's why I was in such a panic.'

'What's the problem?' Harper asked.

Pilger sat on the edge of one of the desks and began unfurling one of his cigars. 'Simply this. It may be our one and only chance to catch him red-handed for possession. But if I do, it'll blow your international investigation. I mean the IRA are going to have to change tactics pretty fast and find a new way of importing. We'll probably never pick up the threads again.'

'You can't let it run?' Harper asked. 'You might get the chance to make a swoop on both sides of the Irish Sea.'

The Drug Squad chief looked pained. 'Can we really expect that much co-operation from the Irish police? And, if we do, can we be sure our information will be secure? In the narcotics business it's always worth somebody's while to tip-off the dealers.'

The timely arrival of WPC Gifford with the coffees gave Harper a welcome opportunity to turn over the possibilities in his mind.

One thing was certain. Pilger was right. On certain levels co-operation with the Irish police was excellent, although security was never one of their strongest points. They tended to be a little too fond of mixing Guinness and gossip. Moreover this business had strong political overtones. If news of the operations reached the ears of a Provo sympathiser in Dublin, the whole operation would be in jeopardy. Besides it also involved the Libyans who were an important trading partner with Eire. There could well be a hundred and one sound political reasons why the Irish Government could decide to be less than enthusiastic about co-operation. Anyway, Harper knew there would soon be more than one way to skin this particular cat.

'I think you should go ahead,' Harper said emphatically as he sipped his coffee. 'Where is the exchange to take place?'

'By the Embankment.'

'Any chance of taking a passenger?'

Pilger scrutinised the major. 'None at all. That would be strictly against every rule in the book.'

Harper's smile was incorrigible. 'I'm a Hereford man, Ray. Never did learn to read.'

The policeman warmed to the Welshman's approach. 'Well, if you happened to be in one of our cars when it was diverted – I don't think the rules apply in those circumstances.'

The major finished his coffee. 'Excellent. I really would appreciate that.'

It was then that the young detective with the Teutonic good looks and steel-rimmed glasses burst into the room.

'What is it, Spicer?' Pilger asked.

'Message from the surveillance team on Lewis. He's at Gatwick Airport.'

'What?' Pilger's face dropped.

Spicer shrugged. ''Fraid so, Guv'nor. Just checked in at the Northwest Orient desk.'

'Ah,' Harper said, 'so he's on his way to Boston at last, is he?'

Pilger turned sharply in surprise. 'You know about this, Bill?'

A wicked, knowing smile graced Harper's lips. 'Just something one of our little birds told me.'

*   *   *

It had been raining steadily since lunchtime, so when Robson arrived in Sutcliff's borrowed E-type that evening, the roads of the industrial estate were gleaming like black lacquer.

No lights remained on in the offices of the warehouse units, as he parked outside the garish red delivery gates of Frank Lewis's premises.

He was surprised to see two vehicles there. He'd been expecting the Daimler, as it appeared that Blair Wallace always drove it when his boss was away. But he had not anticipated Bernadette's bright yellow Metro.

Cautiously he glanced left and right along the wide street. Factory units, storage sheds, exhaust-fit centre, builders' merchants, garden centres – it was strange not to see the place bustling frenetically with activity. Now the only vehicle was an empty dust-encrusted van parked in the forecourt opposite.

He tapped on the small personnel-door set in the gates. It opened almost immediately.

'Quick, get in.' The Rhodesian's welcome wasn't exactly oozing warmth.

As Robson stepped through he immediately recognised the battered freezer-trailer backed against the loading-bay platform. He'd last seen it at the Mulqueens' abattoir being loaded with containers of offal.

'Has everyone gone?' Robson asked.

Wallace looked nervous. His eyes darted suspiciously as though he expected someone to jump out of the shadows at any moment. The tanned skin of his face was greasy with perspiration.

'Of course they've gone,' the man replied tersely. 'You know Frankie's rules.' His smile was twitchy. 'Even got rid of that bloody workaholic Ali. Almost had to boot him out, mind.'

'Is that Mrs Lewis's car outside?'

Wallace's face took on the expression of a man falsely accused of murder. 'I want to tell you – we've got a problem. She turned up half-an-hour ago and refused to leave. Did you know she's had a bust-up with Frankie?'

'No. Where is she now?'

He jabbed his thumb upward. 'In the office.'

'What does she want?'

'To come with us.'

Robson cursed under his breath and pushed past Wallace to the gantry steps that led to the partitioned offices.

He found her sitting on the edge of a desk flicking through a pile of delivery notes. She was dressed in a no-nonsense oiled cotton Barbour jacket, corduroy trousers and low-heeled boots.

'What are you doing here, Bernie?'

She looked up and smiled. 'Hallo, Billy. I've split with Frankie.'

Robson didn't return the smile. 'Even more reason to ask what you're doing here? Are you in on this heroin business after all?'

She tossed the wad of delivery notes onto the desk. 'No, Billy, I would hope you know me better than that.'

'Then you're trying to stop us going ahead with tonight's delivery?'

The head of chestnut hair shook sadly. 'Sure, I'd do anything to stop it . . . if it was possible. I know you've got no option. But himself has got me as much tied-up in this as you, Billy. If your man sinks he'll take me down with him – as well as you. So I've come to protect my interests. The more I know about what's going on, the more I'll be in a position to defend myself should the need arise.'

Robson couldn't help a feeling of admiration for the woman's determination. 'It'll also make you an accessory.'

She gave a short snort of laughter. 'I am already. Legally at any rate.'

'You still shouldn't have come. You could have got hurt. Wallace . . .'

'Wallace is a pussycat—'

At that moment the Rhodesian appeared at the door. 'Time we were going.'

'Where is the awful stuff?' Bernadette asked.

'It's here,' Wallace replied. He held up a string bag containing five hefty, frost-covered ox livers.

'Get on with it then,' Bernadette ordered impatiently. Wallace exchanged glances with Robson, shrugged and allowed the frozen livers to thud onto the desk.

For the next few minutes Wallace busied himself scraping away the layer of frost particles to reveal a thin cut-line around each piece. Then with difficulty he prised the joins apart. The halves were separated to reveal a polythene package of brown powder nestling in the hollowed-out centre of each liver.

Bernadette's mouth dropped. Until now it had all been talk about Lewis's involvement. The actual evidence still came as a shock.

'Ninety per cent pure,' Wallace muttered with satisfaction. 'Twenty kilos. I'll check it.'

'For what?' Robson asked.

'To make sure it hasn't been tampered with,' Wallace sneered.

Bernadette raised her eyebrows. 'By my brothers, do you mean?'

The Rhodesian gave her a scornful glance. 'By *anyone*. And your brothers aren't angels.'

'What about the rest of the hundred kilos?' Robson asked.

Wallace tapped his nose. 'It's already been distributed down the network.'

Robson turned to Bernadette. 'There's no need for you to get in any deeper. There's no reason for you to come.'

'I can't forgive what Frankie's done to you, Billy. I want to go with you. I feel I'm partly responsible.'

'Christ,' Wallace oathed in disgust. 'Isn't that sweet?'

Robson ignored him. 'I appreciate the gesture, Bernie, but I can't let you. If you *really* want to do me a favour you can go home. You're nothing to do with all this. The less you know the safer you are. So just go home.'

He found himself looking closely at her eyes. They were very green, and very sad. 'Okay,' she breathed. 'If that's what you really want.'

Wallace had packed his parcel, and stood waiting with a cloth bag in his other hand. 'We'll take your car, Robson.'

'It's not mine.'

Wallace grinned. 'All the better. I certainly can't use the boss's.'

Bernadette said: 'Good luck.'

Then on impulse she reached forward and kissed Robson quickly on the lips. 'And take care.'

They were approaching Lambeth Bridge before either man spoke. The atmosphere of antagonism between them was becoming claustrophobic in the confines of the E-type's cockpit.

It was Robson who finally broke the silence. 'Look, Blair, I know we haven't seen eye-to-eye, but we'd better try and rub along. I'm sorry I had to do what I did the other day. It was nothing personal.'

Wallace's chin jutted defiantly as he continued to gaze straight ahead through the pendulum swing of the wipers. 'It was all fine till you came on the scene. Nice and cosy, and profitable. I knew you'd be trouble as soon as I clapped eyes on you.'

Robson changed gear as they approached the bridge. 'All good things come to an end, Blair. Think yourself lucky you can get out soon. Lewis is bound to come a cropper sooner or later. And that could mean a long stretch for you.'

The Rhodesian didn't seem impressed. Below them the Thames shrugged by through a drizzly haze. 'Turn left on the far side of the river. Into Millbank.'

'Where exactly is the exchange?'

'After Vauxhall Bridge, Millbank becomes Grosvenor Road. There's a turning on the right off the embankment – that's Lupus Street. We stop on the corner, facing south. If anything goes wrong, we're out into Grosvenor Road before you can say knife.'

'What could go wrong?' Robson asked swinging the car into Millbank, running westwards alongside the river. 'You've dealt with Max before. He's a mate of Frankie's, isn't he?'

Wallace cast a cynical eye in the driver's direction. 'There's no mates in this business. You'll learn that when you've been in it as long as me. Drugs is like gold fever. It turns men greedy. They'd steal the pennies off their dead mother's eyes, some of them.' He reached onto the rear squab-seat and lifted over the cloth bag.

'What's that?'

Again Wallace smirked. 'An insurance policy.' Slowly he drew out the walnut veneered butt of a sawn-off shotgun.

'Jesus!' Robson swore.

Distracted, he wandered momentarily over the centre-line of the road. Headlights flashed. A warning hooter wailed past them.

'Watch the fucking road, will you!' Wallace snarled. 'You have a prang with what we've got on board, and you'll really find out the meaning of trouble!'

'You *don't* need that thing, Blair.'

'Oh, no?' He stared ahead as the junction with Vauxhall Bridge approached. 'Well Max isn't the only one I don't trust. Personally I trust *you* even less.'

Robson shook his head. The man really was a cretin. 'Just keep it out of sight, will you.'

'Slow down,' Wallace snapped. 'Drive slow past the entrance to Lupus Street. Real slow.'

'Past?'

'Yes, past.' Impatient. 'I want to be sure there's no one lurking. No nasty surprises.'

Changing gear again, Robson slowed the E-type to a crawl. The trees and the grey granite wall of the Embankment edged past on their left. On the other side of the road the Sullivan House residential block appeared.

Wallace squinted through the rain-lashed windscreen. The corner of the Lupus sidestreet was deserted. Ten yards down, a line of parked vehicles began. None had any lights on.

'Anything behind us?' Wallace asked.

'Only half of London trying to pass us.'

'Anything *suspicious*?' Wallace demanded.

'A few taxis, a bus, and a clapped-out van.'

Wallace grunted; Robson was sure he was none the wiser. At least he seemed satisfied. 'Take the next free right turn,' he ordered. 'We'll make a circuit round and approach Lupus from the other end.'

'What time is it?'

'Ten-to-ten. We'll be five minutes early when we arrive.'

Robson swung right on Wallace's route that would take them back on themselves. No other vehicle followed.

He felt the tension ebb away. Thank God for that. He hadn't realised just how wound-up he'd become on the journey. His palms were sticky and he could feel a faint fluttering in his chest. It was though he was suddenly transported back five years. Driving the souped-up Jaguar to the bank . . .

'Right here!' Wallace shouted.

Robson spun the wheel and slid neatly from Sutherland Street back into Lupus. He edged cautiously forward whilst Wallace peered at the row of parked cars on each side.

'Can't see a sodding thing,' he complained. Then: 'Jesus, a bleeding courting couple in the back of that one! Would you credit it!'

Robson didn't find it so amusing. 'I'd feel happier if none of the cars were occupied.'

'*Would* you now?' Wallace sneered. 'Relax, you're making me nervous. Snogging lovers'll have their minds on other things.'

Ahead of them loomed the junction with the Grosvenor Road embankment, running east and west alongside the river. The few yards at the end of the street were still free of traffic.

'Pull in on the left,' Wallace ordered. Robson swung the E-type into the mouth of the junction, and backed up to the first of the parked cars. 'Kill the lights, but keep the engine running.'

'Where is Max's car going to stop?'

Wallace inclined his head across the sidestreet to the space opposite. 'There. On the corner.'

'What happens now?'

'I'll get out and wait. I'll leave the stuff on the passenger seat with the door unlocked.' He threw the handle and started to climb out.

Robson reached across and caught his arm. 'Leave that bloody thing behind.'

Wallace gave an evil grin, and patted the cloth bag. 'No way, sunshine, no way. If you think of driving off with the parcel I'll blow you away together with your friend's car.'

'Got it all worked out, haven't you?'

Wallace grinned. 'Some.'

He slammed the door shut and crossed the pavement to the shadows of a tree. Casually he leaned against the wall, lit a cigarette and settled down, his free hand clasping the contents of the cloth bag.

Robson took a deep breath, but it did nothing to quell the pounding of his heart. This was almost unbelievable. Sitting in a deserted London sidestreet with half-a-million pounds worth of heroin on the seat beside him. The reality of it was beginning to sink in. Suddenly Wallace's paranoia seemed to be well-founded.

A movement caught his eye in the rear-view mirror. He reached up and adjusted the angle. Back up the sidestreet a vehicle had turned on its side lights. He'd seen no one walking, but then in the relentless rain it would have been easy to miss someone. Perhaps it was the courting couple? Perhaps the girl was a prostitute. Even as he looked the lights died again. The street was motionless once more.

He glanced up at Wallace. The Rhodesian looked edgy but he evidently hadn't seen the lights. He was watching the continual stream of cars flashing by in front of them along the Grosvenor Road embankment. Waiting for Max.

Robson's eyes followed across to the other side of the road. Thirty yards down, beyond a pedestrian crossing, a van had stopped, facing the other way. It was a rust-eaten Dormobile, or perhaps a Sherpa. He thought the colour was grey, but that could have been the thick coating of dust that had turned to mud in the rain and now dribbled down its side. The driver was having some trouble loosening the nuts on the rear wheel that had evidently got a puncture. The man looked none too happy as he strained with the steel spider.

'Poor sod,' Robson murmured to himself. Then, as he looked more closely, something about the van seemed vaguely familiar.

His attention was caught by a sudden movement from Wallace. Robson's gaze switched back to a vehicle pulled in to the crown of the Grosvenor Road. The steady blink of its indicator said it wanted to turn into Lupus. There was one other man apart from the driver. He gave a thumbs-up sign.

Wallace nodded to Robson. It was them.

A gap appeared in the oncoming traffic and the car swept forward. To Robson's surprise it didn't move into the space opposite, but came straight for him, braking at the last moment. It stopped with its bonnet inches from that of the E-type, its rear jutting a couple of feet into the embankment road. Robson found himself blinded by the lights.

Shit! He was trapped by the car behind and this one in front. His pulse started to race. Anxiously he glanced across at Wallace. The man was stunned, too, his eyes wide with apprehension.

Already one of the newcomers was out of the passenger seat and approaching the Rhodesian. Through the dazzling aurora of light it was possible to distinguish only a man in a dark coat. Light played on a white shirt. He looked smart, a businessman. He was carrying something. An attaché-case?

Robson reached over and wound down the passenger side-window a fraction. He just caught Wallace's voice above the noise of the rain drumming on the roof. 'Are you from Max?'

'Sure.' The voice was muted by the sudden passing of an articulated truck.

'I don't know you,' Wallace said.

The newcomer seemed to be amused 'That's your problem. I've got the cash. That's all that matters.'

'Max didn't say anything about a different team.'

'Stop fucken around.' The man in black was growing impatient. 'Here's Max's money. Where's the stuff? In the car?'

It was the word that did it. 'Car'. The strong Ulster pronunciation. Sounding '*corr*', with a sing-song inflection. Alarm bells began ringing in Robson's head.

Suddenly the Ulsterman thrust the attaché-case into Wallace's hands. 'Thar, count the focken money!' The Rhodesian's cloth bag fell to the pavement with a muffled clatter. The Ulsterman reached for the door of the E-type. Before he could get there Robson threw himself across the seat and flipped the lock.

Wallace rushed at the man who hurled him hard back against the low wall without a second's hesitation. Robson found himself confronting an eerie white face pressed against the glass, distorted with blobs of rainwater. The barrel of the gun was pointing straight between his eyes.

There was no alternative. With his heart pounding he released the lock.

As the man grabbed the parcel of heroin from the seat the whole world went mad.

It was the sickening shriek of tyres Robson heard first. Glancing up he saw the grey van that had been parked by the embankment. It was slewing in a crazy arc of a U-turn against the oncoming traffic. A fountain of spray gushed in its wake.

Suddenly it clicked. The empty van in front of Lewis's warehouse earlier that evening; the grey van trailing two vehicles behind as they had approached the rendezvous. It was the same one.

Lights. The car with sidelights. His heart sank like a lift in a shaft. The rear-view mirror told it all. The car behind him had moved out from the row of parked vehicles. Two blinding headlamps blocked the escape route behind them.

As he glanced around he saw the Ulsterman dashing back to his car. He was screaming at his driver at the top of his voice.

The grey van came to a skidding halt across the mouth of the side-street, its front bumper crunching into the protruding rear of the newcomers' car. Glass tinkled onto the tarmac road surface. Robson gaped in surprise as the rear doors of the van flew open and a group of men came scrambling out. They were a roughly dressed, motley bunch who looked ready for action. At least one wielded a pickaxe handle; another carried a revolver.

'POLICE! STOP!'

Robson gasped.

The vicious bark of Wallace's sawn-off shot-gun shattered all other sounds with its deafening roar. Instinctively the approaching men from the van dived in different directions. One left it too late, and was hurled backwards off his feet. His spine struck the side of the van with a resounding crash as the pellets tore chunks from the surrounding metalwork.

The Ulstermen's car was on the move. Its tyres screaming for a grip on the wet road it ground backwards, forcing the stationary van into the path of the embankment traffic. Cars hooted in alarm. Brakes squealed. Somewhere cars started colliding. The driver of the Ulstermen's car slammed the gears into first and stood hard on the accelerator, the vehicle fishtailing down the road eastwards towards Vauxhall Bridge.

Wallace's shot-gun blasted out its second cartridge. Instantly the sudden illumination of the scene died away as the headlamps shattered in the unmarked police car behind them.

Robson was already moving the E-type forward as the Rhodesian hurled himself at the open passenger door. As he drew level, one of the detectives swung his pickaxe handle at the windscreen. It shattered instantly, spewing a hail of jagged crystal over the interior. Robson swerved violently. He felt the soft thud as the wing caught someone off guard, tossing him aside like a rag doll.

Scraping the front of the van as he went, Robson threw the wheel to the right, carving his way into the westward lane. A passing taxi stood on its brakes, skidded, leapt over the pavement and ploughed into the embankment wall.

With its twin exhausts thundering, the E-type took off along the embankment like a bat out of hell and disappeared into the wet black night.

Ray Pilger staggered unsteadily to his feet from where he'd thrown himself when the shot-gun had gone off.

'Jesus Christ,' he muttered in disbelief at the mayhem around him.

Detective Sergeant Dick Spicer was at his side. 'I've put out an all-cars on both vehicles, Chief. They won't get far.'

Pilger glanced at the man being tended by the van. 'How's Peter?'

'Pellet in the eye,' someone called back. 'Everything else is superficial.'

The occupants of the unmarked police car came forward. A young detective constable said: 'Just cuts and bruises with us. Lucky – that bastard shot straight at us.'

From the roadside, another policeman called over. 'That E-type caught John on the leg, I think it's broken.'

'What a fuckin' balls-up!' Pilger groaned with a rare lapse into barrack-room language. 'And where the hell are the bloody woodentops? I want this bloody traffic-jam sorted out.'

He glanced around again at the carnage and chaos. Then he noticed the stout figure standing quietly in the shadows. The expression of sympathy on Bill Harper's face looked genuine.

'Sorry you had to witness that,' Pilger said.

'It happens to the best of us, Ray,' Harper replied.

'It's never happened to me before.'

'Surely it won't be difficult to pick up Robson and his friend Wallace?'

Pilger managed a bitter smile. 'London's a big place, Bill. They've only got to park the car and dive down the nearest Tube station. With plenty of opportunities to get rid of any evidence before we catch up with them.'

'What about Max's men?'

The detective lit one of his cigars, cupping his hands to protect it from the rainwater that dripped from his flat mole-skin cap. 'D'you know, I'm not even sure that's who they were.

I've got photographs of all Max's known henchmen imprinted on my mind, and I didn't recognise them.' He exhaled a cloud of blue smoke and watched it whipped away into the dismal wet night. 'I don't even know who's got the heroin and who's got the money. If it's the other group who's got the heroin – and they're not connected with Max – then I doubt we can do much to stop one helluva lot of the stuff hitting the streets.'

An ambulance came into view along the embankment and pulled over towards them.

Harper said: 'I don't know about these things, Ray, but I suppose there's no way you can let this ride? Do nothing and bide your time until we get another opportunity to catch them red-handed?'

'That's the galling thing, Bill.' Pilger stared thoughtfully at the glowing tip of his cigar. 'By using shooters, they've forced my hand. It's got to be followed up immediately. I've got no option now.'

He watched as the rain began to sheet down with renewed vengeance, matching his mood exactly. 'It's going to be a long and busy night.'

Robson killed the engine and the lights, and fell back against the headrest with his eyes closed. He was drained, spent.

Wallace, too, found it difficult to think of anything but the closeness of their escape. He was panting as though he had personally run the distance over Chelsea Bridge and around the back doubles until they'd pulled up in the quiet Battersea backstreet.

'My heart's still pounding,' he complained.

Robson opened an eye and looked at him. 'You're a bloody fool, Wallace. Why the hell did you have to bring that thing? We could be wanted for murder now, for all we know.'

'No way,' Wallace returned dismissively, patting the shot-
gun on his lap with affection. 'Just shook the bastards up a
bit, that's all. Too far away to do any damage.'

'He didn't look a picture of health to me,' Robson said
icily.

Wallace was getting irritable. 'I wanna tell you, chum, if I
hadn't taken it, *you* wouldn't be looking too healthy now. Up
before the beak tomorrow.'

That seemed like little consolation. 'If they were able to
spring an ambush like that, then they must know all about
us.'

The Rhodesian wasn't listening. He was pulling the
attaché-case onto his lap, fumbling at the locks in his haste.
'I don't know what the fuck Max was playing at with those
two guys . . . I just hope—' His eyes widened as he opened
the lid. 'Oh, shit!'

'What is it?'

'The fucking bastards!' Wallace was near to tears. He
tilted the case so that Robson could see the contents. Tightly
packed bundles of fifty pound notes held with elastic bands.
'One sodding note on the top of each bundle. The rest is
plain sodding paper! I doubt if there's a grand in total . . . I'll
kill Max, the double-crossing . . .'

Robson couldn't care less about the money; it was trivial
after the events of the past half-hour. 'That's the least of our
worries, Wallace. We're right up shit creek without a paddle.'

The Rhodesian was still staring at the case. 'We've got to
find Max.'

'Fuck Max,' Robson retorted. 'If the police know about
us, they probably know about him.'

'How?' It was as though the thought had never occurred
to him.

'I don't know. Phone-taps, perhaps.'

Wallace paled. 'Oh, God. I've just remembered. The phones were playing up at the office the other day. We called the engineers in.'

Robson remembered something else. 'When I went to Frankie's house the other day, the telephone engineer was leaving as I arrived.'

'Sod!' Their predicament was sinking in fast.

'If we go to Max,' Robson said, 'we'll probably get there the same time as the police.'

The reason for Frank Lewis's low opinion of Blair Wallace was starting to become painfully obvious. Robson decided to take command. 'Clean off that bloody gun and the attaché-case. Use a rag. We'll dump them somewhere. We've got to get away from here.'

Wallace nodded numbly; panic was starting to set in.

Three minutes later they abandoned the car, leaving in opposite directions.

Keeping to the ill-lit backstreets Robson made his way towards the Latchmere near the west end of Battersea Park. The night air seemed full of police car sirens. Every few minutes he heard a distant sound, distorted by the constant hiss of rain. Now and again he caught sight of a flashing blue light as a vehicle shot across a nearby junction. He was being hunted, haunted by the knowledge that the pack was closing in. On the way he disposed of the case in a litter-bin, then he dropped the thousand pounds in notes down three separate drains. He wanted there to be absolutely no evidence of any kind that he'd been involved in the exchange. He just hoped Wallace would make a good job of throwing the shot-gun in the Thames without being seen.

The walk through the blustery, rain-swept streets at least helped to clear his mind. It was all too easy to put himself in the position of the police. If their information had come from telephone-taps, then they would know all about him and Wallace, and Max too. If the van was the same one he'd seen outside Lewis's warehouse, then the police would know they left together.

They would also know that Bernadette had been there. In itself that wouldn't be proof of her involvement, but it would put her under suspicion.

At the scene of the exchange itself half-a-dozen police would have been able to identify Wallace out on the pavement. Although it was unlikely he'd been seen at the wheel, he had little doubt the officers would testify to his identity. They were only human.

If he pleaded ignorance of what was going on – that he was just the driver, that he thought the vanload of plain clothes policemen were a gang of villains – the very least would be his loss of parole. More likely Wallace would drop him in it from a great height.

No, he was well and truly stitched up. Even now he guessed the police would be calling on Andy Sutcliff about the use of his car, and probably visiting Sandy at Fatton Place.

Christ, what a mess!

The telephone box outside the Duke of Cambridge hadn't been vandalised. As he stepped inside a white police car sped past, blue lights pulsating and its modern American-style siren whooping eerily.

Hastily he dialled the number.

'Rich Abbott, please.'

'Who?' It was a bad line and the woman's voice crackled irritably. 'Mr Abbott? Who wants him?'

'Robson. Billy Robson.'

'I'll see if he's in.' She didn't sound hopeful.

Robson cursed as the seconds ticked by. He was nearly out of change. The bleeps started greedily and he fumbled to stuff in the remaining coins from his pocket.

''Allo, Billy-boy, long time no see.' Rich Abbott's voice was unmistakable.

'Rich, I'm in a spot of trouble.'

There was a pause. Then cautiously: 'What sort of trouble?'

Robson looked down at the mouthpiece. 'Big trouble, Rich. I need help.'

'Anything, Billy-boy, you know that.' His offer sounded short on enthusiasm.

'I need to disappear for a few days. I've got half the police in London looking for me.'

'Oh, I see. *That* sort of trouble.'

Robson was getting impatient. 'I'm running out of coins. Can you help? I'm desperate.'

Again a hesitation. 'Of course. Come round.'

'The spieler?'

'No, no,' he said quickly. 'I've got this *pied-à-terre*. A little flat in Norbury the wife doesn't know about.' He gave the address. 'I'll see you there about one.'

'Thanks, Rich.'

'That's okay, Billy-boy. Be lucky—' The pips obliterated his farewell. Robson hung up.

The door opened just as far as the security-chain would allow.

A heavily-mascarared blue eye blinked warily at him. 'Mr Robson, is it?' Her voice was husky with sleep.

'Yes. Is Rich here?'

' 'Ang on, love.' She closed the door to unhook the chain, and opened it wide. She was tall, blonde and just the right side of forty with a figure that belonged to a woman ten years younger. The scarlet lace dressing-gown hardly hid the scanty matching nightdress. Rich Abbott was doing well in more ways than he'd realised. 'I dozed off waiting for him. He phoned just a few moments ago to say to expect you.'

She glanced nervously up and down the corridor before closing and bolting the door.

'I'm sorry to interrupt your evening,' Robson apologised.

She shrugged and smiled, offering her hand. 'Maise. Well, Margaret really, but everyone calls me Maise. Maisie. It's all right. Rich says you're in a bit of bother. I understand.'

Robson smiled weakly. 'Thanks.'

'Fancy a drink? Scotch?'

He suddenly felt relief cocooning him; for the moment at least he was safe. 'I could murder one.'

The twenty minutes that followed were strained and virtually silent as Maisie had evidently been told not to ask questions. The whisky conspired with nervous exhaustion and the dulcet tones of Roberta Flack to drive him to the edge of sleep by the time Rich Abbott arrived.

He was not a happy man. Ordering his reluctant girlfriend into the bedroom, he turned to Robson. 'Well, Billy-boy, you have been busy, haven't you? Stirred up a right little hornet's nest.'

'What have you heard?'

Abbott pulled the dress tie from his tuxedo and plucked open the top two buttons. 'Plenty on the short-wave radio. The police frequencies are full of you. I think every plod on the manor is hunting for you. And a bloke called Wallace. He works for Frankie Lewis, doesn't he?'

'We both do.'

Abbott sauntered over to the vulgar red leather cocktail bar in the corner and poured a large Scotch. 'The plod have been picking up associates of·yours all over the East End. Anyone who's got the remotest connection. I closed down the spieler early tonight. No reason to keep it open. Everyone had gone to ground.'

'Have they called on you?'

Abbott's smile was more of a smirk. 'Not yet. No doubt I'll be blessed with a dawn visit. Dirty bastards, sure they just do it in the hopes of catching blokes humping their wives.' He swallowed a mouthful of whisky.

Robson sensed Abbott's brooding anger. 'Look, Rich, I'm sorry to have imposed on you like this. I just couldn't think who else to turn to.'

For a moment Abbott held him in a hostile gaze. 'Is it true, Billy-boy?'

'What?'

'That this business is about drugs? Heroin? The word is some Irish cowboys were turning you over during an exchange when the fuzz jumped you.'

Robson was reticent. 'Something like that.'

'Christ, Billy, you know how I feel about drugs! God, I never thought you of all people would get involved with that crap! That's not villainy, it's – it's—' he searched for a word, '—it's a perversion. Sick. Blood-sucking.'

'I know how you feel,' Robson kept his tone moderate. 'I feel the same way. I got trapped into it through Lewis.'

'Frankie?' Incredulous. 'Never! We're good mates. He'd never get involved with that sort of skull.'

Robson never ceased to be amazed at the reputation for honesty that Lewis had managed to earn for himself. 'Please yourself, Rich, but it's true. You know he's heavily involved with the Irish through Bernadette . . .'

Abbott frowned. 'You mean you were turned over by a rival Irish gang?'

'It looks like it.'

'This is getting worse by the minute.' Abbott began pacing the room like a caged tiger, the drink in his hand forgotten. 'I hope the bloody IRA aren't tied-up with this. The last thing we need is a bloody gang war between feuding Micks. They're causing enough trouble nowadays.'

'I don't know who's involved,' Robson lied. 'Anyway, what *sort* of trouble do you mean?'

Abbott rediscovered his drink, killed it, and poured another. 'Bloody Irish gangs are muscling in all over the place in recent years. Vicious bastards, too, some of them. Always usin' the threat of the IRA. You never know if they mean it or not. Still, it doesn't matter; the point is, it works. The threat is enough. They control the horses and the dogs. Building site rackets, and bloody great shop-lifting gangs come over from Belfast. They're starting to get big in counterfeiting, too.'

'Rich, this sort of talk is getting us nowhere fast.'

Abbott chuckled bitterly, the drink getting to him. 'It's getting *me* somewhere *fast*, Billy-boy. It's deciding me to get *you* out of here *fast*. You are *definitely* bad blue!' He paused to think, studying the remnants of his drink. 'Just till tomorrow morning. You can kip down on the sofa. I've got you a driving licence and some wheels lined up for you. Nice two-litre Capri. I want you in it tomorrow morning. First thing.'

Robson's growing anxiety subsided again. 'I'm grateful, Rich. Really.'

The other man nodded. 'But our scores are even now, Billy-boy. Remember that. No more favours.' He stared at

Robson for what seemed a long time. 'And shave off that bloody moustache. You left the Marines *years* ago.'

Thoughtfully Robson ran his hands over the bristles. Abbott had a point.

'Come in 'ere, Maise,' Abbott suddenly called out towards the bedroom. 'And bring that blonde hair rinse you use.'

Sixteen

It was with growing apprehension that Bella turned into the dilapidated street of Victorian houses off Kilburn.

All around, desiccated rendering and peeling paintwork exuded an impression of neglect, and of hostility to outsiders. Row upon row of grubby windows looked down on the narrow street – a thousand blank eyes ever watchful, belied the first impression that it was deserted.

The badlands of the inner city. Hundreds of tiny bedsits, like urban caves, with gas-rings and a shared toilet on the next landing. Hundreds of tatty dwellings offering instant anonymity to those wanting to disappear in the vastness of the metropolis, for any one of a million reasons. Just a month in advance, and no questions asked.

A city tumbleweed of newspapers and plastic takeaway cartons scurried along the pavement in the breeze.

Bella shivered and glanced again at the note clutched in her hand. She peered up at the floors of the house towering above her. The railings to the basement area had been taken away during the war for smelting and had never been replaced. The temporary wood and chickenwire fence had long-ago collapsed under the test of time.

Warily she climbed the crumbling steps to the faded blue door. Few of the vertical row of bell-buttons had names. One said Flat Seven. She prodded it with her thumb. There was no sound.

Almost immediately, the door flew open. Two unkempt individuals bustled out, chatting to each other as though she didn't exist. Their accents were distinctly Irish.

She hesitated, then pushed open the door into the darkened corridor. There was a slight odour of must in the air and the smell of cats. A child's pushchair and an old bicycle had been parked against the wall which hadn't been decorated since the Blitz.

Bella creaked her way up the uncarpeted stairs to the fourth floor. Faint strains of *The Jimmy Young Show* filtered through the heavy panelled door of Flat Seven.

Taking a deep breath, she knocked. Instantly she sensed the alarm on the other side of the door. The radio died away. Footsteps scraped on lino.

'Who is it?'

'Billy? It's Bella. I got your note.'

Chains and bolts began to clatter. The door swung open. It took a couple of seconds for her to recognise the tall, fair-haired man with the round wire spectacles perched on the end of his nose. They made him look younger, reminding her of those eternal student types who would never grow up. The jeans and tatty sweater completed the picture.

'Were you followed?' Robson demanded, peering over her shoulder down the dark stairwell.

'I don't think so. I did what you said, changing taxis and all that.'

He stood aside to let her into the dingy bedsit, over-crowded with two single beds and a large ancient wardrobe. A second man she did not recognise stood by the tiny two-ring cooker. He looked at her warily.

'This is Blair. We're in this mess together.'

Bella nodded in acknowledgement, but the man wasn't

interested. He turned back to the dormer window and lifted the yellowing net curtain to resume his watch on the street below.

'Can I get you a coffee?' Robson indicated the bed and she sat down on the edge. As he lit the gas beneath the kettle, he said: 'I'm sorry to drag you into this, Bella. You were the nearest person I could think of who was unlikely to be under surveillance over this business. I was driving my mate Andy's car when it all happened, so they've probably got his phone tapped . . .'

'It's okay, Billy,' she said quietly. '*Really* it is.'

He grinned sheepishly. 'Anyway, I'm bloody glad you came. I've got to get word to Sand in the clinic, tell her not to worry. And Dan, of course. D'you know how Gran Jacobs is managing?'

You poor bastard, she thought, as she watched him prepare the three chipped mugs of coffee. He was so upright and determined, and yet somehow naïve. Unaware that he was fighting a losing battle as his world collapsed around him. When a man was down, there were always plenty queueing up to put the boot in, it seemed. Not for the first time she wondered how different her life might have been if she'd met Robson a few years ago. Sandy never had realised just how lucky she was.

Bella said: 'Dan's been taken into care, Billy. They came for him yesterday. I'm sorry.'

She could see the agony in his drawn face, his mouth contorting around a silent curse.

Bella shrugged. 'I expect it was the Probation people. As soon as they learned you were wanted by the police and Sand was in the clinic . . . Well, you know . . . The Welfare don't miss a chance to stick their noses in.'

Robson nodded. 'It may even be for the best, I suppose. But God knows how the poor little sod'll take this. Do you know where he's been taken?'

'No. But I can find out.' She reached out and touched his arm. 'Shall I tell him you're okay?'

He nodded, but didn't speak. She just saw that his eyes were moist before he turned away as the kettle began to sing.

By the time he'd poured the three mugs, his composure was back under control. 'Would you contact Sand for me?'

'Of course.'

'And also contact a girl called Bernadette Lewis. Or she may call herself Mulqueen. You can reach her at The Czar pub in Peckham. It's the only way we stand a chance of getting out of this.'

Bella's dark eyes were wide with childlike honesty. 'Anything to help, Billy, really.'

He seemed genuinely relieved, and held her hand in an awkward gesture of thanks. 'There's one other thing, Bella. I know you were at Max's club with Sandy the other day when there was that trouble with the Irishmen . . .'

She raised her hand. 'I think I know what you're going to ask, Billy. After Sand and I got away, they forced Max to co-operate with them under threat. It was those Irishmen who turned you over at the exchange.'

'The bastard!' Wallace suddenly spoke from the window.

Bella turned towards him. 'You can't blame Max,' she protested. 'He was scared silly.'

'He'll be scared silly all right when I get hold of him,' Wallace warned.

'Shut up!' Robson snapped, and turned back to Bella. 'Do you know *who* they were?'

She shrugged. 'Only that they seemed to hate the crowd you worked for. Someone said something about them being Protestant paramilitaries from Belfast, but I don't know much about that. It was only hearsay.' She frowned. 'I do remember one of them had an unusual name.'

'What was that?'

'Tom Rabbit.'

When the coffee was finished, Robson hastily wrote two brief notes: one for Sandy, and the other for Bernadette. Then, after Wallace had checked that the coast was clear, Bella slipped quietly back into the street and towards the bustling centre of Kilburn.

As the two men settled back into their long wait, Wallace said: 'Have you been to Max's club? The one they call The Dominatrix?'

Deep in thought, Robson shook his head. 'Why?'

'It's a weird place. Sort of private club for perverts. Sado-masochism, I think they call it. I've seen that girl there. Had her arse tanned till it glowed pink.'

Wallace didn't say any more; he didn't need to. Robson gave him a withering look.

It was five days later when Frank Lewis pulled up outside The Czar public house in his Daimler.

Being just after opening time, he found the place almost deserted. It smelled faintly of lunchtime's smoke laced with the pungent aroma of furniture polish.

Bernadette sat at the corner bar stool in the lounge, casually dressed in tracksuit trousers and a baggy sweater. As he approached, she looked up from the white wine with which she was toying; her expression was less than welcoming.

Lewis glanced warily around at the half-dozen patrons

who had called in to recharge their batteries on their way home from work. 'Is it safe?'

She looked at him long and hard, wondering how she had ever fallen for his charm and self-assurance. Qualities that seemed sadly lacking in the nervous haggard man who stood before her now.

'It's safe, Frankie,' she answered. 'They're all regulars.'

His shoulders dropped as he relaxed. 'Thank Christ for that. I seem to see the busies everywhere I look.' He dumped himself on the stool next to hers. He grinned sheepishly. 'No hiding place, eh?'

'What happened?'

'That's what I should be asking you. I stepped off the plane from Boston and – bang – first I'm turned over by Customs and then the boys in blue take me straight down the nick. Gawd, what a grilling! Forty-eight hours non-stop before they let me out.' He rubbed his chin. 'Haven't even had a shave or changed my shirt.'

'So you *do* know what happened?'

Lewis gave a sneer of disgust. 'Let's say I got the general picture. I gather Billy and Blair Wallace fouled up with Maltese Max. Stupid bastards! I just said I knew nothing about it.'

'Did they believe you?'

'I don't think so.' He shrugged. 'But I was in Boston, so they could hardly prove anything. Mind you, that didn't stop 'em from trying. Eventually I got hold of Hyram, and he came down to put the frighteners on them. Bloody good brief Hyram; had me out within the hour. Just got back to the office when I got your call – came straight here.'

Despite herself, Bernadette felt a certain pity for him. She, too, had been subjected to an extensive interview by officers of the Central Drug Squad. 'I expect you could use a drink?'

'Double Scotch.' He grinned uneasily. 'On second thoughts, make it a treble, love.'

She climbed down from the stool and moved behind the bar. 'What are you going to do now?'

Lewis shook his head in despair. 'God knows! I've got to find Billy and Wallace before the police do. Between them, they could drop me right in it.'

Bernadette slammed his whisky onto the bar. 'Sure, they've enough problems t'be getting along with. That's why I called you.'

Lewis's eyes widened. 'You've heard from them?'

Her expression hardened. 'Well, I didn't ask you over for a reconciliation. Billy daren't telephone either of us in case the telephones are tapped. A girl came over with a message for me. Someone called Bella.'

'Any word about the missing smack?'

'No, Frankie, nothing about that.' She sounded exasperated with him. 'Just a call-box number to ring as soon as you could. She said any day between 12 noon and five-past. Or 8 p.m. and five-past. That's all—' The words froze on her lips.

Lewis frowned. 'What . . . ?'

Even as he spoke, he felt the chill wind from the opening door behind him. A shiver rippled down his spine, and he felt a distinct jolt as his heart literally skipped a beat.

'Good to be seeing you, Frankie.'

Dee walked slowly across the beer-stained carpet. The scruffy individual behind him with the lank black hair and missing teeth looked familiar.

'Remember Timothy?' Dee introduced. 'You met in Buncrana.'

Lewis gulped and nodded in a pathetic parody of politeness.

'Hallo, pretty lady.' Dee leaned against the bar. 'Would you not be offering a wee drink to a couple of old friends?'

Bernadette's face was a mask; she was unable to move.

Dee's thin lips twisted into a smile. 'A couple of Jack Daniels would do grand. On the house? Oh, you're too kind.'

A brittle silence followed. As Lewis motioned frantically with his eyes, Bernadette slowly regained control of her muscles and reached for the optics.

Dee turned his attention to Lewis. 'Well?'

Lewis felt the beat of his heart gather momentum; his palms were cold and damp. 'Look, I don't know. Not yet. The police took me in as soon as I stepped off the plane from Boston.'

Dee took his glass from the bar. He didn't remove his eyes from Lewis as he took a slow, deliberate swig. 'Well, if you don't know, Frankie, it's high time you found out. Because The Man wants to know what you're going to do about it. You see, as far as he's concerned, £½ million worth of our goods has been mislaid in your charge. Perhaps it was that cabbage-hat friend of yours who made off with it . . . ?'

Lewis shook his head vehemently. 'No, no, Dee. Nothing like that, I'm sure.'

'Your faith in your fellow man is quite touching,' Dee murmured into his glass. 'But the word is that the consignment has found its way into the hands of the Proddies. Rumours like that upset The Man. He wonders if perhaps your cabbage-hat friend did a deal with them. Maybe even with your connivance . . .'

'That's nonsense!' Lewis protested.

'Is it, Frankie?' The Irishman's eyes were flat and expressionless.

For a moment, Lewis was tempted to say he'd heard from

Robson; he bit his tongue in time. 'I'd hardly have gone to all the trouble setting up the Boston deal if I've been trying to double-cross you. I *certainly* wouldn't have come back.'

A glimmer of a smile flickered on Dee's face. 'That, I admit, would have been a very foolhardy thing to do.' He drained his glass and placed it on the bar. 'What about Maltese Max? I understand the exchange was supposed to have been with him.'

'I can't call or even phone!' Lewis sounded exasperated by Dee's smooth tone. 'Like me, he's been questioned by the Bill. He's bound to be under surveillance. No doubt his phone's tapped. How can I go anywhere near him?'

Dee watched impassively as Lewis nervously loosened his tie. Beads of perspiration were glistening on the man's face. 'All right, Frankie, you can leave him to us. You've enough on your plate. I'll give you twenty-four hours to come up with Robson – or the three hundred grand cut you owe us.'

'That's impossible!'

At the sight of Lewis's discomfort, the Irishman's smile became genuine. 'The money is needed to finance the Boston deal, Frankie. I'm sure you understand the meaning of cash-flow. The Man certainly does, and so do our Libyan friends.' His white teeth glistened. 'I wouldn't want *you* to become a cash-flow problem, Frankie. Really I wouldn't.'

Slowly Dee turned nonchalantly towards the door. Behind him, Timothy finished his own drink in one gulp and, with a too-friendly toothless grin, followed.

At the exit Dee paused. 'Twenty-four hours, Frankie.'

As the doors swung to a creaky close, it was as though a whirlwind had just swept out of the bar.

Lewis felt his knees go weak, and stumbled to a bar stool. 'Pour us another drink, Bernie, there's a love.'

She watched him, shaking her head sadly.

This time, Frankie Lewis was in it right up to his neck.

Royce was saying: 'I'm sorry, Poppy, but there it is. Since those Irish jokers turned up, the club's been virtually empty. And with this drugs thing hanging over Max's head, it's too risky. The police are likely to be going through all his business interests with a fine-tooth comb.'

Bella looked across the office above the travel agency, where only two weeks before, Royce had ordered Sandy to strip, to the leather settee. Hidden behind the pair of thick tortoiseshell spectacles, Max's eyes were as inscrutable as ever. As usual, he showed as much feeling as a stone Buddha. In fact, she doubted he cared at all what the loss of livelihood would mean to her.

'I'm trying to set up a video deal in Amsterdam,' Royce added. 'But that'll take some time. Obviously I'll be in touch.'

In a sense, she welcomed a break from the work. Just lately she'd been moving into more gruelling routines, and the lash marks were taking longer to heal. Like the heroin she depended on, it was as though she had to absorb steadily more punishment to achieve the buzz she needed. And, she hated to admit, she'd miss Royce.

Max spoke for the first time. 'And obviously I cannot supply you with heroin any more. That's all finished here. In fact, I'm thinking of moving my entire operation into Holland.'

'I'm sorry,' Royce said with finality. It was strange to hear him apologetic; it was so far from his usual role of the unrelenting master.

Bella stared out of the dark rain-lashed window. 'Let's keep in touch,' she said lamely.

Royce's even white teeth showed in a sad smile.

As with so many of his 'slaves', he knew that his power over Bella had long ago become more than a game played for money.

Without warning, Max suddenly became agitated. 'What's that noise?' His short legs wriggled in an effort to get off the settee.

Royce waved a dismissive hand. 'Probably the cleaners, Max. I locked the shop door when I came up.'

His Maltese boss had become a bag of nerves since that incident at The Dominatrix.

Bella's eyes travelled in the same direction that Max was looking. In the lighted frame of the fluted glass door, she, too, saw the dark shape. As it climbed the last stairs from the travel agency below, the huge distorted figure reminded her of a pantomime demon emerging from the bowels of the earth. But this was no illusion. She could almost sense the evil, feel its presence. The skin on her back began to crawl.

Max was paralysed with fear, like a rabbit mesmerised by a car's headlights. Perspiration pumped out of his pores. Royce's mouth dropped in disbelief.

Max suddenly found the use of his muscles. 'Out of the way!'

Barging past Royce, he dived towards the desk where Bella knew he kept an automatic pistol.

By now, the monstrous black shape was joined by another, blotting out the light from the stairway. The handle turned. Bella involuntarily took a backward step.

Slowly, the door swung open under its own weight, the unoiled hinge creaking eerily in the sudden silence.

Max's paralysis returned as he hovered behind his desk, unsure.

'Nice and relaxed, folks. Keep calm and no one gets hurt.'

Bella swallowed. The voice was different from the one she had been half-expecting. It was soft and lyrical, unlike the harsh Belfast tone of the Ulstermen. And the face, that was different, too.

This man had a handsome face with regular features, the skin pale and hued with the remnants of childhood freckles. His hair was soft, brown and curly. His smile seemed as genuine as the laughing eyes.

Then she realised how wrong she was. It was all a mask. Behind it, the eyes glittered like ice chips.

It was only then she noticed the matt black shape of the revolver in his left hand.

With a gasp, she turned her head towards Max and Royce. They had not been fooled for a second. Her master already had his hands raised, his face drained of blood. Max sat at his desk, frozen in shock, his fists clenched on its surface.

'Maltese Max, I assume?' Dee walked slowly towards the desk, arcing his body gently as he moved, so that all three kept within his field-of-fire. He seemed to find something amusing.

Then Bella noticed the second man. A scruffy individual with lank black hair and an evil gap-toothed grin. Half-hidden by a grubby raincoat, his fingers played an impatient tattoo on the breech of a sawn-off shot-gun.

'Who the hell are you?' Max had found his voice. But his words lacked the authority he intended them to convey.

Dee's voice was unnervingly soft: 'Let's just say I am a friend of Frankie Lewis. We have, it seems, a mutual business interest.'

Max feigned confusion, wriggling uncomfortably in his chair behind the desk. 'What business interest? I don't know what the hell—'

Dee sat on the edge of the desk and waved the snout of the revolver under Max's nose. 'Lewis is hardly in the position to come here himself. Not with the police watching you both. So I'm here instead, representing Lewis's masters in Dublin.' He indicated his scruffy companion. 'This is Timothy.'

Max watched the barrel in front of his face as though it was a snake's head ready to strike. 'From Dublin?' he repeated weakly, the significance of the words sinking in.

'Yes,' Dee confirmed. 'You are credited with twenty kilos of heroin. I'm here to collect the amount due or repossess. Get it?'

'I'll have to check my file . . .' Max mumbled, reaching for the drawer of his desk.

Bella winced as the second Irishman lunged forward and rapped the barrel of the shotgun hard over Max's knuckles. The yelp of pain filled the small office.

'Naughty!' Timothy chided as he reached into the drawer and retrieved the small handgun. He held it up for Dee to see. 'A donation to The Cause?' He laughed, and slid it into the pocket of his raincoat.

'Place your hands, palms down, on the desk,' Dee ordered. 'And leave them there.' He waited patiently whilst Max complied, and straightened his bruised hand with obvious difficulty. 'Now talk.'

Max had begun to tremble. His eyes pleaded and actual tears started to mist up his spectacles. His voice was croaked and broken: 'I had no choice, believe me. A group of thugs forced their way into my club. I think they were your rivals from Belfast, you know, Protestants. They were sore over something you'd done. They insisted on me setting up an exchange with Lewis, so they could intercept it. That's all I know.'

'And you went along with it?' Dee breathed.

'I had no choice. It went beyond threats. They started using cigarettes on one of my girls.' Max was now shaking so much that his words were almost incomprehensible. 'It's Lewis's own fault anyway. And your people in Dublin. I'd warned you before I was under pressure. Threats and then they set fire to the shop downstairs. I was *promised* protection!' Anger momentarily broke through his fear.

Dee was unmoved. 'What about that bastard Robson and Lewis's man, Wallace? Were they in on this?'

Max shrugged. 'Maybe. How should I know?'

'I want to know where they are,' Dee hissed.

'I *don't* know!'

Dee's permanent sly smile took on a distinctly frozen look. Carefully, he pocketed his revolver, reached into his coat and withdrew what looked like a small wooden knife haft. With a clean, metallic hiss, the switchblade sprang free, locking into position with its silvered edge trembling in the glow of the desk lamp.

'Your appalling lack of knowledge of everything I ask you, Max, is starting to get on my *nerves!*'

Max gasped and, as he did, Dee swung the fine point of the switchblade down with the full weight of his balled fist.

Saliva exploded from Max's mouth as the razored tip sliced through the back of his hand and thudded into the surface of the desk below, fixing his palm fast.

Max whimpered. The sudden shock prevented the scream he'd started. He stared at the quivering blade that had cruci- fied his hand. A thick gunge of blood bubbled around the flesh, pumped out of a severed artery by his racing heart.

Dee said: 'I think you've been getting your priorities wrong, Max. Compared to us, your Ulster visitors were merely playing games, do I make myself plain?'

Max gulped as both Royce and Bella looked on aghast.

'Now tell me, *where* is Robson?'

'I don't KNOW!' Max screamed, tears now welling from his eyes. He grabbed the haft with his free hand. It wouldn't budge.

Dee's eyes flickered towards Timothy. 'Let's do the other hand . . . Then we'll start on Royce here and the girl.'

'Wait!' Bella stepped forward. 'For God's sake, leave him alone! Max doesn't know where Billy Robson is.' She took a deep breath. 'But I do.'

'Ah!' Dee's smile returned. 'I had a feeling someone here would be in on this.'

Bella's nostrils flared. 'I'm not *in* on anything, you bastard! But I happen to know that Billy Robson just got caught up in this. He knows less than Max. And he certainly hasn't got your bloody smack either. You can find that out for yourself. There'll be no need for any more violence.'

'I do believe the little lady's trying to lay down conditions,' Dee sneered.

Bella was defiant. 'Do you want to speak to Robson or not?'

Dee's fixed smile didn't warm. 'Let's go.' He turned to Royce. 'You get out of here and don't come back. We'll leave Max to contemplate on his true loyalties, by himself.'

Two minutes later, the office was empty, leaving Max seated at the desk, desperately trying to free the knife before he bled to death. He struggled with all his might, ignoring the vicious sparks of pain, as the steel grated against the fine bones of his hand. But all the time, the pool of bright blood continued to expand until it began spilling over the edge of the desk.

His strength eventually drained from him. The fingers of his free hand fell limply from the haft and a red mist began to form in his vision. Deep, thick and warm. Coaxing him in.

Frank Lewis was furious.

'I suppose it was Wallace's idea to take the shot-gun?'

It was a statement that scarcely needed a reply. The Rhodesian glared frostily up from where he sat on the edge of the bed in the dingy Kilburn bedsit.

'It hardly matters now,' Robson interrupted. 'There's no point in recriminations.' After so many days cooped up with Wallace, it was a relief to see someone who might actually have a sensible suggestion. Even if that someone was Frank Lewis. 'The question is what the hell do we do now?'

Lewis glanced back at Bernadette, who leaned against the door, hugging her sheepskin coat morosely around her. 'Don't look at me, Frankie. It's your mess. I just think you owe it to Billy to at least do something to help.'

'For God's sake, woman, stop bleating Billy-this-and-Billy-that!' He was getting angrier. 'I'm hardly in the position to help anyone. I've got the Bill breathing down my neck, and that bastard Dee itching to stamp all over my fingers if I don't come up with that heroin or the money.'

Robson frowned. 'Does Dee think you've double-crossed him or something?'

'Or something,' Lewis sneered. 'That's the trouble with the drugs game. There's always some bastard tempted to try it on.'

Bernadette said: 'Actually, Billy, I think he suspects you more than Frankie. He's got a pathological hatred for Marines. Or cabbage-hats, as he calls them. Even ex-ones. He'd love the chance – or the excuse – to get at you.'

Lewis said: 'Let's not get despondent, Bernie.' He turned back to Robson. 'Trouble is, Dee is also your best chance of getting out of the country. Ireland's not known as the back-door of Europe for nothing. Over there, Dee can organise literally anything. As he's fond of saying, Ireland's got the best politicians money can buy.'

Bernadette's withering glance stabbed him in the back.

Robson didn't look happy. It was a turn-up for the book that was not entirely unexpected. He'd had plenty of time to think about it as he sat with Wallace in the confined flatlet.

Lewis's connections with Dee had offered a fairly obvious way of escape. But even if that could be arranged, it would mean spending the rest of his life on the run; not an idea that he cherished. But what was the alternative? Going back inside for God knows how many years . . .

No, that he couldn't face. And he was certain that Sandy couldn't either. Instead, he seriously examined the prospect of setting up a new life under a new identity somewhere else in the world. He had to admit it had a certain appeal. After all, he'd managed to screw up his life so badly in Britain that he could hardly make a worse job of it elsewhere. In South America perhaps? Or some quiet corner of Africa? Then, when the dust had settled, Sandy and Dan could slip out quietly to join him.

It was then that he realised he was fooling himself. Sandy would never tolerate that sort of existence either.

'What are you smiling at?' Lewis demanded irritably.

Robson lit a fresh cigarette. 'At the irony of it all. The only chance I've got of getting away is through the bloody IRA. The very terrorists I was trying to kill a few years back.'

Lewis shuffled his feet. 'You've got to stay alive, old son, before you get away from anything. As Bernie said, they've got you down as Suspect Number One.'

Robson grabbed Lewis's lapel. 'Well, *you* can put them *right* there, can't you? And don't forget you still owe me that hundred grand for going along with this crazy scheme. And I've a feeling I'm going to need every penny of it.'

He released his grip, and Lewis fell back against the wall. 'Things have changed, Billy. Dee's mob are the preferential creditors now . . .'

Robson was about to reply when someone rapped on the bedsit door. He exchanged glances with Wallace and Lewis. Nervously, Bernadette backed away from the sound.

'Billy? It's Bella.'

His immediate thought was that she had word from Sandy. Without hesitation, he slid the bolt and opened the door. He'd scarcely focused on the figure of Bella, before Dee stepped in front of her. His eyes blazed above the snout of the revolver.

'Back up real slowly, cabbage-hat!' He spat the words. 'And don't try any of your fuckin' Bruce Lee stuff on me.'

Robson's spirits sank.

'Oh, my God!' Lewis gasped.

'You might well indeed call for divine help,' Dee retorted without taking his eyes from Robson. 'Now all of you sit down on the bed on the left. Keep your hands on your heads.' In the overcrowded bedsit, there was an almost farcical shuffle to obey the IRA man's command. 'Timothy, check them all for weapons, then turn this place over thoroughly.'

It was half-an-hour before Dee was satisfied that neither the missing heroin nor money was hidden within the confines of the room. Even the bedding had been ripped apart, as well as a couple of suspiciously loose floorboards.

By that time, Lewis's bravado was beginning to return. 'I told you, Dee. Like me, Billy and Wallace here were set up.

Those two Irish gangsters turned up, posing as Max's men. Just as my blokes smelled a rat, the bloody fuzz appeared. It was total chaos.'

'It was bloody terrifying,' Wallace added with feeling.

Dee wrinkled his nose. 'Well, I smell a rat myself. And he's sitting right in front of me.'

Robson glared up at him from the bed. 'What do I stand to gain from this? I'm in it up to my head.'

'He's right,' Lewis interrupted.

'Shut up!' Dee snapped. 'Once a fuckin' cabbage-hat, always a fuckin' cabbage-hat. Leopards don't change their spots. A tip-off to the police and he'd be in the clear.'

Robson shook his head. 'Maybe that's what I should have done, Dee, but I didn't. Lewis made it quite clear he'd take me with him if he went down. And that your thugs would hunt me and my family down wherever we went.'

Dee almost smiled. 'Our *paramilitaries* would, he was right there. But the police got onto us somehow, which is very strange. Our operation is absolutely watertight. Only a handful of people know any one part of the total operation.'

Wallace said: 'If you think he informed, why don't you just blow him away and have done with it. There's been nothing but trouble since he came on the scene anyway.'

'That sounds like a good idea,' Timothy concurred, fondling the shot-gun as though it was a child. He hadn't forgotten Robson's treatment of him in Buncrana.

Lewis didn't like the way things were going; he had visions of them all being executed. 'Listen, Dee, our operation is still intact. That police raid was at distribution level. Probably one of Max's men turned nark. Or the police had been watching his distribution network. It was just a coincidence that those Irishmen pulled their stunt at the same time.'

Dee watched Lewis's face carefully. 'Ah, yes, *those* Irishmen. Some mysterious Proddy gang, Max was saying. But I'm not sure I believe a word of it.'

'It's true,' Bella blurted. 'I was there.'

Robson suddenly remembered something. 'What was that name you mentioned?'

She frowned. 'You mean Rabbit?'

'That's it. Tom Rabbit. That was the name of one of them.'

Robson looked up at Dee to see the expression on his face freeze. His lips compressed into a thin line.

Timothy blinked. 'I thought he was dead.'

Dee ignored him, and turned instead to Lewis. 'If it's true, this whole thing could make more sense. You're going to have to come to Dublin to explain things to The Man.'

Lewis wriggled uncomfortably. 'I don't think I like that idea.'

The IRA man raised an eyebrow. 'Listen, Frankie, my orders were to execute you if you'd been involved in a double-cross over those drugs.'

'But what about Boston?' Lewis's eyes were suddenly wide with panic.

'They'd have cancelled and re-negotiated,' Dee returned without emotion. 'The Man considers you expendable now, Frankie. You've become a risk all round. So I'm doing you a favour. Come to Dublin and tell them what you've told me. Because if you don't, the chances are I'll be told to eliminate you just to be on the safe side.'

Lewis wasn't convinced. 'Huh, that'd be like walking into the bloody lion's den. It'd be easier to do it there.'

Dee's smirk returned. 'I *can* do it *now*. We'll just take a little trip in the car . . .'

'All right,' Lewis said testily. 'I get the message. But what about Billy?'

'What about him?' Dee sounded irritable. 'He's even more expendable than you.'

Lewis glanced awkwardly at Robson. 'If he stays here on the mainland, the chances are he'll get arrested and that could blow everything. He knows too much about the operation. You've got ways of getting people to Ireland in safety. Get Robson there and we could use him for Boston.'

Dee was incredulous. 'Are you joking?'

Lewis wasn't. 'The police know I was in Boston. It's odds-on they've informed the DEA in the States. You know, the Drug Enforcement Agency. If I turn up there again . . .'

'And what makes you think he can be trusted?' Dee demanded.

Lewis smiled weakly at Robson, and shrugged in a mock gesture of helplessness. 'A hundred thousand pounds.'

Half-an-hour later Dee and Timothy left, taking Wallace with them. Apparently they already had an escape-route planned for him. To Robson, it sounded as organised as the French Resistance movement during the War. It was quite unnerving.

As they heard the footsteps receding down the stairs, Robson said: 'What sort of game are you playing, Frankie?'

Lewis looked pleased with himself. 'You're still alive, aren't you?'

Bernadette was disgusted. 'You mean Frankie Lewis is still alive.'

He stabbed an angry glance in her direction. 'You heard what Dee said, he had orders to execute all of us if we were involved in a double-cross. We've got to persuade them in

Dublin that we're more use to them alive than dead. That's why I suggested using Billy in Boston.'

'Thanks a million,' Robson said. 'I'm trying to get out of this mess and you're just pulling me in deeper.'

Lewis tapped his nose. 'It'll get you out of the country, for a start, Billy. And if we can persuade those gentle Dublin folk to forget about this missing heroin, you still stand to get your hundred thousand. Handy for a new identity abroad.'

'As devious as ever,' Bernadette sighed.

Lewis turned on her angrily. 'And a good job I am, sweetheart, otherwise you, too, might be a target for an IRA hitman. You also know too much, so *don't* rock the boat. Our only chance of ever getting back to a normal life is to play along with Dee's people until we can get out *with* their agreement.'

'You've already found out that won't be easy,' Robson reminded.

'I never said it would be. But the first step is to get them to trust us.' His eyes moved across the room to where Bella sat solemnly in the corner. 'You work at one of Max's clubs, don't you? The Dominatrix?'

She looked up at him with suspicion in her big, dark eyes. 'I did,' she admitted hesitantly. 'But that's all closed now.'

'So I gather,' he paused in thought. 'How do you fancy a job in Ireland? Your sort of work. Say for six months?'

Her eyes narrowed. 'How much?'

Lewis rubbed his chin. 'Say twenty thousand, living in.'

Bernadette reached out for Lewis's arm. 'Frankie, what *are* you talking about?'

'It's none of your business, Bernie,' he snapped back. 'We're finished, remember?'

Bella said: 'I'll do it.'

Lewis smiled, satisfied. 'Good, that's settled. Now I'll get in touch with each of you as soon as I hear from Dee.' He turned to Bernadette. 'Do you want a lift back to The Czar, love?'

She shook her head. 'No, I'm staying here to talk to Billy for a while.'

Lewis shrugged as though it didn't matter to him. 'Well, for Christ's sake, all of you, be careful. Don't relax. The fuzz are still sniffing around.' He turned to Bella. 'Don't tell me you'll turn down my offer of a lift, too?'

She shook her head. 'No. You can tell me more about this job.' She glanced at Robson. 'By the way, Billy, I went to see Sandy today.'

'Really? Thank God for that.' He was as surprised as he was delighted. 'How is she?'

Bella smiled. 'She looked good. No, really. I felt quite envious. Bright and bustling. They keep them very busy there. Chores and therapy, and so forth.' Her smile faded slightly. 'The police had visited her, of course, and that unsettled her.'

'I'm sorry. Did you give her my message?'

'Of course.'

'What did she say?'

Bella looked awkward and stared down at the carpet, then at the other two in the room. 'I'll spare you her exact words, Billy. But basically she doesn't want you back.' She took a deep breath. 'I think she meant it, Billy. I'm sorry.'

That was one thing he somehow hadn't been expecting. As she spoke the words, it was as though someone had thrust a knife into his chest. The pain was almost physical. He stood there in silence, feeling the emotion drain from him.

He felt Bernadette squeeze his arm. 'I'm sorry, too, Billy.'

Lewis gave an embarrassed cough. 'I'll be in touch, Billy. Be lucky.'

He took Bella's arm and led her out through the door. Robson stood rooted to the spot, staring blankly after them.

Bernadette ran a hand through her hair. 'Those bastards have left this place in a right mess. I'll try and tidy it up.' But he didn't appear to hear. 'Have you a drink in the house, Billy?'

'What?' His mind was a million miles and several years away. A bright July morning. Sandy in white lace, he in ceremonial dress. The silver badge on the green beret sparkling in the sunlight. Passing under the arch of crossed swords. Confetti swirling at their feet. 'I'm sorry, yes. There's a bottle of Scotch in the bedside cabinet.'

She smiled at him. Their eyes met and held for a moment too long. It was as though both were asking unspoken questions to which neither knew the answers.

'I think we could both use a drink.' Her voice was hoarse, uneasy.

It was half-an-hour before the bedsit was back in some semblance of order. With any luck, it would pass a cursory muster from the landlady who lived in the basement. Robson had helped Bernadette like an automaton, his mind preoccupied with the news that Bella had brought. The work done, he sat on the edge of the bed and flicked on the single-bar fire. It began to hum, the smell of hot dust starting to fill the room.

'I've got to try and see her,' he said, half to himself, half to Bernadette.

She sat down beside him. 'Have another drink.' He didn't protest as she poured a second generous measure.

'You think it would be a mistake to see her, don't you?'

She shrugged. 'It's not for me to say, Billy.'

He pulled a tight, bitter smile. 'It's obvious what you think. I've screwed up things so badly now that I ought to give her a chance to get on with her own life. That's what you think.'

There was pity in her eyes. 'According to Bella, she's making a brave effort. And I think . . .' She hesitated, unsure how he would take it '. . . I think you really know you can't go to the clinic. At least not without getting caught. The police are bound to be watching. You've got a choice. Go back to prison for God knows how long, or start a new life.'

He swallowed a mouthful of whisky and felt it burn its way down his throat. He stared back at the fire. That was it. Two options. And Sandy could feature in neither. It was that simple. They had reached the parting of the ways. The thought left him feeling empty.

'And Dan?' His voice was a murmur. Outside, the wind rattled at the window.

Bernadette moved closer and rested her hand on his wrist. 'For him, too, Billy. Especially for him.'

He felt the burning sensation in his eyes as the suppressed emotion tried to burst up from inside. He swallowed hard. He tried to speak but didn't trust himself.

Her grip tightened on his wrist and she moved swiftly round to face him, crouching on the floor, looking up into his eyes.

'Don't hold back, Billy. Just let go,' she pleaded. He turned his face away. He was trembling with the effort. She added softly: 'For me.'

It was the way she said it. Two simple words, but they triggered the switch. The dam ruptured and years of fermenting emotional turmoil burst free, sweeping all before it.

★   ★   ★

They talked until the early hours.

After Robson had broken down, they had both begun to talk more freely. Bernadette's total frankness and honesty about her own hopes and despair helped him to open up, too. It was like a warm, soothing wind. Drying the tears and cooling the tortured mind.

At last he picked up the empty bottle. 'Out of provisions. You'll be wanting to get home. There's a phone downstairs. I can call you a mini-cab.' He was aware that his voice was slightly slurred.

Beside him on the bed, Bernadette shook her head slowly. Chestnut hair tumbled over her eyes. She tossed it aside. 'I'd like to stay.'

Robson thought about it. The combination of alcohol and mental exhaustion had slowed his brain. 'Of course. Blair won't be wanting his bed.'

She looked at him curiously. 'I don't want Wallace's bed, Billy.' A pause. 'I want to share *yours*.'

Momentarily, he was stunned. He still thought of her as Frankie Lewis's girl. However much he felt himself drawn to her, he had never once considered that she might have fallen for him.

She smiled a wicked, slightly mocking smile with her head tilted to one side. 'You look surprised, Billy. Didn't you ever think I might fancy you?'

His grin was bemused. 'Are you drunk, Bernie?'

She laughed gaily, the soft Dublin sound still distinct. 'A little maybe. No more than you.' Casually she stood beside the bed and dropped the sheepskin jacket from her shoulders. Beneath it, she wore a plain silk shirt in emerald green. It was tucked neatly into the slim waist of a black pleated skirt. She paused and smiled at his hesitation. 'Undress me. Please.'

Robson reached out his hand to hers and drew her slowly
to him as he stood. His arms slid around her waist. Her lips
parted in anticipation as he brought his mouth down onto
hers. Her lips, firm and moist, tasted sweet and faintly of
whisky. He felt her tongue run playfully along his teeth. The
close fragrant smell of her hair was as intoxicating to him as
the drink had been. He felt it release a new surge of energy
as her hands wound around his neck.

He couldn't remember a long and sensuous kiss with
quite such a disturbingly erotic effect. As he drew back from
her, he noticed that she was trembling.

'Cold?' he whispered.

Bernadette shut her eyes and shook her head with a
half-smile.

Her eyes remained closed and her face took on a more
serene expression as he gently plucked free the buttons of
her blouse. Her trembling intensified. Urgently she tousled
his hair whilst he bent to release the fastening of her skirt.
When it fell away, he wasn't altogether surprised at the loose-
fitting cami-knickers in champagne-coloured silk.

At last, the trembling stopped. She looked up at him, her
mouth slightly open. Her lower lip quivered. Slowly, she raised
her hands and gently eased the thin straps from her shoulders.
The silk fluttered down the length of her body with a faint
rustling noise, to form a rosette at her feet. A statue unveiled.

He swallowed hard. She was more exquisite than anything
he could have imagined. Her skin was taut and milky,
peppered with freckles across her gently-muscled frame.
The smooth swell of her hips gleamed in the glow of the fire.
Her long sculptured legs ascended to a peak of soft chestnut
down. Slowly, he stooped and closed his teeth gently around
the pronounced pink bud that tipped her breast.

'Harder,' she breathed. Again she tremored, and he felt her nails through his shirt. He gnawed with deliberate sensuality, drawing in more of her breast until it filled his mouth. He heard her whimpering softly above him.

'Now, Billy, please.'

Very slowly, they fell back onto the bed. Above him, Bernadette's breathing became more rapid as her hands struggled to free him of his clothes.

The lovemaking that followed was as wild and wanton as anything he had ever known. Instinctively, they seemed to know what the other liked and wanted: the timing and synchronisation was a natural precision masterpiece. They moved and responded together like human machines.

It felt like hours before the finish came. He was kneeling on the bed with Bernadette's legs clasped tightly around his waist. Before him, she lay on her back, her chestnut hair spread over the covers like a halo. Her tight, hard belly glistened with sweat as her muscles worked in unison with his, milking him dry in the final surge of release.

Together, they went into spasm. She bit his lip. She cried out, but it didn't stop. The spasm found more strength, more reserves. He thought his loins would burst. His head throbbed. Bernadette shrieked, uncontrolled. Long and hard. He shuddered violently as he felt it go.

Her hands were still shaking as she reached up for him. 'Oh, God, Billy. Where have you been all of my life?'

He noticed there were tears in her eyes.

Seventeen

Robson did not like the way things were going. He glanced sideways at Frank Lewis.

It was a trial, there was no doubt about that. The meeting in the sombre, timeless atmosphere of the Irish mansion had all the signs. And given that, both Robson and Lewis would have chosen anyone to sit in judgement rather than the three men who sat opposite them at the oak refectory table.

Just three men. But it was all that was needed to pass sentence: judge, jury and executioner.

Robson had no doubt who would play that last role. Tommy Dee. Sitting there in a homely tweed jacket, Viyella shirt and knitted tie. Soft brown hair and a butter-wouldn't-melt smile. Family man with three kids. Robson had only learned that from Lewis an hour ago, during their blind-folded car-ride from Dublin.

'The latest word from Belfast is that the UDF have got the stuff. There's little doubt about that. They're enjoying rubbing our noses in it.'

The man who spoke was gross, his belly half-rested on the edge of the table. Robson remembered the jug ears and slack mouth from the press reception at the Burlington Hotel in Dublin. The man who had set up the canning plant on a Government grant.

That was it. Eamon Molloy. Cattle baron, industrialist,

horse-racer and now, he'd learned, standing for election to the Dáil.

But today it appeared to Robson that Molloy was the jury. Asking questions of both Dee and them, probing, getting the facts straight.

Robson's gaze shifted to the third man.

The judge? It was difficult to tell because the seating arrangements in the gloomy panelled room put the third man's face into shadow. All Robson could tell was that he was dressed expensively in a thin blue silk sweater. The hands resting on the knees of the grey slacks were those of an old man. The nails were beautifully manicured, but the dry white skin was rashed with liver spots.

Robson thought he recognised the quiet modulated voice, but couldn't be sure. Anyway, no names had been used since the meeting began. But the others had twice referred to the mysterious presence as 'The Man'.

'The question is,' Molloy continued, sprinkling saliva as he worked his mouth around the words, 'do we believe that neither of these two were involved?'

Dee placed his elbows on the table. 'Well, you know my view. For safety's sake, we should assume that they are. It's a golden rule I've always stuck by. That's what I'd have done in London if it had been up to me alone.'

'It *would* seem an extravagance to do that *now*.' For the first time in several minutes it was The Man who spoke. 'After having gone to all the trouble and expense of spiriting them away from the noses of the Brit police.'

Dee allowed himself a faint smile. Robson wondered if it was because it had been so apparently easy to achieve. In his case, false banker's-card and driving-licence had been delivered within twenty-four hours, together with a plausible cover-story. With his appearance so effectively changed, he had been able to board the Aer Lingus flight at Heathrow without a single challenge. No passport was required. He had been met by a private car and taken to the first of a number of safe Provo houses and flats. At any time he had been expecting to meet up with Blair Wallace, as apparently he was already moving down the ratline, but that hadn't yet happened.

Dee said: 'It's no extravagance. Bodies on the Brit mainland can lead to awkward questions. Here, a body can rot in a deserted farm well in Galway for centuries before it's found.'

Lewis fidgeted with the knot in his tie.

Eamon Molloy jutted his chin in disapproval at such a blatant threat. He was used to being cosseted from the day-to-day unpleasantness of running a terror-campaign.

But there was a hint of amusement in the voice from the shadows: 'So you would silence our friends, cut your losses and cancel the Boston deal, would you?'

Dee didn't miss the deadly blade hidden in the reasonable tone. 'Only in the interests of our total security. Drugs is our lifeblood now; we can't afford to risk it.'

'There is another consideration,' The Man said. 'The loss of our heroin to the UDF has been a major blow at this particular time. It was to partly finance the Boston deal – which is potentially more lucrative and important to our movement. To scrap Boston and put Mr Lewis here out of business would be – to use the vernacular – to cut off our noses to spite our faces. It would put us out of the drugs market for maybe a year.' He paused, 'I heard today that the Army Council wants the Boston deal at almost any cost.'

Dee was disgusted. 'It's crazy. It's crazy and dangerous. We all know Lewis wants out anyway.'

'There *are* elections to finance,' Molloy muttered, no doubt thinking of one particular candidate.

Lewis suddenly took a deep breath, as though summoning courage before he spoke. 'Er, Sir – er gentlemen. If I might make a word in my own – er – defence, as it were . . .'

Molloy glared at him, but Lewis kept his eyes directed at The Man in the shadows. 'Yes, Mr Lewis?'

'I'd like to have a word in private, if I could?'

'Out of the question!' Molloy blustered.

The Man waved him to silence. 'What about, Mr Lewis?'

Lewis glanced nervously at Robson, his face reddening, then back to The Man. 'Particularly about the girl who came with us.'

The voice in the shadows sounded faintly amused. 'I wondered when I'd get to hear what all that was about. Most intriguing. She came in the car with you?'

Lewis nodded.

'She's outside with one of my men,' Dee confirmed. Suddenly he looked worried. 'I *did* check out Lewis's request with you first . . .'

This time The Man actually laughed. 'I know, I know. It's perfectly all right. Now if you two would be kind enough to leave us alone for just a few moments . . . And Mr Robson here?'

'He may as well stay,' Lewis said.

Reluctantly Dee and Molloy stood up and left the room. As the heavy studded door closed, The Man said: 'Right, Mr Lewis, what is it you have to say?'

For a moment the other man found it difficult to know the best way to start. 'Look, I might be out of order in what I'm about to say. If I am, just forget it, it wasn't meant . . .'

He sensed The Man's growing impatience in the shadows. 'I-I have heard rumours, just rumours, that there are housegirls at this mansion . . .'

If he was hoping for confirmation or denial, he was to be unlucky. 'Go on,' hissed the voice; it was starting to sound angry.

'Well, should there be any truth in it,' Lewis continued awkwardly, 'I've brought the girl as a gift. For your staff . . .'

'You've *what*?' The Man demanded.

Robson stared at Lewis as though he was mad.

'It's a gesture of good faith,' Lewis babbled. 'You know I can't repay that lost heroin money without selling my business. And I *don't* want me, my friends, or associates to end up at the bottom of some well, thank you. I want—' He glanced at Robson – 'we want to work with you until you feel you can trust us to resume our lives normally. Or as normally as possible.' He smiled thinly. 'Perhaps after Boston?'

There was a momentary silence from the shadows. 'And you think the girl will persuade me to have you spared?'

Lewis looked uncomfortable, and shrugged. 'It's all I could think of. She's been paid by me for six months' service. After that, you can keep her or not, it's up to you. She doesn't come cheap, but I understand she's the best there is, submissive—'

'Don't say any more,' The Man hissed. 'I *never* discuss such things.'

'I know it's a grave impertinence,' Lewis babbled, sure he'd blown it.

'It is indeed,' The Man murmured. 'But I think I can understand your reasoning. A peace-offering. For someone completely out of aces, you've played a clever hand. We had better have a look at her then.'

It took a couple of seconds for Lewis to realise that his desperate ploy might have succeeded. Hastily, he rose from his chair and crossed to the door.

A minute later, he returned with Bella. Beautifully made-up, she looked stunning with newly rinsed black hair against her alabaster face, her eyes as wide, dark and as full of child-ish appeal as ever. She stood before the refectory table, in high showgirl-heels, wearing a lush musquash coat belted at the waist. She bowed her head.

'Leave us,' breathed The Man.

Outside in the hall to the mansion, they found Dee and Molloy waiting.

'You're a crafty fucken bastard,' Dee snarled.

But Lewis's spirits couldn't be dampened; he sensed victory. 'I had to do *something* to persuade your people that we're not trying to cause any trouble.'

'Huh,' Molloy grunted. 'You're lucky Yer Man didn't order you executed on the spot. Nobody ever discusses the housegirls here. There'll be blood spilled if he thinks it's generally known.'

Lewis grinned. 'Then it's my lucky day, isn't it?'

The unexpected turn of events had left Robson dizzy. Earlier at a Dublin safe-house, he had been very surprised when Bella arrived in the same Provo car as Lewis. His boss had refused to explain her presence. Now he could see why. To give her as a *gift*! It was as sick as it was incredulous. He felt nauseated.

Lewis read his thoughts. 'It's okay, Billy. She's willing. She's into all that kinky stuff.'

Robson ignored him and lit a cigarette. His mind was reeling. He was thoroughly aware that Bella was bad news.

She paid for her habit by working at some kinky club, and he realised she'd supplied Sandy with heroin. Yet he couldn't forget how willingly she'd helped when he went on the run. His anger at her was tempered with pity, even some affection. When the chips were down she'd been one of the few friends he and Sandy had.

She was obviously a hopeless case, and here was Lewis callously manipulating her weaknesses to his own ends. And there was absolutely nothing he could do about it unless he wanted to end up with a Provo bullet in the back of his head.

His thoughts were interrupted by the noise of a car pulling up on the gravel outside. Moments later, one of The Man's housegirls opened the door.

Sher Gallal grinned widely at the gathering in the hallway. 'Ah, we all wait to meet your big chief, eh?'

A sudden thought occurred to Robson. Quietly, he eased himself out of the knot of people and sauntered towards the huge door that stood ajar. The bright sunlight hurt his eyes after the dark interior of the mansion, and it took a few moments to focus on the gleaming Audi with its CD plates.

Sure enough, the blazered figure of Kevin Shard was leaning nonchalantly against the bonnet, attending his nails with a small pair of clippers.

'So we meet again, Billy Robson.' His recognition was instant.

Robson went down the steps. 'God, am I pleased to see you!'

Shard raised an eyebrow, but continued trimming his fingernails. 'You sound like a man with a problem.'

'You've got to help me. I'm in one hell of a mess.'

'Anything to help an old comrade, you know that.' His even smile was reassuring. 'Tell me about it.'

With a quick glance back at the door, Robson briefly recounted the events of the past weeks. Throughout, Shard listened quietly and impassively.

Finally he said: 'That's quite a story, Billy. Quite a story. And I'll help you. I'll help you with a bit of advice.' He held Robson's gaze steadily with his dark eyes. 'Not that you've proved to be good at taking advice.'

Robson lit a fresh cigarette. 'Try me.'

'If you want to stay alive, don't rock the boat. I warned you to keep out of it, but you insisted on getting in with both feet. You're out of your league.' Shard contemplated Robson for a moment before continuing. 'But now you're in, play along with them until you get a chance to get out with your kneecaps, right? There's nothing I can do to help you, or anyone else.'

His attitude shocked Robson. 'But those Libyans you work for are operating with the bloody Provos, Kevin!'

He smiled faintly. 'I know that.'

'For Christ's sake! How can you continue then? They're helping the bastards who killed and maimed our oppos.'

Shard said quietly: 'Simple, Billy, I'm a mercenary. As far as I'm concerned, that's all in the past. In this wicked world, you've got to earn a living as best you can. It owes you *nothing*. As you're starting to find out. You see, I didn't tell you that I do more than a little driving and minder-work for Gadaffi's lot. I work for one of a small number of British mercenary outfits who work for the Libyans. Mostly internal security. Doing dirty jobs they won't trust their own people to do. We British have got a long reputation as trustworthy mercenaries.'

Robson exhaled a long stream of smoke. 'I don't believe I'm hearing this! You're trying to tell me you know all about this drugs business?'

Shard nodded. 'Some of it. So I've a vested interest, too, in you keeping your head. Just stay cool and play along.' He inclined his head towards the mansion. 'Now I suggest you go back inside before that potato-head Dee decides you've given him an excuse to shoot you. If you hadn't noticed, he's a slight dislike for ex-Marines.'

Robson didn't trust himself to speak. Shard of all people. One of his own. A traitor for a bag of silver.

Grinding out his cigarette beneath his heel, he turned and retraced his steps without a further word.

Back inside the building, the ringing of a bell was taken as a signal by Lewis, Dee and Molloy to re-enter the room.

Robson was immediately aware of a strange atmosphere. Nothing else had changed. The Man still sat in the shadow at the table. Bella stood in front of it, her head bowed, still wearing the coat, but clutching it to her. The belt lay at her feet.

Only as they passed did she look up. Robson noticed that she was visibly shaking. The trail of two tears had ploughed snail-like marks down her cheeks. For a moment her eyes held Lewis's with a look of pure hatred. Then The Man said something and she turned on her heel and left the room.

'Well?' Lewis asked awkwardly.

'The young lady will be staying.' It was said without emotion. 'The interlude has given me time to think. I've also had a few words with Mr Sher Gallal. In view of the Army Council's keenness for the Boston deal to go ahead, I think there is a lot of sense in Mr Lewis's suggestion.'

'It's stupidity,' Dee declared. 'Lewis himself can't go. While he's under suspicion from our police, they'll inform the DEA as soon as he sets foot in the States.'

'And there's the problem with Tom Rabbit at large over

there,' Molloy added. 'If he's now tied up with the Mafia over there, we could be in for all sorts of problems.'

The Man spoke easily; nothing, it appeared, had escaped his consideration. 'That's why I intend doing what Lewis suggests and sending Robson—'

'That fucken cabbage-hat!' Dee's protest was out before he could stop himself.

'Be silent!' The Man's voice hardly raised an octave, but it invited no contradiction. Dee shut up. 'Although he used to serve with the Brit forces, my investigations suggest he can be trusted. He's been involved in a bank robbery, he's done time, and Lewis has had nothing but praise when he's been working for him. As you yourself have found out—' That barb directed at Dee '—to your cost. More than that, he has *everything* to lose if he crosses us – not least his life. He has a wife and child. And a long prison sentence facing him if he falls into the hands of the police.'

Robson shifted irritably on his seat. It was disconcerting hearing himself talked about as though he wasn't there.

'To be certain of his loyalty,' The Man continued, 'we will offer him a new identity abroad if he plays his part successfully. He can then forget all about us, and we about him.'

'I still don't like it,' Dee persisted.

'There is *another* safeguard. Because of our loss of funds on the heroin exchange, we have had to ask the Libyans for a sort of bridging loan to finance the Boston deal.' He paused. His next words would not find favour with his colleagues. 'Because of that, and the danger presented over there by Tom Rabbit, they insist on putting in their own man. Someone in whom they have absolute and proven trust. Someone who will have no qualms about eliminating Robson if he steps out of line.'

'Who?' an unconvinced Dee demanded.

'One of their top hit men,' The Man replied. 'Kevin Shard.'

Billy Robson stared out of the 747's window for a full minute. There was nothing to see in the dull early morning sky. Nothing to take his mind off the newspaper story.

Inexorably, he found his eyes drawn back to the *Daily Telegraph* lying on his lap.

He hadn't really expected to find any mention of the police man-hunt. After all, it had been nearly five weeks since the incident on the Embankment and even then, it had only warranted a small paragraph.

So the blurred photograph of Wallace staring out of the page at him had come as quite a shock.

BODY MAY BE
GANG FEUD
VICTIM

A body found yesterday at a North London building site has been identified as that of Blair Edmund Wallace, 41, who was wanted for questioning by police for a firearms offence.

Wallace, a Rhodesian who had lived in Britain for some years, was a well-known small-time gangster. A warrant for his arrest had been issued, together with William 'Billy' Robson, a bank robber on parole, after a recent shooting incident on the Thames Embankment, involving members of New Scotland Yard's Drug Squad.

The body of Wallace was found buried in rubble by workmen about to concrete-in the foundations of a new office-block development near Brent Cross.

A police spokesman said: 'We are treating this as a murder inquiry. In view of Drug Squad evidence, we do not rule out the possibility that this was the work of a rival gang.'

That was it. Short, sharp and to the point. Robson read it again in disbelief and growing anger.

He recalled the way Wallace had left their bedsit cheerfully with Dee and the other Irishman. The Rhodesian was happy to be on his way out of the country. Robson had even been envious that the arrangements for Wallace had been made immediately whilst he had to endure a further wait.

Now he knew why. Where Wallace had been going, there was no need for documents and identification papers. He was an inept fool who had jeopardised the whole set-up by using his shot-gun indiscriminately. He knew too much and he was the kind who might blab. Wallace's usefulness was over.

With a final effort, Robson folded the newspaper and stuffed it into the pouch in front of him.

That was all over now. The past. He knew he would never again return to Britain, and it gave him a strange empty feeling.

The aircraft dipped suddenly on the last leg of its descent to Logan International Airport on the north bank of Charles River. Above his head, the seatbelt and 'No Smoking' signs pinged musically into life.

Fifteen minutes later, Robson – alias Michael Flynn – stepped down onto American soil for the first time in his life. After an interminably long wait, he reached the row of immigration cubicles. He produced the visa stamped in his new passport, and a letter from a Wicklow bank manager

confirming that he had sufficient funds available for the
duration of his stay.

He could feel himself shaking as the official scrutinised
the documents. Surely the man must be able to smell the
fear on him? Or see the perspiration on his upper lip? Or the
guilty flush of colour on his face?

But no. The man merely asked boredly how long he
planned to stay on his business trip, and accepted Robson's
vague reply without further question.

As he hurried through to collect his suitcase and clear
Customs, Robson felt he was walking on air. It had all been
that easy. A great depressing weight was suddenly lifted from
his shoulders. Freedom! And a new life lying ahead of him.
Exciting and unknown.

He clambered into a huge black Buick taxi and gave the
black driver instructions. Despite the blaring radio, the man
seemed to understand and swung the vehicle out into brilliant sunshine, and straight into the rush-hour traffic jam.

Robson watched, fascinated, as they passed the colourful
two and three-storey clapboard houses that looked curiously
familiar. Except that they were made of timber, the Victorian
designs would have looked at home in many a South London
street. After being swallowed up by the toll tunnel that ran
under Boston Harbour, the cab emerged on the south bank
to filter into the moving swathe of coloured steel pulsing
around the urban expressways.

As they cleared Back Bay, running parallel to the south
bank of the Charles River, the expected image of the United
States began to establish itself more firmly. On either side
of the wide, four-lane road, garish signs invited potential
patrons into the vast parking lots. Gas stations, singles bars,
offices, pizza parlours and burger-joints all vied for trade.

The Fenway Howard Johnson's Motor Lodge was an ugly low-level construction on the busy thoroughfare of Boylston Street on the western outskirts of the city centre. It had been chosen for that reason. Unlike the lush downtown hotels like the Ritz Carlton or the Park Plaza, a newcomer would pass unnoticed amongst the daily comings-and-goings of an out-of-town motel. Robson also suspected that cost might have had something to do with the choice.

The syrupy charm of the manager lasted only until he had secured an advance payment, then he rapidly lost interest. After the bland decor of the endless air-conditioned corridors, the room itself came as a pleasant surprise. It was spacious with deep-pile carpet and a bronze mirror which covered the whole of one wall. The 'king-size' bed was draped in a Japanese cover to match the lampshades. And the Oriental theme carried through to the black-lacquered furniture with its brass trim.

Robson just had time to change after a quick shave and shower before the bedside telephone rang.

'Mike?'

It threw Robson for a moment. The voice at the other end laughed. 'You'll have to do better than that, Mr Flynn. It's Kevin here. Let's meet.'

The voice of a friend and ally – even a dubious one like Shard – was welcome. 'Where are you?'

Kevin Shard was in the motel bar, a drink at his elbow, as he plucked happily at a bowl of popcorn. He seemed unperturbed amidst the gathering of plump middle-aged women with Southern accents, whose over-made-up eyes said they'd be happy to devour anything in trousers.

'What'll it be?' Shard asked.

'A beer will be fine.'

The lethargic barmaid with a T-shirt that explained she was a day-time student at Harvard University on the north bank went to the brass Bud-lite tap to fill the glass.

Shard said: 'Let's grab a quiet seat.' As they found a table away from the bar and the burbling television behind it, he added: 'Glad you came when you did. Those bloody women are from some divorcees' club in Florida.'

Robson grinned; he could sense the lascivious stares from the bar even now. 'What's the attraction of Boston?'

'Baseball. The Fenway Park Stadium's at the back of the motel. They're all ardent Boston Redsox supporters. All on vacation, all milked their ex-husbands for every cent, and all without a man.'

Robson found it hard to reconcile the cheerful ex-Marine in front of him with the hard-bitten mercenary he'd spoken with outside The Man's mansion only ten days earlier. 'Do you know Boston well?'

'Not very. I've been over a couple of times on courier work for the Libyans. They're just about as popular as the Iranians with the Yanks, so they like the way I can move around. Without let or hindrance, so to speak.'

Robson sipped at the beer. 'I still find it hard to accept your attitude to working for them.'

Shard's eyes hardened. 'You'll get used to it. You have to take your breaks when you can.'

'I've certainly got no option now,' Robson conceded.

He was looking past Shard as he spoke to a denim-clad man with a check shirt who had sauntered through from the reception area. Cold blue eyes were set in a blunt face that could have been chiselled out of granite. He fixed his sights on the two men. He indicated Shard's blazer. 'Pardon me. You look like an English guy. Wouldn't be Shard by any chance?'

Shard grinned. 'The very same.'

The man glanced at Robson. 'And you'll be Flynn.'

'That's right.'

The man smiled and dropped his heavy frame into a spare chair. 'Dan Dooley's the name. I work with Sean Brady's set-up. He's just been on the wire to me. Says he wants you to come over right away.'

Robson knew he and Shard would have to wait until the Irish Mafia contacted him, but he wasn't expecting things to move this fast. 'Mr Brady doesn't hang about.'

Dan Dooley's rock-like features cracked into a smile-shaped fissure. But the glitter in the pale blue eyes suggested wariness rather than friendliness. 'Sure don't. Let's haul it.'

Shard leaned forward. 'Sorry to be a spoilsport, Dan – if I may call you Dan? But how do we know you're from Sean Brady?'

The fissure sealed up again. 'Yer don't. Now are you comin' with me or ain't yer?'

Robson and Shard exchanged glances, and shrugged. Obviously this was Brady country.

'I'm takin' you to a bar up Cambridge way,' Dan Dooley explained as he swung the wide Cadillac towards Harvard Bridge.

'On the north bank?' Robson asked.

'Yeah,' Dooley replied. 'It's near the University. Reckon that's the real reason it's Sean Brady's favourite waterin' hole. Plenty of young ass, see? Pretty young things who find old war-horses like Brady an' me a bit of a challenge.'

Robson and Shard looked at each other doubtfully, but the Irish-American was warming to his subject. 'At that age, everyone's a rebel without a cause. Then they get to hear

about the Troubles in Ireland, the songs an' all. Real folksy
hero stuff. Gets 'em right here.' He thudded a giant balled
fist against his chest and laughed. 'So, if they've got an Irish
name or ancestry, they say, "Hey man, this is *injustice!* The
Irish are still fightin' the Brits like we had to over here!" So
old soldiers like me 'n' Brady give 'em all the old stories, and
some of 'em really get into it. Especially some of the gals.
That gives old 'uns like me 'n' Brady the chance to get down
their pantie-hose!'

Dooley jabbed a thumb over his shoulder. 'But the real
Irish community's down to the south of Boston. Pretty much
a no-go area for most Bostonians, but we kinda like it that
way.'

'What about the Italians?' Shard asked. Robson realised
he was concerned about Tom Rabbit's connections with the
Mafia.

Dooley laughed. 'Our area's *especially* no-go to the
Ities! They got their little community at the North End
of Boston. Like the Chinese got theirs. Each to his own.
That's how we like it.' Again the chuckle. 'That's how we
keep it!'

At that moment, they pulled up outside the bar on a street
corner. As Robson and Shard crossed the pavement after
Dooley, they could hear the guitar music and singing voices
raised from inside.

As they pushed their way through the tightly packed
crowd of drinkers in the narrow bar, Robson felt himself
transported back in time and place. The guitar and maud-
lin voices, the rebel songs, the fog of cigarette smoke, and
the thick, woody smell of Guinness. Except that the voices
were more American than Irish, it could have been a Provo
shebeen in West Belfast. His skin crawled.

The barmaid, a woman in her late thirties, with a croissant of fair hair plaited on top of her head, waved at Dooley.

'Yer man's in the corner as usual.' Her voice was distinctly Dublin.

The table and chairs at the far end of the long, narrow bar had obviously been reserved for them. Two people waited. It took a moment for Robson to recognise Sean Brady. He looked younger than the man he remembered from the bar in Buncrana. It was probably the casual sports zip-up and the Harvard sweatshirt that did it.

Robson remembered the too-perfect smile of artificial teeth. 'Nice to see you guys. I gather it's Flynn now?' he asked provocatively.

'That's right. Mike Flynn. And this is Shard.'

Brady nodded. 'Hope your manners have improved since our last meeting.' He didn't wait for Robson to answer. Instead he flipped over his hand in an introductory gesture to his companion. 'Meet Crystal.'

She was extremely attractive, a student-type who Robson assumed came from the university. Long, straight strawberry blonde hair worn in a fringe. Distrusting blue eyes appraised him from above the red pout of a mouth.

'Sit down,' Brady invited.

As they selected their chairs, Shard said: 'This is a bloody stupid place to meet, Brady.' He sounded very angry.

The Bostonian blinked rapidly – a device he used to check his temper. 'You're in my neck of the woods now, Mr Shard. We're amongst friends here. This place is a bastion of IRA support. Strangers stick out like a sore thumb.'

'Exactly,' Shard hissed. 'Anyone with an interest will know we're here. I don't call that smart thinking.'

Sean Brady smiled slyly. 'You don't want to worry about the Boston police, friend. A lot of them go by the name of Brady. Or O'Mara. Or O'Toole . . .'

'It's not the police I'm concerned about,' Shard replied testily.

'Ah.'

Brady and Dooley exchanged grins.

'This guy called Rabbit?' Dooley asked.

Shard nodded. '*And* the company he keeps. Dublin thinks he's tied up with the Sicilians and the Protestant paramilitaries from Belfast.'

Dooley leaned his broad shoulders across the table. 'The *Irish* run Boston, Mr Shard, not the *Cosa Nostra*. We know exactly where Rabbit is. If he so much as farts we'll know about it.'

Shard drew back, reluctantly. Robson said: 'Kevin's right, Brady. It's still taking an unnecessary risk, meeting like this. So let's get it over with. What's the latest?'

Brady turned to the girl beside him. 'Go and get our friends some beers while we talk, Crystal.'

With a glance of disapproval at the two Englishmen, the girl obeyed, sent on her way with a slap on her denim-clad rump by Brady. 'A dedicated follower that one,' he said appreciatively. 'Her grandfather took part in the Easter Rising.'

'So?' Robson was anxious to get on.

Brady grunted. 'I don't like the last-minute changes in plan over money. It usually comes from Dublin via one of the Continental banks. This time it was paid from some Arab outfit via a Maltese account. That suggests Libya to me.'

'It's not your concern,' Robson replied, 'now that you've got the payment.'

'It arrived through the Deak-Perera Bank this morning,' Brady confirmed. 'But I still don't like it. If it smells like Libyan money, someone over here could smell a rat.'

Shard said coldly: 'Next time, we'll do it differently.'

Brady narrowed his eyes. 'All right, just make sure you do. Meanwhile the petfood consignment is due out of the container port tomorrow. As soon as we've checked that the contents makes up the balance, we'll release the coke.'

'When?' Robson asked. The sooner this was all over, the happier he'd feel.

'Tomorrow night.' Brady shoved a business card across the table. 'Be at that warehouse at 10 p.m. If everything's in order, we'll exchange then.'

'And the boat?' Shard asked.

Brady smiled thinly, his porcelain teeth glittering. 'Anxious to be going, eh? It's ready at the Fish Pier. The *Boston Dawn*. The weapons are already hidden aboard, and she's expected to sail before first light. She's a fifty-foot deep-water trawler, so she'll make the trip in good time.'

Robson nodded slowly, as he went through the mental checklist of things he'd discussed with Frank Lewis before he left. 'Will we have any trouble getting aboard?'

Dooley plucked at the sleeve of Shard's blazer. 'Only if you dress like that! You're supposed to be fishermen. You'll just walk through with our guys when they join the boat. It'll be dark and the security ain't that clever on a fish wharf. You'll just replace two regulars on this trip. Don't worry. Nothing can go wrong.'

'Anything else?' Shard asked.

Brady shook his head. 'Guess that's it.'

Without exchanging a word, the two Englishmen stood up. 'Then we'll see you tomorrow,' Robson said.

Brady looked irritated. 'What about your drinks, boys?'

'Some other time,' Shard said.

'Wanna lift?' Dooley offered. 'I'm going in a few minutes.'

Robson shook his head. He was learning fast from Shard's professional caution, and he'd seen enough in Malta and Ireland to know this wasn't the sort of game that people played by the rules. 'We'll make our own way back on the subway. I've little doubt Tom Rabbit's friends know you use this pub.'

Brady laughed. 'I told you boys, this is *our* town.'

The two Englishmen didn't argue further, they just began to make their way through the crowd.

The student called Crystal arrived back at the table with a tray of drinks. 'Those guys gone already?'

Dooley sneered. 'Typical limeys. Scared of their own shadows.'

'I didn't like them,' the girl said.

Sean Brady fondled her rump absently. 'You don't have to, sweet child. They're helping The Cause. That's all that matters.'

Five minutes later, Dan Dooley finished his drink and left for his car.

It was another few seconds before he reached it and turned the ignition. The explosion momentarily lit up the street outside as though it was daylight. As the shockwaves rattled the windows of the bar, everyone was stunned. Then someone screamed.

'They couldn't find his legs apparently,' Shard threw down the edition of the *Boston Globe* in disgust. 'Nor much else of him by all accounts.'

Billy Robson stared out of the motel window at the swimming-pool. 'Like being back in Ulster. As soon as I heard the noise, I knew what it was.'

'It's not the sort of sound you forget.' Shard propped himself against the wall.

Robson turned. 'I thought you *had* forgotten, Kevin.'

'Let's not start that again. Just let it remind you the danger we're in. Brady's lot were too complacent by half. They've lived in a fantasy gangland over here for too long. They don't realise what they're up against. They don't appreciate just what a dangerous bastard Rabbit is.'

Robson reached for a cigarette; just lately he'd been back on two packets a day. 'And who the hell is this bloke Rabbit anyway?'

Shard shrugged. 'A disaffected Provo. He's gone over to the Ulster Protestants and tied them in with the Mafia.'

'Why?'

Shard raised an eyebrow. 'You were in Malta. Friend Dee tried to assassinate him at Mellieha Church. Trying to cut him and his Mafia connections out of their heroin run. Only for once, Dee fouled up – which left one *very* disaffected Provo who'll now stop at nothing to stop this deal going through.'

'So *that's* what it was all about in Malta.' Robson took a deep lungful of smoke and exhaled slowly. 'Christ! I could kill Lewis for getting me into all this.'

Shard smiled. 'Well, I did try to warn you off. Anyway, we can't be too careful tonight.' He glanced at his watch. 'Eight-thirty. Time we got ready.'

He stood up and went to his suitcase, flipping open the lid. He extracted a business-like automatic pistol wrapped in soft leather holster webbing, and handed it to Robson.

'It's a 9mm Beretta 92F,' Shard said. 'US Army issue. The holster's a special Price Western design with a snap-release. You wear it on the upper thigh with the butt tight up in the crutch. Easily missed in a body-search. Unstitch and remove your trouser pocket for access.' He paused and grinned. 'Only problem is you're inclined to punch yourself in the balls if you draw too fast.'

Robson inspected the weapon with interest. To his own surprise, he didn't baulk at the idea of using it if it was going to be necessary.

He checked the breech was clear. 'Nice bit of kit, Kevin. But why the concealment?'

Shard shrugged. 'It's just a hunch, but I don't think friend Brady is going to want us to be armed at the exchange. Or aboard the boat for Ireland for that matter.'

'Everyone in this business seems paranoid,' Robson observed.

'With good reason. Anyway, I'll also pack some hardware in a shoulder-holster, which they'll find if they search. That might satisfy them. It doesn't matter if we don't get away with it – they'll understand our wish for protection. But it's worth a try.'

'I'd feel happier,' Robson agreed. He didn't trust their Bostonian contacts or the IRA, let alone this Tom Rabbit character and his Mafia friends.

Shard grinned. 'Life is full of surprises, but I like 'em to be nice ones. Preferably mine.'

At the bedside, the telephone trilled. It was Brady confirming that the meeting was on. He sounded edgy – the sudden death of Dan Dooley had obviously done nothing for his nerves.

Half-an-hour later, Robson and Shard slipped out of an emergency side exit of the motel, each dressed in casual clothes. Their holdalls contained anoraks for the sea-crossing to Eire.

They took the back road – past the Fenway Stadium where gathering fans waited to see another Redsox fiasco at the hands of the Royals – to Kenmore subway station. A standard 60-cent token got them through to the low platform with its square tiled pillars, which gave a clue to the fact that it was the oldest underground system in America.

Climbing up into the plastic-seated interior of the tram carriage, they rattled down the Green Line to Park Street. There they changed, taking the Red Line to the big South Station terminal.

Satisfied that no one had followed, they hailed a taxi to take them to the address Brady had given. The short journey took them over the narrow Fort Point Channel which fed into the Inner Harbour, and past the famous Boston Tea Party ship tourist attraction into the bleak dockside area. This formed the northern flank of Irish-dominated South Boston, a tough, working-class neighbourhood of small terraced houses.

By the time the cab pulled up in the darkened street lined with warehouses and storage compounds, a chill wind was gathering momentum. It carried with it stinging droplets of rain and the salty smell of the Atlantic.

They waited until the taxi had disappeared before proceeding cautiously alongside the high link fence of the container compound. Inside the steel bodies were stacked three deep. The tall double gates were locked with several heavy-duty padlocks and chains.

'This is it,' Shard breathed. He peered beyond the wire but there was no sign of life.

Robson faced outward, scanning the shadows for signs of danger, while his companion produced a pencil flashlight and flicked a quick four-burst signal at the unseen building somewhere within the compound. The expected reply signal didn't come. Shard tried again. The rain gathered strength, suddenly eddying across the container compound in wind-driven gusts.

'Nothing,' Shard muttered. Once more he flashed the signal.

'Light!' Robson said suddenly. 'At two o'clock. Just a chink.'

A dark figure emerged from the blackness of the compound, bent against the torrent.

The man slowed as he approached the gate, his face hidden by the hood of his waterproof. The dazzling beam of his torch blinded them.

'Put that bloody thing away!' Shard protested.

It was a second or two before the man was satisfied as to their identity and the light was doused. He opened the gate, gestured them through, then laboriously re-secured the padlocks. No one was taking *any* chances.

He led the way through the puddled quagmire of the compound until the warehouse itself came into view. Without knocking, he pushed open a small personnel-door. Cautiously, Robson and Shard followed.

The cavernous interior was dimly-lit by just a couple of fluorescent tubes beneath the upper-level gantries. Sean Brady was waiting for them. Beside him was the girl Crystal they'd met the night before at the Plough and Stars. She wore the same snug-fitting denim outfit and the same sullen pout.

The Ruger machine-pistol did nothing for her femininity at all.

'What's this?' Robson asked warily. 'Does Annie Oakley here know where the safety-catch is?'

Brady grinned reassurance. 'Don't worry, boys, it ain't nothin' to worry about. Just takin' precautions. An' yes, Crystal here *can* shoot the rocks off a gnat at fifty.'

The man who had shown them in stepped up behind them, his Ruger now drawn from beneath his dripping waterproof. With the hood now down, the bald crown looked incongruous with the long hippy hair and drooping moustache.

'This is Dick Quirke,' Brady introduced unnecessarily. 'Now just turn around, and let him check you out. I'd rather we're the only ones with hardware round here.'

Shard pulled a wry smile. 'Pity you weren't this cautious *before* your chum Dooley got himself blown up. *Was* it Tom Rabbit's people?'

Brady looked uneasy. 'Dunno.'

'I thought you had everything under control?' Robson challenged.

'We *had*. But Rabbit's gone missing. We had his place under surveillance, but he must have slipped out somehow.'

Robson looked sideways at Shard, and met the same exasperated expression. There was no point in antagonising Brady by rubbing it in.

Shard said: 'Save Dick the trouble, Brady. I'm carrying.' He held open his jacket to reveal the butt of an automatic at his armpit.

'May I?' Quirke's voice was unexpectedly quiet and gentlemanly.

Shard grinned widely. 'Be my guest.'

The man drew out the revolver, broke open the chamber, and emptied the bullets. He then dropped them into one pocket of his waterproof and the gun into another.

Robson said quickly: 'Is that our shipment?' He began walking towards the battered red container nearest to them.

He made his move before Brady realised that he hadn't body-searched them both. 'Let's get it unloaded. The sooner this business is over with, the happier we'll all be.'

Crystal said to Brady: 'I'll keep watch.'

He indicated the upper-gantry. 'Use the top window. It won't show so much light.'

For the next twenty minutes, the warehouse was filled with the chugging of the yellow forklift. Quirke expertly unloaded the pallets of petfood cans that had crossed the Atlantic from Eamon Molloy's new canning factory in the Mulqueens' meat processing works. As each pallet was dumped, Robson used the ultra-violet torch device to detect the invisibly-marked cans. Then began the laborious process of opening each, pouring out the top-covering of 'Choice Meat-chunks with marrow-bone and added vitamins', and extracting the sealed polythene pack of brown powder in each.

The job seemed to be taking for ever and Brady was leaving nothing to chance. Each pack was opened, weighed and tested for purity. It was a massive single consignment.

'Thirty kilos,' Brady confirmed. His eyes had the bright gleam of a prospector who'd discovered his first seam of gold ore.

Shard was growing impatient. 'It's two in the morning, Brady,' he reminded. 'If you're satisfied, let's have that consignment of coke.'

Like a miser interrupted during his umpteenth recount, Brady reluctantly drew back from the neat polythene stack. Within hours it would be on its way along the well-established clandestine distribution network throughout New England. Cut with a mixture of weird and not-so-wonderful substances at each stage by greedy dealers, it would filter down the pyramid. The end result would be one of thousands of thirty-gram foil packages for sale on the streets of New York.

Brady crossed the concrete floor of the loading bay to where he'd parked his car. He returned a few moments later with the brown paper package.

It was dumped unceremoniously on the trestle-table beside the heroin. 'Forty kilos of happy powder,' Brady announced casually. 'Plus two hundred thousand dollars of assorted arms already aboard. I'm satisfied it's covered by this shipment of heroin – plus the funds transferred from Malta.'

As he stared at the packages on the table, the vast dimensions of the deal began to dawn on Robson. In Europe's burgeoning cocaine market, the stuff was fetching up to £80 for a mere gramme. Forty kilos would gross over three million pounds. The enormity of it! A caterpillar of fear began crawling along his spine as he realised this must be one of the biggest drugs transactions in history.

Shard had already begun opening the large cocaine packages. Inside the paper were a number of smaller oilskin envelopes. Rapidly, he began testing each and placing them to one side.

'Billy, I've got two attaché-cases in my holdall. Can you get them out?'

Robson quickly obliged and began fitting the oilskin envelopes neatly into place. Quietly Shard said in an aside: 'They're made of bullet-proof fabric. If it's snatched, it lets off an alarm and emits a smoke dye. And if the thieves still get away, there's a tracking transmitter which sends out a signal that can be traced by a direction-finder.'

Robson grinned at the shared confidence. 'The miracles of modern science, eh?'

It was Brady's turn to become impatient. He and Quirke had now finished loading the heroin into his car. 'It's nearly three. The *Boston Dawn* is scheduled to leave at four.'

'All done,' Shard replied easily. He closed the lid of the second attaché-case, set the combination lock, and handed it to Robson. 'Handcuff it to your wrist.'

It had been quiet outside ever since their arrival, so the sudden growl of a heavy truck engine sounded alarmingly loud.

Robson forced himself to relax. No doubt it was the early arrival of someone with a delivery for another warehouse. With the others, he listened to the vehicle grumbling along the road. There followed a slow grinding of metal as the driver changed gear. It wasn't the sound of an artic. Something a lot heavier.

In the sudden frozen silence of the vast warehouse, they were like submariners listening to the deadly ping of an enemy sonar. The noise of the vehicle filled every inch of the black void around them. It did not recede.

Whatever it was sounded as though it had slowed. Right outside.

Eighteen

'Crystal!' Brady bawled. 'What's out there?'

No reply came from the girl who was supposed to be keeping watch.

'Shit!' the American cursed. 'Stupid bitch has probably fallen asleep . . . Dick, check it out!'

Quirke was already on his way. In half-a-dozen strides, he reached the personnel-door. Slipping the bolts, he peered out. The rain had cleared and the approaching dawn allowed him to see the menacing silhouette on the road beyond.

'Christ!' It was the only explanation they got from him as he stared, rooted to the spot.

'What is it?' Brady yelled.

Outside, the heavy motor gunned up the power, the roar of it sending a trembling shock-wave through the concrete floor of the warehouse.

Quirke at last found his voice. 'It's a fuckin' great dumper-truck—' His words were lost in the sudden crash of wrenching steel as the dumper hit the compound gates at maximum throttle. The steel girder supports were ripped from their mountings as the hinges refused to give. Sparks flew around the cab as the vehicle steam-rollered into the compound. The mesh gates flapped like ears on either side of its huge snub nose. Above, the twin stacks belched exhaust, giving it the appearance of some grotesque metallic dinosaur.

Quirke blindly let rip with his machine-pistol. Round after round spat uselessly at the dumper as it rolled inexorably towards them.

'Quick!' Brady snapped. 'The back way . . .'

'FREEZE!' The high-pitched yell carried above the sound of the dumper.

For a split second, it occurred to Robson that, somehow, their attackers had already infiltrated the warehouse; perhaps they'd even killed the girl.

As all eyes turned up to the voice from the gantry, he realised he was wrong. It was the girl who was giving the orders.

The muzzle flashes from her Ruger pistol dazzled from the darkened gantry and she poured a full half magazine into the floor by their feet. The bullets sang as they ricocheted in all directions, kicking chunks out of the concrete.

By the time they had recovered, Crystal was inching her way down the gantry steps, her pistol held in a double-handed grip so rigid that the weapon wavered. Her eyes were wide with panic.

With her back jammed against the safety rail, she edged down the last remaining steps to their level.

'Throw down that gun, Dick!' she ordered. 'And get with the others!'

Quirke obeyed instantly. She was so obviously nervous, that she was likely to squeeze the trigger if anyone so much as coughed.

Brady just shook his head in disbelief. 'Crystal? You . . . ?'

'Shut up!' she snarled, and inclined her head towards the personnel-door. 'Okay, guys, come in!'

The first of the two armed men to enter had the dark features of a gypsy. His shoulder-length hair was grown into scimitar-like sideburns on his cheeks. A gold ring glittered in his left ear.

'Tom Rabbit,' Brady breathed. It was easy to recognise the distinctive features from the photographs he'd been sent from Dublin.

The second man looked Italian, probably from the north of Boston. Short-cropped black hair over an expressionless, swarthy face. Black slacks, black leather jacket and expensive black leather shoes. Triumph radiated from Rabbit's eyes as they fell on the attaché-case fixed to Robson's wrist. 'This looks like an *interesting* party we've interrupted. Very interesting.'

He sidled forward, enjoying the moment like a wolf deciding which part of its prey to devour first.

Crystal said: 'The heroin's already stashed in the car.' She gave a nervous chuckle. 'You can just drive it away.'

Rabbit laughed. It was a sound full of menace. 'That was thoughtful of them.'

'Bitch!' Brady spat.

The girl sneered at him. 'It's no more than you deserve, you dirty ol' bastard. It'll be the last time you paw me.'

'She's got you taped,' Rabbit said. 'The Family over here's had you infiltrated for years. All those girlfriends you've had in the past. Apparently they've nearly all been plants.' He seemed to think it was a huge joke.

Brady's crestfallen face suggested he didn't see the funny side.

'The two English guys have got the coke,' Crystal added. 'In the cases.'

Rabbit turned his attention to them. 'Which of you two is Robson?'

'I am.'

The lips twisted into a smile. 'So *you're* the joker who tried to kill me in Malta?'

Robson looked at him with contempt. 'I had nothing to do with that. It was one of your own Provo friends. The one they call Dee.'

That stopped Rabbit for a moment. The disappointment showed clearly in his eyes. Robson's statement had an earnest ring of truth about it. 'It doesn't matter, you're going to die anyway. It'll be a warning to your friends when this place goes up in flames with you inside.' He leaned back towards the Italian. 'Get them tied up and douse them in kerosene.'

'Don't forget the coke,' the girl reminded.

Robson smiled thinly as he held up his case. 'Locked on, I'm afraid.'

Rabbit sneered. 'Then, we'll chop it off at the wrist.'

'No need,' Robson answered evenly. 'I've got a key in my trouser pocket. Okay?'

He didn't wait for a reply but slowly lowered his hand into his pocket, his fingers urgently seeking the hole through to the Beretta strapped to his inside leg.

Beside him, he sensed Shard stiffen.

'Damn, it's here somewhere . . .' Robson mumbled to give himself extra time.

Shard said: 'Mine's not hand-cuffed. Have it.'

Involuntarily, Rabbit reached out for the offered case. As he drew back with it, he suddenly realised Shard still had hold of the trigger cord.

The shriek from the built-in siren was ear-splitting in the huge, echoing warehouse. It shattered Rabbit's tetchy nervous system like a bolt from a crossbow. In panic, he dropped the case. As it hit the floor, thick blue smoke burst out of the internal tanks, engulfing everyone.

Robson's Beretta was out. Rabbit saw it and swung his machine-pistol up defensively. It was the last move he ever made. The 9mm round caught him full in the mouth and blasted into his brain. He hit the concrete like a sack of potatoes. Deadweight. Blood oozed from his shattered lips and a fine vein of crimson seeped from the corner of his right eye.

Shard had moved like lightning. He was only a split second behind his companion, and the single shot from his own Beretta caught the Italian dead-square in the centre of his chest. A marksman's aim.

'The girl!' It was Brady's voice, raised in warning.

Instinctively, Robson swung his case up to shield his face as he saw her swivel the snout of the Ruger in his direction. The crack of gunfire was ear-shattering. But he was aware only of the numbing force of the two rounds that slammed into the case, wrenching it from his grasp. He stumbled back under the impact, the flesh on his face and chest pulsing with the bruising pain.

As he regained his senses and peered up, he was aware of the sudden awesome silence in the warehouse after the violent cacophony.

He swallowed hard. He hadn't even been aware of Shard firing back at the girl. But he must have done, because now she lay sprawled inelegantly on the floor. In the centre of her abdomen, two small holes bubbled out their contents. Like red spring water, the stuff pumped out, seeking the easiest course over the white blouse, to the spreading reservoir on the concrete. Then, suddenly, the flow stopped. She was dead.

Brady looked shaken. The drained face showed his years. 'Where the hell you learn t' shoot like that, my limey friend?' He stared down at the girl who had betrayed him.

'Pheasant shoots, old boy,' Shard retorted acidly. 'Now let's get aboard that boat. I trust your people *are* competent to clear up this mess efficiently?'

Brady smarted, but under the circumstances he could
hardly protest. 'Follow me.'

Frank Lewis wasn't sure.

The man who sat across the table from him in the sunny
bay window of the Hinchley Wood pub in Surrey was not
the sort he was used to doing business with. It made him
feel uneasy.

He was accustomed to smart villains who knew their way
around. Smart in every sense. From the desire not to do
another stretch inside to the way they dressed.

But this character ... ? Lewis guessed he was in his early
thirties. He had eternal student and Leftie stamped all over him.
From the cropped fair hair and National Health granny glasses
to the bloody silly Bolshevik cap he'd been wearing when he
came in. And five miles of woollen scarf wrapped around his
throat. Compared to that, the worn cords and tatty crewneck
sweater with the CND badge were almost forgiveable.

'Well, do we *do* a deal or not?' Even the man's quiet,
assured voice irritated Lewis. The hint of cockiness got to
him. That and the furtive way he flickered his eyes from side
to side whenever he spoke. Like a bloody lizard.

'Listen, lad, there are certain rules to this game,' Lewis
said patronisingly. 'And if you want to do business with me,
you have to stick to them.'

The man smirked. 'Is that so, Daddy-O?' he mocked.
'Like what?'

Lewis drew in his breath. 'Like not deliberately trying to
get up my nose for a start,' he hissed. 'And taking things one
step at a time. Being *absolutely* discreet. And that includes
your girlfriend. She's giving me the bloody 'eebies just sitting
there.'

The girl, who was in a seat a little apart from them, looked to be in her mid-twenties. Her hair, like her baggy clothes, was a mess. She had been fidgeting with her glass ever since they'd come in, and her eyes continuously roamed the bar as though she was terrified someone would notice she'd forgotten to put her knickers on before she came out.

'Brenda's okay, man. She and I have been dealing dope down the line since the Vietnam protest meetings.'

A nerve flickered in Lewis's temple. 'We're not talking hash, lad. The stakes for this stuff are a lot higher. And I'm telling you, your Brenda's a liability. So next time just you and me. Right?'

The man nodded with resentful agreement.

Lewis continued, talking quickly. The sooner he was out of this character's company, the happier he'd be. 'Now, before we do a thing, I need to know something about you. Something that's *verifiable*. Understand?'

'You got the recommendation,' the man reminded.

'That's true,' Lewis admitted. And it was. The phone call had come out of the blue from Bernadette the previous morning. It was a total surprise but a pleasant one. Apparently she had been helping her mother in The Czar when an old friend, Rich Abbott, came in for a drink. In conversation, he'd mentioned off-handedly that there were a lot of new faces around lately. 'New wave' villains, as he referred to them disparagingly. Reading between the lines, he'd gathered that some were in narcotics. One in particular was in a bad mood because his source of supply had dried up unexpectedly and he was desperate to meet his commitment to his customers.

Bernadette had pricked up her ears, but said nothing. Was Lewis interested?

He was taken aback for a moment until she made it clear that she was only concerned in pulling out of their joint business arrangement with some of her investment intact. She realised that the lost heroin shipment would have left them financially crippled if the IRA demanded their cut. A once-and-for-all deal would at least give her something to salvage.

Lewis had smiled to himself. He didn't tell her that for once the masters of the IRA had been forgiving in return for completion of the Boston deal – and the services of a masochistic sex-slave.

Instead, he'd telephoned Rich Abbott, casually enquiring if he'd anyone amongst his contacts who was looking for goods to supply? Not for himself, of course, but for an old associate to whom he owed a favour.

At the end of the conversation, which Lewis sensed was a little tense, a name was delivered. Wal Atkins. And the telephone number of an intermediate.

'Wal Atkins,' Lewis murmured. 'Real name?'

'Yes,' the man confirmed, his irritation clear. 'I'm a lecturer in chemistry at Surrey University.'

'Guildford? And how long have you been moving smack?'

'Four years. As I told you, we started in dope years back.'

'And what size of consignment are you looking for now?'

Wal Atkins's eyes glittered with hard humour. 'I'm looking for twenty kilos.'

Lewis almost spat out the drink he'd just sipped. 'A score? Christ! *What* sort of set-up do you run?'

At the surprised outburst, the lecturer allowed himself a gloating smirk 'My network stretches to just about every university, college and poly in the country, Mr Lewis. Everything from smack, which is the current favourite, to dope, barbs, Methadone and speed which we make at our own labs. Oh, and coke – when we can get it.'

Lewis was genuinely astounded and impressed. He tried not to show it. 'Coke, eh?' An idea was forming in his mind.

Wal Atkins shrugged. 'It's the new craze. Once the street price comes down, it'll take over from smack.'

'And who's been your smack supplier until now?'

The lecturer's eyes narrowed. 'Now what the fuck's that got to do with you?'

Lewis tried one of his most disarming smiles. 'Security, Wal. It's in your own interests that I know the sort of outfit I might be getting mixed up with. Mutual trust and all that. It means a lot in the regular underworld.' The slight emphasis on 'regular' was meant as a jibe and the lecturer saw it.

He said: 'Do you read the papers?' Lewis didn't reply, he just allowed the younger man to go on. 'Three days ago there was an explosion in a flat in St John's Wood. Two Irishmen were killed. Names of Robinson and O'Rourke, if that means anything to you? The police thought it was a gas mains 'til they discovered fragments of a Gaz cylinder in the debris.'

The names *certainly* meant something to Lewis. It looked as though the gang war between the Provos and the Proddies was hotting up, with Dee's men gaining the upper hand. Lewis felt suddenly cold.

'So you see,' Atkins continued, 'I've huge commitments to meet and no supplies. So I want twenty kilos, and I can get through that in two or three weeks.'

Lewis felt his excitement rise. This was an incredible break. Wal Atkins's network would more than double the loss of Max's business now he was pulling out. Not only that, but it would be at the expense of the Proddies. Retribution!

And it offered a ready-made outlet for the cocaine on its way from Boston.

'The Man' and Dee would be delighted, he was sure, and everything would settle down nicely again.

'Look, Wal, I think we can do business. But you're still a new face to me. That means we never exchange more than six kilos at a time. It's a golden rule. I took a chance recently on a bigger consignment and came horribly unstuck. So it's back to six.'

From behind the National Health glasses, the hard eyes bored into him like gimlets, but Atkins didn't speak.

Lewis added cautiously: 'And the price will be high for the first score. Then we'll renegotiate a long-term contract which will bring a smile to your face. And I think I can say you'll find us a lot more reliable than your mates in St John's Wood.'

It was another half-an-hour of intense bargaining over unnoticed empty glasses before the provisional deal was struck. Sensing Lewis's keenness, Wal Atkins managed to push the first consignment up from six to ten kilos. The time and place to be fixed the next day.

That would give Lewis enough time to check up on the chemistry lecturer at Surrey University, and his jittery girl-friend, Brenda.

Through the window, he watched them climb into their battered lime green Citroën 2CV and chunter noisily across the car park to the main road.

As it turned into the traffic flow, it passed the bright yellow Metro coming in. In seconds, Bernadette had parked, entered the pub, and found Lewis.

'You're lookin' great, doll,' he greeted. The new deal had restored his confidence. 'Perfect timing.'

She sat down, but didn't smile. In fact she seemed to find it difficult to meet his eyes at all.

Afraid she'll allow me to charm my way back into her knickers, he mused. Just give her time; she'll be back.

Bernadette said: 'I parked across the way till I saw them leave, Frankie. So, what do you think of him?'

Lewis grinned. 'He'll do.'

She pulled a tight smile. 'He looked a bit of a creep to me.'

A genuine laugh. 'That, too, doll! But he's got an interesting set-up, and assures me he's got the wedge. Ten kilos. Looks like it could be a good long-term runner. We've agreed to do one deal initially to see how it goes. We could be back in business, love. What ya say?'

At last her beautiful green eyes narrowed as they focused on his face. The single dimple deepened as she pulled a bitter smile. 'I'm not interested, Frankie. I just want a straight half of your profit on the first deal. That'll give me enough to buy a place of my own. Straight cash. It'll be better than going through a long legal battle to get back my rightful share of the business. You can keep it.'

Looking at the soft tumble of chestnut hair, Lewis realised just how much he'd missed her over the past few weeks.

'We could still make a go of it together, Bernie.' He reached out his hand to hers.

Bernadette pulled back before he got to her. 'Forget it, Frankie. Half the deal, that's all I'm going to want from you, ever. When Billy's set up safe in the States or wherever, he's going to contact me. I'll join him and see he gets a real break this time. A new life.'

Lewis wanted to tell her what a stupid, romantic cow she was. That there was no way it would work. That, of all the

things he'd ever regretted in his life, introducing her to Billy
Robson was the one he regretted most.

But all he said was: 'Okay, Bernie, if that's the way you
want it.'

'God, Andy, it's good to see you. I can't tell you.'

But she had told him. Five times in as many minutes.

He grinned and shook his head again in wonder. It was
hard to believe it was the same Sandy Robson he and Billy
had brought to Fatton Place just six weeks earlier. Then
she had been almost a skeleton. Thinly fleshed, with sunken
eyes and hollow cheeks.

Now, sitting in the bright sunlight at the old pine table
in the communal kitchen, the transformation was stunning.
The beautiful but lack-lustre eyes now sparkled with life and
vitality. Her sandy-gold hair bounced with shine and health.

She noticed his eyes on her waist. She laughed happily and
tugged at the belt of her jeans. 'You've noticed! I've put on
so much weight, I'm almost bursting. I'm eating like a horse.'

He laughed to see her so happy. 'But how do you *feel*?' he
asked anxiously.

Sandy tilted her head to one side. 'Wonderful, Andy. Just
wonderful.' She frowned suddenly. 'Oh, the first week was
absolute hell. I really thought I would die doing turkey. But
as the weeks went by . . . it just got better and better. Oh, I
can't say I don't still get the twinge for a fix – sort of.' She
leaned towards him. 'But, Andy, do you know what really
made the change?'

'Tell me.'

She fixed him with her eyes. 'They've got a shrink here.
A sort of psychiatrist or psychologist – something like that.
Nice, friendly sort of bloke. Well, he talked things through

with me. We covered everything. My life, Billy's.' She paused uncertainly. 'And you.'

He smiled. 'I don't mind if it helped.'

She nodded. 'It did, Andy. I realised I didn't want Billy any more. Maybe I'd never really wanted him. I married the wrong man. It should have been you from the start.'

He reached across the table and clasped her hand. 'Well, Sand, it will be from now on.'

'I'm so happy, Andy. Really. As soon as I decided I'd finished with Billy – *really* decided there was no going back – I felt like a new woman. It's been great from that moment.'

Andy nodded sagely. He wasn't sure how Billy would eventually take the news, but he no longer really cared. The chances were his old friend could never return to Britain, and if he did, he'd be locked up in the slammer as soon as his feet touched the shore. 'When will they let you out, Sand?'

She shrugged. 'That's up to me. But Doc Swinburne says maybe next week. He's happy I'll be moving in with you. Although he's a bit worried about your financial security.'

Andy Sutcliff's beard split into the widest grin yet. 'Bit of good news there, Sand. I've got a new VAT inspector who's done a deal with me. And I've got a new contract to supply posh motors to the Middle East.' He didn't mention that Rich Abbott was behind the operation to ship stolen top-market cars out of the UK to wealthy Arabs.

'God, Andy, that's fantastic news!' She was jubilant. 'And the Doc reckons there's a good chance the Welfare will let me have Dan back in a few months.'

Sutcliff had grown fond of the lad: he was looking forward to the new life with a ready-made family. When Billy had told him it was time he settled down, he could never have imagined it would be with his own friend's wife and son.

At that moment, the matron peered around the kitchen door. 'Mr Sutcliff? Dr Swinburne wondered if you might have a word on your way out?'

'Sure. I'm just leaving. I'll pop in.' He turned back to Sandy. 'I can't wait to have you at my place.'

She kissed him on the mouth. 'Neither can I. Roll on next week.'

Andy Sutcliff turned and strolled nonchalantly over to the doctor's book-lined study.

Dr Swinburne was waiting. 'I gather you're taking over responsibility for our patient, Mr Sutcliff?' He raised a hand; he wasn't expecting a response. 'We've had the police around, so we know all about Mr Robson's background. And Sandy has filled me in. No need to explain. I'm happy for you both.'

Sutcliff was relieved; he still felt an acute guilt that somehow he'd betrayed Robson's trust. 'She seems to be doing well.'

Dr Swinburne smiled tightly. 'It's still early days, but she appears to be making excellent progress. If she leaves us as soon as next week, I'd like her to continue as an out-patient.'

'What does Sand say?'

'Fine. At the moment. It'll help if you persuade her to keep to it.' The doctor watched him carefully as he nodded his agreement. 'There's just one thing of which you ought to be aware.'

Sutcliff frowned. 'Yes?'

'I believe Mrs Robson has no other close relatives?'

'With Billy disappeared, there's only her mother. She's in an old people's home. Not quite *compos mentis*, if you get my meaning. And she doesn't have contact with any aunts or uncles. Leastways, not for years.'

'Right,' Swinburne said. He seemed to be finding difficulty in selecting the right words. 'Then you're the best one
to tell. Especially as you'll be – I gather – cohabiting, as they
put it.'

Sutcliff felt a mild flutter of panic. 'Tell me what, Doc?'

'Sandy's blood-tests have shown up an abnormality.' He
said it tersely through his teeth; his eyes looked at Sutcliff
frankly. 'It has been confirmed that her blood carries the
acquired immune deficiency syndrome virus.'

'What?' Sutcliff didn't understand. The words sounded
familiar, but he couldn't quite recall where he had heard
them.

'AIDS' Dr Swinburne explained patiently. 'Sandy carries
the virus. It's not uncommon for addicts. Using a needle
that's been used by someone else usually. They're never too
concerned about hygiene . . .'

The words exploded in Sutcliff's brain like a grenade. He
felt breathless, winded. He fumbled blindly for the support
of a chair. 'Does – does she know?'

Dr Swinburne shook his head. 'Not yet. Giving news like
that to an addict trying to get off would not be exactly helpful. I'll tell her at the end of her treatment, or pass her file to
her own GP for his decision.'

'Jesus Christ.' Sutcliff stared blindly at the rows of leather-
bound volumes behind the doctor. 'So what does it mean?'

Dr Arnold Swinburne tried his best to smile reassurance.
'Well, for a start, it doesn't mean that she'll develop AIDS.
But she carries the virus. That means that she could pass it
on. Not easily, of course. There's no real evidence that it can
be passed on by touch or saliva. But sexual intercourse, vagi-
nal or rectal, could – just could – result in the transmission
of the disease.' He hesitated. 'Careful use of a sheath would

greatly reduce any element of the risk. But, you must understand that the risk could never be eliminated.'

Andy Sutcliff was trembling. He could do nothing to stop
his eyes from burning as he felt the tears coming.

Frank Lewis had arrived before dawn. He was taking no
chances.

A hundred feet below him, he could see the Leith Hill
lay-by through the gap in the vegetation, as the first pale
wash of sunlight allowed him to identify individual trees.
Birds began their excited early morning chatter.

He shivered. The damp had penetrated his bones over
the previous two hours while he had waited, watched and
listened. Feeling slightly foolish, he had seen nothing, just
the total blackness of the night. All he'd heard was the drip
of condensation on the underbed of dried leaves. Only two
cars had passed down the remote winding lane.

But it had been worth it for his peace of mind.

The incident of the intercept with Max's consignment
had left him unreasonably anxious. Now at least he was
certain that this was no set-up. From his side, *only* he knew
the location of the exchange. The rest was down to Wal
Atkins.

He glanced at his watch. The minute hand swept towards
the hour. Exactly 5 a.m.

Immediately, he detected the uneven chatter of the 2CV's
engine as the vehicle strained up the misty forest road.

He smiled.

It was three further minutes before the lime-green Citroën
with its ugly slab sides pulled into the lay-by and stopped.
Wal Atkins looked nervous as he stepped out into the chill
morning air. He glanced at his watch, grimaced and began

walking the length of the lay-by. Under his arm he carried a brown paper parcel.

Lewis waited another five minutes. Thankfully, the Citroën was empty; as promised, the lecturer had left his girlfriend behind.

Lewis made his move. He half-fell and half-slid down the steep slope, bursting suddenly through the young vegetation just feet behind Atkins.

The man started. 'Christ!'

'It's okay!' Lewis assured. 'Don't panic. Is that the money?'

Atkins nodded. 'Used notes.'

Lewis held out both hands, one empty and one holding a hessian shopping bag with the ten kilos of heroin.

'The smack?' Atkins queried.

'Here,' Lewis snapped irritably. 'Check it now, while I go over the money. Be quick.' He paused as he heard the distant sound of a car. 'Sod! Let's get on . . .'

He hesitated. There was something odd about Atkins. He wore the same scarf as before. The same sweater. The same CND badge.

'Oh, my God!' Terror struck at Lewis's heart as realisation dawned too late. Beneath the tin badge was a small black plastic button. Just an inch of the flex showed. The bastard was wired!

Before he could retrieve his offered hand, the wrist was grabbed by the lecturer. It was a grip like steel. Expertly, his arm was wrenched around until the pressure was forced against the joint.

As Lewis gasped for breath, Detective Sergeant Dick Spicer grinned with satisfaction. 'You're nicked, Frankie-boy!'

There was a sudden stirring in the undergrowth as half-a-dozen burly plainclothes Squad officers, most of them wearing khaki or camouflaged anoraks, appeared. Some were armed. Lewis was speechless.

He was securely handcuffed before the two unmarked cars arrived at either end of the lay-by to seal it off.

'He could have picked a more comfortable place for a stake-out,' one of the detective muttered, blowing into his hands.

'I've got a flask,' another replied. 'Let's get a swig.'

Lewis's eyes narrowed on the man he knew as Wal Atkins. 'You checked out at the University.'

Spicer smiled cynically. 'I would, wouldn't I? Our friend exists, and his girlfriend. Only he doesn't know the first thing about the sort of muck you've been moving. We just borrowed his identity.'

Lewis shook his head in despair; he still couldn't believe it. But his sudden capture wasn't the last of his surprises. His heart sank as he recognised Bernadette climbing out of one of the newly arrived cars with two senior-looking plain-clothes men. They came towards him.

One of them was slightly built with pale skin that showed in contrast to his dark raincoat. The ginger hair was short and neat. 'Detective Chief Superintendent Pilger of Central Drug Squad,' he introduced himself in a clipped, matter-of-fact manner. 'Frank John Lewis? I arrest you under the Misuse of Drugs Act for conspiring with others to import and distribute controlled drugs or substances. You are not obliged to say anything unless you wish to do so, but whatever you do say will be taken down in writing and may be given in evidence.'

Those words, that cliché that everyone in the country knew by heart from countless television dramas. But this time, they were for real. Lewis felt sick. Literally. An empty, frightened feeling crawled around in his gut.

'Anything to say?' Pilger demanded.

'Why's *she* here?'

Pilger raised an eyebrow. 'Miss Mulqueen? She's here because she wanted to be, that's all.'

Unlike their previous meeting, this time Bernadette found no trouble in meeting his gaze. 'I'm here because I wanted you to know why I did it, Frankie. It was to try and give Billy a chance. And the only way I could do that was to sacrifice you.' She bit on her lower lip. 'I'm sorry it had to be like this. But you tricked and used me like you did him. So really, you've no one else to blame. I'm sorry, Frankie.'

Panic grabbed at Lewis. He turned to Pilger. 'God, you don't believe her, do you? Jesus, she's been in on it all along. This is just – just vengeance.'

'Please, Frankie, don't say any more,' she pleaded. 'You'll just make it worse for yourself.'

Detective Sergeant Spicer urged Lewis towards the waiting car. 'No one loves a drug pedlar, Lewis. Even that old lag Rich Abbott didn't take much persuading to co-operate with us. The old school think people like you are a bloody subspecies. And I think they might just be right.'

Pilger waited until the girl and Lewis had returned to separate cars, before he turned to Major Harper who stood beside him. 'Well, Bill, you were right.'

'After losing that consignment it was pretty certain he'd clutch at a straw.' The sing-song Welsh accent was even more buoyant than usual. 'And the Provos aren't known for their forgiving nature.'

'The girl was a Godsend, though. Coming to us like that. Not the sort of luck we're used to. She must be pretty keen on Billy Robson.'

Harper chuckled. 'Or mad with Lewis. Hell hath no fury, and all that.' He watched the first of the cars drive away with Lewis inside. 'How will Robson stand legally? I mean, strictly speaking, it's the girl who's turned Queen's Evidence, not him.'

Pilger frowned; it was a puzzle he wasn't yet able to sort out himself. 'Well, if the Mulqueen girl is right, and he was blackmailed into going on that exchange with Maltese Max, then the court might take a lenient view – if it can be established that it was Blair Wallace who shot at our blokes. But, frankly, Bill, it's all going to depend on how Robson himself reacts to events.'

'And, more importantly, if we ever get him back on British soil,' Harper thought aloud. He shivered. The morning chill was getting to him. 'What d'you say to a spot of breakfast?'

The *Boston Dawn* had been rolling like a bitch all day and all evening.

It seemed like he'd only just gone to sleep when Billy Robson was awoken by the crash of tin mugs from the galley. Someone cursed.

He stirred in the half-world between dream and reality. A second before he'd been holding Emy Graziani in his arms, making love to her before he realised she was dead. It was a deeply real and disturbing nightmare, and he was thankful to leave it behind.

The familiar smell of damp wood and diesel greeted him as he unglued his eyes. Across the aisle of the small forecabin, Kevin Shard was stretched out on his mattress, his hands behind his head.

'Welcome back to the life on the ocean wave, Billy.'

Robson swung his legs off the bunk. 'God, this takes me back. I'd forgotten I hated it so much.' He peered up at the storm-lashed scuttle. 'What time is it?'

Shard didn't need to consult his watch. 'Just after eleven.'

'And we're still steaming in the face of that north-easterly?'

'Afraid so.'

Robson scratched thoughtfully at the stubble on his chin. Today was the big day. The trawler had been struggling manfully across the Atlantic for eight days now, and somewhere out there, beyond the heaving swell of cold grey water, was the dark coast of Eire. If they were still on schedule, they'd rendezvous with the fishing-boat from Buncrana around midnight.

'When d'you reckon we'll make it?'

Shard shrugged and propped himself on one elbow. 'If he stops pissing about, the skipper reckons it'll be nearer one or one-thirty. But it'll be a rought ride.'

Robson was uncomfortably aware of the nerves chewing away in his stomach. In conversation it had sounded easy enough when Dee had said, 'You just rendezvous with the boat. There'll be nothing else about. Signal by Aldis. Pull alongside and transfer the arms. When that's done, pass over the two attaché-cases of cocaine.' No mention of an alcoholic skipper, or a heavy sea, or the possibility of an Irish Navy patrol.

He lit a cigarette. 'Well, just as soon as it's over, the better. I only want to get back to the States and see if Bernadette still wants to join me like she promised.'

Shard said: 'I think you'll see her before that.'

Robson wasn't sure he'd heard right. 'Pardon?'

'I've something to tell you.' Shard's expression had changed. In an instant, the relaxed devil-may-care look vanished from his eyes. He motioned Robson to remain seated and made his way to the bulkhead hatch. He opened it a fraction to check that there was no one within earshot. Closing it firmly and quietly, he returned to his bunk.

'Listen, Billy, I've got a confession to make.'

Robson didn't like the sound of this.

'When I met you in Malta that time, I told you I'd been out of the Royal Marines for four years. Well, that wasn't strictly true.'

'Oh?'

Shard's eyes were ice cold. 'That was when I left Four Two Commando and joined the SBS.'

It took Robson a second to recall the old service slang. An 'SB' was a member of the Special Boat Service – the covert Royal Marines equivalent of the Army's Special Air Service Regiment – and, if anything, even more secretive.

'Are you saying . . . ?'

Shard nodded. 'I'm *still* with them.'

Robson was stunned. 'Sweet Jesus . . . You mean this is some sort of undercover mission?'

'Exactly that, Billy. I was with the SBS in the Falklands and after. Since then we've been doing more and more of the sort of work the 'Regiment' has always done. I'm afraid demand's been outstripping supply in the anti-terrorist business.' He studied Robson's reaction carefully. 'I don't know if you heard about the two bodyguards to the British Ambassador in the Lebanon last year. He was visiting the US Embassy when those Islamic lunatics tried their lorry-bomb trick again. The two bodyguards with our Ambassador shot the bastards stone dead before they struck.'

Robson recalled the story. 'The press said they were SAS.'

Shard smiled thinly. 'In the old days it would have been. It suits us to let them take the credit.'

'How did you get involved with the Libyans?'

'It's true what I told you about the British mercenary outfits working for Gadaffi. What I didn't mention was that they tend to retain their old personal ties with the Forces, or Whitehall, on an informal basis. Just the odd word if they think something's of interest. That's how we got to hear that Gadaffi's lot were meddling in the heroin business. I was infiltrated and worked from there. The connection with the IRA was becoming apparent to me at just about the time you came on the scene.'

'So what to God do you think you'll do about this . . . ?' Robson's voice petered away, as the realisation dawned on him. 'Is that what you meant by seeing Bernadette sooner than I thought?'

Shard nodded. 'When the Provo's boat is in territorial waters, it will be seized by the Irish Navy. With a little help from the SBS.'

Robson let out a low whistle. 'Were the SBS involved in the seizure of the *Marita Ann*?'

The SBS man smiled slyly. 'That's for me to know, and you to guess.'

'Incredible,' Robson murmured. He lit another cigarette. 'But where does that leave me now, Kevin?'

Shard smiled gently. 'That rather depends on you. I can't guarantee any legal niceties, but obviously I'll do all I can to explain how you were innocently caught up in all this. As the expression goes, you're either with me or against me.'

'Do you need to ask?' Robson grinned. A great weight seemed to lift from his shoulders. 'It'll just be a bloody relief to be out of this.'

'I'm glad you said that.'

It was only then that Robson realised that all the time a 9mm Beretta had been pointing at him, concealed beneath Shard's blanket.

In fact, it was to be nearer two in the morning before contact was made.

Wrapped in oilskins, Robson and Shard made their way to the pitching wheelhouse where the skipper fought against the wheel to hold a course. Icy pellets of spray spat at the windscreen as their eyes strained to penetrate the blackest of nights. The sea was only discernible from the inky sky by the curling white phosphorescence on each shrugging wave crest. Heavy mountains of black satin rolled alongside as they pitched into another trough. It was an angry, tormented sea, stirring restlessly as though undecided as to the exact foulness of its mood. Outside, the wind screamed through the jumbled paraphernalia of navigation equipment.

'It'll be a bloody miracle if we don't pass within a few feet of each other and never know,' muttered the skipper. As usual, the bottle of whiskey had made him morose.

'Can we heave-to in this?' Robson asked.

Bloodshot eyes left the windscreen momentarily and blinked at him like an owl. 'We'll just have to see, Mr Robson, won't we?'

Without the use of radar, which could have alerted the Irish Navy or coastguard, it took twenty minutes of circling the rendezvous area before the blurred flash of the signal lantern was finally spotted through a squall off the port bow. It was a mere thirty-five-footer. An MFV of timber construction, which must have been its owner's pride and joy when it was launched fifty years earlier. But today the *Pumila* was showing her age as she nosed creakingly into the rollers, the water streaming off her paint-peeled foredeck.

The gusting wind had slackened perceptibly and the helmsman of the smaller craft decided to edge gently in as a couple of deckhands began putting out the heavy sisal fenders. It took a couple of attempts before the lines came across and she nuzzled gently alongside the mother ship. A man in yellow oilskins stepped across the dangerously shifting gunwales from the *Pumila* to start supervising the transfer of the sealed and waterproofed cases which contained the arms.

Satisfied that everything was under way, the man from the *Pumila* made his way to the *Boston Dawn*'s wheelhouse. Wind and spume whipped into the meagre warmth as he entered and slid the door shut behind him.

It was only when he ripped off the steaming oilskin hat that Robson realised it was Dee.

'You could have picked a better night for it,' Shard observed.

Dee's face was pinched and blue, the skin taut after the constant lashing of rain and spray. 'Thought this was how you tough cabbage-hats like it,' he sneered. He peered out of the windscreen. 'At least a filthy night like this suits our purposes. Visibility's down to a few yards.'

The skipper was thankful his mission was almost complete. He handed over a flask. 'Expect you could use a drop of this?'

Dee took it and swigged on the burning liquid, but just the once. It had been almost empty. 'You've had a hard night yourself, I see,' he accused, and handed it back to the skipper. He turned to Robson: 'You've got the other consignment?'

Robson smiled sweetly and indicated the two attaché-cases stowed by the door. 'Safe and sound.'

Dee nodded slowly. 'I heard you had problems?'

Shard said: 'Tom Rabbit's dead.'

A thin, humourless smile spread over the Irishman's face. 'Then that'll save me doing the job.' There was no hint of thanks or congratulation.

'There's a small change of plan,' Shard added.

'Oh?'

'Robson here's coming ashore with us.'

Dee snorted. 'Like fuck he is! We've just got rid of the bastard to the States. We don't want him back.'

It was Shard's turn to smile. 'It's not up to you. My Libyan bosses want to talk to him. They think he could be useful to them.'

Dee opened his mouth to speak, then stopped. Robson knew what he was thinking. His initial inclination would have been to radio Dublin for confirmation – until he remembered they had to observe strict radio silence.

'Sorry, old lad.' Shard seemed genuinely apologetic. 'But I assure you it's what my people want.'

Dee had no option. Besides, one of the crewmen had just waved to indicate that the transfer was complete. It was time to go. As the three of them left the wheelhouse, Robson glanced up at the thick black clouds pressing down on them. From what Shard had told him, he knew that somewhere up there, high in the calm world above the clouds, a Nimrod maritime surveillance aircraft of the Royal Air Force was tracking every move they made.

There were only three men crewing the *Pumila*. That included Dee, who ushered them into the foc's'le. The bulkhead lamp threw a feeble light over the four bunkbeds and the untidy shambles created by its temporary occupants. It stank of diesel and mildew and the shifting bilge-water was distinctly audible beneath the deckboards.

Dee's first words took both men off guard. 'Get up against that bulkhead. Hands, feet and legs spread.'

Shard tried to make a joke of it. 'What's up, don't you trust us or something?'

The Irishman's eyes glittered like granite. 'That's a fucken stupid question! We've got a boat here with three crew, three hundred assorted firearms, and a million quids' worth of coke – and now you two fucken ex-Brit cabbage-hats. You're not kiddin' I don't trust you.' The sudden appearance of the revolver made his statement superfluous. 'Now turn!'

As they obeyed, Shard caught Robson's eyes and shook his head imperceptibly. The unspoken message was clear. Don't try anything; we'll bide our time.

Dee was more thorough than his counterparts on the *Boston Dawn* had been. His find of the two thigh holsters and the pair of Berettas put him in a better mood.

'As tricky as ever, I see,' he said triumphantly. 'The only way I'd ever trust bastards like you is with your legs and arms off.'

Robson felt his bile rising. The Provo's festering hatred and callous disregard for human life turned his stomach. 'Just what the hell have you got against Royal Marines, Dee? You and your thugs have killed and maimed God knows how many. So how many more to even the score?'

Dee looked at Robson curiously. 'Oh, a lot, Robson. A lot.'

Shard was intrigued. 'And why? Just for The Cause. Or is it more personal?' he guessed.

'It was in '71,' Dee said slowly, as though it was painful to recall. He looked at Robson. 'In your time. Some slick-talking cabbage-hat started dating my kid sister. She was still at school. Hardly sixteen, a child.' His eyes became hard and distant. 'He was married, but he couldn't wait to get his rocks off with a child who thought it romantic to have a secret liaison with a Brit soldier.'

'Love knows no boundaries,' Shard muttered provocatively.

Dee's glare could have drawn blood. 'Love had nothin' to do with it. He took her to this bar in Derry. A Proddy bar used by his off-duty cabbage-hat mates.'

'And?' Robson pressed.

'And then the fucken bomb went off,' Dee hissed. 'It took three months for her to die. Three long months in the knowledge that her hands were just two burnt stumps. And that she'd never see again.' His voice had dropped to a whisper that was scarcely audible against the noise of the sea beyond the hull. 'Maybe the blindness was a blessing. She never knew what it had done to her face.'

Robson took a deep breath. 'The bomber never knew she was in there?'

Dee appeared to be in a trance. 'No, I never knew.'

It was touch and go whether the *Pumila* would reach the haven of Lough Swilly before the dawn. The wind had slackened but the sea remained high and sluggish, making the old marine diesel feel its age.

Robson and Shard went on deck as the first fingers of cold light probed through the bruised clouds in the east. It cast a steely sheen on the waves. They sat together on the folded foremast below the wheelhouse and watched the darker smudge on the horizon take on a solid form. The rugged coast of Donegal.

Shard saw it first. He'd been expecting it, and knew the direction from which it would come. Not ahead where all other eyes were anxiously waiting.

There were no lights on the 972-tonne Irish patrol vessel *Emer*. She was just a grey blur against a grey background of sea and sky, spray and mist as she closed rapidly on her prey.

He nudged Robson. 'One of them's closing.'

Robson felt a sudden charge of anticipation like electricity. 'Where?'

'Don't look, but she's astern.'

'What about our radar?'

Shard shrugged. 'Maybe it's as wanky as everything else on this tub.'

As though in answer to Robson's question, they suddenly heard the skipper's voice from the wheelhouse calling Dee, who had seated himself up in the prow.

'What is it, Seamus?' he yelled back.

The skipper beckoned him fiercely, and Dee left his look-out position immediately, making his way back over the anchor chain and coiled ropes towards the wheelhouse.

'What's up?' Robson asked, as the Irishman passed.

Dee shook his head tersely.

Shard nodded to Robson for them to follow the Irishman back to the wheelhouse.

The bearded skipper Seamus looked uncomfortable. His eyes flickered back and forth from the compass to the primitive radar-set. 'I think there's something behind us.'

'*Think?*' Dee demanded.

Seamus shrugged. 'Fucken thing's been on the blink again. At first I'm thinkin' it's sea -clutter . . .'

Dee turned and looked back across their wake.

'I don't see anything,' Shard said helpfully.

Dee did. 'Oh shit!'

Seamus turned and squinted against the increasing glare of the rising sun. 'Dammit, you're right! Navy grey. Must be fishery protection.'

'We'll outrun them,' Dee decided.

The skipper laughed bitterly. 'In this, my friend? Never! It's better just to brazen it out. They'll just want to know if we've been fishing. We'll tell them it was too rough.'

Dee began to get agitated. 'That's the mistake the *Marita Ann* made.'

'We've no option,' Seamus snapped. 'I can hardly get ten knots out of her on a good day.'

'Try!' Dee yelled, his eyes widening with anger.

Seamus shrugged and reached for the brass handle of the telegraph. It clanked to a Full Ahead. However, it was a good forty-five seconds before the engineer responded, and the deck plates began to tremble as the diesels wound up to maximum revs. Despite the noise, the difference in speed was negligible.

Robson sighed in relief.

Dee suddenly prodded a finger at the radar scope. 'What's that ahead?'

'Rocks,' Seamus suggested. 'They've been stationary for ages.'

'Don't you *know* these waters?'

'Yes. And these are rocks.'

Dee was exasperated. 'Well, these rocks are fucken well *moving*!'

He threw open the door and peered out to get a closer view. Two more vague grey shapes mingled with the haze around the shore. He couldn't have known they were the *Aisling* and the *Deirdre*, completing the Irish Navy's triangle.

He glanced astern. The *Emer* was now clearly visible and giving up all pretence of stealth as she bucked speedily through a head sea, gaining remorselessly.

He pulled back inside the wheelhouse and spoke rapidly to Seamus: 'Give it all you can and keep 'em chasing for as long as possible. We'll start throwing everything over the side. Come on, you two, start to earn your keep.'

Shard suddenly smiled. 'I tell you what, Dee, you were right not to trust cabbage-hats—'

He struck before he'd finished his sentence, his elbow smashing hard into the Irishman's solar plexus. As he doubled up with pain, Robson grabbed Dee's left arm and twisted it into an armlock, forcing it against the joint with such force that the Provo squealed aloud. He'd hardly straightened up before Shard had relieved him of his revolver.

Seamus was staggered by the speed of events. 'What the hell?'

Shard calmly reached for the telegraph and rang down Slow Ahead. 'Just heave-to nice and steady, skipper. No need to alert your engineer. I think the IRA have had more than their fair share of martyrs, don't you?'

His head now forced against the side of the wheelhouse, Dee's face was contorted with pain and rage. 'You bastard, Robson! I knew you were bad news from the start! I should have bloody killed you when I had the chance.'

Robson strengthened his grip; he was actually enjoying this. 'I think you'll find, Dee, your killing days are over for a while.'

Shard kept the Irishman's revolver steadily at the skipper's head as the *Emer* overhauled them with her siren blaring. Seconds later, the black rubber Gemini dinghy came bouncing around the patrol boat's after deck, and across the intervening stretch of water. It pulled alongside and half-a-dozen troopers with blackened faces scrambled warily aboard. Without any orders being given, they divided into three pairs, one taking the engine room abaft, and another the fo'c'sle.

The third pair approached the wheelhouse, Heckler and Koch submachine-guns aimed. There were no insignias or badges of rank on the dripping camouflage smocks nor on the woollen hats. But they weren't needed as far as Robson was concerned. You could always tell a fellow Royal Marine.

Shard grinned. 'Took your time.'

The SBS lieutenant raised an eyebrow at the sight of the gun held at the skipper's head. 'Now, let let me guess. You're Shard?'

'Nice to see you've been well-briefed. And the gent behind with that Provo ape is Billy Robson.'

The lieutenant nodded sagely. 'We wondered if he'd be with you.'

Shard laughed as the tension of the past few hours ebbed away. 'Be nice to Mr Robson. He's one of us.'

Billy Robson's grin was irrepressible.

Epilogue

'The Man' waited until the housegirl from England had left the room after delivering the silver tea service.

She would have to go. It was a shame because she was undoubtedly the best he'd ever had. Her capacity for pain and humiliation seemed limitless, and her total obedience even unnerved him at times. Never before had he met someone with such a need to be hurt.

But she would have to go. After the recent events he could take no chances. At least with no friends or relatives to worry about her, Bella's disposal would not present a problem. He might even arrange for her to go in the way she would most enjoy. The idea excited him.

'The Army Council wants a meeting tomorrow.' Eamon Molloy's slurping voice interrupted his train of thought. As usual the fat man was panicking. 'What shall I tell them?'

The Man knew what concerned his colleague. Since the interception of the *Pumila* off the coast of Donegal the IRA hierarchy had been holding their breath. But The Man wasn't concerned. Dee was the only one on board who could do real damage, and he was too consumed with hatred of the British and Irish Governments to even consider grassing. Besides he had a nice nestegg waiting if he kept his mouth shut.

Of course the Libyan's man, Shard, knew a little. He'd met The Man and had been to his mansion. But nothing

could be proved. Even if it could, The Man had long ago
made sure that his influence had reached the upper echelons
of the police, the judiciary and even the Government. If any
over-zealous policeman got too nosey he'd be told quietly
but firmly to look for clues in another direction.

Of course The Man didn't tell Eamon Molloy that. It was
good to see that big slob sweat for a while; it amused him.

The Man said: 'Tell the Army Council I'll be pleased to
meet whenever they wish to confirm that the *Pumila* incident
will not affect the heroin routes. Tell them that ever since
Mr Lewis first became unco-operative we started planning a
new routing. Besides he was only one of several.'

'But the Boston deal . . .' Molloy blustered, imagining
the grilling they would get from the Provo leaders. He had
visions of himself lying in some gutter with his kneecaps
shattered.

The Man laughed lightly. 'We were fortunate that the
British agent was working for the Libyans. It put the ball
in their court. After all, it was *their* money up-front. Sher
Gallal had little option but to renew the funds. So it's a
mere delay.'

That seemed to please Molloy. He helped himself to tea,
and slurped it noisily from the delicate porcelain cup. 'By the
way, we've had a message from Dee in Port Laoise Prison.'

The Man raised an eyebrow. 'Oh yes?'

'He says while we're working out how to get him released,
he wants something done about that Brit bastard Billy
Robson.'

'Ah, the redoubtable Mr Robson. Bit of a black sheep. I
think we all underestimated him. I'm not surprised Dee has
taken it personally.'

'So what do I tell him?'

The Man smiled gently to himself, relaxed back in the deep armchair, and stared at the ceiling. 'Just tell him we'll think of something.'

The Russian Embassy in Malta is a picturesque two-storey building of yellow stucco with green sun awnings. It stands in its own well-kept grounds on Kappara Hill, separated from the quiet surrounding residential suburb by six-foot high wrought iron railings.

It was through the gates of the embassy that the smart limousine flying the Libyan flag sped, leaving a trail of dust in its wake.

It was watched by a man who stood in the shadow cast in the office by one of the sun awnings on the second floor.

Marat Kopylova's first name was unusual. His father had called him after the cruiser on which he had served during the Great Patriotic War.

Now in his forties, the tall, thin KGB officer was engaged in an extension of that war in his own right. Not against Nazi Germany, but the Western imperialist states that had declared the Soviet Union its sworn enemy, and strove to interfere and destabilise it at every opportunity.

Of course the weapons were different now. And Kopylova smiled as he imagined how his father might react to their clever and insidious methods of waging battle today. It was doubtful if the old boy would even have begun to understand.

The sun was beginning to sink low in the western sky. It was time he made his report. Soon his comrades would be expecting him to play flood-lit tennis with them in the grounds. That always made him smile because they knew that, when all the lamps came on, it caused a reduction of power to all the nearby houses. Beautifully timed for when suppers were cooking in the ovens. It was quite a cause for amusement.

Kopylova returned to his desk and prepared an encrypted memorandum for his Department chief about the conversation he had just had with the Libyan Sher Gallal.

Briefly it informed his masters in the Department that one of the heroin routings into Western Europe had been severed.

He knew the information would not cause any great stir. It was just one routing of many. Nor was it the first to be cut by Western police or customs. Indeed another ring run by air hostesses from the Yugoslav airlines JAT had just been smashed and that, although far less important, could prove embarrassing.

What was it his KGB boss had been fond of saying? 'Drugs rot the very fabric of society. Preying on the disillusioned whilst creating apathy, crime and corruption. It diverts billions of dollars into otherwise unnecessary policing and medical care. And when the fabric gets that rotten it just falls apart like an old curtain.'

And during his posting to Malta he'd seen it starting to work at first hand.

The ciphered memorandum complete, Kopylova locked his office and took his sealed note personally down to the dispatcher's office.

Tomorrow morning it would leave in a diplomatic bag for the airport and the first flight to Sofia in Bulgaria, the nerve-centre of the KGB's vast international drug distribution network.

The summer sun angled through the dormer window of the top floor flatlet, and bathed the double bed in warmth.

Billy Robson stirred into life, and instinctively reached across for Bernadette. It was a novelty to have a woman who enjoyed being woken from the deepest slumber to make love.

She wasn't there. From the small kitchen he heard the rattle of cups and could smell the thick aroma of toast and coffee. He glanced at the bedside clock.

Nearly midday. He smiled. It seemed lately that he'd been sleeping a lot. It must be contentment, he mused. Never had he been happier. Over the past few months it was as though the trauma and tension of the years had been gradually drained away from him.

It had begun the day he learned that all charges against him had been dropped. Shard had been as good as his word and the police, after being reluctant at the start, had gradually changed their attitude as Robson told them everything he knew. He sensed that behind the scenes a lot of rules were being bent and a lot of arms were being twisted to be co-operative.

But it was really all down to Bernadette. If she hadn't turned in Lewis, it could have been very different. Knowing her far better now, he realised how much it must have hurt her to make the decision. It had also meant a complete split with her entire family.

His freedom was not all he owed her. She'd cocooned him in a loving passion, good humour and optimism – a combination of feelings he desperately needed. As broke as she was after her split with Lewis, she had enthused about starting a new business. It was infectious, and Robson found himself filled with a new sense of ambition. Bernadette had drawn on her legitimate contacts in catering to get the new firm off to an encouraging, if slightly shaky, start. She was a natural saleswoman, and soon the orders were flowing in to the

telephone in the flatlet where Robson organised the administration. They made a good team.

A tousled head of chestnut hair peered around the door.
'I see our hero has condescended to wake up.'

'It was a heavy night.'

She nodded and smiled her lop-sided smile. 'But nice.
Especially the last part.'

He grinned. They had been out with Rich Abbott until
three. A thank-you for his somewhat reluctant help when
Robson had been on the run, and Abbott's subsequent once-
in-a-lifetime co-operation with the police.

On their return Robson and Bernadette had made hard,
demanding love for an hour before falling asleep in total
exhaustion.

'Come back to bed,' he said.

'Breakfast's ready.'

'Let's have it in here.'

'You're a slob.'

'I love you.'

'I'll bring it in.'

The doorbell rang. They exchanged glances. Robson
shrugged.

Bernadette said: 'I'll go.'

When she opened the door, Robson thought he recognised the voice. Bernadette certainly seemed to and the
conversation went on for a few moments.

Somehow Robson sensed that something was wrong.
He had just slipped on his dressing-gown when Bernadette
appeared at the door. She looked pale and shaken.

'Billy, it's Detective Sergeant Spicer.'

Robson remembered the Teutonic-looking young Drug
Squad officer with the steel-rimmed glasses. He'd given

evidence at Lewis's trial where he and Bernadette had been witnesses.

'I'm sorry to trouble you, sir.' Spicer sounded very apologetic. He also looked decidedly uncomfortable.

'What is it?'

Spicer said: 'We're acting on information received. An anonymous tip-off, I'm afraid. But we are *obliged* to follow it up.'

'What sort of tip-off?' Robson didn't follow.

'Is there a suitcase under the bed, sir?'

'Huh?' Robson looked at Bernadette. 'No. We keep them on top of the wardrobe, don't we, love?'

She nodded in confirmation.

'Then there'll be no objection if we take a look?'

Astonished, Robson stepped aside as the detective knelt down and reached beneath the bed.

The old leather suitcase scraped on the lino as it was extracted. An Aer Lingus baggage ticket hung from the handle.

Robson's mouth dropped.

Spicer flipped up the lid. For a full thirty seconds he stared at the single polythene package. The brown powder inside was clearly visible. It looked like about half-a-kilo.

'God,' Robson breathed.

'It wasn't there yesterday when I cleaned . . .' Bernadette began.

Robson's mind raced. 'It must have been put there last night. While we were out.' He turned, ashen-faced, to Spicer. 'We've been set up.'

Spicer's lips moved imperceptibly. His eyes were moist. 'Yes, sir, I think you might be right . . .'

'What are you going to do about it?' Robson demanded.

Spicer took a deep breath. Slowly, very slowly, he said: 'You see it's in your possession. I'm afraid, sir, that I have absolutely no choice. None at all. I'm *very* sorry.'

Seven miles away Andy Sutcliff was working in his garden. For the first time ever his weed-ridden plot was seeing the sharp end of a hoe. To his own surprise he'd discovered he had a latent nest-building instinct.

Sandy watched him from the window. She had never felt happier in her life. She had a new husband – albeit common-law – and her son would be home in a week.

She glanced at the sideboard. Andy would be a while yet. She just had time. It was a week since she'd last had one. Just a small one. She could handle it now. Another wouldn't hurt.